The critics on Liz Evans

'Another winner . . . The mystery is even better this time with unexpected twists and a cast of believable characters . . . Grace is developing into one of my favourite sleuths' Susanna Yager, *Sunday Telegraph*

'It is fun and fast-moving. And above all a wonderfully easy page-turning thriller. Liz Evans certainly is one to follow regularly' *Publishing News*

'Humorous and sharply written, this pacey novel . . . will keep you guessing to the end' *Good Housekeeping*

'An entertaining broth of a book, packed with comic set pieces and cracking one-liners' *The Times*

'A good start . . . funny and engaging. Give her a go' *Literary Review*

'This is not a book to make you a better person; it will not change your life nor enhance your sex appeal . . . but you might enjoy it' *Oxford Times*

'With a cast of colourful characters (including a feisty and witty heroine) and sparky dialogue, this is an energetic, fast moving and confident novel. Worth checking out' *Sunday Mirror*

'The whole story spins along at a fast pace, and the details are well observed . . . Evans . . . her propensity for cliff-hang is amusing'

Liz Evans was born in Highgate, went to school in Barnet and now lives in Hertfordshire. She has worked in all sorts of companies from plastic moulding manufacturers to Japanese banks through to film production and BBC Radio, eventually ending up as contracts manager for a computer company. She now writes full time.

Also by Liz Evans

Who Killed Marilyn Monroe?
JFK is Missing!

DON'T MESS WITH
MRS IN-BETWEEN

Liz Evans

ORION

An Orion paperback

First published in Great Britain by Orion in 2000
This paperback edition published in 2001 by Orion Books Ltd,
Orion House, 5 Upper St Martin's Lane, London WC2H 9EA

A CIP catalogue record for this book is available
from the British Library.

ISBN 0 75284 297 8

Typeset by Deltatype Ltd, Birkenhead, Merseyside

Printed in Great Britain by
Clays Ltd, St Ives plc

In memory of
Mary Louise Wright

I

One of my favourite fantasies consists of someone saying: 'I'm filthy rich, and I've decided to make a will leaving the lot to a complete stranger. I've chosen you.'

This morning Barbra Delaney looked me in the eye and said: 'I'm filthy rich, and I've decided to make a will leaving the lot to a complete stranger. I've chosen you . . .'

But that was later. My day started early because – for pressing personal reasons – I needed to get to the office before the postman did. Unfortunately it didn't start as early as I'd originally planned since Sod's Law dictated that today was the day my alarm clock would finally decide to rust in peace.

When I fell out of bed, my watch said eight thirty. Generally the office post arrived around seven thirty. Janice, the receptionist from hell, didn't get in until nine if we were lucky. (If we were *really* lucky, she didn't show up at all.)

There was always the chance, I realised, dragging on a T-shirt and trousers, that one of the other private investigators who shared the offices of Vetch (International) Associates Inc. would be in early, but they wouldn't open any mail addressed to me. It was only Janice who made a point of largely ignoring the common post but invariably opening the envelopes that were marked 'Private & Confidential' or 'Strictly Personal'.

I shot round the corner at a fast trot. My watch now read eight forty-five. The first thing I saw was Janice, standing on the steps outside the office, scanning the street.

Normally Jan tends to dress in black with metallic and leather jewellery by Torture-Chambers-R-Us. It gives her the appearance of being the Bride of Dracula, and last night it seemed the Count had finally struck lucky. Her hair – usually as pitch as her outfits – had turned white overnight. She looked like a badly developed negative.

'What the hell's going on?' I asked. 'Did you have a shock or something?'

'I'll say. Vetch phoned me at home. Made me come in early.'

'Not that. This.'

I drew out a strand of my own hair. I keep it short in a hacked-by-nail-scissors style. Janice seemed to have gone for shorn-by-hedge-trimmer.

'Oh, me hair. I thought I'd try being a blonde. All those girls who get on the telly are blondes. I want to be famous, you know.'

'You said.' We'd already established that Janice had no discernible talent for anything – including typing (especially typing, actually) – but she figured it didn't really matter. And given some of the celebs that regularly appear in the show-biz gossip columns, I suppose she might have a point.

Janice rubbed the ends of a couple of clumps together, sending a small cloud of glinting fragments rasping into the breeze. 'My sister did it. I don't think she read the instructions right. She says I've just got wonky hair. What do you reckon?'

I reckoned stupidity and inventive lying ran in Janice's family, but I didn't really care right at that moment. I had a crisis of my own to sort out.

'Dye it back if you don't fancy it. Has the post come?'

'No idea.'

'Haven't you looked?'

Since the husband of an ex-client had taken exception to the information we'd provided on him and reciprocated with a bottle of petrol and a match through the letter box, all our mail is now held in the heat-proof cage clamped to the back of the open door that Janice was currently leaning on.

'No. I've not come in early to work.'

'So when do you come in to do that, then?'

Janice folded her arms and glared down her nose at me. At five feet eleven she's about the only person in the office who tops me in height. 'I do as much as you, Smithie. More, I'll bet. You haven't exactly got clients queuing up, have you?'

'That's because Vetch pinches all the best cases for himself. If he passed a half-decent job my way occasionally he might get his rent on time for once.'

'Sweet thing,' purred a voice behind Janice. 'Is that a promise?'

I threw her a dirty look. She could have warned me that our esteemed leader, Vetch-the-Letch, was in residence.

Janice smirked, then called over her shoulder, 'There's no sign of them yet. I could have got in at my proper time.'

'But you so rarely do that. Good morning, sweet thing.'

I sauntered into the reception area. 'Morning, Vetch.'

I refused to apologise for my earlier grumble, since it had some justification. Vetch was the only official employee of the business. The rest of us were self-employed. In theory, by working under the one name we benefited from a Corporate Identity (the brass name-plate outside); Shared Office Facilities (Janice and a fax machine); and the chance to re-allocate clients when one investigator was overly employed and the rest of us had a window in our schedules. Recently I seemed to have had enough windows in mine to give the Empire State Building an inferiority complex.

Leaning over Janice's desk, I hooked out the top drawer where the key to the mail box was usually kept and shuffled the assorted debris.

'Lost something, sweet thing?'

'I wanted to see if I had any post.'

I tried to keep my tone light. Judging by the glint in

3

Vetch's eyes, I didn't succeed. I sensed the tops of his pointed ears were pricking.

For once Janice did something useful. 'Is this them?' she yelled from the step.

The engine roar announced a heavy vehicle just before the body of the truck slid into the kerb and blocked out the sunlight. The writing on the side announced it belonged to Speedaway Removals. My first thought was that Vetch had finally sold the building out from under us.

Three men clambered from the cab. Two headed for the back of the lorry, while the third climbed the office steps with an expression of deepest gloom. I revised my opinion. It looked like we were about to be hit by the bailiffs.

Vetch beamed. 'Good morning, Mr Ifor. Beautiful day.'

'If you like that sort of thing, I suppose.'

'Everything's ready. You'd better bring the larger items through the internal stairway. I doubt they will fit down the outside one.'

'It makes no odds. They're bound to break something,' sighed the joyful one, gesturing to the carriers before disappearing into the depths of the cellars.

'What's going on?' I asked Vetch.

'I've rented out the basement.'

'Why?'

Like the rest of the buildings in the street, this one had started life as an Edwardian boarding house. When Vetch had inherited it from his granny, he'd converted the upper storeys into office accommodation, but as far as I knew the basement had always been closed up.

'Cash flow, delicious, cash flow. And Mr Ifor Ifor will provide a useful aid to our own business.'

What was he into? I wondered aloud. Surveillance equipment? Credit checks?

'Instant printing,' Vetch said.

'That would have been my next guess,' I agreed.

'Sarcasm does not become you, Grace. Mr Ifor will do

wonders for our turnover. Do you know one of the main reasons we lose clients before they've even set foot in our offices?'

'They see Janice?'

'Publicity,' Vetch elaborated. 'Very few people want to be seen going into a detective agency. It tends to alert their nearest and dearest to the fact there is something nasty in the wood pile.'

This was true enough. We often got clients from a radius of anything up to a few hundred miles away, simply because they didn't want to consult a local agency for the reasons Vetch had just outlined.

'I'm not acting as his receptionist too,' Janice protested, extracting herself from between the door frame and the photocopier that had just arrived.

'You won't have to,' Vetch assured her. 'In fact, I have added a couple of large bolts to the cellar door to ensure there is no access between us and those wandering the lower regions. Normally Mr Ifor and his clients will use the outside stairs to the basement.' He inflated his puffball cheeks and prepared to elaborate but was interrupted by a shrill whistle from the street.

'Are these the barricades, Vetchy, or is someone nicking your furniture?'

'Barbra!'

'Hi, sweetheart. All right to come in?'

The female he helped over the jumble of Ifor's possessions currently blocking the entrance didn't seem to mind the way he kept his arm around her waist as he ushered her into the former residents' lounge that now served as his office. In fact, she dropped an affectionate kiss on the top of his bald head. Because, like most of the world, she was taller than him, this was his most accessible spot.

Janice and I exchanged raised eyebrows.

'I blame care in the community myself,' I said.

'Yeah. And she looked dead normal, didn't she?' Jan

5

nodded. The movement set the couple of huge haunted-house-type keys she was wearing as earrings jangling, and reminded me why I'd dashed in here in the first place.

'Where's your mail-box key?'

'No idea.' Taking out a bottle of dark green varnish, she prepared to paint her nails, but was forestalled by Vetch asking for coffee. With a heavy sigh, she rescrewed the bottle and started sorting out three cups.

I needed that key. It wasn't in the right drawer, nor any of the wrong ones. It wasn't on top of the reception desk and, by crawling on the floor, I confirmed it wasn't amongst the drifts of dust under the thing.

'For heaven's sake.' I straightened up as Jan returned from her waitress duties. 'Can't you remember where you put it last night?'

'I never put it anywhere. It's been missing for days. I've been getting Vetch to open up. He's got a spare.'

'Why didn't you say so in the first place?'

'You asked if I knew where my key was. And I don't.' Crossing her ankles on the desk, Jan drank her coffee and squinted at her reflection in the computer screen. Wrinkling her nose, she crumbled another load of split ends. 'God, this is chronic, ain't it? I just hope I don't see anyone I know before I can get it fixed.' Delving inside her handbag, she extracted an enormous pair of sunglasses and slid them on her nose.

Frustrated, I went back to the door and pushed my fingers in the slot to see if I could detect any envelopes in there. I had a lock-picking set back at the flat. But if the postman hadn't already called, and he delivered while I was out . . . I glanced speculatively at Jan. Ordering her not to open anything addressed to me would be the equivalent of slashing my wrists and shouting 'Grub's up!' to a great white shark. On the other hand, Vetch was distracted, and if I stuck my head round his door and casually asked for the post key . . . Hopefully, I might even interrupt something personal and highly embarrassing.

Vetch frustrated the potential high-spot of my day by opening his door before I could reach it and asking me to spare him a moment of my time.

'Got the key to the post box?' I asked at the same moment as Vetch said, 'I think Grace might suit you, Barbra. Unless you've a prior engagement, sweet thing? Parachuting behind enemy lines, for instance?'

This was a crack about my choice of clothing. Vetch tends to favour made-to-measure conventional, whereas I'm more Oxfam-groupie. My trousers this morning were patterned in camouflage khaki and brown splodges and had been a real snip at fifty pence. I assured him the SAS would just have to manage without me this week as I perched on the other visitor's chair.

'Mrs Delaney,' he explained, 'requires our services. Barbra . . . Grace Smith. My most . . . available investigator.'

I nodded my hellos. She was in her forties, I guessed. Sleek blonde shoulder-length hair, light make-up, plain gold watch and wedding ring.

'So how can I—' I was about to say 'help' but was interrupted by another wave of deliveries crashing through the front door.

Since I hadn't shut Vetch's office door completely behind me, we could all enjoy the leading bloke asking Janice, 'Where d'you want this lot, darling?' as he decanted what sounded like several large cardboard boxes on to the reception floor.

'What is it?'

'Nexon Printing Supplies. Here's yer delivery schedule. Want to check them off?'

'No, I flaming well don't! I'm nothing to do with that lot downstairs.'

'Give them a shout then. We're in a bit of a hurry ourselves. Stick 'em there, Paul—'

From where I was sitting I couldn't see the delivery man, but I guessed from the crash his load had touched down.

Murmuring his apologies, Vetch levered himself once more from behind his executive-style, over-large desk and slipped out to the hall.

'I believe the gentleman you require is currently working in the basement. Kindly take this lot downstairs.'

'We're running late.'

'Then run a little harder,' Vetch advised. Returning to the office, he took one of my new client's hands and raised it to his lips. 'Now. Where were we?'

'Cut it out, Vetchy.' Barbra reclaimed her fingers but used them to give his pointy lobe an affectionate tweak. 'Me and your mate here have got serious money to discuss. Fancy breakfast, Grace?'

I always fancied food if someone else was paying. But my suggestion of a trip to my favourite greasy spoon was vetoed.

'The Rock Hotel,' Barbra said firmly.

'Fair enough. Hang on a minute, Mrs Delaney.'

'Barbra.'

'OK. Vetch, have you got the key to the mail box? I want to collect my post.'

'I don't think it's arrived yet.'

'There's a strike at the sorting office, isn't there?' Barbra said. 'I didn't get a delivery this morning.'

A large black cloud lifted from my heart. There was a kindly fate out there rooting for me for once! 'Let's hit the full English fry-up then.'

We stepped out into the hall. Through the open front door I could see it was a beautiful morning where the sun was shining, the gulls were singing (off-key, but who was complaining?) and the sky was cloudless. The happy trill of a local maiden filled the air.

'Oi! You! Hold on!' Waving a piece of paper, Jan charged past us, down the front steps, sprinted along the pavement, and planted herself in front of a van that was just pulling away from the kerb. The printing suppliers, I assumed.

They seemed to be having a row. Jan's foot was braced against their front bumper and Speedaway's truck was blocking them from reversing out of the gap. Eventually the back doors of the van were thrust open and a hand threw a box on to the pavement. With a self-satisfied saunter, Jan retrieved it as Paul and Co. sped away.

'What was that all about?' I asked.

'That order came to more than fifty pounds.' She waved the copy of the delivery note under my nose. 'It says here you get a free desk diary for this year if your order comes to more than fifty pounds.'

'It wasn't your order. It was Laughing Ifor's. Anyway, what the hell do you want a desk diary for? It's August.'

'I don't care. It's the principle of the thing, innit?'

'I like a woman who knows what she wants,' Barbra Delaney said. 'I always did. It just took me half a lifetime to get it. Come on.'

She marched me to the Rock Hotel and waited until we were seated overlooking the beach with a full English breakfast en route to our table before explaining the reason for our meeting.

Looking me straight in the eye, she said: 'I'm filthy rich, and I've decided to make a will leaving the lot to a complete stranger. I've chosen you . . .'

2

'. . . to trace them for me.'

'You what?' The fortune that had so nearly been mine for a good two seconds was rapidly galloping over the horizon.

'Find them,' Barbra reiterated. 'I know I said "stranger",

9

but when I thought about it, I decided it might be safer to split it a few different ways.' Taking one of those glossy folders they give you in Boots developing shops from her shoulder bag, she passed it over the table. 'All you've got to do is get me their names and addresses so I can stick them in the will. And I'd like to know if they've ever been in bother with the law.'

Life was beginning to feel a little surreal. I couldn't quite believe she was intending to leave everything to a collection of photo snaps she'd never met. A sudden nasty suspicion that this was all a wind-up – courtesy of Vetch-the-Letch – took root.

'Mrs Delaney,' I said, deciding to go for the dignified professional approach, 'if this is a joke, it isn't particularly funny.'

'Who's laughing?' she said, helping herself to a slice of toast. 'And I thought you were gonna call me Barbra. That's Barbra without the second 'a', like in Barbra Streisand. Do you want the honey?'

I shook my head and twisted the cap off a Mr McGregor's Genuine Chunky Highland Marmalade with a Whisper of Drambuie. The small print on the back indicated the Tartan Army had colonised further than anyone had previously suspected, since the stuff was produced in Minneapolis, USA.

'So why the beneficiary hunt?' I asked. 'Don't you have any family?'

She took a large bite from the corner of the toast triangle before asking me if I was married.

'No.'

'Ever been?'

'No. I lived with someone for a while, but we never made it legal.'

'I have. Twice. First time I was eighteen. Sean Delaney. Bought me frock from a catalogue. Got married in the register office. Had our reception down the local pub.' She whipped out a leather holder and passed it over, open at a couple of snaps.

Barbra the first was pure seventies: white calf-length crocheted frock, a big floppy-brimmed matching hat, pale face and eyelashes like tarantulas. The two bridesmaids were squeezed into matching maroon crocheted numbers and encircled by the arms of the best man, who towered over them by a good head.

The prettiest thing in the shot was the groom. Even the naff flared trousers, velvet jacket, sideburned hair touching his collar and Zapata moustache didn't detract from the fact he was male crumpet.

'Good-looking bloke,' I said neutrally.

'And he knew it. He and Bri spent longer in front of the mirror than us girls.'

'Bri?'

She tapped a manicured nail on the large bloke cuddling the bridesmaids. 'Best man. Best mate. Him and Sean worked the fairgrounds together. Me and my mate double-dated them. Only she had the sense to say ta for a great summer and marry a butcher from Birmingham. And I thought I was so flaming clever getting Sean to the register office.'

A wistful dreaminess clouded her eyes for a minute as she focused beyond my left shoulder. 'God, he was hot. Sex on a stick. I don't reckon we went outside the flat for the first three months. Still, all good things . . . He went off the idea after I got pregnant with Carly. Well, off it with me – he was on anything else with good legs and a pulse around those flats.'

'I'm sorry.'

She shrugged, poured out more coffee, tasted it and wrinkled her nose. With a shrill whistle, she lifted the silver pot and told the waiter to fetch a fresh one.

'It was my own fault. I knew what he was like before I bought me wedding frock. I thought I could change him. By the time our Lee came along, I'd given up trying. I finally slung him out just after Lee started school.'

'Do you still see him?'

'Only when I've had a few too many vodkas. He died eight, nine years ago. Place he was staying in burnt down. They got me to identify the body. What was left of it. Rotten job. I don't know how the ambulance and fire lot do it year after year. They ought to pay 'em a bleeding fortune, if you ask me.'

'And speaking of fortunes . . . ?' I tapped the folder sitting beside my plate.

'Sorry, I'm rambling. Thing is, my Lee's been going down the usual route since he was old enough to climb out of his cot—'

'Action Man, space monsters, football, acne, girls?' I suggested.

'Car theft, breaking and entering, drugs.' Barbra cleared space for the fresh coffee. 'Shall I be mother?'

'Why not? You sound better qualified for it than me.'

'Nobody's ever qualified to be a parent.' My client spoke with feeling. 'I mean, you see those cute kids in their prams and you figure it must be a doddle. Everyone does it – right?'

'I haven't.'

She looked me over. 'You've still got plenty of time to try it, lady. How old are you? Twenty-seven, eight?'

'More or less.' Hastily, I changed the subject back to her efforts at carrying on the Delaney clan. 'So Lee was never going to qualify for Kid Most Likely to Succeed?'

'Not unless they're giving out medals for being evil little Ess-Oh-Bees.' She added two artificial sweeteners to her own cup and pushed the sugar in my direction. 'I tried to bring him up right, I really did. Sean never gave us a penny after he left. Oh, he'd turn up with an armful of sweets and toys for the kids about twice a year, but it was me had to pay for their clothes and food and keep a roof over them.

And I never scrounged for it like some. Always paid my own way. Managing a classy underwear shop was the best number I ever had. But it was hotel work mostly – until the burglaries. Lee must have done a couple of dozen, but he only got caught twice. Word got round: steer clear of Barbra Delaney. I think I was officially listed as a hazard on insurance forms in the end – *Tick box if you have now – or might at any time in the future – consider employing Barbra Ann Delaney.*'

'What about Carly?'

'Carly?'

'Doesn't she have any influence? Big sisters can apply a particularly subtle form of arm-twisting. I know – I am one.'

Barbra stared blankly for a moment. 'Carly died when she was nine. Leukaemia.'

I refused to feel guilty. It was her own fault for mentioning the other kid without giving me the full story. 'Where's Lee now?'

'I've no idea. He's like his dad. He'll turn up when he wants something.'

'Fair enough. So, getting back to the fortune . . .'

'Oh yeah. That. Few years ago I answered this ad for a live-in housekeeper out at Wakens Keep. You know it?'

I did. We had a lot of similar villages scattered over the Weald. A few hundred years previously they'd been collections of run-down farm workers' cottages grouped around whatever passed for the pub and the local church. Essentially I suppose they still were, except the cottages had been converted into 'desirable period country dwellings' and were now priced far beyond the few remaining farm workers' pay packets. Wakens Keep was about twenty miles inland from Seatoun and located at the northern edge of the Downs as they started to rise from the flat farmlands and salt marshes that stretched to the coast.

'Barney had just retired and bought a place out there. He

wanted a bit of company more than anything, I reckon. He was a widower, see. No kids.'

'Barney being . . . ?'

'Barney Syryjczyk. My second husband.'

'So how come you're still calling yourself Delaney?'

'I got fed up having to chant S-y-r-y-j-c-z-y-k every time I gave my name.' She squeezed the last dregs of coffee from the pot. 'Anyhow, fifteen months later I'm saying "I do" again. Only second time round, I got hitched on a beach in the Seychelles in a designer frock that cost two thousand quid.'

She flicked the plastic sheets in the leather folder again. It was much as you'd imagine a tropical wedding to be: palm trees, yellow beach, sparkling azure ocean and everyone trying to look like they don't feel like idiots standing around dressed like this amongst a bunch of bikini-wearing spectators.

Barney was half a head shorter than his betrothed. He appeared to have bought his wedding suit in the hopes of growing into it, which seemed a bit optimistic, since I'd have put him at seventy if he was a day.

'Sixty-five,' Barbra corrected me. 'He was already ill. I know everyone thinks I married a sick old man for his cash, but I don't care. Truth is, I never even knew he *had* that kind of money. Oh, I guessed he was comfortable, but rich – no way. I mean, the house was just ordinary, not some fancy big mansion. Then he lets me have it: he's a flaming millionaire.'

'Tough break.'

'Yeah.' She grinned again. 'Sorry. Didn't mean to go on, only I don't get the chance very often. I'm not trying to kid anyone I was *in love* with Barney. But I did love him in a way. He was a real treat after the losers I'd picked up with after Sean. Ever heard of McCurrie's Foods?'

'Can't say I have. What are they into – haggis tikka?'

'They started off in jams, marmalades, pickles, and then

moved on to cooking sauces, pre-packed spice mixtures, all that sort of thing.' She picked up another jar of Mr McGregor's Genuine Chunky Highland Marmalade. 'They make this stuff. At least they used to until they got taken over by some American conglomerate. Barney's first wife was a McCurrie. He inherited her share of the business, and when they sold out, he did very nicely, thank you, ma'am.' She replaced the jar and sighed wistfully. 'We had a great time together, me and Barney. We did all the things he'd ever wanted to do: the Grand Prix in Monaco; Empire State Building; Great Wall of China; Honolulu beach. First class all the way. Then he died.'

'Unexpectedly?'

'*I* didn't expect it, but maybe he did. We never saw the doctors much except for the last few weeks. His first wife had all the treatments and it hadn't helped, so he decided not to bother, and live each day as his last. So I guess when it *was* the last day, it wasn't such a surprise to him.' She lit up a cigarette.

One of the waitresses opened a window, allowing a fresh breeze to carry the scents of ozone and seaweed into the room. Then she spoilt it all by turning on the portable TV in the corner. A solemn-faced reporter stood in front of a hospital somewhere, informing the country in tones of mock concern that two more cases of diphtheria had been diagnosed. It was the third cluster of cases in as many weeks, with the other patients being held in isolation in London and Dover. The picture cut to an equally solemn shot of the local MP in a businesslike Gucci-style navy jacket and pearls, earnestly assuring everyone that the authorities were doing all they could to trace the source of the outbreak and there was no need for anyone to panic.

'Turn the flaming thing off, love,' Barbra called. 'I can't stand politicians. They just love the sound of their own voices. I never watch them. It's time the Government got their act together and threw them out.'

'The politicians?'

'The foreigners. The so-called political refugees. Bringing all their illnesses over here. They don't have the same standards as us. We used to have 'em at some of the hotels. Good rooms too, not any old rubbish. I wouldn't like to tell you what we found in some of those rooms after they'd gone.'

She made no attempt to keep her voice down, despite the fact that the waiting staff in Seatoun tended to be moonlighting foreign language students or catering staff from the continent doing a year over here to improve their language skills.

I must have looked uncomfortable, because she smiled and waved at the waitress resetting tables. The girl nodded shyly and returned the salute.

'You don't need to worry I'm offending anyone here,' Barbra said, flicking ash into a saucer. 'I'm only saying what most people think but haven't got the guts to say out loud. They don't all stick together just because they come from across the Channel. Most of them treat foreigners worse than we do.'

With its back terrace which had steps leading down directly to the beach, the Rock Hotel had one of the best positions in town. Striped deckchairs, raspberry-pink sun-worshippers and pale-skinned castle-builders were already staking out their places. It looked like a seaside town ought to look like for once; and I wanted to get out there and enjoy.

'The will?' I prompted, abandoning subtlety in favour of the direct prod.

'The will,' Barbra repeated. 'Well, I've told you what I want.'

'To find the names and addresses of some complete strangers so you can leave all Barney's worldly goods to them.'

'Vetch said you were a bright girl.'

'What about Lee? Aren't you going to cut him in?'

'Lee spent most of his life messing up my chances. I don't intend to leave him a penny. In fact, that's why I want you to find out if any of that lot have been in bother with the law. I'm not talking about parking tickets. Or someone who was inside twenty years ago. I can live with that. But I'm not cutting my Lee out just to leave a flaming fortune to some other—'

'Mother's pain in the arse?'

'You said it.'

'Why this, though? Leaving it to the local dogs' home would have the same effect.'

'I thought about that, but see this?' She held back the corner of her jacket and pinched a fingerful of the T-shirt underneath. 'Two hundred – give or take. I know I could have got it cheaper down the local shops and most people wouldn't know the difference. But *I* know. I like sitting here knowing me knickers cost more than most folks spend on a night out. And I like the idea of passing that feeling on to someone else when I'm gone. I've got enough cash now to do anything I damn well like. So if I get this idea in me head to hire someone to run around fetching me names and addresses, I don't have to think that's five years' gas bills I'm blowing. I think; I call Vetch; I get you.'

'Fair enough.' I put the folder of photos in my own bag and asked how she'd chosen the lucky legatees.

'That was the trickiest bit,' she admitted. 'I had all these ideas, but in the end it was giving me a headache. Finally I woke up with the birds one morning and thought, to hell with this, it's getting to be no fun at all. So I drove out to St Biddy's and snapped the first three out of the local store. And here you are.'

I took a notebook from my bag. 'You'd best give me your own details and I'll get a contract drawn up. Did Vetch tell you my rates?'

'Sure. I'll pay, but I don't expect to be ripped off.'

I thought she already had been, by whoever had sold her the two-hundred-quid T-shirt, but I gave her a look which I hoped radiated professional outrage at the very idea – and moved the leather folder to rest my notebook on the tablecloth. It fell open at another shot of Barbra. But this one looked to be about three stone heavier than bridal-Barbie, with badly streaked hair, prominent nose and dimpled flesh larding its way from under the shorts and stretch top. The other side of the double spread was of a young girl with too-thin arms and eyes too large for the face that peeped out from under a floppy-brimmed hat.

'Yeah, that's me too,' Barbra said, reaching across to retrieve her property and placing a palm over the girl's picture in a way that shut me out.

She twisted a lock of her fair bob. 'Personal stylist.' She tweaked out the suit jacket again. 'Personal style consultant.' Both hands smoothed the flat midriff. 'Personal fitness trainer.' She tapped her slim nose. 'Plastic surgeon. Believe me, whoever said money couldn't buy happiness was shopping in the wrong store.'

'Speaking of shoppers, do I tell your beneficiaries the reason you want their personal details?'

'Absolutely not! Don't get me wrong, I have every intention of living to an extremely old age and spending every damn penny I've got in the bank. But since they reckon the best way to make God laugh is to tell Her your plans, I'm just planning for the unexpected. What I definitely don't want is for any of my lucky choices to start thinking of me as a loan company and turning up on me doorstep asking for a sub on their future fortune. These names stay between you, me and my solicitor – and I want that put in the contract. Got it?'

'Whatever you say.' I glanced around. The dining room was completely deserted except for us. 'So,' I said, 'why don't you tell me the real agenda here, Barbra?'

'Sorry?' She'd been about to reapply her lipstick. The tube froze two inches from her lips.

'You said you'd decided it would be safer to split Barney's cash a few different ways. Safer for who exactly? Barney's hardly in a position to worry. It makes no odds to me; just bumps up the number of hours I'm going to bill you. So I guess that leaves you.'

For a moment she stayed still. Then the lipstick continued on its trajectory. 'Vetch was right. You are smart.' She snapped the mirror closed. 'Yeah, OK. There is something else. Last month I was up in London seeing my solicitor. I'd come out of the offices and was waiting at the lights to cross, and somebody pushed me into the traffic. If it wasn't for a taxi driver with fast reactions, I wouldn't be sitting here now.'

'Did you see who did it?'

'No. By the time all the shouting was over, whoever it was had gone. But the taxi driver said there was a bloke behind me, about six feet tall, wearing one of those grey sweatshirt tops with the hood up. Said the man had his hand out towards my back just before I took a nose-dive under his wheels. I guess driving a taxi you get used to keeping your eye on the pavements.'

'Did you report it to the police?'

'No.'

'Why not?'

'Because I couldn't prove anything. Anyway, who wants to admit their only kid is prepared to murder them?'

'Are you sure it was Lee? It doesn't sound like much of a description to go on.'

'Who else has a motive? I haven't any other family. If I end up as strawberry jam under a bus, Lee will get the lot.'

'Hence the will.'

'Exactly. I'll feel safer when Lee knows there's no chance of getting a penny if I drop off the twig. And just in case he gets ambitious, I'm dividing the cash up. Even the dimmest copper is going to work out who dunnit if a bunch of strangers with only that will in common start having fatal accidents.'

'I wouldn't bet on it,' I said, thinking of the dimmest copper I knew. I also thought it unlikely that a small-time crook like Lee Delaney was suddenly going to evolve into a mass murderer. But then again, it was a no-hassle fee for easy work, so why argue?

I said goodbye to Barbra on the steps of the hotel, promised to drop the contract over, and strolled back to the office through sun-filled streets in a mood to love the whole world.

As I came into sight of Vetch's premises, a large black weight engraved 'Gotcha, Smithie' descended from thirty thousand feet and knocked the complacency straight through the soles of my shoes.

The thing I'd dreaded was here with a vengeance.

3

And vengeance had used her talons to slit open the envelope.

It couldn't have taken me more than five seconds to sprint to the office doors after I'd spotted the postman strolling away from the steps. But in that time Janice had managed to home in on the one letter I would have given my last bottle of plonk to keep away from her, and whip out the contents.

I have to say it didn't exactly require the eyesight of a bald eagle to spot it. Amongst the pile of white and buff conventional-sized offerings, a twelve-inch-high green envelope addressed in the sort of deep black copperplate that used to win school handwriting prizes sixty years ago does tend to scream 'Open me immediately!'

And Janice had taken Great-Aunt Gertie's invitation straight to her malicious little soul, and was doing just that.

'Is that yours?' I asked, trying to keep my voice from rising.

'Of course it's not. My friends send birthday cards to me home, not work. Doesn't this Gertrude know where you live?'

She did. But unfortunately I'd once let slip to G-A Gertie that I didn't pay any rent for my flat. This was principally because the owner didn't know I lived there, a situation that wasn't entirely my fault since none of the tenants in the house had any idea who actually owned the property. We'd all moved in and established squatter's rights to the part-converted flats at various times, and nobody had ever challenged our right to be there. Except for G-A Gertie.

It had never occurred to me she'd have a problem with the situation. By and large Gertie was one of my more reasonable relatives, but I'd forgotten that she came from an era that prized 'strong moral fibre'. Having found out I was illegally in possession of my current address, she'd refused to legitimise the situation by sending mail to it. She insisted on sending my post to the office. Normally that didn't cause me any problems. Except for today.

I'd telephoned her last night to ask her to divert her birthday card to my friend Annie's place (a legitimately mortgaged flat that wouldn't sully her principles), only to find out she'd posted the damn thing two days early – viz., yesterday afternoon. Hence my dash to the office this morning.

'I thought,' I said, glaring at the pile of post on Janice's desk, 'that there was some kind of problem at the sorting office.'

'Fixed.'

She was still examining my birthday card with interest. I considered snatching it away, but decided that would just draw more attention to it. Maybe if I played it cool she wouldn't notice. Some hopes!

Her voice acquired the purr of a cat that's just spotted a mouse with a broken ankle. 'You said you were twenty-eight. So how come this card says "Happy Thirtieth Birthday"?'

She turned it so I could see G-A Gertie's choice in all its glory of rioting crimson roses, lacy hearts and a blazing great gold foil figure 30 in the centre.

'Because my Great-Aunt Gertie is an octogenarian.'

'They don't count birthdays different abroad, do they? You needn't—'

She was interrupted by a salvo of sound drumming on the cellar door behind her.

I grabbed the opportunity to divert her. 'It sounds like the Grim Reaper below is trying to get out.'

'He's supposed to use the outside entrance. Vetch said.'

'Hello? Hello! Is anybody there?'

I strode across, slammed back the two huge metal bolts Vetch had had fitted and dragged on the ring handle. The door swung back and Ifor-squared fell on to his knees.

'You're supposed,' Jan told him, finally leaving her desk and walking over to scowl down at him, 'to use the outside door.'

'I've been trying to do so, but the lock is defective. It keeps sticking shut. It's a little oil or some tools I was hoping for the loan of?' He looked hopefully at Jan – a sure sign he was new.

While Ifor Ifor was discovering Jan's legendary talent for unhelpfulness, I scooped up my card and headed for the stairs.

My office was on the top floor of the premises. It shared the landing with my friend Annie's office and a bathroom left over from the days when Vetch's gran had run this former boarding house on principles laid down by the Ghengis Khan School of Hotel Management.

22

As I went to unlock the door marked 'G. Smith' in uneven black paint, the one opposite decorated with a small plate engraved 'A. Smith' swung open.

'Hi,' Annie said. 'What's this about you lying about your real age?'

'Flaming hell! Do MI5 know about you?'

'Jan just rang me on the internal line.'

'Great. She'll have a web site set up on the Internet by lunchtime.'

'It's true then? You have been lying?'

'No. Well, I might have been economical with the truth.'

'Why?' Annie stood aside to let me into her office.

It was a tough one to explain. I hadn't deliberately set out to deceive anyone. In fact, it wasn't really my fault.

My ex (the one I'd lived with but not married, if you were paying attention earlier) had decided to throw a twenty-sixth birthday party for me. He'd set up the usual essentials of booze, food, helium balloons and music but he hadn't been able to find a Happy Birthday banner reading '26'. So he'd brought a '25', intending to fill in the gap in the 5 and turn it into a 6. Somehow he'd never got around to it, and I'd ended up having a second twenty-fifth birthday.

After that everyone had assumed I was a year younger than I actually am. It had never seemed to matter before. I mean, there was no big difference between twenty-seven and twenty-eight. Or twenty-eight and twenty-nine. But trying to pretend you're twenty-nine when you're actually thirty suddenly seemed. . .

'Like trying to hide the fact you've reached the summit and hit the down skids?' Annie suggested.

'I can't think how you failed that audition for the Samaritans,' I said, accepting a cup of coffee. 'I was going to say pathetic, actually. Like all those celebrities who are thirty-nine-and-holding when everyone knows darn well they must have hit the big five-oh.'

Annie poured herself a cup of black, and added cream and sugar. Plainly we were in one of the spells of self-contented calm that occurred between the diet storms when she tried to shift two stone of stubborn blubber.

'Well, you're out now. There's no chance Janice will keep this to herself. Better take it like a woman. A thirty-something one. Anyway, it's not so bad being thirty-odd. I've been there for three years, remember.'

I gave a noncommittal grunt and fished a lump of floating digestive out of my coffee. I didn't really want it after my full breakfast, but Annie's usually so possessive about the contents of her office pantry that I didn't want to refuse and discourage her from offering again.

'You working on anything interesting at the moment?' I asked, in a feeble attempt to change the subject.

Annie let me get away with it. 'A few more personnel checks for my tame securities company in the City; a missing hubbie; and a wavering Pasdirp.'

(Pasdirps were Annie's shorthand for: Probable Adulterous Spouse; Do I Require Proof? An awful lot of clients book an investigation in the first heat of suspicion, call a few days later to put the whole thing on hold, and eventually decide they prefer to bury their heads in the sand and hope the situation will go away. Apparently this one was in the second stage at present.)

'What about you?' she asked.

'Vetch recommended me to one of his girlfriends.'

'As what?'

'A doorstop – what else?'

Annie's eyes twinkled behind the large, red-framed glasses that were the preferred spectacle-design of the moment. 'So what's her problem?'

'She's having a bad heir day.'

'Seriously.'

'I am being serious. She's taken some snaps of a bunch of

24

complete strangers and wants me to track them down so she can leave them a million in her will.'

'Is she nuts?'

'No. She suspects her only offspring might be trying to shove her under a bus. The will is a sort of insurance policy so she can wallow in retail therapy in peace.'

'Wouldn't leaving it to the Salvation Army have the same effect?'

'We've already done that conversation. She's a bit of a control freak, I suspect. The idea of having that much power over them – and me for as long as this takes – is a turn-on, even if the legatees aren't going to find out about it until she's gone. But then again, why should I worry? It's landed me a client with serious money.'

'All our clients have serious money if you think about it,' Annie remarked. 'Even a simple job is going to run up a fair-sized bill. It's not the kind of money someone on income support is likely to come up with. We're another one of those areas of society from which the deserving poor are excluded.'

'On that deep thought, I think I'll leave you to it and get down to work.' I swung my feet off the table and stood up as Annie jokingly told me to let her know who benefited from the mad millionairess's will, particularly if they were male and unattached.

'Sorry. Client wants total shtum.'

I mimed a zipper across my lips. Annie shrugged philosophically but didn't argue. It was a sort of unwritten rule in the company that The Customer Ruled – OK?

After the soothing and beautifully decorated quiet of Annie's office, my own bare-floored, dust-challenged pit felt . . . homely. The sun was pouring in through the windows, illuminating my natural talent for ignoring the housework. I eased them open to let in the sea breezes and the gulls' incessant squarking, and then spread Barbra's photo collection over the desk.

She had a camera with an automatic motor; by keeping her finger on the shot button she'd captured half a dozen views of each person from the moment they left the shop door until they were a few yards down the street.

I grouped them into subjects. There were three of them. Barbra Delaney was intending to leave her money to a man, a woman . . . and a parrot.

4

I checked the developer's wallet. The strip of negatives was missing. My guess was that Barbra was hanging on to it as insurance against my producing any old names and addresses providing their owners vaguely resembled the pictures on my desk. This way, she was letting me know, she had the option to check against the print herself.

Turning one of the snaps over, I discovered her camera had automatically recorded the date and time on the back of each shot. They'd been taken on the twelfth of August, which was last Wednesday. Assuming Barbra had got there for the store's opening, the woman had been their first customer, at 7.12 a.m.

Age isn't that easy to judge – particularly in two dimensions – but the woman was late thirties to mid forties, I'd say. She was dressed in a loose-fitting white T-shirt with a brightly coloured abstract design, over wide-legged black trousers and flat slip-on shoes. Slimly built and of average height, using the shop doorway as a perspective guide. Her dark hair was cut in a short, feathery style that framed a face that might have been heart-shaped, although it was hard to be definite because she'd kept her head tilted downwards so the strands fell forward and hid parts of her features.

She was holding a package in her left hand and sunglasses in her right. The specs were being raised with each successive shot, and by the last they were perched on Mrs X's nose. This particular picture was in profile and must have been taken as the woman crossed in front of Barbra's lens. I wondered where she'd been as she'd shot off the film. Her models didn't give any indication they were aware they were being captured on celluloid.

The man was next. He'd left the store at 7.30 a.m. Rangy was the first word to come to mind. He was certainly over six feet, but leanly built as far as I could see under the crumpled checked shirt and jeans. The narrow, long-nosed face was capped with sandy-coloured hair cut close to his head at the nape but slightly longer in the front. I'd have bet anything the style was to hide a receding hair-line. He was about a decade older than the woman: late forties to early fifties was my best guess.

The parrot had fluttered in last: departure time 7.45 a.m. She was slightly shorter than the bloke, perhaps nearer my own height of five feet ten inches. It was hard to tell her build because of the bizarre clothing. She was wearing one of those buckskin thigh-length jackets usually seen on early American backwoodsmen who favour dead raccoons as headgear. Its fringed bottom was flapping over the sort of patchwork skin skirt and boots generally worn by said backwoodsman's Native American life-partner (or Red Indian squaw, for the politically incorrect amongst you), except in her case the natural hide colour had been dyed into jewel shades.

What made the whole thing truly bizarre was the feathers. Somewhere in the Amazonian rain forests, a couple of parrots were flying around like a pair of oven-ready chickens while their modesty was attached to Hiawatha here. She had a whole plumage spiked into her hair. It was dark and fringed like Mrs X's, but that was about the only resemblance. These locks were thick and straight, hanging to the bust and adorned with single feathers of brilliant blue, red and green twisted in an apparently random pattern across her head.

The ensemble was completed by an almost dull pair of beige suede boots and a thonged duffle bag slung over one shoulder.

At least, I decided, shuffling the pictures back into their paper holder, number three should be a breeze to trace. How many parrot-fixated Indian squaws could there be wandering around a small country village?

My first problem was getting to St Biddy's. I have a car, according to the log book. According to the police, I have an unroadworthy collection of mechanical parts and they'd just love me to make their day by taking it on a public highway. At present it was lurking in a friend's yard while a new set of stables for his donkey string was built around it.

Annie turned down my request for a loan of hers. 'Get your own fixed.'

'I did. Something else went wrong. Well, several something elses, actually.'

'Then buy another car.' Straightening up from the bottom filing cabinet drawer, she swore softly as the button of her skirt fired across the room.

Normally I'd have cracked a joke, but today I needed a favour.

'I know damn well you've got money stashed away,' Annie grunted, struggling to insert a safety pin to secure the skirt zip.

'How?'

'I can count. You've had decent-sized fees from at least two recent cases I know of. You don't pay rent for your flat, you shop at charity stores and you scrounge everything else off the rest of us.'

'I'm conscientious about recycling the earth's resources.'

'You're tighter than this damn skirt,' she informed me, closing the pin at last. Letting her breath go with a gasp, she dragged her blouse out of the waistband and smoothed it over her stomach. 'How does that look?'

'Porky.'

'Bitch.' Annie grinned without rancour. The effort had left her round face slightly pink and made her mousy hair stand out. 'Go get a cash extraction. It can be quite painless if you're brave.'

Not for me. I hated spending my own money and only did it when the last resort failed. In this case the last resort proved surprisingly obliging.

'Of course I can lend you some transport, sweet thing. What else are colleagues for but to share and share alike?'

I was stunned enough to bite back a flip reply and simper my thanks.

'Walk this way – and swallow the joke about talcum powder that I just know was on the tip of your tongue.'

I turned towards the front door, since Vetch normally parked outside the office. He swung right, however, as he headed for the back of the premises.

'This way. I presume your efforts this morning are devoted to Barbra's cause?'

'Yep. Did she tell you what she wanted?'

'Naturally. How else could I have decided to whom I should pass the file?'

'How d'you know her?'

'Business.'

'Our business?'

'Hers. Here we are.'

Taking a large key from its hook by the back door, he inserted it in the lock of the substantial door installed by Grannie Vetch when she'd terrorised holidaymakers into arriving for high tea at six thirty PROMPT and leaving ALL BUCKETS AND SPADES OUTSIDE THE PREMISES. The general opinion was that she'd had this door and the metal window bars added to thwart a bolshie boarder who'd been trying to form an escape committee.

Vetch disappeared into the small brick outside shed.

I stared in disbelief as he wheeled out a bicycle. Not a modern lightweight model, but the sort of robust bone-shaker that I last saw free-wheeling across the TV screen in a documentary on the 1920s Depression. Its name – according to the gilt lettering – was Sunbeam.

'You've got to be kidding!'

Vetch's grin extended to the top of his pointed ears. 'Not at all. Grannie swore by it.'

'I'm not surprised. I can think of a few swear words that I bet Grannie never used.'

'I doubt that, sweet thing. Well, I'll wish you happy hunting.'

'I suppose it's pointless to suggest you might want to lend me your motor?'

'Totally. Both now and in the forever more. Take care. You shouldn't overexercise – at your age.'

They say you never forget how to ride a bicycle. They lie.

The fastest way to St Biddy's was straight along the main east-to-west A road, but there was no way I was risking it with my cycling synchronisation still struggling in the fledgeling stage.

Slinging my bag in the wicker basket fixed to the handlebars, I aimed for the country lanes that meandered between the farm fields. Up until now my contact with horticulture had been confined to supermarket freezer cabinets. I had no idea what they grew out here beyond the fact that I sometimes drove past rows of green that I assumed were vegetables and an occasional patch of pale gold waving stuff that was obviously some kind of cereal crop. Most of them seemed to have been harvested already.

My combats had come with a sleeveless khaki singlet and a peaked forage cap. The sun was still beating down from a sky flecked with puffy pockets of clouds, but the gentle breeze skittering over my bare arms and shoulders kept me pleasantly cool, and the cap shaded my eyes. It occurred to me that now I'd got into the rhythm of cycling without thinking about it, I was actually enjoying myself. I was sure that wasn't Vetch's intention – which made me even more determined to go on doing it.

I had to join the main road for the last half-mile of the approach to the village. But hey – long stretches of black tarmac and white lines were no longer intimidating to an old hand at pedal power like me. Standing off the saddle to check the right was clear, I swung confidently left – and just glimpsed a large bonnet and headlights before he clipped me.

He'd been pulling out and turning right from a track that joined the other side of the main road. Flat on my back, and pinned under the full weight of the bike, I watched him pull up a few yards in front of me and heard the sound of the window sliding down.

I guessed he was watching me in the wing mirror. As soon as I demonstrated enough movement to make it a fair bet I wasn't about to peg out, he let the clutch in and left me to watch Mr Timpkin's Farm Fresh Vegetables roar away in a cloud of diesel fumes.

With my skin intact and my cycling confidence shot to pieces, I remounted and wobbled to the right turn down to St Biddy's – or St Bidulph's-atte-Cade to give it its full title.

The village proper lay half a mile from the main road. The general store could have been built any time within the past forty years and was neither new nor old. It was a plain, stolid sort of building with a grey tiled roof, a central chimney stack and three pink-curtained upper windows. The ground-floor shop area had pane-divided glass windows either side of the door, a board for ads, and a small notice giving the opening times for the sub-post office.

I'd intended to flash Barbra's photos inside as a reasonable starting point for the legatee hunt. However, it seemed sensible to take a circuit of the rest of the place first. There was no point doing it the hard way if the three lucky winners were currently enjoying the tipples of their choice outside the local pub.

They weren't. Neither were they inside either of the two public houses that faced each other across the narrow road in alcoholic competition. The Royal Oak, on the left, seemed to be winning. A quick scan of the bar and tiny restaurant confirmed my trio weren't in residence, although a reasonable number of the locals were. The Bell – for no discernible reason, since there was nothing between them that I could see – was empty.

Now I was in the central portion of the village, the buildings were of the uneven brick-and-exposed-timber construction that had been in vogue around the time Shakespeare had started sharpening his quill. Narrow tracks twisted away down side streets, leading to small rows of cottages in some cases, barns in others, and occasionally just losing interest and running out a few hundred yards from the back of the village. The church was massively intimidating, and the last building in the village, apart from the St Biddy's sheltered housing complex, which comprised a newish two-storey block of flats around a small green and a toy-town bus shelter.

I walked the bike back to the general store, suddenly conscious of aches in places I didn't expect to ache unless it was preceded by unusual activities involving whipped cream and swinging from chandeliers.

Delving into my bag, I took out a clipboard with an attached pen and a form with lots of interesting-looking boxes for ticking. With the photo folder held under the bull clip at the top, I sashayed inside. 'Hi. Lovely day, isn't it?'

The woman behind the grille that fenced off the post office section looked up from a column of figures she was totalling. The girl lounging against the shop counter continued to draw a tattoo on the back of her hand with fibre pens.

'Carter! The lady wants serving.'

Carter flicked a bored look in my direction. 'Yeah?'

The voice and the odd name made me realise I'd got the gender wrong. Carter wasn't a pug-ugly girl. He was a slightly effeminate-looking boy.

'Carter, we don't want to see Mr Sulky, do we? Now, let's open that mouth and let Master Smiley out, shall we?'

The woman came out from behind her cage. She was a plump little body with creamy-white skin, pink cheeks, black-rimmed glasses and a cloud of thick white hair that was pinned up into a fluffy bun. The colour scheme was continued in her outfit of black skirt and silky white blouse with huge black spots. She'd accessorised with yellow plastic earrings and a pair of neon-pink terry-towelling slippers. The latter, I assume, because they were the only shoes that would fit her heat-swollen feet.

'How can we help you, my dear?'

She pronounced the 'my' as 'moy', with a touch of that country accent you sometimes hear in the older locals here (the younger lot mostly talk in estuary English).

I bought chocolate because a girl can never have enough, and ate it as I browsed along the dull product displays, ticking off boxes on my clipboard form. I could feel their eyes following the back of my neck. Just when I thought they'd crack, shrieks and thundering music from outside distracted them.

An old Ford Escort was cruising up from the centre of the village and swerving erratically – mainly because the driver was probably having trouble seeing the road. There seemed to be eight of them packed inside a motor designed for four. One of the boys – a skinny runt with tattooed chains around his biceps and green-striped hair – was standing up with his top half thrust through the open sun-roof. As the car came opposite the shop, he yelled over the thumping boom box: 'Yo, Mr Saddo, how ya doing?'

Something whistled through the air and hit the metallic

sign advertising *Ice creams sold here*. It went flying. With an exclamation of annoyance, the woman ordered Carter to go and pick it up.

'I have a good mind to report the whole lot of them to the police.' She stepped to the window and gestured for them to get off the forecourt. This had the inevitable effect of increasing the catcalls. As the car sped away, one of the girls pushed her bottom up against the back window and mooned us. With screams of laughter, they headed out towards the main road.

The postmistress and I exchanged small, tight smiles at the manners of the modern young.

Carter retrieved the sign. But instead of a thank you, his employer asked him what on earth he was wearing. Since he was in a rather oddly formal short-sleeved shirt tucked into a pair of blue jeans, I couldn't see there was much to upset her.

'It's the holidays, Gran.'

'You are at work, Carter. We have our standards. Now go and change into some proper trousers.'

'They're all creased.'

'Then you should have told me. As soon as I've finished here, I'll press them.'

Carter muttered something that might have been 'Terrific,' and slouched back to droop himself moodily over the shop counter. I returned to box-ticking with a vengeance.

The woman cracked. 'May we help?'

'It's for my thesis. I'm doing a course at the university: socio-economic trends in the last decade and their effect on down-sized rural-centred retail units. I've already had a hint it could be published commercially.' I unclipped the photo wallet. 'I was here the other week. Took some snaps of typical customers. I'd really like to use them, but I don't want to put anyone in without their permission. Have you any idea where I can find these people?'

I fanned three prints. The woman barely glanced at them before shaking her head. 'We don't know them.'

'Are you sure? If you took another look—'

'I'm quite sure. Now, if you're not going to buy anything else, perhaps you'd be going.'

The temperature had gone down by ten degrees. I'd hit a nerve somehow and I wasn't going to get any further here. With a casual shrug, I turned away.

The bike was leaning against the shop front. Leaving it there, I walked forward to the position I judged Barbra must have been in when she fired off that film. At first glance it didn't look feasible. The small dirt track was called Cowslip Lane. It was bounded on one side by someone's stone garden wall, and appeared to be in full view of the shop doorway. There was no way the trio could have failed to notice Barbra snapping away.

I took a few more paces and saw what wasn't visible from the main street. A tiny stone seat was set into the wall and hidden by a profusion of exuberant bush branches leaning from the cottage's garden.

I eased myself on to the slab and drew my legs to sit cross-legged. I just about fitted and Barbra was shorter than me.

Forming a round with finger and thumb to imitate a camera lens, I closed one eye and squinted through the leaves, pretending I was snapping the shop doorway. Carter's bored face stared back at me from about eighteen inches away.

Schlepping over in a desultory amble, he slapped his butt against the wall. 'You really from the uni?'

'Why shouldn't I be?'

He raised an indifferent shoulder. 'I dunno. Just wondered.' Hooking a thumb in his waistband he pulled it down a fraction to reveal a hoop pierced through his navel. It was complete with a diddy padlock in the shape of a grinning skull. It was a working model, as Carter demonstrated by snapping the bar open and closed mindlessly. 'Put it in myself. What you think?'

'You'll get blood poisoning.'

'I put it in disinfectant first.'

I looked him over now that I could see him clearly. He was a plain, overweight cherub with light brown hair tinged with ginger. His round, wide-lipped face was liberally dusted with freckles and, judging by the lines of angry pink sunburn glowing along the neck and sleeves of his shirt, he also seemed to have been cursed with that non-tanning dead white skin that often comes with reddish locks. The tattoo he'd been drawing on his hand was a skull with dripping fangs.

'You finished at the shop for the day?'

'No. Gran's gone up to the flat. I can watch the door from here.'

'She seemed a bit upset when I asked about the photos.'

'She thinks you're a Social Security snooper. We had one last summer. Checking for benefit claimants doing casual work on the farms.'

'Do you get many of those?'

Carter raised a bored shoulder. The movement pressed those pubescent breasts that had fooled me into thinking he was a girl against his shirt. 'Some. Asylumers from the ferries and sun-tanners from the cities who move to the beach in summer. Not that Gran cares about *them*, but some of the locals got into trouble last time. And they're our bread and butter.'

'Well I'm not from the Social – honest. I'm a student.' And if you say *Aren't you a bit old?* kid, you're dead, I thought.

Instead Carter announced he couldn't wait to leave school and go to college.

'What are you going to study?' I enquired. I'd have laid

money on an NVQ in Terminal Boredom and Body Mutilation.

'Astrophysics,' he said. 'I'm gonna do stuff about space: quasars and black holes and all that. Like in *Star Trek*.' Moodily he blew air over those thick lips, forming tiny bubbles of spittle on the bottom one. 'I hate this place. There's nothing to do, and you can't get out unless you've got wheels.'

'What about the bus? I saw a stop.'

'Did you read the timetable? We get two a day. One early morning, one late afternoon. Nearest evening stop's a mile down the main road. And the last bus gets back at nine thirty. It's deadsville, this place. It's where lobotomy donors go to retire.' He threw another weary look around the idyllic country scene. 'Give me a twenty and I'll sort your photos for you.'

'Make it a fiver – if you can give me names and addresses.'

'Twenty.'

'I could show them around the village.'

'No one will tell you. They'll just think you're a Social Security snoop like Gran does.'

'How come you don't?'

'I don't care if you are.'

It was going on Barbra's bill anyway, so I delved into my trousers and rescued two notes I'd pinned inside. Holding them between my middle and forefinger, I said, 'OK. Grass.'

'If I had any, I'd do it myself.'

'No, I meant—'

'Yeah, I know. It was a joke, right?'

'Right,' I said meekly. I passed up the photo folder.

Carter shuffled the prints quickly, interest finally replacing the flat stare in his pale green eyes.

He passed back the shots of Mrs X with a head shake. 'I

don't know her. She's not from the village. But this one's easy.' He handed back the snaps of the bloke. 'That's Harry Rouse. 'S funny, Gran was saying just before you came that he hadn't been in all week. He's big on humbug mints – buys bags of them. He lives up at Tyttenhall Farm.'

'Has he lived there long?'

'He was born there, I 'spect. The Rouses have been around for ever. Why?'

Because there would be plenty of local gossip to establish whether Harry had ever enjoyed the hospitality of HM Prisons, that was why. However, since that information wasn't included in Carter's pieces of silver, I contented myself with a vague mumble of the 'just curious' variety, and asked about the parrot.

'Bloody hell, what is she like? Will you look at those *feathers*.' Carter snorted. 'They reckon they're a few braves short of the full war party up there.'

'Up where?'

He handed the final clutch of snaps back and jerked a thumb in the direction of the church end of St Biddy's. 'It's about a mile outside the village. Opened this spring. Listen for the drums and if they stop—'

He paused. I fell for it. 'Yes?'

'Be afraid. Be very afraid.' Twitching the tenners from my fingers, he started back towards the shop.

'Hang on. Where do I find Tyttenhall Farm?'

Carter swung back to shout, 'Straight back to the main road, turn left, take the first track on the left. You can't miss it.'

He was right, I couldn't. It was the road Mr Timpkins's lorry had emerged from just prior to our near fatal connection.

There was no obvious sign of a house as I wheeled the bike up the hard-baked track, and I was just beginning to wonder if Carter had sold me a dummy when I got to the

38

top of a slight rise and discovered the farm lurking in a natural hollow.

For some reason I always expect farmyards to look like those twee illustrations on calendars set in some cod-Victorian era: fat hens, jolly pigs, big-eyed cows and rosy-cheeked kids romping in the barn. A sort of cross between Old Macdonald's place and the-Waltons-go-scrumping.

This one fell well short of the picture. Apart from a scrawny ginger cat, there was no sign of life – animal or Walton – at all, although there was a pungent aroma that became stronger nearer the house and which gave it an air of four-legged things doing what comes naturally.

The door knocker echoed inside an apparently empty house. It looked like I was going to have to make another trip out here to verify that my photo was who Carter claimed it to be. Mildly irritated, I started walking backwards, my eyes on the windows for a curtain twitch or movement inside.

The collision came as a complete surprise – to me at least. The old boy I'd collided with seemed unfazed. Staring from under a lank fringe of white hair, he acknowledged my automatic 'Sorry' with a laconic 'Ahr.'

'I was looking for Harry Rouse.'

'Ahr.'

'Do you know where I can find him?'

'Ahr.'

'Are you going to give me a clue?'

Life improved. His next sentence expanded our verbal contact by fifty per cent. 'Stop here,' he said.

He produced a key tied to his belt by a large lump of string, went inside and closed the door firmly behind him. It seemed unlikely Harry hadn't heard my onslaught earlier, but perhaps he was deaf and the old boy would rout him out for me.

I'd decided to stick with my mature student's thesis story. Maybe I could even invent a few questions about the decline in rural farming around here, I decided, contemplating the silent outhouses and deserted yard. Creaky hinges and turning handles announced the arrival of someone from inside the farmhouse. I swung back with my best welcoming smile, clipboard poised professionally – and froze.

The dangerous end of a double-barrelled shotgun was pointing straight at my head.

5

I found I'd put my hands up. Keeping them in what I hoped was a placatory position, I started to back away, placing each foot carefully in case he interpreted a sudden movement to keep my balance as threatening.

After we'd executed a one-hundred-and-twenty-degree circuit, it occurred to me we weren't doing a random dance: he was deliberately manoeuvring me so that I ended up with the barn at my back. As he advanced he forced me to back up to keep a respectable distance between my head and those barrels.

'Look, why don't I just get on my bike and pedal off into the sunset? Wouldn't that be a great idea?'

Evidently not. The barrels kept coming and I kept demonstrating one of physic's basic laws: viz., for every action there is an equal and opposite reaction. Eventually I was forced to a stop by the immovable roughness of the barn door.

'So what now?'

The barrels came several inches closer. They looked like a pair of sightless eyes. Despite the weight of the gun and the fact he'd had to follow me over the uneven ground, the line of his aim hadn't shaken or wavered once.

'Gorin.'

'Pardon?'

'Gorin . . . Gorin . . .' The barrels were jerking in an alarming way by now as he repeated the word. 'Gorin.'

I guessed I was supposed to go in. The doors didn't give when I leant my full weight against them. Fumbling behind my back, I tried to locate the handle. I couldn't. My failure agitated the geriatric Ned Kelly in front of me even further.

'Gorin . . . Gorin . . .'

'I'm gorring . . . er . . . going.' I desperately didn't want to turn my back on those barrels, but I was going to have to in order to get the damn door open. With fear clomping up and down my spinal bones like a line of boot-scoopin' centipedes, I wrestled with the bolt and handle, half expecting a couple of cartridges to smash straight into the small of my back and erupt from the front of my bowel. I was trying to recall some more of those school physics lessons. Did sound travel faster than bullets? Would I hear the bang before the blast hit me or after?

The doors opened outwards. Ned Kelly stepped away to give me room to swing one of them wide.

The interior was a surprise. Despite the lack of an Old Macdonald set outside, I was still expecting hay bales, four-legged creatures and the sort of pungent atmosphere that you tend to get when you combine the two.

The place was empty. There were several wooden horse stalls down one side, an even smaller pen away in one corner and assorted implements hung from wall hooks, but not a sniff (literally) of livestock or a wisp of straw on the bare concrete floor.

'There . . . There . . .' The barrels jerked in small, sweeping motions towards the far stall.

With more descriptive circles of those deadly pipes he indicated I should sit down. Without taking his eyes off me, he backed slowly away until he came to the opposite wall. He felt behind him and slid a thin leather strap from one of the hooks. Using his teeth and one hand, he tied a slip noose in the end. In order to do so he had to put the shotgun under his arm and clamp it against his waist. Several times he fumbled the operation and had to glance at what he was doing.

No doubt you're now thinking that that was my opportunity to do something heroic in the 'with-one-bound-Jill-was-free' mode. Fling myself forward and whip out his feet with a cunningly placed kick while I wrested the weapon from him, perhaps? Or distract his attention by throwing something to the opposite end of the barn while I sprinted through the doors, maybe?

Listen, that's your fantasy. When I was in the police I saw the results of shotguns up close on two occasions. The first was a domestic argument. The woman's loving other half had blasted her in the back as she tried to escape from the house. Luckily for her he had been too drunk to aim properly. The blast had glanced off her right shoulder and gouged out a large lump of flesh, muscle and sinew. I saw her again two years later – despite plastic surgery the area resembled a moon crater covered in puckered greyish skin. It looked ugly and it always would.

The second time it was self-inflicted. The victim had crouched on the floor by his kid's cot and put both barrels in his mouth. They recovered some of his brain tissue from inside the lampshade hanging from the rose in the centre of the room.

So to sum up: if you want to rush a loaded shotgun – be my guest. Personally I intended to do everything Ned Kelly told me to, which in this case meant slipping the noose over one wrist and wrapping the rest of the thong several times round the corner post of one of the stalls.

He edged forward and grabbed the spare end from me. 'Hand up,' he growled.

I put it in the air. A rumble of annoyance behind his teeth told me I'd made the wrong choice. Swiftly I stuck it against the one that was already tethered. Right choice. The rest of the strap was whisked round in fast, competent movements, until the post and I were irrevocably joined until death or a deal did us part. I was rather hoping we could achieve the latter now I was safely trussed up and no threat to him any more.

'Listen, maybe we should try names? I'm Grace Smith. What should I call you?' (Apart from raving, I added mentally.)

For a moment I thought I wasn't going to get an answer. Then he mumbled: 'You knows. You ain't catching me that way.'

'I'm not going to catch you any way like this, am I?' I flexed the bonds and was pleased to discover that keeping my wrists side by side instead of crossing them had given me the play I'd hoped for. 'I've got to call you something, haven't I?'

'No need. We got nothing to say. I ain't coming with you. I can't. I've got to look out for Madge, see?'

He had the old local accent I'd heard in the postmistress, with the 'I've' coming out as 'Oi've'.

'Hey, I certainly wouldn't want to come between you and Madge. Er . . . what does she call you?'

'Atch.' The barrels mercifully had been drooping nearer and nearer to the floor as we spoke. Now that I was no longer mesmerised by those two deadly tubes, I looked at their owner with more attention. He'd lost muscle and fat as he'd aged. In addition to the slight stoop, his clothes hung on his skin and his skin hung on his skeleton. In fact the only bit of him that didn't seem to have shrunk with the years was his teeth. Whenever he spoke, I got the full glory of a mouthful of yellow paving slabs that would have looked at home in the plough-horse that ought to be in this stall instead of me.

'Any chance of you getting Madge over here?'

'What for?'

'Just to get her side of the story. Maybe the three of us could work something out. How about you fetching her?'

A worried frown flickered over the weatherbeaten features. 'I can't find her. I been looking, but she ain't nowhere.'

'She might have gone to the village. St Biddy's, you know? I could help you look, if you like.'

He shook his head; the thatch of white hair lifted for a moment, then resettled. 'I can't let you go. You'd take me away. I've seen you all looking for me. But I'm smart, see. I hid from your mates. They never caught me, not once.'

'That's great, Atch, but I think there's been some kind of mix-up. As far as I know, none of my mates have ever been here. Must have been some other mates.'

'You're not from the same mob?'

'Absolutely not. In fact, I'm the most antisocial person I know. I never join anything. Never volunteer, that's my motto.'

Unexpectedly he chuckled. 'Government got you too, did they? Didn't know they was taking women. They'll not take Madge, though – not in her condition, I don't reckon.'

'Definitely not. I'd say Madge was OK.' I had absolutely no idea what he was babbling about, but agreement seemed the simplest option.

He beamed, and I felt quite pleased with myself. We were definitely making progress here. Another half an hour and we'd be exchanging holiday snaps. 'You fancy a cuppa?' he asked.

'I sure do, Atch. Wouldn't mind a biscuit too. Or a bit of cake. Good cook, is she, your Madge?'

'Ahr. She's a fine cook, my girl. We'll do well here. We're going to have pigs.'

'That'll be a nice change for the midwife.'

'How's that?'

He squinted from beneath the fringe fronds. I sensed I was losing him and quickly suggested I'd like to meet Madge.

'I'll go fetch her.'

He shuffled back towards the barn doors – taking his damn gun with him. I'd been rather hoping he'd untie me, but getting rid of him so I could work at the straps myself was the next best option.

It was slow going. A parallel bar between the two upright posts prevented me from heaving the strap up and over. The timber looked old and might have been rotten. It wasn't.

I had a go at shoulder-charging the plank and then balancing on one foot and kicking with the other heel. All I achieved was a shorter temper and a bruise. My mouth was drying up; I sucked my thumb vigorously to work up some spittle, then licked and spat over my wrists.

I don't know how long I worked at the damn things. Atch had a pretty mean style with knots, I discovered. The thongs had been twisted and secured in a way that prevented me from getting free but didn't obstruct the blood flow in my hands. It was a neat trick. Maybe it was the sort of thing you learnt on a farm.

Every few minutes I stopped jiggling and listened hard. There was no sense yelling for help if the place was as deserted as it had been when I arrived; but the first hint of intelligent life out there and I intended to bawl my head off.

It was warm work. Sweat oozed out of my pores and stuck the singlet to my back and bust. All my spittle had gone and I could have murdered for that cup of tea.

I assumed Atch had wandered off into whatever dimension he cruised in, and forgotten all about the offer of refreshment, but he proved me wrong. I'd just got the strap halfway over rubbed-red knuckles, and was leaning back to give it one more heave and rip, when the door lock rattled warningly. I froze as the steel barrels nudged open the door and Atch shuffled in behind them, clutching a blue and white mug in the other hand.

'Tea.' He nodded. 'Didn't forget.'

'You're a hero,' I said, trying to inject love, empathy and

friendship for life into my voice. Please like me, I projected silently. Be my pal. And untie me, you stupid old idiot.

'No, I'm ain't.' The barrels jerked up less than two inches from my stomach. 'I don't want to be no hero.'

'OK. Fine. You're the biggest yellowback this side of the Thames,' I agreed hastily. 'Can I have that tea then?'

He seemed to rediscover the mug attached to the end of his fingers. I'd hoped he'd untie me so that I could hold it myself. Instead he held it to my lips, but at least that meant he had to angle the gun barrels away from me.

I gulped the sweet liquid down greedily. 'Any sign of Madge?' I asked, when I finally came up for air.

'I can't find her. 'Spect she's gone for the shopping. Ought to have told me first. She knows I worry.' Setting down the mug on top of the post, he tested the leather straps. And discovered how far I'd got the left hand out.

I half expected him to turn nasty – I'd noticed in the past that those who tie you up have an unreasonable attitude to escape attempts. Atch, however, merely muttered under his breath, shuffled over to the far wall and picked up another length of what I reckoned had been some kind of horse's rein at one time. It was three more loops, two twists and no chance of getting free this time, Grace.

'Hey!' I yelled at his disappearing back. 'Where's Harry Rouse?'

He paused briefly, one hand on the open door. The sun was behind him, so that all I could see was a featureless silhouette.

'No one's going to find Harry Rouse. I seen to that.' He raised the gun in salute. The light caught both barrels and a shaft of white brilliance sprang from them like fire. They looked beautiful, and very, very deadly.

Suddenly I could hear Carter's voice: 'That's Harry Rouse. 'S funny, Gran was saying just before you came that he hadn't been in all week . . .'

6

It was a very long afternoon – which, when you consider the alternative, was better than a very short one.

My thoughts kept going back to Atch's comment on Harry Rouse, like a tongue niggling at an aching tooth even though you know damn well every probe is going to make it worse.

I got flashes of the figure in Barbra's photos lying somewhere inside the house with a large hole in his chest. Supposing he'd been shot soon after Barbra snapped him last week? In this weather he'd be smelling the place out by now, rather like that distinctly pungent whiff I'd caught near the farmhouse when I first arrived here, when I thought about it. I decided I'd rather *not* think about it, and concentrated instead on positive images like chocolate, sex and chips.

Finally, after what felt like several hours, I heard the sound I'd been praying for all afternoon: a human voice, shouting and whistling in an effort to attract someone's attention.

Flinging back my head, I tried to join in. My first screech came out as a pathetic croak before I dissolved into coughs. Terrified my rescuer would end up captured – or shot – before he could get me out of this mess, I spat, breathed hard and YELLED.

I held my breath and listened hard. It wasn't until the door fastening rattled that I was certain he'd heard me.

Because the light was behind him and my eyes had to adjust after the gloom of the barn, all I saw was height and leanness. He plainly had a better view of me, judging by the exclamation of: 'Bloody hell. What's happened?'

'I was held up by a geriatric lunatic with a set of teeth he borrowed from a cart-horse, and a loaded shotgun.'

'That'll be Dad,' Harry Rouse said, leaning over the top bar to test the leather bindings.

'That's it?' Relief that he wasn't decomposing somewhere, plus the imminence of rescue, was restoring my courage. 'Just *That'll be Dad* ! Is that the best you can come up with?'

He'd taken a penknife from his jeans pocket and was sawing at the knots. With a crack, one parted from its thong and the rest of the straps fell away. 'OK?'

'Of course I'm not bloody well OK.'

He tried to help me up. I elbowed him aside and stood by myself, shaking and waving my arms to get the blood flowing properly again. He was a bit too flaming casual for my liking.

'Does your dad make a habit of this? Or is it just a weekly thing since he can't get out to the over-sixties' bowls club?'

'Sorry.' He looked embarrassed. 'Look, come up the house, and I'll fix up those wrists and some tea. Or something stronger, if you like. Please. Just give me a chance to explain.'

I hesitated. My first instinct was to put as much distance as possible between me and that gun. On the other hand, I was going to have to find out some more about Harry if I wanted to collect my fee from Barbra. And he seemed fairly confident his dad wasn't about to start blazing away.

'All right. I'll have tea and what had better be a bloody good explanation if you don't want the police up here in the next half an hour.'

'Thanks. Thanks a lot, Miss . . . er—'

'Grace Smith.'

'Harry Rouse.' He offered a hand. I polished a palm on the seat of my combat pants before accepting it.

The bike was where I'd left it, propped outside the farmhouse, with the contents of the basket still intact, as far as I could see.

'Wondered who it belonged to,' Harry remarked, ushering me into a dark hall, its wooden floor protected by old strips of faded carpet that seemed to have been flung down randomly as the one underneath wore out. At least this bit looked like my mythical olde-worlde farm. So did the kitchen.

The assorted china displayed on the Welsh dresser had probably been in the family for a hundred years or so, judging by the worn patterns and cracked glaze. The kitchen table was solid wood, scarred by a hundred chopping knives and decorated by the shotgun balanced across one corner.

The sight of those barrels reminded my legs and stomach just how scared I'd been.

'You OK?' Harry turned as I grabbed a chair and sat down quickly. Following the direction of my gaze, he leant over, broke the gun and showed me the empty chambers. 'It's safe.'

'It's not safe,' I snapped. 'It's a *gun*. You're supposed to keep them secure, not hand them out to the odd passing psychotic parent.'

'Dad must have found the key to the cabinet. I'll move it. You don't have to worry, though.' Fishing inside his pocket again, he hauled out a bunch of keys and separated two small ones with his forefinger. 'Ammunition box. I always keep it separate.'

'Oh, great. You realise he wants locking up?'

'Aye, I do,' he agreed calmly, dropping tea bags into a pot and adding boiling water. It had heated so fast it was pretty obvious the kettle hadn't been long switched off. The thought made me nervous again. I inched the chair around so I could keep an eye on the door. Who knew how many murderously inclined relatives Harry had?

'He went off to look for someone called Madge,' I said.

'That's my ma.' Harry set two mugs of tea on the table, took half a bottle of whisky from the drawer and added an inch to each.

'Is she around? Or has she popped over to the neighbours with some home-baked cookies and the chainsaw?'

'She died when I was thirteen.'

Why does that always happen to me? Just when I'm in the right for once, I somehow end up in the wrong again. 'Sorry,' I mumbled, taking several quick mouthfuls of the brew.

'It was a long time ago now.' Like his dad and Carter's gran, he had that slight trace of old local accent in his voice, that should have been West Country but wasn't. Rummaging in a drawer, he drew out a lethal-looking knife and then produced a part-cut loaf from an old bread crock. 'I'm having toast. Fancy some?'

'Sure.'

He hacked off slices – thick at one end and transparently thin at the other – and set them under the grill before joining me at the table. Elbows resting on it as he cradled his mug, he said: 'Dad has dementia. It's been coming on for the past few years. But this last eighteen months, it's just got . . .' He made a chopping motion with the side of his hand, indicating the end, I suppose.

'And you leave guns where he can play with them?'

'I don't. I told you. I didn't know he'd found the keys. As a rule, I'd not have left him, but I had to go out unexpected for a few hours. He was fast asleep when I went. I thought he'd be OK. He sleeps a lot now. Anyway, what else could I do? There's no one else to do the minding.'

'No other family?'

'My wife walked out to live with a mortgage on a centrally heated semi ten years ago. There's just me and the old man now.'

Snatching the toast from the griddle with bare fingers, he dropped it on plates and added an assortment of mismatched knives, a butter dish and a large pot of lemon curd. 'Help yourself.'

I did, but the sight of more bread going under the grill and another tea being served up was taking away my appetite.

'It'll be OK,' he said, interpreting my expression correctly. 'Take your cap off.'

I'd forgotten I had the thing on. But I whipped it off and shook out the locks, combing them down with my fingers. Harry hitched a brushed cotton man's shirt from a peg on the back of the door. 'Stick this on over your top and haul your chair up to the table a bit. Get those trousers out of sight.'

'Why?' I asked, shrugging myself into the shirt, which smelt – of Harry, I assumed.

'Because you look like you're in uniform – and army uniform at that.' He added the new toast to the table and rasped butter thinly over the unevenly browned surface, then stuck two fingers in his mouth and sent a shrill whistle into orbit. 'Ever heard of National Service?'

'The compulsory conscription of male civilians into military service for a period between eighteen months and two years. It was finally scrapped in this country in nineteen sixty,' I said promptly. (It had come up in a pub quiz last month, in case you were wondering.)

'Right. Dad got called up just after he got Mum in the family way with me. Some blokes might have reckoned that was a lucky break, but not Dad. He was desperate to stay with her. She was barely seventeen and he thought they'd take her off to one of those homes for unmarried mums and make her give the baby up. They did that back then. Girls didn't have no choice, according to Dad. It was keep quiet, read your Bible and sign the forms when they told you. So he goes on the run from the training camp, marries my mum and brings her back here to stay. Trouble was, by that time they'd started a war in Korea. Do you know about that war?'

'I've seen *M.A.S.H.*' I accepted the lemon curd pot from him and slapped a large dollop on my toast.

'Right. So Dad starts thinking, what's going to happen if he gets himself killed out there?'

'So he bunked off National Service?'

'Hid out whenever they came looking for him. Used to be exciting when I was a kid. A bit of a game, like. Dad hiding and everyone swearing blind we'd not seen him.'

Given the limited number of possible hiding places and the fact Atch must presumably have had to work outside on the farm, I found it hard to believe the local coppers hadn't managed just a glimpse over the years.

'Of course they did,' Harry laughed. 'The local sergeant was in the same darts team as my grandad. But it was a game; everyone understood the rules. If they weren't looking officially, they didn't see him. And when they got an official request to investigate—'

'They tipped you off beforehand and Daddy made himself scarce?'

'That's the idea.' Levering back his chair, he opened the window, and repeated the earlier whistled signal. 'Dad! You out there?'

He tilted his head as he listened. I found myself doing the same. We both heard the soft click of a door opening at the back of the house and the shuffle of footsteps somewhere.

Satisfied, Harry returned to the table. 'They gave up looking years back. About the time they ditched National Service. I reckon Dad's records just got lost somewhere. Problem is, these last few years he forgets things that happened this morning, but fifty years ago is like yesterday. He thinks they're out to catch him. Anyone in a uniform sets him off.'

'Must be fun for the postman. Have they issued him with a bullet-proof vest?'

'I told you, this was a one-off. He just hides normally. Hello, Dad. Come and have your toast. I got you some of your special mints.' A red bag with the logo of a motorway service outlet slid along the table and came to a halt millimetres from the edge.

Atch came in slowly. I half expected an apology, or further rage. Instead I appeared to have cracked the secret of invisibility.

'Don't report this, please,' Harry said abruptly. 'It wouldn't do any good, would it?'

'It'll protect the next idiot who wanders up here in uniform.'

'He won't get the gun again, I promise. And what do you think would happen if he's arrested? They'll put him in a psychiatric ward for a few weeks until he can be assessed, then tell me what I already know – that he's incurable. Then they'll send him back here while they look for a place to put him.'

I'd hissed my own comments under my breath because Atch was in earshot. Harry, however, simply continued to use his normal tone, ignoring his father, who was now dosing the cat with sugared tea. Looking up, I caught the old man flicking a puzzled sideways glance at me and realised he hadn't a clue who I was, or how we'd last met.

Harry was waiting for me to promise I wouldn't shop his dad. Barbra's camera lens had been kind to him. Seen in the flesh, he looked older and more care-worn. He'd been lucky: the genetic code for Atch's buck teeth and nondescript pale blue eyes had been overridden by quite an attractive mouth and hazel irises. I wondered if they'd come from the dead mother. I also felt pretty pleased that I'd won my private bet with myself that that haircut *did* hide a receding widow's peak.

'Look,' I said, not ready to go soft on him yet, 'I've just been threatened with a shotgun, spent several hours trussed up, and if you hadn't come back, I'd probably have died out there of dehydration. What happens if the next victim isn't young . . . ish, fit and healthy? Supposing the visitor is older than—' I jerked a thumb in Atch's direction, and discovered he'd disappeared. Judging by Harry's expression, he hadn't noticed his dad slipping away either. 'Have you got any more guns?' I asked sharply.

'They're secure. Don't get yourself in a frazzle.'

'Being frazzled I can cope with. Being a corpse takes more talent than I'm currently prepared to invest in my future. Let's get back to your plans for Atch. Is that really his name?'

'Nickname. It's H really. H for Harry. He's Harry Rouse too.'

And I'd turned up in my camouflage gear and told the old boy I was looking for Harry Rouse. No wonder he'd gone into psychosis-overdrive. But he was still a menace and needed looking out for.

Harry Junior agreed. 'I *know* I can't manage like this. I've been looking for help, someone to live in. Even offered free board and lodging, but no one's interested once they see the place. And having full-time carers come in costs.'

'What about Social Services?'

'He needs watching all the time, even nights. He wanders, you see. I've tried locking all the doors, but he has tantrums; screams the place down. They say he'd be better off in a residency place. But I might as well put those barrels to his head. He's never lived nowhere but this.' He looked at the old, stained room. It wasn't everyone's idea of desirable living, but I guess if it was all you'd ever known . . . 'I just need a bit of time,' Harry continued, 'to get something sorted. Will you keep this between us?'

'I don't—' My 'know' was interrupted by the shrill of the telephone. Harry excused himself and my innards finally signalled they'd unfrozen enough to make it a good idea if I did the same. The loo was at the top of the stairs, and surprisingly clean for a bachelors' pad. Despite the partially open window that was letting in a gentle breeze, the odours of pine cleaning fluids and bleach were catching at the back of my throat as evidence that one of the Rouses was a conscientious cleaner.

It overlooked the outhouses. The doors of the larger one were standing open now, revealing the muddy back of an old truck. Down below I could see Atch pottering up and down as if he was looking for something. Hopefully it was this morning's memories that were proving elusive, and not the DIY sub-machine-gun kit.

Flushing and hand-washing like a well-trained house guest, I stepped out on to the landing and couldn't resist a quick peek in the nearest door. It was much as the downstairs had suggested: old-fashioned furniture and fading rugs.

The top of the dresser was covered in old photos. I found Atch and Madge's wedding picture easily enough. I'd been right about young Harry looking like his mum. There were a lot of pictures of him growing from toddler to adult, but none of his wedding or the ex-Mrs Harry Rouse (OK, I was snooping, but every girl should have a hobby).

I tried another door. It was a near-identical room, except in this one the bed was stripped back to the bare mattress and once again there was that slightly pungent, unpleasant smell I'd detected outside. Following my nose, I found it partly emanated from a plastic sack full of dirty bedclothes. It looked like it wasn't just Atch's mind that was slipping out of control.

There were two other bedrooms in the same stripped-back state. One containing a double bed and a single, the other with two ancient singles of the lethal-and-rusting-bedsprings variety. It was a family house this, built back in a time when loads of kids were the norm. It must feel desperately lonely with just the two of them rattling around in here, particularly in the winter, when the fields froze over and darkness fell by mid afternoon.

The last door opened on to a long, narrow cupboard. The shelves were stacked with cardboard cartons from a cash-and-carry warehouse in south-east London. I delved inside one and found non-brand-name tinned peas. A second held two dozen cans of carrots. All the cartons contained variations of the same: groceries whose packaging screamed frugality. It looked like the Rouses did their shopping in bulk once a year from the cheapest source they could find. My fantasy of ye jolly farmer harvesting fresh produce from his lovingly nurtured vegetable patch withered a little further, but my find tended to confirm Harry's assertion that he couldn't afford home help for his dad.

I got back to the hall just as Harry reappeared from the back of the house. 'What are you doing?'

'Using the facilities.' I mimed a chain flush.

'You could have asked.'

Well, pardon my manners, I thought rebelliously. 'I've had to keep my legs crossed all afternoon, remember?'

He looked like he'd have argued it, but I didn't give him the chance. It wasn't just the cleaning fluids that were getting up my nose around here. Swinging round with what I hoped was an icy dismissal, I marched out of the front door and grabbed the bike.

'Wait!' Harry seized the handlebars as I kicked the pedals into position. 'You haven't said what you're going to do about Dad.'

'That's because I haven't decided yet. Now let go!'

I heaved, he pulled. We were just getting into the spirit of a real tug-of-war when Atch shuffled round the corner.

'I can't find it. It ought to be there. Where is it?'

Harry's attention was distracted sufficiently for him to relax the grip on my handlebars. I twisted them free and backed off a few paces.

'You can't find what, Dad?'

'The thing. What's it called?' An expression of panic started to flow over the old boy's face. I could see him straining to remember and felt his misery. 'Water comes out of it.' One hand swished back and forth as if he was holding a baton.

'The hose, Dad. Is that what you're looking for?'

'Hose. Yes. That's it.' A smile of relief lit up his eyes. 'I'm going to wash the truck. Just have time before I go pick up your ma from the shops.'

'Ma died, Dad. A long time ago. Don't you remember?'

'She did?' Atch peered around in a bewildered fashion and appeared to notice me for the third time that afternoon. 'Who's she?'

'This is Grace, Dad. She's—'

'Just off.' Kicking the pedal down, I stood on the bike and shot away before either of the Rouses could get between me and the farm track.

It wasn't until I'd put ten minutes' pedalling between me and Tyttenhall Farm that the oddest thing about the afternoon occurred to me.

During the entire time, Harry Rouse hadn't once asked me why I was there.

7

I'd intended to get Barbra's contract typed up first thing next day and take it out to Wakens Keep. But as soon as I woke up, I hit a major drawback to this plan, which was best summed up by Annie asking why I was doing John Wayne impressions.

'The hell I am,' I drawled, walking with wide-legged caution to the foot of the office steps and clutching the package I'd just got from the chemist tightly to my chest.

'Sweet thing! How are you getting on with Grannie's pedal power?'

'I left it at the flat. I presume you aren't in a hurry to have it back?' I gritted my teeth and smiled at the smirking gnome who'd whipped the front door open before we could reach it.

'No hurry at all. Keep it as long as you like. Dear me . . . life continues to offer new experiences, doesn't it?'

The subject of this cryptic remark was stomping towards us with a scowl on her face and a slice of turf on her head.

'It's your fault,' Jan said, homing in on me. 'You told me to dye it.'

'So? What is that shade, incidentally? Swamp-à-gogo?'

'It's called Zanzibar Twilight.' A squashed and water-stained carton was waved under my nose. 'It's supposed to be black.'

Annie removed the box from Jan's fingers and scanned the small print. 'It says here, don't use on bleached hair.'

'Does it?'

'Didn't you read it first?'

Jan shrugged. 'It's only flaming hair dye. Who needs instructions?'

'Apparently you do, dear thing,' Vetch put in. 'Are you planning to do any work today?'

'I'm traumatised. I ought to get the day off.'

'I shall arrange counselling for you.'

'Honest?'

'No. I was lying. Now, if you could make some attempt to pretend you're earning the wage I pay you . . .' He unlocked the post cage and handed her a bundle of letters.

Jan slung the envelopes on to the reception desk and her coat on to a handy chair. It gave us a chance to appreciate the rest of her bizarre appearance. She'd abandoned black and leather in favour of a bright orange blouse, leggings in a psychedelic swirl of tangerine, lime green and banana, and emerald stilettos with a five-inch heel.

'Bloody hell.' Annie more or less summed up the general opinion.

'What? Oh yeah, this. I thought I'd make it look like a proper style 'stead of another screw-up. They got a sale on up the charity shop. You can buy them off me later if you like, Smithie. They're the sort of naff gear you like.'

'Cheers, Jan. Can you pick up my calls for the next half-hour? I've got something important to handle.'

I followed Annie up the staircase to the top landing. A familiar Welsh-tinged drone drifted up the central well, apparently apologising for having to use the internal cellar door again.

'Have you met the Grim Reaper yet?' I asked, as Annie jiggled with her office door keys.

'Yesterday. Not exactly a bundle of laughs, is he?'

'Not even a solitary chuckle. What's Vetch up to, foisting him on us?'

Annie paused with her door half open. 'Haven't you heard? Barnfeather's left.'

Barnfeather was one of the other investigators who rented floor space (and 'office facilities') under the general Vetch (International) Associates Inc. banner. But apparently since last month – he didn't.

'How come?' I asked. 'Where's he gone?'

'I'm not sure. He said he was starting something on his own – specialised work of some kind – but he wouldn't say what. Got very cagey when Vetch asked. Anyhow, he's cleared his office and handed in his door key. Hence Laughing Ifor in the crypt. I don't think Vetch had a rush of investigators wanting to fill Barnfeather's floor space. Which reminds me, I've been meaning to say ...' She hesitated and looked vaguely uncomfortable. 'Look, come in a second ... have a coffee ...'

A small knot of anxiety tightened in my stomach. This wasn't like Annie. She didn't break things gently to me, and she was offering free coffee rather than making me beg for it.

I got chocolate biscuits too. Served up with the news. Annie's pet securities company in London were suggesting she might like to move in with them permanently.

'I could have my own space in their block, work freelance if I liked, but they'd have first call on my time. I'd be establishing a reputation . . . making the right contacts . . .'

'Sounds great.' I forced a smile. 'When are you leaving?'

'I'm not sure. I mean, I haven't said I'll take it yet.'

'Go for it, girl. After all, you're not getting any younger.'

'Neither of us are,' Annie came back with an attempt at sisterly bitchiness.

Normally I'd have batted the insult back with interest, but today I wasn't in the mood. I helped myself to a handful of the biscuits (without any protest from the lawful owner), slung the Delaney file into my own office and bolted myself in the bathroom.

Lying back in the old-fashioned cast-iron tub (another leftover from the reign of Grannie Vetch), I watched the verdigris tendrils under the overflow outlet being distorted by the trickle of hot water, licked the chocolate that was being melted by the steam off my biscuit – and brooded.

I don't have many friends. People don't seem to like me (I can't imagine why) and Annie was the closest of that select club. OK, London wasn't exactly in the Arctic Circle, but we both knew it wouldn't be the same once we had to 'make plans' rather than wander round for a drink, a pizza, or a bitch, whenever the mood took us.

On top of that, there was the problem of what might happen to Vetch's with two operatives flown. And to cap a perfect morning, my mother had rung to say she'd prefer it if I didn't come home for my birthday. Not that she put it in those words. It had all been dressed up in tangled explanations about baby-sitting my sister's kids, hospital appointments at the pain clinic for my dad, and suggestions that an all-girl night out in town in a few weeks would be more fun, wouldn't it?

I got the message. My father didn't want to see me and he'd make life hell for Mum, before and after, if I put in an appearance. Some days she can take it, some days she can't. This was obviously one of the latter. I assured her I had millions of plans for my birthday and was far too busy to come up, and heard the relief in her voice as she swallowed the lie.

I wallowed in self-pity and Vetch's free hot water for another twenty minutes, then got my head back together and told my subconscious to stop being such a pathetic little bundle of neuroses and get on with life.

Heaving myself out of the tub, I patted off the water with a towel in some areas – and with extreme caution in others. Unwrapping my chemist's parcel, I applied a large dollop of gel guaranteed to soothe away nappy rash to the inner patches of my thighs. It stung like mad. No wonder the poor little sods are always yelling their heads off.

Retrieving my clothes from the floor, I discovered they'd been soaked by a tidal overflow from the bath. The bra and black T-shirt weren't too bad – they'd probably dry off with a bit of body heat behind them – but the trainer bottoms were sopping. I left them dripping over a pipe, and padded back to my office to sort out Barbra's contract.

There was a typewriter back at my flat, or I could drop it into the Bermuda Triangle that passed for Janice's in-tray and wait for whatever incomprehensible horror emerged. Since there was no way I was up to pedalling twenty miles to Wakens Keep at present, I figured Janice might as well do her worst. I did ring Barbra, however, to suggest a deposit.

'I put a cheque in the post to Vetch yesterday afternoon,' she replied. 'How you getting on?'

'Oh, you know. Early days. I've got a definite lead on one and pretty good clues for the others. Should be back to you in a few days with news.'

(I felt the above statement contained just about the right amount of optimism. The idea being to keep the client hooked for as long as you think they'll pay without actually lying or conning them.)

'You haven't forgotten I want this kept quiet?' she said sharply.

'My lips are sealed.'

'So what are you telling them?'

'At present, I'm a mature student wanting to publish their pics in my thesis.'

'Not bad,' she admitted. 'You'll keep in touch, won't yer? Come out here for lunch.'

'Great. Say one day next week?'

'Sunday.'

'I'm not sure Sunday's good for me—'

'It is for me. I'm paying for your time, aren't I? I'll see you at one o'clock.'

She hung up. Bobbing a curtsy, I muttered: 'Yes, ma'am, Missy Barbra. Ah sure will do as you says, ma'am, just as soon as I finished toting dem cotton bales.'

I picked up the scrawled draft contract. It might be less hassle to type it myself if I could cadge half an hour on Annie's computer. I bounced in without knocking, and stopped dead when I realised she wasn't alone. Her youngest brother was sprawled on the small couch, sipping at a mug of black coffee.

A quick glance downwards confirmed the T-shirt was long enough to cover my confusion – if not much else.

'Hi, Zeb. Excuse the flashing.'

He flicked a half-hearted wave in my direction. ''S OK. I hadn't noticed.'

I decided he wasn't being diplomatic. This was a real facer. Not only was I rapidly sliding over the hill, but my pulling factor was fading fast.

(Not that I *wanted* to pull Zeb. He was a pleasant enough looking bloke, with the eyes – and occasionally the friskiness – of a labrador puppy, but not my type at all. However, a girl has her pride.)

I guess the pique showed on my face, since Annie felt obliged to explain Zeb was a bit tired as he'd just come off duty at the local CID office. 'He's undercover. He's had to put in a bit of hard graft for once.'

'For heaven's sake, Annie,' he objected. 'Undercover means you don't tell the whole bloody world, in case you've forgotten.'

'It's only Grace, she's not going to blab to the bad guys, is she?'

'Well, you never know,' he muttered.

'Zeb!' Annie snapped in her best don't-mess-with-me big sister voice.

I decided to give him the benefit of the doubt. I knew his remark hadn't been intended as an oblique knock at my ignominious departure from the police while I was under suspicion of taking bribes from local low-life. He was just displaying his normal talent for sucking his own toes.

The import of what he'd implied finally got through the thatch of untidy light brown hair. 'Oh? Yeah! Sorry, I didn't . . . I mean, we're still not certain who's involved, so you might say something to someone . . . quite innocently, you know . . .'

It was like watching a fluffy bunny squirm on a meat hook. I put him out of his misery by telling him his grovel was accepted. Anyway, Annie was right – he did look rough.

With an enormous yawn, he swung his ankles over one arm of the sofa whilst he wriggled his shoulders into the cushion at the other end. The movement let his coat swing back. I caught a glimpse of an identity badge clipped to the belt of his jeans. I was interested to see that Zeb was now calling himself Craig Stillwell. (A change that probably came as something of a relief when your parents have lumbered you with 'Zebedee' and the world regularly greets you with 'BOING!') I just managed to read the last fraction of the company name ('ainers') before he saw me noseying, and thrust it into a pocket.

'Don't get comfortable there,' his loving sister ordered. 'I've work to do. Go home to your own bed.'

'Yeah. In a tick.' With another jaw-cracker, Zeb stretched and arched his back.

My request to borrow the computer was turned down on the grounds it was already surfing the net on Annie's behalf. It looked like I was going to have to throw the contract to Jan (and pray that God had mercy on its syntax).

The only spare clothes I had at the office were my best three-piece suit, which consisted of a dark grey pin-stripe jacket with interchangeable short skirt and trousers. I pulled the skirt on and retrieved the photo wallet. If my thighs and butt couldn't make the twenty-mile trip out to Wakens Keep, at least I might be able to manage the three miles to St Biddy's and start on my search for Barbra's second lucky legatee (please God Hiawatha was an orphan!).

I slung Barbra's contract in Jan's typing tray on the way out, and after a quick trip home to exchange the skirt for jeans, I bumped Grannie Vetch's Sunbeam up the iron steps from my basement flat and sat down with great care. I found if I stayed sitting fairly still and pedalled with my legs bent outwards at the knees, I could get along quite well.

About a mile outside St Biddy's, Carter had said when I asked about the Indian parrot's possible roosting place. When people say you can't miss it, you usually can – by miles. However, in Carter's case, he'd been right. The insistent thrumming of a drum beat could have come straight out of a John Ford Western (generally the scene before the wagon train's attacked by hordes of whooping Apaches).

The estate looked like it had once belonged to someone who thought they were important. The driveway curved away from the chained iron gates with their large '*Keep*

Out' notice. There didn't seem to be any bell or other means of attracting the owners' attention. Luckily the ten-foot brick walls on either side were crumbling sufficiently to provide a decent set of footholds. Tucking the photos in my waistband, I laid the bike down in the overgrown grass along the verge and heaved myself up and over the parapet.

I had to jump for it but the soft carpet of leaf loam on the other side provided a good enough shock-absorber. The trees and shrubbery must have been planted by the house-owners. Out here we were too near the flat marshlands of the coast for such a profusion to be natural. At present they were in full midsummer leaf, which meant that most of the sunlight was obscured and it was oddly cold and gloomy. It was almost as if I'd entered another dimension.

The timpani section, which had been working itself into a frenzy in the distance, fell silent with an abruptness that made my heart jump into my throat. I recalled Carter's joke about being afraid when the drums stopped. It *was* a joke, right?

There were sounds in here I hadn't noticed before. Rustlings and murmurings – as if something, or things, were stalking me.

A dried branch cracked loudly behind me. I swung back. And was confronted by a seven-foot nightmare of horns, yellow eyes and brown fur, its huge mouth a gleaming cavern of ivory teeth and red flesh.

8

I did what any reasonable woman confronted by a demon from Hades would do: prayed that devils kept their family jewels in the same place as mere mortals and brought my knee up – hard.

It seemed to have the required result – well, required by me, at any rate. The roar that erupted from the slavering jaws indicated he was going to find biking as uncomfortable as I did for a few days.

I headed in what I hoped was the direction of the house. Why I felt that way was any safer, I can't think now. After all, Mrs Moloch and her little devils could have been heating the oil in anticipation of someone dropping in for lunch, for all I knew. But unless you're a bat, daylight somehow seems to offer more hope than darkness and I could see the bushes thinning out and the promise of open ground ahead.

I was aware that the whispers and rustles around me were getting nearer. I'd got close enough to make out the vein patterns on the last leaves before open country when the first arrow whistled past my head and drove into the earth ahead of me.

A blow against my left shoulder blade knocked me off my stride. I staggered, trying to regain my rhythm, flailed out into the light, and landed nose first in the grass. Rolling on to my back with my arms across my midriff, I lifted and bent my legs ready to deliver the soles of both trainers into the most tender area of whatever reached me first.

What did reach me was a skinny kid of about ten, liberally daubed with paint over his face and bare chest, and wearing a couple of feathers in a head band.

A dozen more little savages slid silently out of the growth and huddled to stare down at me. They were carrying small bows and wearing the sort of expressions that I'd last seen on a pack of lager louts at chucking-out time. It was like being trapped in a production of *Lord of the Flies*.

'Who's she?'

'How'd I know? You shot her, git-head.'

'Didn't.'

'Did.'

'I know who she is. She's a grass. My dad says so.'

This last comment came from the smallest member of the hunting party. One look was enough to place him. He belonged to the tribe of my least favourite copper. Terry Rosco's seed had gone forth and multiplied four times (that his wife knew of). This was the oldest Rosco sproglet.

'Your dad wants to watch his mouth, Junior. There are laws against slander – and shooting people.'

I wrenched the spent arrow from the earth. The one that had hit me in the back had bounced off and fallen a few feet away. Examining them both, I discovered the bouncer had had its tip bound tightly in foam rubber, hence its failure to make itself at home in my back – and probably my lung, judging by the point on the second shaft.

'You can't touch me. I'm under the age of criminal 'sponsibility, I am.' The arrogant thrust of his bottom lip was pure Terry.

'You know, Junior, if I didn't already feel sorry for your mum, one of the joys of my life would be waiting for you to grow into your rebellious genes and make your dad's life pure hell.'

One of the others sniggered. 'Joooonior.'

'That ain't my name. She's soft. Brain rot. And there ain't nothing wrong with my jeans neither. They fit OK,' he finished in a rush, grabbing the arrow from my hand just as my devil limped slowly from the undergrowth. His John Wayne impression was much better than mine.

In the light it was plain that the fur was a zippered body suit and the yellow-eyed, red-toothed, horned head was a full elk mask. Worn over his own head, it must have added another couple of feet to his natural height. At present, it was being clutched under his arm, which allowed the owner's real eyes (blue – not yellow) to glare at me over the collar rim of the costume.

'Are you completely out of your mind?' he snarled.

Coming from someone prancing around the woods in a pantomime costume, I thought this was a bit like the pot accusing the kettle.

'How the devil did you get in here?' he demanded.

'I climbed over the wall. The gates are locked.'

'And did it occur to you that that might be because we were trying to keep people *out*? Did that large notice annotated "Keep Out" not give you the tiniest clue that this was private property?' He was panting heavily, partly from pain and anger, but also from the heat inside his costume, I suspected. I decided the time had come to proffer the peace pipe and start again.

'Look, I'm really sorry about kneeing you. It's just that you scared the hell out of me. I was looking for someone who can give me some information. I'd really appreciate the help. Why don't we get inside out of this sun?'

I half expected to be told to leave the hunting grounds before he whistled up Crazy Horse or something. Instead he grunted and told the war party to head back to the house.

'What about our elk hunt?' one protested. 'We ain't shot nothing yet.'

'You nearly shot me,' I reminded him.

'It's not that dangerous,' the elk said. 'The arrows are covered.'

'Not all of them.'

The vague ripple of guilt as the boys jockeyed for the positions furthest away wasn't lost on either of us. The elk held out a hand. 'All right, let's have them.'

No one moved. The elk grabbed a couple of shafts at random. Their metal tips gleamed wickedly in the sunlight.

'You stupid little . . . Do you realise you could have maimed me – or each other?' he added a trifle belatedly.

'Lighten up, Grandad,' the biggest kid said. 'It's supposed to be a frigging hunt. Can't have a proper hunt without drawing blood.'

A few of the others laughed, braver now they knew any comeback was going to be homing in on their spokesperson.

'If you don't get out of here *this minute*, the only blood spilt, you little moron, will be yours.'

The big kid had to keep face. 'You can't hit me. I'll have the law on you. It's assault. I'll have you slung in prison.'

The war party backed away hastily, spreading out around us like ripples in a pond. They still murmured support, but kept out of whacking range.

'Frankly, you unpleasant lump of excrement,' the elk hissed in short, clipped tones, 'I couldn't care less. I doubt if prison would be any worse than a day in the company of you stupid, mannerless louts. Now go away and do your worst. Go on . . . GO!'

'We're not supposed to leave. Not till we get met,' one of the smaller braves said.

'Then wait by the gates. But GO AWAY!'

A raised fist sent them flying towards the house. Once they were safely out of range, several turned round to semaphore anatomically impossible suggestions. Rosco Junior contributed by yelling that he'd tell his dad. He got the arrows the elk was still holding bowled overarm at him. They fell well short and brought a few more jeers from the war party.

Breathing hard, the elk turned his attention to me. 'Well, come on.' He stalked away awkwardly, handicapped by the costume and my recent assault.

I put the house at late Victorian. Lumps of other styles had been grafted on erratically: rusting metal fire escapes, window frames that didn't match, plastic gutterings. A newly painted board outside announced it was 'The Purbrick Centre for Native American Studies'. Inside there was more paint, and the aromas of linseed oil and wood stain. And an echoing hollowness that said there wasn't enough furniture or soft furnishings in the rooms yet to absorb normal everyday sounds.

'In here.' The elk led the way into a room on the right of the front hall. Large uncurtained windows at the far end let in a flood of sunlight that poured over the bare floorboards and a dust-sheeted jumble of furniture that had been pushed to the far side of the room. A woman was perched on a step-ladder by the left-hand wall, transferring paint from a palette to a tiny figure galloping across the plains of buff-coloured emulsion. When she turned to see who'd come in, she proved to be younger than the streaks of grey in her auburn hair had suggested.

'Esther, this is Miss . . . Smith, was it?'

'Grace. Hi.'

Esther abandoned the palette on the top step and climbed down, casually pushing the boyish cut from her face and adding more paint smears to the fringe. Extending her hand, she said: 'Esther Purbrick. Pleased to meet you.'

'My wife,' the elk said. I am Selwyn Purbrick.' There was a note of pride in his voice. '*Professor* Selwyn Purbrick. You might have seen a précis of my piece on the Windigo legends of the Sub-arctic in *Reader's Digest* last month.'

'Of course she didn't. Most people don't read those things until they're at least four years out of date. And then only if they're stuck in the doctor's waiting room for hours.' Esther grinned. She had one of those big-mouthed, rubbery sort of faces that looked their best during a smile. 'Well, that's the introductions done. Selwyn, hadn't you better change? You look like you've sweated off ten pounds. How did the hunt go?'

'It was hellish. I dismissed them.'

'What do you mean, "dismissed"?'

'I mean I told the bunch of morons to go home. And don't look at me like that. I am a professor of anthropology, not a children's entertainer. This whole concept was a ridiculous idea. We should be a serious study centre – instead of which we're in some kind of sub-standard Butlin's. Well, I, for one, have had enough.' He waddled in the direction of a side door, calling back over his shoulder, 'Miss Smith wants some information on the centre. Can you sort her out?'

Before I could correct the mistake, Esther whipped up a corner of dust-sheet and removed a sheaf of stapled paper from the desk underneath. 'This is our new programme. It's only provisional at present until we get ourselves settled in.'

Further unpeeling of the dust-sheet had unearthed a cardboard pallet of mineral water bottles. Clawing back the thick plastic coating, Esther jiggled two free and raised an interrogatory eyebrow. At my grateful nod, she flicked one over.

I hadn't realised how dry all that sun, exercise and fear had left me until I took several large gulps of the slightly warmish liquid. Esther sipped hers more decorously. Glancing down the prospectus, I discovered the centre offered courses in all Indian arts, from quill-weaving and basket-making to canoe-building and totem-pole-carving. They appeared to exclude buffalo-hunting – which was the subject of Esther's wall mural.

'It's good,' I said, toasting it with the mineral water.

'Thanks.' Head on one side, Esther scanned the panorama of small mounted warriors firing arrows into a distinctly cheesed-off buffalo. 'It's not original, of course. It's a copy of Howling Wolf's work. Do you know him?'

'Not unless he's the DJ on the pirate rave station.'

'Possibly he is. But this Howling Wolf was a nineteenth-century North Cheyenne artist.' She took another sip of water and asked me what had happened with the hunting group.

'They were playing with live arrows. I nearly got skewered. My own fault, really. I was trespassing.'

'And Selwyn? Just how abusive was he?'

I discovered I felt no loyalty to Selwyn. 'He threatened to thump one.'

'Oh, no.'

'He didn't.'

'That's hardly the point, is it?'

'The point to what?' enquired her husband, rejoining us.

He'd swapped the elk costume for a pair of jeans and a cerise shirt topped off with a natty yellow bow-tie. His trimmed hair and beard were a lightish grey, and by my estimate he was at least fifteen years or so older than his wife. Nonetheless he moved easily, and from what I could see his body had the well-toned definition of a much younger man.

'For mercy's sake, how much longer do we have to put up with that racket?' he exploded as the Apache drum section outside suddenly burst into life. This time they'd been joined by a chorus of what sounded like constipated wolves.

'Only half an hour to go. We advertised a week's course for children on Native American activities: making music, body-painting, constructing a teepee, tracking skills, that sort of thing,' Esther explained for my benefit. 'It's proved amazingly popular. I think we'll have to make it a regular event during the school holidays.'

'Over my dead body,' Selwyn snapped. 'I won't be taking part in this farce in the future. Is that quite clear?'

All three of us wandered down to the window to stare out at about thirty little savages beating the hell out of assorted drums, hollow logs and filled gourds under the supervision of several teenage helpers wearing matching grey sweatshirts with the yellow legend, *How? (Ask Me!)*.

'How long have you been here? I didn't even know this place existed until yesterday.'

Selwyn hitched a chair out from under the dust-sheeting. 'Four months. We were lucky to get the lease for a song.'

'More like a whole opera,' Esther muttered. She'd taken a bundle of letters from under the drinks pallet. From where I was standing, most of them appeared to be bills. Except for one.

Selwyn pounced, twitching it from her fingers. 'Is that from the grant committee?'

The thousand-watt light that had sprung on behind his

bright blue eyes started to fade as he absorbed the contents of the letter. When he'd finished, he crushed the paper slowly and deliberately between his long fingers and pitched the ball into the far corner of the room.

'That's not going to help,' Esther said quietly. 'They said it wasn't personal. Necessary economies—'

'Economies! They practically promised us that research money. You know I was counting on that field trip. We must go.'

'We can't afford luxuries—'

'Since when has a major excavation been considered a luxury by a dedicated scholar?'

'Since she started feeling physically ill every time a bill drops on to the doormat. Please, Selwyn, since we're stuck with this house, we need to put in some hard work over the next few years. You've seen how well the children's course has gone. Once we've got trained instructors in, started to show a profit—'

'We could end up in *The Times* list of the top one hundred companies? I hardly think so. I've already told you, I want no one under eighteen on these premises again. And if you must be so relentlessly cheerful, perhaps you could do it out of my hearing? This place is a dump and there's no sense in pretending it will ever be anything else. Why don't you cry? Or yell?'

'Because,' Esther said quietly, 'if I started, I might never stop.'

There was a silence. I was conscious of holding my breath. I got the impression they'd both forgotten I was there for the minute.

'I'll be outside making sure those louts haven't inflicted too much damage on the instruments, if you want me,' Selwyn finally said.

We both waited until his footsteps had faded before either of us spoke again.

'Sorry if I've added to the problem, Mrs Purbrick.'

'Professor, actually. But call me Esther. We're both anthropologists. Selwyn specialises in the sub-arctic cultures and I'm interested in the south-western tribes. You'll have to excuse him today. It's been a while since he's managed any pure research instead of . . . well—'

'Capering around like a pantomime cow?'

'Yes. This has been about the lowest spot in a bloody awful year. It should have been a buffalo, of course, but have you any idea how hard it is to find a buffalo robe around here?'

'They speak of little else in the amusement arcades of Seatoun.'

'Is that where you're from? It will be easy for you to get in to the courses, then. You won't need the residential package.'

It was probably just as well, I thought, given the unfinished state of this place. But I had to tell her the truth – well, part of it. I trotted out the mature student line again. 'I'm sorry about the misunderstanding, but I'm not used to being accosted by elks. I really would like to get these people's permission before I stick them in my thesis as typical village store customers.'

I fanned the prints. She pounced on the overdressed Indian squaw as I'd hoped. 'That's Rainwing.'

'Also known as . . . ?'

'Also known as Rainwing. I have no idea what her real name is. Some of the clients like to get into the spirit of the place: choose an Indian name and remain in character for the duration of the course. Rainwing is one of those.'

'But you must have some idea. An address? Telephone number? Bank details?'

'No. I don't. She started turning up a few years ago, paid for her course in cash and declined to provide any address for future mailings.'

'Is that usual?'

'No, but we can't afford to be picky.' Esther's voice had taken on a slightly impatient edge now I was no longer a potential customer. But PIs can't afford to be picky either.

I pressed on. 'I thought you only opened four months ago.'

'Opened here. Originally we had other premises, about fifteen miles away, until we . . . well, never mind. I'm afraid I can't help you. Now, if you don't mind, I have to get cleaned up. I've a class to prepare materials for.'

'Didn't Rainwing ever mention where she came from? You must have talked while you wove or whatever?'

'I got the idea she came down from London – although I can't tell you why. Apart from that . . .' She shrugged. 'She rings up, books a course, immerses herself in the whole experience . . . and, well, blends into our world.'

'Hardly blends in that get-up, I'd have thought.'

I waved the photo that showed the exploded parrot outfit in its fullest technicolour glory.

'She likes colour. I've noticed that in her work. But she can be more restrained. Here.' She scrabbled in the desk drawer and drew out an album. It seemed to contain mostly end-of-course group shots. She selected a group posing by the steps of a large house and pointed to a figure in the front line.

It was my second legatee, but in this one she was wearing a fetching little above-the-knee buckskin dress in a restrained shade of, well, buckskin, I guess, plus calf length boots and a woven band of beads round her forehead. Her pose with one leg slightly bent and her hands on her hips was pure model-girl chic.

Esther plainly wanted rid of me. I had to resort to leaving my phone number and asking her to get Rainwing to call. Normally I'd have given the office number, but since Vetch's would hardly tie in with the student story, I had to scribble out my flat's.

'I'll pass your details on if she gets in touch,' Esther promised. 'Although I'm sure you could publish those pictures without her permission. I don't suppose Rainwing has anything to hide.'

A statement that – with hindsight – was on a par with Custer's famous '*Don't worry, men, we'll easily surround all those redskins.*'

9

The centre was using a side gate as the main entrance to the property now. Possibly because the flatter verges gave better parking for the cars that had arrived to collect the assorted paint-daubed savages who were pouring out as Esther shepherded me firmly off the premises.

I had to skirt back to pick up the bike. Unfortunately it was still where I'd hidden it.

Approaching St Biddy's, I came across a familiar lump hunched on top of the churchyard wall.

'Cheers, Carter.'

'Hi. D'you find those people?'

'I found Harry Rouse. And his dad. You could have warned me he was a few chickens short of the full coop.'

'Atch's OK. My great-grandad's sister was his grandmother.' He sent a chip of church wall whirling through the air. It cracked off a distant stone buried amongst the untrimmed grass on the far side of the burial plots. 'That's him. Great-Grandad Elijah Cooper. And his wife, Jeanette, née Tanner. And that,' another stone soared into the air and made contact with something, 'is his brother, Great-Uncle Carter. We got a special connection, me and him. And his daughters: Susannah, Sophia, Maria . . .' A fusillade of pebbles whizzed around the burial mounds.

It was a pleasant enough spot if you didn't mind sharing it with the dead. Heaving myself up beside him, I listened to the hum and chirrup of unseen insects, and enjoyed the sun warming my face and arms for a while before taking out the photos and staring at the blank shiny images again in the vain hope that they would give me some clue to their lives: name, address and current phone number, for preference. Carter continued to target the dead. Every so often my concentration was interrupted by the 'ting' of a direct hit and Carter's hissed 'Yesssss.'

'Are they all your relatives?' I asked.

'Most. My family's lived around here since . . . since for ever. They're pretty much all buried here. 'Cept my mum and dad; they're up the cremmy. They don't bury people in here no more, except for the mixed doubles.'

'The whats?'

'You know, when one of them's already buried here. If they bought a double, they open it up for the other one.'

'When did your parents die?'

'Six years ago. My dad crashed his van.' He pronounced my 'moy', with that slight trace of local accent.

'Do you live with your grandparents?'

'Just Gran. First of all I was in foster care, then Gran said she'd take me.'

'That was good, wasn't it?'

'Suppose. 'Cept she's old. She was old when she had my mum. And she just doesn't see about . . . things. It was OK at the foster home. We used to play football and have rumbles at night when they put the lights out.'

'So why didn't you say you wanted to stay there?'

'I couldn't do that. My gran would have been upset. She's all right really. She just thinks how things were when she was young is how it ought to be now. Only it's not, is it?' He hunched along the wall a bit, pushing a plump thigh into mine. 'D'you want to give me another tenner?'

'Why should I want to do that?'

'I could ask around about the other two in your pictures.'

I wondered briefly if he'd known all along who the others

were and was just holding out until I'd upped the ante. But apparently not.

'I told you,' Carter said indignantly, 'I've never seen them before. How about that tenner?'

'Dream on, Carter.'

I shuffled the shiny prints for the umpteenth time. Whichever way I looked at them, they weren't prepared to give up any secrets. Carter leant across me to help himself to a couple of shots and repeat his offer to flash them around the village. 'What about a bluey?'

'I haven't a small kangaroo about my person just at present, Carter.'

'It's a fiver. A five-pound note, you know?'

'What happened to my other money?'

'I'm saving for . . . something.' He hauled up his shirt, exposing more spare tyres than Kwik-Fit and those girlish breasts, in order to examine the ring in his navel. 'I'm thinking of doing my nipples next. Or maybe getting a tattoo. What d'you think?'

'Ouch,' I said succinctly.

'The pain doesn't bother me. I can take it.' His coolly unconcerned shrug unbalanced him. He regained his balance by grabbing at my waist.

I jabbed a finger into his soft midriff. It was like poking proving dough. 'Shift those raging hormones away and get your thrills somewhere else.'

Carter blushed at being caught out before taking his hand off my waist, his right nipple off my left arm and putting a few inches between my leg and his right thigh. 'Are you going to give me any money?'

'Carter, I told you, I'm a student. Students are among the great financial inadequates of the world. So why the hell would I want to throw cash at you?'

'Not all students are. Some have money. Especially the old ones. They've had jobs and things, haven't they, before they joined up. Some of them get redundancy payments.'

'Well, I didn't. I'm poor. Very poor. Far too poor to want to dish out fivers to bored self-mutilators. And I'm not old.'

'OK.' He slewed round on the wall and went back to pitching at long-dead ancestors. 'Luke wasn't poor when he was a student. His uncle gave him cash.'

'Lucky old Luke.' Swinging my legs round so I was facing the same way as him, I surveyed the grassy mounds and engrimed monuments. 'Which one's Luke?'

Carter shot out an arm. 'That's him.' Leaning back, I made out the bonnet of a car just nosing into sight around the far bend in the narrow road. 'Awesome motor, isn't it? He's got a brill motorbike too.'

It was an open-topped red sports car. The old sort, with enough chrome, leather and 'vroom-vroom' noise to rate it a 'classic' tag and to have his motor insurance agent salivating at the thought of sufficient commission to cover two weeks in the Bahamas – five-star class.

Carter waved. The driver raised an arm in salute. I squirmed round again to re-face the road. And kicked Grannie Vetch's bike straight into the path of the rapidly approaching bonnet. I dived to rescue my only form of transport.

He had great brakes. And terrific reflexes. In fact, all of him could be classified under one of those headings. Just under six foot of bronzed muscles which rippled under a clingy white T-shirt, with a stomach and bum to die for in lycra shorts. His face was partially obscured by a blue peaked baseball cap and a pair of sunglasses. Vaulting out of the car, he whipped the glasses off, fixed a pair of anxious tawny eyes on me, and asked if I was OK.

'Just fine.' I gave him a relaxed smile to show it was no big deal and I regularly worked out by taking a tumbling somersault off a wall. I'd ended up on the far verge with the bike clasped to my chest and generous proof that Vetch had

79

been keeping the damn thing well greased smeared down my front.

'Here, let me.' He pulled the cycle clear to allow me to scramble up. 'You sure you're OK?'

'A hundred per cent, thanks.' I flexed and bent each leg in turn to demonstrate, and discovered I'd thrust the photo folder down the front of my pants before my dive. It crackled embarrassingly, but I didn't feel inclined to retrieve it with Luke watching. 'Grace Smith.'

'Luke Steadman. Great save. Ever played American football?'

'Nope. Haven't even played the British version.'

'Luke's lived in the States,' Carter announced, mooching back to join us. His concerned reaction to my imminent flattening under Luke's tyres had been to stick his head sideways into the car as soon as Luke vaulted out and examine the dashboard. Polishing the bonnet with tentative fingertips, he asked if Luke was going back to the States soon.

'Hope so, champ. Should get the house sale sorted in the next few weeks. And then I can start getting the crew in place. But don't sweat it. Few more years and you'll be out there yourself.'

'Be another five years at least.'

'You heading Stateside then, Carter?' I asked.

'Thought I'd do my degree out there. There's scholarships you can apply for. After that I'll get a place somewhere smooth; California or Florida maybe. One of those ocean-front condos like on the TV. And a car.' He smoothed another wistful stroke over the shiny metal.

I glanced at Luke, half expecting to see amusement at the very least at the fat kid's ambitions. But he didn't appear to find anything odd in Carter's grand plan. He asked if I was staying in the village.

'She's a student,' Carter pushed in before I could answer. 'She's looking for these. You ever seen them before, Luke?'

He produced two photos which he must have held on to when I'd left the wall so hurriedly.

Luke stretched across to the passenger side to take them. It gave me the chance to hoick the cardboard album out of my nether regions.

Carter pointed out, needlessly I should have thought, that they had been taken outside his gran's store. 'Last week. The date's on the back.'

Luke twisted his fingers to verify the thin line of printed figures running across the developer's logo. He shook his head. 'No. Sorry. Doesn't hit any home runs with me.' The warning blare of a horn announced an oncoming driver couldn't get past him. 'I'd best move. If you're walking back into the village, Carter, I've got something for you.'

'Great. Thanks, Luke.' Carter's face lit up. 'You going in the store? Only Gran said to remind you you've not settled your paper bill yet.'

'My mistake. I'll get it sorted.'

Luke returned the two snaps to Carter, who passed them back to me. I thrust them in among the other prints without checking which ones he'd been looking at. Which – with hindsight – was a big mistake.

10

The car behind Luke's was the Ford Escort from my first call at the village. It screeched past us in a cloud of exhaust fumes and thundering sound system.

I walked the bike in the same direction. Carter seemed determined to stay latched on to me. Scuffing small clouds of dust with the toes of his trainers, he provided a running commentary on the village and its inhabitants. 'That's the Thatchers' place. They only come weekends. That's the Grieves'. That's the places for old people. My gran says she'd crawl on her hands and knees before they get her in there.'

I stopped, staring at the small block of newish flats, a sudden idea forming. 'Hold this a sec, Carter.'

Carter took hold of the handlebars I'd just leant on his stomach. I scrabbled through the prints until I'd sorted out the ones of Rainwing and dealt them into their correct time sequence.

Harry Rouse had turned left out of the store, presumably walking back to the farm track; the woman had passed down the lane in front of Barbra's hiding place; but Rainwing had turned right into the village. By the final frame, her front leg was lifted well off the ground as she started to run. And what was there to run for at that time in the morning?

I scanned the timetable on the toy-town stop in front of the flats. It wasn't a long read since, as Carter had already told me, there were only two buses a day. The earlier one left at seven forty-five a.m.

'Do you ever catch the early bus, Carter?'

'Every morning, term-time.'

'Is it always the same driver?'

"'Cept when he's on holiday. Or sick.'

'What's he look like?'

'What's it worth?'

'Nothing. I'll ask someone else.'

'A fiver.'

'One quid. Final offer.' I dug deep into my jeans pocket and disentangled the handkerchief I'd pinned in there. Knotted in one corner was my handful of telephone change. I crossed Carter's hand with five pieces of silver. 'Now, give – what's he look like?'

'Gross.'

'Can you be a bit more specific?'

Carter stuck his hand over his face, squashing the nose

flat and inflating his cheeks. 'Dross,' he trumpeted nasally. 'He's called Spencer.'

'Thanks.' I remounted and started pedalling at walking pace. Carter trotted beside me, his breath coming in short gaspy little 'hurrs'. It sounded like he had asthma on top of all his other disadvantages.

Since I was stuck with him, I figured I might as well put in a little work on Harry Rouse's suitability to inherit Barbra's fortune. 'This bloke I know was in prison with someone called Harry Rouse. Came from around this way, I think.'

'What did he do? Something really gruesome?' Carter's face was alight with the possibility of some vicarious carnage.

'Tax fraud.'

'Boring.'

'Very. Don't suppose your Harry Rouse has ever been inside, has he?'

'Shouldn't think so. I could find out. Cost you, though.'

'What's to find out, Carter? If Harry Rouse had disappeared for a time, everyone's going to know. His farm wouldn't run itself.'

'It's not his farm. It's old Mr Rouse's.'

'Who's an ee-eye short of the full Macdonald.'

'He wasn't always like that. *Hurr.* When I was a little kid, he used to let me go up there and play. And he taught me how to drive over the fields in his truck. It's not his fault he's got Alzheimer's.'

We were approaching the twin pubs. The Escort was parked in front of the Bell. To make amends, I decided to sacrifice what was left of my change. 'Want a lemonade?'

'That's a kid's drink.'

'Please yourself. Which bar's best?'

'Doesn't make any difference. Mr Benting's taken over the Bell as well now.'

A girl had emerged from the Royal Oak on our right to

83

clear glasses from the forecourt. Her appearance was the signal for the driver of the Escort to lean on his horn. It blasted out to the accompaniment of shouted invitations to join them from the half-dozen leaning out of the windows.

A shake of her head just made them redouble the noise. She ran across to say something. The tattooed moss-head who'd been clambering through the sun-roof last time reached out and grabbed her wrist, trying to pull her inside. She was struggling and laughing at the same time. For a moment it seemed as if they'd drag her in through the back window.

Then an angry roar erupted from the Royal Oak. 'Kelly! Get back here. Now!'

He'd come round the corner from the car park, the sinews in his arms bulging under the weight of two crates of mixers. He had the look of the sort of bloke who was capable of pitching the whole load through the Escort's windscreen if they tried to drive off with Kelly. Evidently the driver thought so too. He let her go and took off in a roar of screaming tyres and blown exhaust.

Kelly smoothed down the belt that was passing as a skirt and sauntered back to the Royal Oak forecourt with a casually provocative butt-sway that said she knew she was being watched. The man – Mr Benting, I assumed – had disappeared inside.

Carter's breathing was beginning to sound like a steam engine. I glanced round and found that his tongue was on the floor. He managed to reel it in long enough to pant, 'Hiya, Kelly.'

The girl started to swab up beer spills from the wooden trestle tables. ''Lo, Carter,' she called over her shoulder. Unlike Carter, she didn't have any local accent. I thought I detected a slight hint of London East End, however.

She finished with a last swipe and turned to face us. Her attractions were obvious – mainly because the tight skirt and silky cobalt-blue slip-top weren't doing much to hide them. Neither was Kelly. Casually slipping one blouse shoulder down, she adjusted her bra strap, tweaking it up so that we got a brief glimpse of the lacy cup with its dark brown nipple beneath. Carter's steam engine was threatening to blow its safety valve.

Calmly Kelly replaced her strap. Her face was all wide-eyed friendliness, but there was a glint beneath those lashes and a provocative tilt to her hips that said she knew exactly what she was doing to Carter.

'What's it to be, Carter?' I asked. 'Tequila slammers all round?'

'I can't get yer nothing from the bar,' Kelly said. 'I'm not allowed.'

'What about a soft drink?'

'Sure. What d'ya wan'?'

'Carter?'

Squaring his shoulders, Carter delivered his order with what I imagine was meant to be a macho sneer. 'Coke. No glass.'

'And leave the tops on,' I added, entering into the spirit of the thing. 'We like to take them off with our teeth. Right, Carter?'

'Yeah.'

We hitched a bench out to sit on. Carter's eyes remained fixed on the door through which Kelly had just wiggled her bottom.

She was leggy without being very tall, with a tumble of dark curls and deep brown eyes to match. Her skin had an olive tone that wasn't entirely due to tanning. The overall impression was of a more exotic origin than St Biddy's – eastern Mediterranean, perhaps. I asked Carter where she'd come from.

'Balham. Mr Benting took over the licence five years back.' He pointed at a black-and-white plate screwed over the door that informed the world that Keith and Maria

Ageneta Benting were licensed to sell intoxicating liquors on the premises.

We'd both been facing the inn. The sudden arrival of something thudding on to the table made the pair of us jump.

'Sorry,' Luke apologised. 'Didn't mean to pitch it that hard. It's for you, Carter. Maps and guide books on the States. Thought it might help with some forward planning.'

'Thanks.' Rosiness flooded Carter's freckles at this kindness from his hero. 'Shall I come round and clean the car again this after?'

'It's already so polished it dazzles low-flying pilots.'

'I don't mind. Honestly. I'll vacuum it out too.'

'Please yourself, champ. You know where everything is.'

'Leave it to me. I'll sort it.' Carter drew the rubber-band-bound package to him with both hands, stroking it as if it were . . . well, any part of Kelly Benting's anatomy, I guess.

The tease in question arrived with our drinks at that moment. 'Two Cokes. Hello, Luke. Fetch you something?'

'I'll pass, thanks.'

'He brought me some stuff on the States.'

'That was really nice of him,' purred the little minx, slipping her hands on to Carter's shoulders and lightly massaging them with open fingers. 'Perhaps I'll borrow them some time. I'd just die to visit the States.'

'Sure. Any time. You could come up the house. I could show you loads of stuff about the States if you like,' Carter gabbled. 'In fact, I was going to ask . . . About Friday. It's my birthday. I've been saving for ages . . . We could go out . . . anywhere you want . . . I'll take you anywhere you like. Kelly, will you?'

'Sounds like a good offer to me.' Luke had picked up a tinge of American in his accent. Nothing too heavy. Just enough to add an interesting edge.

'Well, I could fancy going out,' Kelly cooed. Her fingers slid nearer Carter's windpipe, whilst her thumbs kneaded the soft base of his neck. 'A club, maybe.' She abandoned Carter's massage. I doubt he noticed. He was floating in a fantasy of his own. 'I had *my* sixteenth birthday weeks ago. Dad bought me this.' She rested both palms on the table top and leant forward to show off the heavy gold rope chain around her neck. The skimpy top didn't even try to fight gravity. 'What d'ya think?'

'Very desirable,' Luke said, deadpan, as he stared into the valley. 'But perhaps best kept for a special occasion?'

'Think so?' Straightening up, she gave him another one of those sexy-but-oh-so-innocent glances before sashaying over to pick up glasses from the next table.

Watching the performance made me miss what Luke had said to me.

'I said,' he repeated, 'which direction are you heading?'

'Seatoun.'

'Want a lift? I'm going that way myself.'

'I've got the bike.' I indicated the metal monster leaning against the pub wall.

'No problem. We could probably lash it on to the trunk. I'll go get something to fix it with.'

Passing behind Carter, he pinched a handful of top arm lightly. 'Muscle tone's coming along nicely there, Carter. You still doing those work-out routines I showed you?'

Carter deepened to an even rosier shade. 'Yeah. Yeah, I am, Luke.'

'Good.' He punched the soft flesh. 'Don't run off,' he said to me.

'I'll be waiting.' I toasted him with the Coke bottle, remembered it was still sealed and slammed the crimped top off on the edge of the table.

Kelly pounced. 'My dad doesn't like yobs doing that to the furniture.'

'If I see any yobs I'll be sure to mention it to them. Cheers!'

Kelly turned her attention to an easier target and asked

Carter if he didn't have some place else to go. 'Dad doesn't like people holding on to seats over just one drink, yer know.'

Carter jumped up immediately, nearly knocking over his bench in his eagerness to please. 'Yeah. Sure. Sorry. What about Friday? Are you going to come out with me?'

'I'll think about it. Push off now. I've got work to do.'

Clutching his Coke bottle to his damp shirt, Carter pushed.

I wandered inside in search of the loo. It was an inviting sort of bar room. Plenty of brass and farm implements which seemed to be genuine local mementoes rather than having been bought as a job lot from olde-worlde-pubs-are-us. And a good selection of personal items: old family photos; Kelly's 'best pet' rosettes; judo cups and trophies that sent out the unspoken message that Keith Benting wouldn't have any problems dealing with drunks; and an assorted collection of Arsenal football memorabilia. I would have lingered there longer if certain areas of my anatomy hadn't been indicating that another three-mile bike ride wasn't a great choice at present.

I could see what looked like a beer garden out the back with yet more tables. A big sign on the back door announced: 'Delicious cream teas served in our secret garden from 3.00 p.m.'.

A woman bustled out of a door to my right, her hands full of dishes of thick cream, ruby-red jam and still-steaming scones. There was enough resemblance in the coarser middle-aged face to let me peg her as Kelly's mum. 'You want something?' she asked.

'Looking for the Ladies'.

She dipped her forehead at the door behind me, backing up the corridor to manoeuvre the garden door open with her backside.

The wash-basin mirror was opposite the door, so I got the full horror as soon as I stepped into the tiled room.

Staring back at me was a wild-haired woman with two large black stripes of bike grease smeared from the corners of her mouth to her ears. Why the hell hadn't anyone mentioned it? Did they think I normally made up like this?

Snatching down a handful of paper towels, I lathered liquid soap down my arms and over my face. The door swung open as I threw a final handful of hot water over my face.

Leaning against the door, Kelly removed a stick of chewing gum from her pocket, fed the wafer into her mouth, and watched me.

'Something bothering you?' I asked.

'No.' She chewed open-mouthed whilst I dried myself. From somewhere in the pub, her mother was calling for her. Kelly ignored the shouts. 'You live in Seatoun then?'

'Yep.'

'Wish I did. This place is dead boring.'

'So Carter was saying.'

'Carter's a real dork. Don't see how he could find anything more boring than himself.'

'You think so?' I said, balling the sodden towels into the rubbish can. 'Personally, he's just the sort of cutie I'd adore to have as my love slave. All that soft white flesh . . . Grrrr . . .' I snapped in a tigerish snarl. 'Don't you just long to sink your teeth into it?'

Her mouth hung open for at least a minute. 'Are you taking the piss?'

I held my hands up. 'OK, I admit it. Carter is all yours. He's obviously crazy about you.'

'Yer've got to be joking. Do you know, he used to wear short trousers to school until he was twelve? And now he wears a suit. From Marks and Spencer. I mean, my God . . . Sad or what?'

I was tempted to go all sanctimonious on her and point out that looks aren't everything – let's consider personality, sincerity, reliability, and half a dozen other ities. But I

89

couldn't do it. Any girl who went out with Carter might as well be wearing her 'Totally Desperate' T-shirt. 'He could be a good long-term investment. He reckons he's going to university in the States. High-powered science degree of some kind.'

The expected snort of derision didn't come. Instead, Kelly said that he probably would.

'You mean he really is bright? I thought he was talking himself up.'

'No. He's a nerd but he's dead brilliant at all that maths and physics stuff. The teachers say he'll get into Oxford or Cambridge easy. They're always showing him off when the inspectors come snooping.'

A teacher's pet as well. Life really had stacked the odds against Carter. No wonder he wanted to leave the country.

'So he could be living in a luxury condo in California in ten years' time?'

'Yeah. I 'spect he could.'

'You'll probably like him then.'

Kelly bit her bottom lip, thought about it for at least two seconds, and then agreed with me. 'Yeah. I expect I will.'

I left just as Kelly's mum finally figured out where she was hiding. 'Kelly. What you doing? There are customers.'

'Coming, Mama.' With a weary sigh, Kelly levered herself from the wall and slouched in the direction of the back garden.

Luke had already lashed the bike to the sports car's boot and was waiting for me to join him.

'Hop in. If you're ready?'

I hopped. He cruised up to the junction at a prowling pace, signalled left and roared out on to the main road. The wind caught our hair and whipped strands at my cheeks. The sun had bleached strands of gold into Luke's brown shade and they wove and danced together in the slipstream. The throaty note of the engine settled to a steady sexy purr.

'Great car!' I shouted.

'Thanks,' he yelled back. 'It was my uncle's. He had it from new.' He jerked a thumb over his shoulder. 'He left it to me. Along with the house in St Biddy's and . . . well, just about everything else.'

'Lucky you. I don't have rich relatives – at least not that I know of.'

'You live in Seatoun?'

'Yes.'

'With your family?'

'No. I left home a long time ago.'

'I meant husband, live-in lover, kids?'

'None of the aforementioned. How about you? What do you do in the States?'

'Film studies. I'm putting together a project for my own production company at present.'

'Sounds impressive.'

He shot one of those chocolate-fudge-sundae smiles at me. All irresistible smoothness. At least the dental segment of it was. I couldn't see whether it reached his eyes since he'd put the sunglasses back on. They were the designer-wrap-around style: very now and very, very expensive.

'It does, doesn't it? Mind you, I have to confess that everyone in LA has a project. That's why I come back here; to do a bit of real quality-time boasting. And to sell up in St Biddy's.'

'You're moving out there permanently?'

'No choice, really. It's where the work is. Besides, I need the money from the house sale to get the film off the ground.'

'I thought the British film industry was hot?'

'Distribution isn't. Anyway, my script is centred out there.'

'What's it about?'

'Life. Death. Good. Evil. Redemption.'

Not a comedy then. 'Isn't it difficult to get work permits or visas or whatever?'

'I've got dual nationality. My dad was a Yank.'

'Is he in the film business?'

'Owned a meat company. Supplied a lot of the big restaurant chains. He's dead now. Mom too.'

So he hadn't picked up that sexy accent recently. 'Did you grow up in Los Angeles?'

'Chicago. I was a kinda wild kid who ran with the gangs. In the end, my folks packed me off to this rehab place in the midwest. Thought it would sort my head out – getting in touch with the roots of the country.'

'And did it?'

'Amazing doesn't even begin to cover it. Lying out there under the stars with just the sounds of the desert – no cars, no electricity, no phones. And the dark so tangible you almost feel you can reach out and touch it. Have you any idea what that feels like?'

'Like being in an *X-Files* episode just before the alien ship hovers into view?'

He laughed. 'You're not one of the world's great romantics, are you, Grace?'

'I tend to prefer the great outdoors when viewed through the windows of a five-star hotel.'

'I'll sure keep that in mind.'

For what? I nearly asked.

The exterior sights were changing as we left the open countryside and entered the beginnings of the ribbons of development along the coast to the west of Seatoun.

'How about you?' Luke asked. 'What's your story? A student, Carter said. What are you studying?'

'Urban development and decay, rural trends – that sort of thing.'

'Are you aiming for some special field?'

'Not really. It's for my own personal growth.'

'So what line are you in? For paying the bills, I mean?'

'This and that.'

'Don't give much away, do you?'

I was aware I sounded uptight. But my natural instincts were always not to confide too much in strangers – mainly because in the past some of them had turned out to be very strange indeed. 'I've only known you for two minutes. It's too early to be getting in touch with our feelings, don't you think?'

'We could always fix that.'

'I guess we could. Except I don't have any plans to move across the Atlantic at present.'

'No sweat. I'll be around for a while yet, if you fancy a drink or something?'

I made a noncommittal noise to see if he'd push it. He didn't. Instead he concentrated on steering through the small shopping area of West Bay. The weather had brought the strollers and gawpers out in force, and the traffic was being forced down to walking pace by wandering holiday-makers with drooping shorts, peeling sunburns and melting ice-cream cones.

Luke handled the car with easy movements, giving me plenty of chance to notice how the muscles rippled under all that smooth brown skin. He plainly took his own advice and worked out regularly.

'You can drop me off anywhere along here, thanks.'

'This where you live?'

'Closish. Over there will do.'

He glided to a stop in one of the many roads of small private B&Bs that run at ninety degree angles to the sea front and came round to help me unlash the bike. As I kicked the pedals into position, Luke handed me a pen. 'Got something to write on?'

I hadn't, apart from the inside of the photo wallet.

He spelt out the address and gave me his mobile number. 'Drop by, or give me a ring if you fancy that drink sometime.'

I added his name (as if I might not be able to place the

address amongst the dozens that eligible blokes regularly pressed into my hands) and thrust it in my pocket.

He was looking expectant. 'No reciprocity?'

I dodged the question. 'That's OK. I'm not into these foreign beers. Thanks for the lift.'

I free-wheeled down the small street to the front. As I paused to take a right turn, I glanced back. He was still standing by the driver's door, watching me. He looked like an advert for masculine fragrances straight out of a monthly glossy. I wondered briefly why on earth I hadn't tattooed my phone number on his bare flesh before he got away.

Seeing me looking, he raised one hand in salute. I waved back. It was the last time I saw him alive.

11

I kicked off my thirty-first year by nearly killing someone.

They say a summer's morning has an appeal that no other time or season can match. And they're right. The air is fresher, the light is clearer, the colours of the flowers are brighter, and the birdsong sounds sweet and melodic.

That said – take my tip – it's not worth losing a couple of hours' sleep over: buy yourself stronger spectacles and a cassette of bird calls – and snuggle down until a civilised hour.

I'd set the alarm for six thirty, since I had to be in St Biddy's in time to catch the seven forty-five bus. But I woke up at half four to a feathered barber's-shop quartet harmonising on the basement rail outside, and after a futile half-hour of twisting and turning I decided to give up and find out if the early hours had improved since I'd pounded the late shift in my WPC uniform.

Firstly I took out Auntie Gertie's card and set it on the 'mantelpiece'. In the days when this had been yet another one of the ubiquitous Edwardian boarding houses, my little kingdom in the basement had formed the original kitchens and pantries. This main room where I largely lived had been the kitchen and still had the gap where the cooking range had stood. Along the wall above was a thick strip of wood, so solid and weathered that it looked like it might have started life as a ship's timber (after it had gone through the acorn and spreading branches stage, you understand). I stood Auntie's card in the middle. It looked a bit pathetic at present, but the next few hours would soon fix that.

It was, I realised, crunch time. Either I entered my thirties with a coffee and a slump in front of the early-morning news, or I hit the ground running.

Pulling on a tracksuit and shoes, I strolled down to the front nursing that smug, self-satisfied glow that comes from knowing you're going to suffer when the other bed slugs are still cosied up beneath the duvets.

There were already a dozen dawn swimmers out on the main beach, leaping and crashing into the rollers of the outgoing tide. I jogged my way along the promenade until I reached a smaller beach around the next bay but one. As I'd hoped, I had it all to myself at this time of day.

Making my way down to the water's edge beside one of the wooden groynes, I left my clothes folded on the large black boulders that piled against the slimy, algae-covered struts, and plunged in.

The first shock of the water hitting my face knocked the breath from my lungs. It was freezing! Gasping with shock, I duck-dived under the waves, swimming parallel with the shore until my body adjusted to the temperature. It was a long time since I'd swum in the sea. I'd forgotten how buoyant it was and how great it felt when the roll picked you up and swept you along with a roar that filled your ears with water and sent a lacy crest of creamy froth slapping into your eyes and nose.

Turning on my back, I swam with lazy overarm sweeps, watching the sky above losing the milky pearl-greyness of dawn as the sun grew stronger, and turning a pale blue that would deepen to the colour of cornflowers if the heat wave held. And by the looks of it, it would, I decided, rolling over again and powering back with a vigorous crawl. Once you got used to the hypothermia, the water was great. I did a diving turn, plunged down towards the sandy bottom, and powered up and out of the waves in a butterfly leap.

I managed another six laps before lack of breath and the retreating tide forced me towards the beach again. The edge of the water had receded several yards beyond the final pile of boulders, forcing me to pad across the wet ridges of khaki sand and soft worm casts to reach my clothes.

Out here, with the sun barely up yet, my skin erupted in goose-bumps. Swiftly I wriggled into the tracksuit and patted myself dampish dry on its fleecy inside. Sauntering back up the powdery sand, I found myself staring at the soles of two pairs of worn trainers. I followed the legs, up the creased jeans – over blankets draped round their shoulders – to two heads resting against the battered knapsacks they'd been using as pillows. They must have been sleeping rough up against the retaining wall. I'd missed them in the deep shadows at the land end of the beach.

The older one was an odd shade of maggot white and his mouth was hanging open wide enough to show a collection of nicotine-stained teeth.

'Is he OK?' I asked.

'He is now,' the other said, holding up a brown off-licence bag with the top scrunched to form a breathing mouthpiece. 'I thought his ticker was going to explode for sure there. Blimey, darling, that's the best alarm call Oi've ever had. Are yer coming back tomorrow?'

'Afraid not.'

'Ah well, have a happy life.' He toasted me with the

remains of the bottle that had come out of his mate's improvised breathing aid. He wasn't bad looking, in a battered sort of way, with his deeply tanned skin, iron-grey hair cropped close to his head and a roguish twinkle in his brown eyes. He dropped one in a wink as he wished me happiness.

I winked back. 'And you too.'

I skipped up the stone stairs to the promenade. There was no big deal about being thirty. I still had a lot of living to look forward to. Bring on the world – I could handle it!

It was a mood that not even seeing a police patrol car free-wheeling down the pedestrian ramp could affect. My least favourite copper in the entire world stepped out from the driver's side and ran across to the metallic promenade rails, using his linked fingers as a sun-shade while he scanned the glinting grey swell.

'Hello, Rosco. Looking for mermaids?'

'Eh? No.' He dragged his gaze back reluctantly. 'What are you doing here this early, Smithie?'

'I rose with the dawn, Terry.'

'Yeah? Who's she? You batting for the other side now, or can't you find a fellah – now you're getting a bit past it. Tell you what, I don't mind sorting you out.'

A smug smile spread over his face, whilst he flexed the body he was convinced was God's gift to the opposite sex.

'That's very generous, Terry. But how do I know you're up to it?'

'I've never had any complaints.'

'No? You should read the walls in the ladies' loos more often. Byeee . . .'

I started up the slope to the road above. As I got higher, I could see another police car pulling into the kerb and a blue Vauxhall – which I recognised as an unmarked CID vehicle – parking up behind them. Two officers leapt out and ran to the edge of the wide grass verge on top of the cliff. One called down to Rosco to ask if he'd got anything yet.

'No. Maybe we're in the wrong area,' Terry bawled back.

'Can't be, the informant lives just over there . . .' He pointed back to the detached houses that lined the opposite side of the road, their large balconied windows facing the sea.

One of the CID men had taken out a pair of binoculars and was sweeping them back and forth over the horizon.

'What's up?' I yelled to Terry. 'Invasion fleet of drug-smugglers expected?'

'Someone reckons they saw a naked blonde in the sea. You see anything?'

I was spared having to answer by the CID officer with the binoculars, who shouted he thought he'd spotted something.

'Where? Let's see.' His colleague half choked him grabbing the glasses away.

I left them to it and strolled home. Well, how else is a girl to celebrate her thirtieth birthday but with a spot of skinny-dipping?

12

The postman had been by the time I got back to the flat. I wondered if the postal strike was on again. The small pile of coloured envelopes seemed strangely . . . small.

I identified the handwriting as I slit the backs open. My parents' card was in my mum's handwriting. *Daddy sends his love and kisses*, she'd written. Only if his saliva was infected with rabies.

Ever since I'd been invited to resign from the police a few years back rather than face an inquiry regarding my supplying a false alibi for a local piece of nastiness who'd seriously injured another officer, the relationship between me and my dad had been strained, to say the least.

Mum had enclosed a fifty-pound note with instructions to *buy yourself something nice, darling*. I was tempted to send it back. In the end I tucked it in the back of Barbra's photo wallet.

My sister's card included love and inky fingerprint signatures from my nieces, plus a scrawled instruction that my present would need regular feeding. I just hoped she wasn't sending me her kids' hamster – although I wouldn't put it past her if the price of sunflower seeds had gone up again. She and her husband have always lived so far beyond their means that they need satellite tracking to get back to the original budget.

Nick's card was signed from *Nick and Simone*. My brother's cards are always from Nick and someone. But never the same someone. (I send my own cards addressed to Nick and whom-it-may-concern.)

The other two cards were from a distant cousin I wouldn't recognise if I fell over her in the street, and my mum's sister.

The indignation I felt at finding none of my so-called friends had bothered to send me anything festered whilst I towelled myself dry so vigorously I raised friction burns. Then I calmed down. Given the recent trouble with the post, they'd probably decided it was safer to hand them over personally.

Cheered that I hadn't been forgotten, I dressed, cleaned my teeth, threw a few things in my shoulder bag, tucked the photos safely into the inner pocket of my jacket and, on an impulse, added my lock-picking kit before bumping the metal monster up the iron steps from my basement.

I didn't really expect to find anyone at Vetch's at this hour. However, the door was on a single lock and the alarm was switched off. My dropping the bike on the hall floor brought Vetch to the door of his office.

'You're not thinking of leaving that there, are you, sweet thing?'

'Two seconds while I check my office. You're in early.'

'Needs must. I've a meeting. In Southampton. So I must love you and leave you.' He kissed the tips of his fingers to me and headed for the front door.

'Haven't you forgotten something?'

'I don't think so.' He patted down the swanky tailored overcoat he always wore when he wanted to impress clients. 'Give me a clue.'

I hummed 'Happy Birthday'.

Vetch frowned. 'Dear me. Is that today? I didn't realise. Well, let me wish you many happy returns. Thirty of them, I believe. Now I must fly.'

There was no sign of anything remotely resembling a birthday card in my office. Thirty was beginning to lose its attraction already. Stepping out and locking up again, I was surprised to hear the sounds of a printer in Annie's office. It appeared that everyone at Vetch's was suddenly suffering from insomnia.

'Meeting,' she said crisply when I invited myself in. 'I need to get through the rush-hour traffic.'

'Where you heading?'

'Heathrow. My client has a forty-minute window between flights.'

'Flash.'

'Flush. It's my Pasdirp. I might need some help on surveillance later if you're interested.' Her fingers flashed, switching off the computer icons and snatching up the sheets spewing from the printer.

'What are you doing later?' I asked. 'This evening, for instance?'

'I'm not sure yet. Why?'

'I thought if Tom Cruise doesn't ring in the meantime, I might have a few birthday drinks.'

'Oh, hell, is that today? Sorry, it just went clean out of my head. Yes, sure, if I'm around we'll get a bottle of wine or something. See you.'

The echo of her high heels had faded by the time I slouched back to the hall. And discovered Jan had completed our quartet of insomniacs. Unmissable in orange leggings and a knee-length cardigan in broad stripes of tangerine and lime, she stalked the reception area like an animated stick of seaside rock.

'I can't work,' she said.

'I know. I've seen your attempts at it.'

'Ha bloody ha. I meant, I'm not starting at me desk until nine. I'm only here to help Ifor with his decorating.'

'I thought you couldn't stand the Welsh whinger?'

'He's OK when you get to know him. He thinks I'm artistic.'

I looked from the tip of Jan's green barnet to her emerald stilettos and realised Ifor Ifor had a handicap that made him totally unsuitable for running a print shop – daltonism (look it up!).

'I just popped in to see if there was anything anyone had left for me. Is there?'

'No.'

'Well, you could look.'

'Look yourself. I'm going downstairs.'

I sorted through the rubbish on Jan's desk and – recalling her bizarre filing system – inside her waste-paper bin. She was right. There were definitely no cards there. There was one last stop to make before I headed for St Biddy's.

My favourite café – Pepi's – was lost in a fifties time warp of red and white formica, huge plastic squeezy tomatoes of ketchup, and a chrome and neon jukebox stocked with the hits that had had them rocking in the aisles forty years ago. It was run by a man called Shane, who'd started life as Hubert before he'd turned himself into the greased-haired, lip-curling, snake-hipped rock star that sneered from the black-and-white stills pinned around the walls.

The hair had almost gone and the snake-hips were lost

somewhere behind the elephant's belly, but Shane still reckoned he had what it took. Just a lot more of it, as the straining jeans and white T-shirt proved.

But he was one of my mates. We shared an interest in cholesterol-laden fry-ups. He enjoyed cooking them and I enjoyed scrounging and eating them. It was a munch made in heaven. Surely he'd remember my birthday?

Shane was frying to the accompaniment of Chuck Berry blaring from the jukebox. I watched his rump jiggling and his knees swivelling for a minute whilst he twirled the frying utensils like a set of cheerleader's batons and urged us all to twist again like we had last summer.

Eventually he swept the contents of the pans on to plates and swung round bawling, 'Two full English! Morning, Smithie. What can I do you for?'

'Coffee. And a bacon sandwich on brown. Make it a double. I'm celebrating.'

'One double porker's lament coming up.' He poured a mug of coffee. 'Two pounds seventy to you.'

'Suppose you wouldn't like to put it on the house? Seeing as it's a special day?'

'Sorry. No can do. You've had so much free nosh off me, the missus is beginning to think we're an item.'

'That's ridiculous.'

'I know. I told her I'm saving myself for Michelle Pfeiffer, but there's no reasoning with the woman.'

'Don't you want to know *why* this is a special day?'

'Go on then.' A doorstep of rashers and wholemeal was plonked in front of me. 'Help yourself to sauce.'

'It's my birthday.'

'Really? You should have said.'

'Why? It's the same day every year. You've only got to count forward twelve months.'

'Sorry. Life just keeps lapping me these days. Tell you what ...' He fished into the jar where he kept the pre-decimal shillings that fitted the jukebox and offered me one. 'Here, stick yer favourite song on. My treat.'

'My favourite song hadn't been written when that lot was being recorded. In fact, the writer was probably a hopeful sperm practising its racing crawl. I'll take this to go.' Slapping two pound coins and a handful of silver on the counter, I sloshed the coffee into a polystyrene cup, gathered up my sarnie and departed with dignity – subtly disguised as a hair-tossing flounce.

There's nothing like a bit of brooding resentment to improve your cycling skills. Steering one-handed whilst I ate from the wicker basket and my legs pumped the pedals in a furious up-down-stuff-the-lot-of-them motion, I soared along at a pace that intimidated any car in less than fourth gear.

Swinging right into the lane to St Biddy's, the bike inclined at an angle of forty-five degrees to the road, I free-wheeled down the empty main street and arrived at the tiny bus stop with five minutes to spare.

My plan had been to check if Spencer was on duty, and if so, to catch the bus into town and subtly prise the information I needed from him during the journey. The drawback to this plan occurred to me as I balanced the bike. I was used to parking the car, if necessary, and retrieving it later. But I didn't even have a chain for the bike.

I was going to need somewhere to leave the thing – fast. Standing on one pedal, I scooted down to the store in the hopes of finding Carter in residence, only to find a notice announcing they weren't opening until eight o'clock this morning. Which left one possibility.

My intention to fling myself on Luke's mercy was thwarted by the sight of the bus turning in from the main road. Flinging was time-consuming; dumping was better.

Pedalling like crazy, I discovered Brick Cottage was several hundred yards down the otherwise untenanted rutted track. Heaving the bike over the stone wall, I dropped it behind the bushes at the far end of the garden, where it would be out of sight of casual passers-by, and hoped Luke would recognise it if he decided to do a little pruning.

Sprinting back, I found the small green-and-cream single decker had already turned round and was heading back up towards me. I stood in the centre of the street and windmilled my arms, until he drew in and released the doors. I swung into the front seat across from the driver's cab-hole. 'How far do you go?'

'That'ud be telling, wouldn't it? Tell you what, though, my sex life is so good, even the neighbours have a cigarette afterwards.'

'Tell you what, why don't I just stay on board until I get bored with your witty conversation – or kill you, whichever comes sooner – and I'll pay you then. OK?'

'Can't say fairer than that. Want to hear a joke?'

'Not particularly.'

'What did the hangman say to the condemned prisoner?'

'Surprise me.'

'First time, son? Don't worry, you'll soon get the hang of it! Hang of it . . . gettit? Want to hear another?'

Like I wanted to hear the Dutch telephone directory recited backwards. But since I needed his help, I gave him an encouraging 'Go on, then.'

Twenty minutes later, I realised that Spencer needed encouragement like a cannibal needed a knife and fork. This bloke had written down every Christmas cracker joke since he'd first hung a stocking on his cot for Santa.

A couple of other passengers travelled a few stops with us, but apparently school kids made up the bulk of his fares on this run. And since it was the summer vacation, I had the benefit of Spencer's performance all to myself for most of the journey.

We were actually swinging into the one-way system that

would feed us into the bus station before I managed to interrupt a joke about a dry cleaner who fell into his own vat (he came out insolvent, in case you're wondering) and thrust a picture of Rainwing under his nose. 'Do you remember her?'

'Certainly do. How d'you get four elephants in a Mini?'

'No idea. About her—'

'Liquidise them. Gettit. Gettit?'

'You're a riot, Spencer. You ever thought of doing this professionally?'

'Matter of fact, I have. I've been trying out at those comedy clubs. Never get a spot, though. It's because I'd show these youngsters up, I reckon. I mean, they don't tell jokes, now do they? Just keep going on about their boring lives. Where's the humour in that, eh? Alternative, they call it. Alternative to sleeping pills, if you ask me. Me now, I tell jokes. I'm thinking of bypassing the live performances. Take me act straight to screen – get a wider audience—'

Inspiration struck. 'I've a friend who owns a nightclub.' (This was true.) 'He'd love to hear your act.' (That was the biggest lie since Henry VIII told Anne Boleyn not to fret, he was just measuring her for a new necklace.)

It had the desired effect. Spencer couldn't wait to tell me everything he knew about Rainwing. Which boiled down to the fact that she was a really smashing-looking squaw but not one to powwow much. And she'd got off at the bus station. 'But I reckon I can put you on to where she went,' he said, anxious not to lose his ticket to the big time. 'I've seen her before, see? Not on the bus; that was the first time I ever picked her up.'

That made sense if the Purbricks' study centre had only moved to its present location within the last few months. 'Where, then?'

'I've got this friend, see? Regular date. I've seen the Indian going into a house in her street.'

'Which one?'

A sly look flowed down the planes of his face. There were no hills. Carter had been right about his looks: Spencer seemed to have crashed into a brick wall at thirty miles an hour – without his bus. 'What about my audition?'

'I'll fix it. Trust me, Spencer. I'm a fan. You deserve a break.'

The sap fell for it. He gave me the address and added the news that Rainwing had a boyfriend.

'Is he into buckskins and war paint as well?'

'No. He's normal. City type. Plenty of cash too, I reckon. He's got a flash car. Silver Audi. Top of the range. Probably thinks a motor like that pulls the birds.'

'It does, Spencer.'

He stared through the windscreen, threading the steering wheel through his broad fingers with professional ease as we glided to a stop in the bus station. 'Yeah, I know. But when I'm famous, eh?'

'You'll make Rod Stewart look like a monk. What's this boyfriend look like?'

'Like? I dunno. City boy. Thirtyish. Dark hair.'

I was standing on the platform, ready to leap down as soon as he opened the doors. But not even the promise of fame and unlimited bimbos was going to make Spencer forget his obligations to the bus company. I had to pay up before he let me off.

The street he'd described was just outside the old city walls. It was called Loveluck Lane. A throwback to the time when the world's oldest profession had a monopoly on business down here. The woman who opened the door had a rosy-cheeked, beaming smile that soon disappeared when I produced Rainwing's picture and started into my 'I heard she stays here sometimes' speech.

'No. You're mistaken. I've never seen her.'

'Hang on.' I had to wedge a foot to prevent the door swinging shut. 'I'm not mistaken. I've got witnesses, Mrs . . . er?'

'Miss. Miss Violetta Schlesinger.' She peered up at me through the gap left by her efforts to close the door and mine to keep it open. 'Please. It's only a few days. Just a few pounds, really.'

I got the message. She'd been renting out rooms without declaring the income. It was a popular pastime in this tourist trap. Providing they weren't too greedy and didn't have vindictive neighbours, most of them never got caught.

'I don't want to cause trouble for you,' I said with my best heavy-sneer. 'So you help me, and I'll help you. That's fair, isn't it?' I backed her into the house as I spoke.

'I don't know, I'm not sure ...' Miss Schlesinger fluttered. It was hard to tell whether she'd picked the habit up from the dozen caged birds scattered around the sitting room – or she'd chosen them as pets because she felt at home in a flock.

'Now what could possibly be wrong about telling me her real name?'

'That is her name. Rainwing. So pretty, don't you think?'

'What about the boyfriend?'

'Does she have one?'

'Come on, Miss Schlesinger. He's been seen. City type? Flashy silver car?'

'Oh dear.' Her feathers shivered again. The menagerie went into a collective spasm of mirror-bashing and bell-ringing in sympathy.

'Has he got a name?'

'Daniel,' she whispered.

'Surname? Address? Phone number?'

'I don't know. I truly don't.'

'You must have some idea. What about when they reserve the room?'

She was near to tears as she assured me they telephoned whenever they wanted to stay and paid in cash on arrival. Much like Rainwing's arrangement with the Purbricks.

They were a strangely elusive couple. I asked what Daniel did while Rainwing was off carving totem poles.

Miss Schlesinger didn't know that either. 'I don't pry. I respect my guests' privacy.'

She stuck her chin up, lips firming. Now she'd got over the initial shock of my arrival, her backbone was returning. I pressed on quickly by suggesting I didn't believe she knew nothing about her guests.

'I think I'd like you to leave now.'

'Fair enough. Let's see . . . the tax office for this area is where, exactly?'

'Oh no.' The feather-ruffling went into overdrive. 'Please. I've only my pension.'

'I should care.' I thought mega-bitch and sneered at her again. I'm really no good at this intimidation lark, but I seemed to make an impression on Miss Schlesinger. She begged me to wait.

'There is something. Wait here a moment.'

I heard her pit-pattering up the stairs, and drawers opening and closing above my head. The birds had stopped twittering and fallen silent, and the only sound in this room was the faintly sinister click of their little claws as they shifted on their perches. I was beginning to feel like I was trapped inside a scene from a Hitchcock film when Violetta finally crept in again and handed me a paperback.

'He left it behind. Well, lost it, really. It had slipped behind the dresser. I meant to return it the next time he came.'

It was a book of poems by Walt Whitman. I fanned the pages and found a faint pencilled note on the front flyleaf. *Daniel Sholto, Flat 32, St Stephen's House, City Road. £2.00 to pay.*

I'll spare you the details of the train trip. Imagine being trapped in a tin can with no air-conditioning and no buffet car for a couple of hours and you'll get the general idea. It was, however, an improvement on London. The heat wave that made life a joy at the coast turned the days into hell in London. The heavy air seemed to push the heat down, trapping it at street level, where it broiled up the traffic fumes and added a layer of dust and exhaust emissions to everything it touched.

The main entrance to St Stephen's House was in a smaller street off the City Road. It was a solid four-storey red-brick structure with a marbled step entrance, an echoey marble décor inside and one of those old-fashioned brass cage-type lifts. It had probably been built about the same time as those Edwardian boarding houses in Seatoun. Unlike them, its location so close to the City of London no doubt meant the flats here cost the equivalent of a small country's defence budget. Which made the choice of a room in Violetta's aviary all the more odd. Why not a four-star hotel? Daniel could plainly afford it.

Flat 32 was on the third floor. There was no answer to the doorbell. Scouting around, I couldn't find any silver Audis parked in the residents' parking spaces.

I picked a seat in the pub opposite, where I could keep an eye on the entrance, and waited. And waited. And waited. No one even vaguely resembling Spencer's dark-haired, thirtyish City boy went in. In case there was a back entrance, I slipped across every so often and tried the flat bell.

By six o'clock I was sick of nursing halves of lager, and the barman was beginning to hint that if I was on the game he knew where I could do better business. In the end I caught the tube to Oxford Street and spent a few hours mooching in and out of the department stores with the American and Japanese tourists.

By the time I returned, the streets were filling up with those out to make the most of the warm evening, but there was still no Audi parked in the neighbourhood. He might have a garage somewhere, of course. Although it was unlikely in this area, where I'd heard it was dearer to park your wheels than to park your butt. The flat was still in darkness and there was no response to the bell.

He could work late. On the other hand, he might have gone off on a month's business trip. I didn't fancy constant visits to the metropolis on the off chance of one day catching Daniel at home. I could leave a note asking him to contact me. On the other hand . . .

Slipping the lock pick in, I eased the tension wrench in below it and started probing. It wasn't a good lock. From the tenant's point of view, I mean. For anyone breaking and entering, it was a dream. It needed a double turn to lock it securely, and whoever had used it last hadn't bothered.

It also had a couple of internal bolts that hadn't been engaged. I discovered this fact when the door was suddenly ripped open.

Crouched down, I found myself looking at a pair of long, prehensile feet. My eyes slid up the smooth legs, the striped towel worn like a sarong, the hairless chest with another towel draped over the shoulders, and the narrow, dark-eyed face capped by tousled dripping hair. He smelt of fresh soap, damp hair and shampoo.

'What the hell do you think you're doing, may I ask?'

'The light wasn't on.'

'I find the dark relaxing.'

'You didn't answer the bell.'

'I can't hear it when I'm in the shower. Forgive me. If I'd have known there was a burglar waiting, I'd have changed my whole ablutions routine.'

He flicked dripping fronds out of his eyes and dragged the neck towel up to sop up the excess water.

His knees weren't bad, but I was getting a bit tired of staring at them. So I stood before asking why he thought I was a burglar.

'My mistake. This is just a hobby, is it?' His thumb and forefinger shot out and twisted the pick from my grasp.

I bit back the witty reply I would no doubt have thought

of in the next nanosecond. The towel he was using was dark brown. When he'd flicked it over his head the ends had draped down each side like long strands of hair. I looked into the angular face, now softened by the frame of material, and saw what hadn't been obvious before.

'You're Rainwing!'

13

Rainwing/Daniel stood aside. 'You'd better come in.'

There was a fish tank set into one wall, full of tiny darting chips of jewel colours swimming between the sunken remains of drowned ruins. It gave enough light to see polished floorboards, walls in pale non-colours, scattered sofas, low tables, abstract art, horizontal blinds and all the doors replaced by walk-through arches. It felt wrong somehow. I'd have expected Rainwing to live in a world of colourful clutter. Her *alter ego* seemed to be her complete opposite in more than the biological sphere.

He touched the base of a lamp and a yellow glow spread from beneath the Japanese-style paper globe. 'Hang here a minute, whoever you are.'

'My name is Smith.'

'God, how boringly unoriginal. Can't you make up something better than that?'

'I could. But my parents couldn't. It really *is* my name.'

'Please yourself.' He strode away through the left-hand archway, leaving a trail of damp footprints that evaporated from the polished wood as I watched. Another lamp came on, giving me a glimpse of a floor-level bed and the shadow silhouette of Daniel discarding the towels for more conventional clothing.

I took a quick glance around while he was busy (just on the off chance of coming across his appointment card for the probation office, or his year photo from

Wandsworth Prison, you understand).

It was an empty place. Not just the furnishings, but the whole atmosphere. The CDs were music club collections. Apart from half a dozen airport blockbuster paperbacks of the lone-hero-saves-world-from-psychotic-dictators/aliens/rampaging-viruses variety, the rest of the books were dictionaries, road maps, restaurant guides and assorted worldwide train and air timetables. Even the fish proved to be plastic fakes. There was a two-drawer filing cabinet, but it was locked, and getting caught twice picking locks seemed like exceptionally crass manners (even for me).

The kitchen area had more stainless-steel implements than a TV hospital drama, but most looked like they'd never encountered a hot plate or chipped a spud. The noticeboard was decorated with business cards for taxi firms, laundry services, a housekeeping agency, courier firms, and takeaway menus that catered for every ethnic foodie craving, from sushi to kangaroo steaks.

The only area I really liked was the balcony. I discovered it by chance when I opened the blind slats on what I'd taken to be a window and discovered instead a set of narrow french doors. It overlooked a small walled garden at the back of the building.

It was unexpectedly peaceful out there after the continuous jostle of traffic and humanity all day. I stood for a moment, enjoying the summer air now it had lost some of its heat.

The mood was spoilt by the roar of a jet beginning its descent towards the City airport. I thought briefly of Annie and wondered how her Heathrow meeting had gone. Well, probably. Annie generally impressed clients. She'd plainly impressed that City securities company. Who knows, in a few months perhaps she'd be staking a mortgage on an overpriced London flat like this. In which case, she could at least have remembered my last birthday as her closest friend – geographically speaking.

'It's lovely, isn't it? A little treasure amongst all the chaos.'

The hairs had prickled on the back of my neck. He'd come up behind me without my hearing a thing.

Rainwing/Daniel squeezed on to the balcony beside me and leant his arms on the parapet. He'd changed into dark cargo trousers and a light silky shirt.

'I often come out here at the end of the day and just stand and enjoy the night.' He tilted his head and breathed deeply and evenly. 'Can you smell the night-scented stock?'

I gulped in a mouthful of air. 'That flowery thing?'

'That flowery thing.' He'd turned towards me; his features were still in shadow. 'Doesn't it make you think of *Romeo and Juliet*?

> *'What's in a name? that which we call a rose,*
> *By any other word would smell as sweet;*
> *So Romeo would, were he not Romeo call'd,*
> *Retain that dear perfection which he owes,*
> *Without that title. Romeo doff thy name;*
> *And for thy name, which is no part of thee,*
> *Take all myself!'*

It was eerie. I mean, I knew he was a bloke now, but the voice, the gestures, even the way he was standing – I could have sworn it was a fourteen-year-old girl whispering urgently beside me. It was easy to see how he'd deceived the Purbricks into believing he was a woman.

Light spilt over the patio terrace below, infusing colour into the flower petals. A high-pitched laugh shrilled out, shattering the moment.

'Whoops,' Daniel tutted, reverting to type. 'The ground floor's coming out to play. We'd best make a tactful retreat. They like to do *it* al fresco. One doesn't like to be a peeping Tom.'

He drew me back inside and shut the blinds. I asked him

who he did like to be – if not Tom. 'Should I call you Rainwing or Daniel? You are Daniel Sholto, I take it?'

'Yes, I'm Daniel. But Dan will do. Was my performance that inspiring? I seem to have moved you to tears.' He reached out and wiped a thumb down over my cheek.

I hadn't known I was blubbing. That neglect of my big day had hit me harder than I'd been prepared to admit – even to myself. Perhaps that was why I blurted out, 'It's my birthday. And no one remembered.'

'So you decided to cheer yourself up by stealing a present? Should I be flattered that it was my taste above all others that you coveted?'

'I wasn't going to take anything. Honestly.'

'Well, no. One usually takes things *dishonestly*, as I understand the rules.'

'I meant . . . It's a bit tricky to explain.' But I'll have a convincing lie on the tip of my tongue any second now, Danny boy – if you can just keep talking for a little longer.

Luckily he did. At least he said, 'Come into the kitchen.'

I perched on a wooden stool by the breakfast bar and watched him flick open an overhead cupboard. He set two champagne flutes on the counter, went to the fridge, took out a bottle of bubbly and whisked a clean white napkin from a drawer. He had a way with the foil, wire and cork that a wine waiter would have envied.

Filling the two glasses, he took one by the stem and toasted me. 'Here's to your birthday, Miss Smith. Am I allowed to ask which one?'

'Thirty.' I picked up my own glass. 'Cheers.'

It tasted expensive. I hoped it was. 'You're taking my attempts at breaking in very coolly. Is it a lifestyle thing, karma against crooks or something? Or are you just incredibly laid-back?'

'The truth?'

'Why not.'

'I'm bored. And you're an intriguing diversion.' He

waved the crystal in a vague sweep that encompassed the kitchen area and whatever was visible through the archway. 'Look at this place. It's not a home – it's pit-stop between meetings.'

'Meetings for what?'

'I work for a bank. Negotiating finance packages for businesses. Far Eastern, mostly. Although some of the Latin American countries are coming on line now.'

'Isn't it interesting?'

'It was, once. But now – you get tired of facing the same greedy-guts across the same board tables. It doesn't matter where you are, they all want the same thing: bags of dosh and no responsibility if the whole thing goes down the toilet.'

'So why do it?'

'Money. I intend to retire at forty and spend the rest of my life on a beach somewhere.'

'How long to splash-down?'

I thought there was the slightest hesitation before he admitted to twenty-nine.

'Top-up?' Champagne fizzed to the top of the flutes again. 'So, Miss Smith, if burglary isn't your career of choice, what is?'

The student-anxious-not-to-publish-without-permission wasn't going to pass the credulity test under these circumstances. I decided to stick to as near the truth as I could without prejudicing Barbra's anonymity.

'I'm doing a correspondence course. You must have seen the ads: "Train to be a Private Investigator"?'

'I think so. Amongst the classifieds for kinky lingerie and adult videos in the tabloid papers?'

Well, call me common as muck, do, Daniel dear, I thought, whilst keeping an ingratiating smile stretched over my lips. 'You have to do exercises and send them in. For my latest assignment I had to take random photos of people and then try to trace them – without cheating and following them home right there and then.'

'And you took my picture, did you? May I see?'

'I didn't bring it with me,' I lied. 'You were in your Indian kit. The bus driver at St Biddy's remembered you. And then I traced your landlady in Canterbury ... Miss Schlesinger.'

'She doesn't have my address.'

'You left a book behind.' I extracted the Walt Whitman from my bag and passed it over, the cover open so he could see the pencilled note.

'How careless of me. And I went to such trouble to conceal my tracks.'

'Why? If you don't mind my asking?'

'No, I don't mind. Although I'm not sure I'm going to answer.' He threw back the rest of his champagne and ran a wet finger around the rim. It set up a high-pitched whine that made me long to knock his teeth in.

Which would have been a pity. They were nice teeth. Now I had a chance to study him, I could see what made him such an attractive woman. The narrow face with its high cheekbones and large dark sloe-eyes was the sort of look that kept supermodels in work and plastic surgeons in super-tax havens. Without the long sweep of Rainwing's wig to soften the edges, the image was slightly gaunt, but he still registered as 8.5 on the Smith Fanciable Scale. Even if he did have at least one teeth-itching personal habit.

'Are you trying to call the cat in?'

'Pardon?' He refocused on me.

'The noise.' I nodded to the slowly circling middle finger.

'Oh? Sorry. It's a stupid habit. I don't realise I'm doing it. Are you hungry?'

'Almost invariably.'

'Will you have dinner with me? If you don't have any more sleuthing to do this evening?'

'Nope, I'm all sleuthed out.'

He ordered a Chinese takeaway on his credit card,

demonstrating his facility with numbers by reeling off the whole sixteen-figure code without even bothering to get the plastic out. We finished the champagne whilst we were waiting for the delivery. He put some smooch music on the sound system and fetched a fresh bottle from the fridge.

We'd graduated back to the living area by then. Daniel sat on the floor with a sofa at his back. I liked that. I always sit on the floor too, for preference.

The cork came out with a disappointing lack of exuberance once again. 'No pop? Is it flat or something?'

'Firing it off like a cannon is the mark of an amateur. Those of us who appreciate good wine prefer not to waste it.'

'Is this good?' I twisted the label. It meant nothing to a dedicated aficionado of supermarket plonk. 'How much does it cost?'

'About ninety a bottle, I think.'

'You don't know?'

He shrugged. 'I didn't really notice. Drink up, Miss Smith.'

'Grace.'

Pressing the palms of his hands together in a prayerful gesture, he intoned, 'For what we are about to receive, may the Lord make us truly thankful. And I, for one, am.' He tipped the straw-coloured liquid down in one smooth movement whilst I admired the way his silky skin caught the lamplight. The light tan glowed like liquid gold in the V of his shirt neck.

He lowered his head quickly – saw me looking – and leant over. I half expected him to try for a kiss and was debating whether to pucker up or fend him off. Instead he surprised me by very gently rubbing his nose against mine.

It was an interesting sort of manoeuvre. I tickled back. Out of the corner of my eye I could see that the second bottle was two thirds empty already. And I hadn't had anything to eat since Shane's double bacon sarnie this morning. I hoped that Chinese arrived before I had to decide whether or not to take this a bit further. Or did I? 'I meant my name is Grace.'

'Really?'

'Grace Smith isn't the sort of name anyone would make up. It's too dull. My friend Annie is a Smith too, and her parents gave the kids all really outrageous first names. To make up for the ordinariness.'

'Annie isn't outrageous.'

'Anchoret is. And her sisters have been lumbered with Tennessee and Tallahassee.'

'That is . . . unusual.'

'It's not as unusual as Rainwing . . .' I could hear my tongue slipping and sliding whilst it gave away personal details of a fellow investigator – which is a real no-no. The bottle on the table was empty. He'd refilled my glass again when I wasn't concentrating. I should have slipped the contents into the vase behind me, but it seemed such a waste at ninety quid a bottle. Especially when no one else had even bought me so much as a Ribena for my birthday. So I kept sipping.

'Rainwing isn't my real name, though, remember. It's my spirit name, I guess you could say.'

'Yep. Don't suppose you get many Sioux called Daniel.'

'No, I don't suppose you do.'

The bubbles fizzed up to the glass rim again. I asked him if Miss Schlesinger realised Rainwing and Daniel Sholto were the same person.

'Naturally she does. Although I didn't realise she knew my surname. Careless of me, that. Dear Vi minds the suit and the car for me whilst I'm at the centre.'

'And she doesn't mind?'

'Is she shocked, do you mean? If she is, the scandalous cost of millet and cuttlefish these days tends to override her finer feelings. After all, it's not as if I'm doing anyone any harm, is it?'

He was doing a reasonable amount of harm to my earlobe with his teeth by that point. It felt terrific. Two drop-dead gorgeous blokes showing an interest in two days – was I hot or not!

So I relaxed and enjoyed the sensation until the intercom buzzed and Daniel uncoiled himself. 'Can you answer that whilst I sort out more drinks?'

I signed for two huge carriers that smelt heavenly. It wasn't the standard takeaway collection of tin-foil packages. This lot came in wine-red bowls that could have passed for china. The rice bowls *were* china, with a message inviting us to keep them as a souvenir of our experience. There was even a dish of lemon-scented towels to be heated in the microwave.

Daniel spread the banquet over the low coffee table. 'I ordered the Emperor's Birthday Feast. It seemed appropriate.'

I sneaked a look at the menus under the pretence of fetching some kitchen roll to act as a serviette. Supper had just cost him a hundred and twenty quid – plus tip.

I'm not naturally overimpressed by guys who flash the cash, but if a bloke's going to try for the full seduction scene, it's always pleasant to find he doesn't see you as his for the price of a lager and a chicken vindaloo. I looked out at the vast array of dishes on offer and was aware I had a decision to make here. Was I going to sleep with the biggest dish of all – or not?

14

Piling Peking duck on a pancake, I rolled it up. 'You were going to tell me about Rainwing.'

'Was I?' He wielded his chopsticks with enviable dexterity. 'What do you want to know?'

All I needed to know – for the purposes of Barbra's brief

– was whether he/she had a criminal record. But what I really wanted to know was: 'Why?'

Dan sighed gently and tucked his legs under him, resting an elbow on the sofa and twisting slightly so he could look directly at me.

'Because I have to. Most of the time I can handle this . . .' He circled a chopstick, flicking grains of boiled rice on the cushions. 'I switch off, concentrate on the insanity of the banking world and hold on to the thought of that beach. But sometimes the pressure gets to me and I just have to escape.'

'And become Rainwing?'

'Yes. I've always needed to dress in women's clothing. Not all the time, just occasionally – to relax. At first I only did it at home. But then I found myself wanting to mix with other people – as a woman. I tried the club scene at first, but it wasn't me. There was too much of everything: too much make-up; too many sequins; too much backcombing and hairspray; too many posturing and pouting drag queens. I wanted to be accepted as a woman in the *real* world. And then I discovered the Purbricks' place. It's a study centre for the exploration of traditional teachings and crafts amongst what I suppose you'd call the Red Indians.'

'I know the place. Just moved to outside St Biddy's, hasn't it?' I asked artlessly.

'The very one. It was like a sign finding them. Native American studies had always been a bit of a hobby of mine anyway, and students often came in costume, it was part of the fun. There I could just unwind. It was so liberating. I was devastated when they had to leave their last place. Selwyn – that's the owner – has no business sense at all. I don't know how his wife copes with him, frankly. Well, I do. She loves him, it's as simple as that. She confides in me. Woman to woman.'

'Doesn't that make you feel rotten? Deceiving her like that?'

'You don't understand. When I'm Rainwing, I'm not a man pretending to be a woman. I *am* a woman. I can't tell you how totally at peace I feel after a few days at the centre. But the bank might not understand. In fact, they definitely won't. That's why it would be a disaster if anyone were to give them even so much as a hint.'

Those peat-dark eyes were holding mine. I saw the question in them.

'They won't hear it from me. But are you sure it would be such a big deal? From what you read in the papers, some of these high-flyers lead pretty bizarre lives.'

'Oh, they do. But the trick is not to get found out. There's the public face – which has to be beyond reproach. And the private one – where anything goes and you can sell tickets to consenting adults if you like.' He held his hands palm upwards in an elegant gesture, supporting the two unseen halves of his life. 'Would you say you were an open-minded kind of person, Grace?'

'Pretty much, I guess.'

'And if someone were to give you a million pounds tomorrow, could you honestly say you'd be happy to entrust it to a bank where the male employees wear dresses and make-up?'

I wish I could have said sure – no problem. But there's nothing like coming face to face with your prejudices to find out just how conventionally boring you really are. He was right, of course: my windfall would have gone to the professional grey-suit not the bloke on the left in the buckskin mini.

'I can see the answer is "no way, ma'am",' Daniel said, reaching across to take a spare rib. 'You should try these, they're delicious.'

He handed me a sticky bone. He was right. It was great. I gnawed off lumps of crisp, juicy meat and asked if he hadn't ever run into anyone he knew when he was in his Pocahontas kit.

'Not that, no. But I did nearly get caught once. This was a few years back, when I was still doing the club scene. I'd got myself up in the full outfit – dress, wig, make-up, false nails, the lot – and there's this ring at the door. So I'm tripping over to answer it – assuming it's the taxi driver – when suddenly this voice calls out asking if I'm in. And it's only my boss. That was the closest I ever came to experiencing what it's like to be a real woman. I nearly gave *birth*!'

'What did you do?'

'I broke the world record for getting my kit off. Then I just *flung* myself into the shower. The tray looked like Hannibal Lecter had had a snack in there – just ten red fingernails and a wig swirling around on the tiles.'

I laughed. The sounds whirled around inside my head. Despite the padding from the Chinese chow, I was getting well and truly sloshed, but who cared – it was my birthday.

'Anyway,' Daniel continued, 'I eventually open the door to him and he takes one look at this scene – me starkers under my robe and the carpet covered in black stockings and frilly underwear – and gives me this big knowing wink and tells me he's sorry to have called at a bad time. Next thing I know, I've got a reputation as the office stud.'

He explored what was left of the untouched bowls and asked if I could fancy a toffee apple.

I most definitely could. He retopped our glasses with fizzing cream yet again.

'You trying to get me drunk?' I asked. 'So you can have your wicked way with me?'

'No.'

'Not your type?'

He slipped closer so that those large brown irises were a few inches from mine. 'I'm not gay, if that's what you mean. And I don't want to be a woman – not in any permanent biological sense.'

'So what's the problem here?'

'I just tend to prefer my partners sober.'

'Pity.' (Did I really say that?)

He offered me a toffee-coated slice of apple. The heat exploded in my mouth and I gasped, sending a dribble of juice and hot sugar down my chin. Dan mopped it up with kitchen roll and finished up the cleaning with his tongue. He was very thorough; he even washed off the back of my teeth with it.

'I thought you liked your girls sober,' I murmured when we finally came up for air.

'I think we should all try to be a little flexible in this life. I've tried sober. Perhaps it's time to move on. Experiment.'

'That's prob ... prob ... because you're drunk too.'

'Am I?'

'I'll check.' I locked my lips around his and took several deep breaths. It wasn't a method much favoured by the traffic police, but I have to tell you, it was a lot more fun than a breathalyser kit.

When we disentangled this time he was flat on the floor and I was straddling his waist. The lamplight was still gleaming off that triangle of golden skin at the V of his collar. I just had to see if the tan went all the way down to his belly button. I flicked open the top button. Then the second.

He caught my wrists just before I reached the answer to that intriguing question. 'I've never done it with a private investigator before.'

'Trainee private investigator.'

'When do you get your badge?'

'When I've passed all my tests.' I debated whether to bite him and make him release my wrists. In fact I'd bent over, my teeth hovering over the curve of that deliciously smooth, hairless chest, when he abruptly let go of my arms and reached up under my T-shirt to locate the fastening of my bra.

In the interests of equality, I got his kit off too before we

123

ended up in a tangle on the bed. There was a slight hiatus in proceedings at that point whilst he rummaged in cupboards, drawers and pockets in search of condoms. I lay on top of the bed and watched. His growing frustration when he couldn't find any was both hilarious and reassuring. A giant economy pack in the bedside drawer would have been a real turn-off. Eventually he found a box and abnormal service was resumed.

His bed linen was dark blue with an undulating pattern of lighter blues. It was like being in the ocean again. It seemed like a very tidy end to my birthday. I'd started the day bouncing stark naked in the waves with a couple of drop-outs for company, and I was ending it the same way but with a rich, good-looking banker appreciating my assets. Age definitely had its compensations. (The golden tan did go down to his navel, incidentally. In fact, it went all over.)

Later, when we were both curled up like a couple of warm spoons under the duvet, he returned to the subject of my (supposedly) new career path. 'It seems a strange choice. What did you do before?'

'Worked for the community,' I said truthfully.

'Care homes?' Dan asked. 'Mental health cases?'

'That sort of thing.' It wasn't a total lie. Some of the people I came across in the police certainly qualified as mental cases.

'That's strange. If I'd had to guess, I'd have put you down as something in the artistic line. Painter or writer, something like that.' He ran his fingers up my arm until they entwined with mine above our heads. 'You have artist's hands. They're very expressive. Very deft.'

I demonstrated my deftness with my free hand until he told me to pack it in, he had to get up early in the morning. 'It's all very well for you idle artists, but some of us have to graft for a living.'

'I'm not an artist.' I applied a bit more deftness.

'Bet you are. I'll bet you're a secret sculptress. Or a clandestine crayoner. No, I have it. You're a frustrated writer. I'll bet you've got the beginnings of the great unfinished novel of the century hidden somewhere, haven't you?'

'Not even a great unfinished shopping list. But you're right about one thing.'

'What?'

'I'm definitely feeling frustrated over here.' I rolled on top of him and the waves started crashing again.

I guess we both fell asleep after that. The next thing I remember was light, a raging thirst, a drilling headache, and the early-morning news on the portable television.

Daniel was already in the shower. I padded into the kitchen, found some aspirin, swallowed two with a couple of pints of water, and switched on the filter coffee machine. Whilst it brewed, I collected my confiscated tension pick from Dan's discarded trousers and my clothes from the living room floor. The square bulge of the photo wallet was still there in my inside jacket pocket, but being a suspicious little bunny I checked anyway. The Boots logo was getting a bit battered now. I eased a finger inside and counted: eighteen snaps all present and correct.

Carrying the coffee back to bed, I drank it listening to an earnest-looking health minister assuring the nation that the Government was doing all it could to trace the source of the diphtheria outbreak and there was really no need for anyone to panic. He was followed by a doctor describing the symptoms of diphtheria (just in case we all wanted to panic) and some outside shots of rent-a-rabble demonstrating outside a hostel of refugees.

We returned to the bright-as-a-button studio presenter as she told us how lucky we were to have the MP Faye Sinclair with us this morning. Gucci and pearls slid into focus; she must go to bed in them.

'Mrs Sinclair, many of these cases have occurred in your

constituency. As someone who is widely tipped as a future cabinet—'

I clicked the remote and consigned Mrs Sinclair's solution to the current medical crisis to the digital other-world.

Dan was using the brown towel on his hair again. I raised a hand as he emerged from the bathroom: 'How!'

'Very inventively, as I recall.' He took the mug of coffee I passed over. 'Look, I'm really sorry. I know this is going to look like I hit and run, but I've got to get going.'

'No problem. I wasn't expecting an engagement ring with my boiled egg and toasted soldiers.'

When I came out of the shower, he'd cleared up the debris of my birthday dinner. 'Want a hand?'

'It's OK, thanks. Like I said, I really have to be out of here.'

'OK. I'm gone.' I started climbing into my clothes, trying to remember how you make a graceful exit from situations like this (it had been a while, as you may have gathered).

'Can I see you again?' Dan asked.

'If you like.'

'I like. My number is written on the phone.'

'Right.' I patted down my pockets and found only the bundle of picks and tension tool.

'Here.' Dan flicked a pen. I caught it and scribbled down the figures on the back of my train ticket.

'And?' he prodded.

I gave him the office number and then – because I had a sudden nightmarish vision of Jan fielding the call – added my home number. 'I'm out a lot,' I said, giving it the cool, busy-busy, girl-about-town performance. 'But, you know . . . if you catch me . . .'

'I'll do my very best.'

'Great.'

Goodbye was awkward. In the end we settled for a peck on the lips.

There must be an awful lot of worms in London, judging by the early birds flocking at this time of the morning. I surged down the tube with them and wedged myself in amongst the tabloids, polystyrene containers of breakfasts eaten on the hoof and breaths of last night's curry suppers. Occasionally I caught glimpses of myself in the train windows as we went through the tunnels. I had a great big stupid grin plastered all over my face.

The ticket clerk at Victoria managed to wipe it off by telling me the day-return I'd bought yesterday was no longer valid. I needed a new ticket to travel today. It didn't matter that it was going on Barbra Delaney's bill in the end – I hadn't enough cash on me to get home.

'It's only a third of that price if you travel after nine thirty,' the clerk said helpfully.

That was fine by me. I bought a cappuccino and croissant from the café and sat out at one of the tables on the concourse, watching the wage slaves tearing off the commuter trains.

I had a lot of time to waste people-watching, and there's a limit to the time even I can stretch out one cappuccino. I spooned the froth at the bottom of the cup and wondered whether to use up the last of my change on a refill. That was when fate decided I'd been enjoying myself for a tad too long. I remembered the fifty-pound birthday present.

Breakfast probably wasn't what my mother had had in mind, I reflected, disentangling the photo wallet from my jacket pocket, but so what – it fitted my definition of 'something nice'.

Something was wrong. It took a second to register. There was no time and date stamp on the back of the first print. I snatched out the snaps from their pocket and spread them across the table.

They were a varied assortment taken over a period of time, judging by the different weather and lighting. A pagoda-shaped pavilion with a curly red roof was bathed in intense sunlight; a lake with a mother swan spreading its wings threateningly over its cygnets was dull and overcast; whilst an odd teapot-shaped rock on a cliff edge and a city street with a van propped on bricks were lit by that bright, sparkly sheen that said 'perfect spring day'. There was nothing remarkable about them – except for the fact I'd never seen any of them before in my life.

At least he'd had the good manners to leave my fifty pounds alone. I found it tucked inside the slot for the negatives. It must have given him a nasty taste in his mouth to find that they were missing. At least I hoped it did. I couldn't decide which upset me most, the knowledge that he didn't trust me enough to keep my promise not to flash those photos of Rainwing around, or the idea of him sneaking out of our bed in the night to search through my stuff. He must be a hell of an operator. Normally I'm a light sleeper and someone moving around a strange room like that would have disturbed me. On reflection, though – given the amount of champagne I'd drunk – perhaps it wasn't so surprising. Had that been the idea all along when he'd started pouring ninety-pound fizz down my throat? I headed for the phone booths, rehearsing some of my better insults.

The answering machine picked up at Dan's flat. His voice sounded less attractive over the phone. Or perhaps I'd just lost my rose-tinted ear lobes since last night. Instead of the usual leave-a-message-after-the-tone it instructed callers not to bother 'because this damn tape always runs out', but urgent messages could be left with his secretary at Bundell-Heishmann's Bank, number as follows . . .

His secretary was sorry that she couldn't put me through to Dan. 'Look, tell him it's Grace. Tell him . . . tell him it's about eliminating the negative.' I figured that the promise of getting his hands on those might at least bring him to the receiver so I could tell him what I thought of his cheap little trick. I hummed a few bars of the tune: '". . . *accentuate the* positive . . . *eliminate the negative . . . and don't mess with Mrs In-Between, buster . . .*"'

'I meant,' she said, interrupting my recital, 'I can't put you through, because Daniel isn't here. He's away from the office at present.'

'When do you expect him back?'

'Six more weeks, perhaps.'

What did she mean, *more*? 'Sorry? Where is he exactly?'

'South America. He's been out there for a few weeks. Is there a message . . . ?'

'No message.'

I didn't believe it. Well, maybe I did. But I had to confirm it anyway. Before I did, I rang Barbra down at Wakens Keep. She wasn't too thrilled to hear I'd ruined all her photos by dropping them in the bath, but she agreed to get another set run off.

'I'll drop them off. Something's come up,' she said. 'I need to see yer anyway. Thought we'd have a chance for a natter last night. See yer.'

The library was my first stop. Leafing thought the yellow page directories I pinpointed a shop selling work-wear off Regent Street. Some of my fifty pounds went on a plain navy nylon zippered boiler suit edged in red binding and a peaked navy cap. An office stationer's yielded pencil, sticky tape, cardboard, scissors, brush and paint. I spent a couple of hours in Regent's Park neatly tracing and cutting out letters from the cardboard sheet, sticking it to the back of the boiler suit and carefully painting inside the makeshift stencil.

The pub where I'd staked out Dan's place yesterday was already buzzing. Lunchtime starts early and finishes late on warm, sunny August Fridays. I breezed into the block of flats with the confident poise of a bona fide caller. A couple emerged from one of the ground-floor doors as I made my way through the lobby. I tweaked my cap a little lower; they barely glanced at me. Once on the third floor, I laid out my picks and tension wrenches openly on the landing and got to work on Daniel's door.

A good lock-picker can open a door in seven seconds. I'm not a good lock-picker and I rarely practise. Hence it took me fifteen minutes of jiggling and cursing under my breath before I finally managed to get inside. Whilst I was working, a forty-something female with a mobile clamped to one ear and a briefcase in the other hand rushed from another flat on the third floor landing, and an elderly woman cradling a tiny dog rode the open-cage lift past to the top floor. They took no more notice of me than that couple on the ground floor.

Why should they? Who sees workmen? I'd become invisible in that cap and overall with its newly painted 'Acme 24-Hour Locksmith Service' logo on the back.

I padded through the empty rooms half hoping he'd be here, even though the dead stillness told me he wasn't.

In the bedroom the ocean-inspired duvet had gone; the bed linen was a geometric mixture of black and white. The brown and striped towels Rainwing had used were also missing. In fact there were no damp or crumpled towels in the place at all – just a neat stack of dry white and blue ones in the bedroom cupboard. I checked the shower tray – it was bone dry.

Daniel had expensive taste in clothes. All the stuff hanging in his fitted wardrobes screamed money. What he didn't have was a pair of black cargo trousers or a plain silky white shirt.

The rubbish bin was empty. The stainless-steel inside gleamed back mockingly as if asking whether I really expected to find it full of takeaway Chinese dishes and empty champagne bottles. I even went over the sofa we'd leant against last night – I couldn't find one solitary grain of cold rice stuck to the cushions.

Finally I used the picks to open the filing cabinet. The stacks of household bills, travel invoices and bank and credit card statements confirmed this was Daniel Sholto's property.

As a last resort I went down to the offices of Bundell-Heishmann in Blackfriars. Despite the ancient location, it was a modern corner block of gleaming whiteness, silvered windows and curved lines. Bundell-Heishmann occupied the top four floors. They must have had a terrific view out over the Thames from there. I never found out, because the only way up was via lifts guarded by a couple of muscular security officers and Daniel Sholto's secretary decided to come down to the reception hall on the ground floor. She was a stick insect in a mini-skirted designer suit and big hair who didn't take my hint that she was just being overprotective, and Daniel was really hiding in his office, too well.

'I've already told you, Danny is in South America.'

'I had dinner with Daniel last night. Perhaps he flew back without telling you.'

'I hardly think so.'

'Could he have loaned his flat to a friend? Late twenties, my height, dark-haired?'

'That's Daniel. And I can assure you he hasn't loaned his flat to anyone. If he had – I'd know.'

'How about giving me his phone number in South America? I'll give him a ring myself. See if I can work out what's going on here.'

'Oh, I think we both know that already, don't we, desperate?' Her eyes swept me from head to toe with all the gentleness of a wire brush encountering oil-stained concrete. I'd lost the boiler suit and returned to jeans and top mode. Her cute little nose wrinkled. 'Look, face it, you're history. I mean, you're not the first to try this one, you know . . . *Oh, Jemima love, I've lost Dan's number, which hotel was he staying in again . . . ?* Get this – Dan is no longer available. He's taken . . . he's not on the market any more. Do you want me to spell it out for you?'

'No thanks. I think I can manage that for myself. Let's see. C.O.W. and D.E.L.U.D.I.N.G. plus S.E.L.F. It's just a question of getting them in the right order really, isn't it?'

It wasn't until I left the building that it occurred to me she probably thought I was referring to myself. Perhaps she was right. Whoever Rainwing was, it would seem he wasn't Daniel Sholto. Whichever way you looked at it, I'd been well and truly screwed by the conniving Crow.

I got back to Victoria to find the lines to Seatoun had been closed by a landslip, and ended up spending the night on the station concourse along with several hundred other commuters who couldn't afford the price of a London hotel room.

They finally started running the service again after lunch on Saturday. Seats were a lottery in which I drew the third train out. As compensation they had taken any restrictions off our tickets, so I used the opportunity to hop off and tackle Violetta about her tax-free lodgers and that oh-so-convenient book she'd happened to come across in 'Daniel's' bedroom.

She'd done a flit.

'Gone visiting for a few weeks. My son's seeing to the birds,' a neighbour explained. 'Do you want to leave a message?'

'Yes. But I won't. Wouldn't want to shock the little fellows out of their feathers, would we?'

I caught the next train back to Seatoun – to the news that my office had been burgled.

15

Well, to be strictly accurate, all the rooms on the upper floors had been trashed. But I was principally concerned with the devastation in mine. Which was fair enough, because Annie was plainly right out of empathy for anyone's misfortunes but her own. Kneeling on the floor, she oozed get-out-of-my-face from every pore.

'Bloody stupid idiot, if I had enough energy left I'd kill him,' she raged, slapping files into piles. It was like watching a demonic game of snap.

Apparently she'd spent the best part of the day reassembling the contents of her office files, which had been dumped over the carpet. My own office was in much the same state. I made a few ineffectual attempts to clear up and decided I just couldn't be bothered at present.

One advantage of having an office that's taste-challenged is there's not much to mourn. Annie, on the other hand, had put a lot of effort into decorating her territory. She feels it's important to make clients – particularly the female ones – feel relaxed, since it makes them talk more freely. To which end she'd set up one half of the room to reflect a homely atmosphere. At present it was only going to feel that way if you happened to be shacking up with a couple of acid heads.

I turned as she swore loudly and found her clutching the upper section of her computer. The base lay on her foot in a tangle of boards and wires.

'Do you want a hand?'

'No, I've got two of those. It's a new set of toes I need.' Easing off her shoe, she massaged the bruised ones. I asked how they'd got in.

'Bathroom looks like the point of entry.' She jerked a thumb in the direction of the third door on our landing.

There was only one small window overlooking the back yard in there. Or there had been. Now there was a hole framed by glass shards. I wriggled my head cautiously into the gap and squinted upwards. The gutter next door was partially detached, and by easing out a little further I discovered the nearest window to us was wide open. There was nothing surprising about that – it was, after all, the middle of a heat wave. But that house was being converted to bedsits and was currently unlet – according to the police.

'They checked this morning. Asked a few questions, filled in a few reports, you know the form,' Annie explained, disembowelling her computer. 'It looks like the visitors swung across the roof. It's a pity they didn't break their flaming necks.'

'Do our finest have any clues?'

'None.' A lump of computer innards was added to one of the filing piles. 'And since nothing much seems to be missing and no one was injured, we aren't exactly top of their list for the allocation of resources. I shouldn't hold your breath for an arrest, unless you've got the lung capacity to swim the Atlantic – underwater.'

And she should know. Annie is also ex-police service. Like me, she'd resigned for personal reasons. Unlike me, she retained an excellent unofficial working relationship with all her old contacts.

I asked how come the alarm system hadn't activated.

'Why don't you ask him?' Annie snarled through her splintered door frame at Vetch, who'd just climbed the stairs with an armful of planks.

'Ask me what, sweet thing?' he panted, depositing the load and removing hammer and nails from his pocket.

'Grace was wondering why the alarm didn't go off.'

'It did. And the security company's response was everything they promised, I assure you.'

'What did they promise?' I asked, surveying the debris. 'To take a round trip via the Orkneys before they dealt with any trouble?'

Annie was packing the computer's hard disk and a dozen plastic files into a bag. 'They offer a six-minute response time. And judging by the amount of damage to Jan's desk, I'd say that was about right. Needless to say, they didn't have time to enter Vetch's office at all. You see, the alarm triggered when our vandals got bored trashing the upper floors and decided to wander down to reception. And do you know why it went off at that particular juncture?'

I was beginning to have an idea. But Annie was in full rant and not about to be interrupted.

'See that?' She dragged me on to the landing and pointed to the winking red light of the security sensor nestling in a ceiling corner. 'It's a fake. It's nothing more than a plastic box with a battery-powered bulb. The only genuine ones are those on the ground floor.'

'Since when?'

Vetch gave a shrug. 'The past two years or so.'

'But why?'

For once the smug self-assurance had been wiped off his round face and even the tips of his ears seemed to have a hangdog droop. 'Cash flow, delicious. The tide has been ebbing so I decided we'd have to economise.'

'No, you decided the rest of us should economise. Your office still had the benefit of the security system,' Annie snapped.

'It is on the ground floor. It made sense.'

'To you, maybe, you cheap little . . .'

'Gnome,' I supplied helpfully.

'I was going to say chiseller. The sooner I move, the flaming better.' She heaved the packed bag on to her shoulder and waved a hand over the rest of the stacked files. 'You see that lot. Well, I expect to find them stored in your safe when I get back.'

'It's rather occupied at present.'

'Unoccupy it until you've got my filing cabinets and office door repaired. I'll let you have the bill for replacing the carpet and furniture.'

'But if you're leaving anyway, dear thing . . .'

'As the others will be, I should think, when they see the state of their offices. Which will leave you two cheapskates to see who can scrounge the most off each other.'

That was too much after the last couple of days. 'Listen,

when it comes to cheap, you could win medals, lady. What kind of best mate can't even remember to buy a birthday card?'

'You what?' Sparks glittered behind Annie's lenses.

'I said . . .'

'I heard. Come here.' Her hand locked around my wrist like a handcuff. She had more weight and a surge of energy fuelled by adrenalin and a whole day of furious filing. I was dragged downstairs, into the street, and marched past the strolling gaggles of day-trippers making the most of the warm Saturday evening along the promenade.

The mood she was in, I wouldn't have been surprised if Annie had hauled me down the beach and tipped me straight into the rollers. But she swung inland again part way along the prom and stormed up a familiar side street.

The tables were packed with beach bunnies tucking into fry-ups before they hit the arcades and pleasure park for the night, and the jukebox was jumping to 'Chantilly Lace'. Ignoring the fact I was bouncing off the tables, Annie charged up to the counter with me in tow. 'Evening, Shane!'

Swinging round with his arms wide open, Shane metaphorically embraced us to his T-shirt. 'Here she is at last – the original birthday girl. Great party you missed there.' He swept the arms out again, embracing the whole of his café.

For the first time I noticed that Pepi's was somewhat more gaily decorated than usual. There was a large sign strung behind the counter with holographed letters spelling out 'Happy Birthday'. I let my eyes slide further round the walls. Bunches of balloons were stuck up at regular intervals; some had shrivelled and shrunk but there were enough left to read the birthday greetings, '30 today', and assorted erotic suggestions. I completed the three-hundred-degree sweep and locked on to Annie's glittering eyes.

'We had a surprise birthday party for you. Shane shut the café for the evening so we could use it.'

'You never said.'

'That is rather the point of a surprise party. You said you'd be around Thursday evening. In fact, you asked me out for a drink.'

'I sort of forgot.'

'Obviously.'

'Sorry.' There didn't seem a lot else to say. She'd plainly gone to a lot of trouble to give me a good evening. And I'd not only missed it but slagged her off as well. Fortunately I was saved from further abasement by another arrival.

'Barbra,' Shane yelled. 'How's the best little bopper in town?'

'Tired. I haven't jived like that for years.'

I remembered Barbra's cryptic remark on the phone Friday morning about hoping to catch me 'last night'. 'She came too?'

'Vetch brought her,' Annie confirmed.

'And you had dancing?'

'Moved the furniture into the back yard so we could bop in here. It was so good we had people queuing up outside to get in. Thought we were the latest club, didn't they, Barbra?'

'Yeah, it was a belting do,' Barbra confirmed. 'You get a better offer?'

'You could say that,' I murmured. 'Were you looking for me?'

'Went round the office. What a bleeding mess – reminds me of some of Lee's visits. Vetchy thought you'd be here.' She took another photo wallet from her bag. 'Here. Don't go washing this lot.'

I checked the front. Still no negatives.

She saw me looking but didn't offer any excuses. I guess since it was her case she didn't need to, really. Or perhaps she was just having a bit of trouble competing with Jerry Lee Lewis who was really ripping it out.

'Why did you want to see me?' I shouted.

'Warn you. Lee's back.'

'Has he tried anything yet? Matricide-wise?'

'Even he's not that thick. He's not going to make it that obvious.'

'Does he know about . . . ?' I held up the wallet.

'I made darn sure he did, darling. Take care now. And don't forget lunch tomorrow. You and Vetch. One o'clock. Bye, sexy . . .' She blew a kiss at Shane. He smiled smugly. And then asked me if I wanted the rest of my cake.

I glanced at a still steaming Annie. 'A cake?'

'Looked like a giant cheeseburger with trimmings. Full buffet as well. And the booze could have filled a bathtub. Well, I wouldn't be surprised if that's where some of it started out, actually . . . but still you found something better to do. How did you spend your birthday, as a matter of interest?'

'I started off skinny-dipping and ended it getting bonked by a complete stranger who wears a frock and spent the entire evening lying through his teeth to me, if you must know.'

My announcement happened to coincide with a switch-over in discs on the jukebox. It blasted into all four corners of the café. The clink and scraping of cutlery came to an abrupt stop.

'Blimey.' Shane's jaw dropped. 'No wonder you hadn't got time for the party. Tell you what, wait until the rush dies down a bit and I'll cook you both supper on the house. Steak, onion rings, fries, the works. And you can pick up yer presents. I got them all in the back.'

'I love you, Shane.' Leaning over, I smacked a kiss on his lips.

'I'd love you too,' Annie assured him. 'but I've given up men for the present. We'll take two teas to go and wait for the lull outside. Come on, you . . . I want every salacious detail.'

She had to wait until we were seated on the largely deserted beach before I gave her the full story.

'So where do you go from here? Are you still going to go looking for this charmer?'

'You bet. For one thing, I've got to find him in his Rainwing mode for this . . .' I tapped Barbra's photos that were sticking out of my jacket. 'And for another, I want to tell the rat what I think of him. Preferably in a way that will ruin his chances of future fatherhood.'

'Why? I mean, it's not like he forced you into doing anything – is it?'

'No.' I drove my bare feet into the warm sand, watching it creeping up until they were buried up to the ankles. 'No. He didn't. But it's just . . . I don't know how much was real now. And I feel such a *victim*.' I wrapped my arms round my knees and rested my chin on them so I was looking out to the retreating tide rather than at her. 'I don't make a habit of one-night stands. I know everyone does it these days . . .'

'I don't.'

It didn't seem very polite to point out I didn't suppose she got asked all that much. 'You read about it in the papers and mags. All these columnists going on about who – and how many – they've had this week.'

'That's probably because admitting they go home to watch *Coronation Street* with a microwave meal and the cat doesn't make good copy.'

I looked round. Annie was flat on her back, staring at the small wisps of clouds drifting in from the Channel.

'You think so?'

'Yep. You know that girl in your class who came in every Monday morning to tell you how she'd got dead drunk/ stoned over the weekend and been at it with at least six drop-dead-gorgeous boys since Friday?'

'The only one who was still a virgin when we all left?'

'That's the one. Well, I reckon those columns are the

literary equivalent. They're the twenty-something match of the diary you hoped your mum would never read when you were fourteen – ninety-eight per cent wishful thinking.'

'I'm not sure that makes me feel better about leaping into bed with a bloke I'd only known a couple of hours.'

'Write it off as a mistake. You're entitled to one a decade. And you've got a whole new decade to screw up in now.'

'Cheers.' I finished my tea, emptied out the dregs and stared out across the sands whilst I assessed if I felt any better about last night. I guessed I did, I decided.

I let my eyes wander around the sweep of the sands. Some diehards were still pitched in small groups around the sandcastles and holes, but most people had moved off to join the traffic jams home or pack into the cafés and private hotels for dinner. Which was why the couple plodding through the soft sand drifts towards the steps caught my attention. They didn't notice me until they were practically tripping over my feet. In Carter's case that was probably because his eyes were fixed on Kelly Benting's backside as she stalked ahead of him.

'Hi, Carter.'

'What? Oh, hiya.' He stood awkwardly, his arms full of a beach bag, towels, two pairs of trainers and shirts. 'Kelly and me's been doing the beach. We went to the amusement park yesterday evening. Didn't we, Kel?'

'Don't call me Kel. I told yer, it's Kelly.' She'd paused a few steps beyond us. When her two-sizes-too-small clothes might have been appropriate, she was wearing an overlarge sloppy T-shirt that brushed her knees, and a pair of shorts underneath. Standing now with both hands in the shorts pockets, she ordered Carter to get a move on.

'OK, Kelly. You sure you don't want an ice cream? Or some chips? We could go up the fish bar.'

'I've told you, I don't want nothing to eat. Saturday's our

busiest night. I have to help out Mum in the restaurant. Now go get us a taxi quick, before they all go.'

'Sure, Kelly.' He turned clumsily in the sand and nearly fell over when she told him to leave her shoes and he had to change direction again.

Thumping down beside us, Kelly dragged the trainers on, heedless of the film of dried sand clinging to her skin.

'I thought Carter wasn't your type? In fact, I thought Carter wasn't anybody's type.'

Kelly raised her shoulders. 'I got to thinking about what we said – about how Carter could be into big money in ten years. I mean, it's not like I have to just stick to him. He'll be off to university anyway. But when he does start earning big bucks and gets a place in California . . .'

'You're making sure he remembers who you are when you turn up with the suitcase?'

'Yeah. Investing, that's what I'm doing.'

She sounded uncertain. I had the distinct impression that not even the prospect of a condo on the Pacific was going to keep Kelly 'investing' for long.

'Anyway,' she added, 'I just dumped Ricky – my boyfriend – and I've got to have someone to go round with. You can't not have a boyfriend. Only pogs don't have a bloke.'

Carter arrived back in a flurry of kicked sand and asthmatic *hurring*. 'Taxi's waiting on the prom, Kelly.'

'Coming. See ya then.'

'Interesting couple,' Annie remarked once they were both out of earshot. Her eyes were closed and I thought she'd been dozing. 'Where'd you meet them?'

St Biddy's. My legatee hunt. Oh, hell!'

'What?'

'I've left the damn bike there. I'd forgotten all about it. I wonder if Luke's found it.'

'Who's Luke?'

'A would-be film producer with a car to die for who gave

me his phone number. He wants me to have a drink with him.'

'Short, ugly and married?'

'Tall, gorgeous and available.'

'Well, haven't you struck the jackpot lately.'

'After yesterday's farce, I'd say it was more like the booby prize.'

'Now don't get all bitter and twisted on me. It's very ageing.' Annie extracted her mobile from her bag. 'You know what they say about getting back on a bike after a fall.'

'You could have put that more delicately.' But perhaps she was right. One louse did not a lice convention make. I punched in the number quickly, before I could lose my nerve. The phone rang distantly while Annie browsed through the useless snaps 'Rainwing' had foisted on me. Eventually Luke's mobile message service clicked in. I left a message that I was still up for that drink and facetiously added I hoped he was being faithful to me – or else.

'Looks like we're both going to be pogs – whatever they are,' Annie said, locking her phone again. Before she'd finished, it rang. Her face changed as she listened to the caller. She was scrambling up, banging sand grains off her bottom, before the call had finished.

'Trouble?'

'It's Zeb. Something's happened. I have to go.' She ran for the promenade steps.

'Do you want company?'

'No,' she shouted back. 'I'll call you.'

My birthday supper wasn't quite the same on my own. Although Shane did his best to make up for the deficiency by letting me choose the evening programme on the jukebox. And I had my presents to open, and a stack of belated cards. By the time I wandered home past the neon-lit arcades, with their whistling game machines, and the distant throbbing rhythms and excited screams from the amusement park rides, I was in a mood to love the whole world.

It lasted until I manoeuvred my way carefully down the outside basement steps, trying not to drop my genuine Elvis statue that jigged to 'Jailhouse Rock' when you clapped your hands (Shane's present). The rawer wood where they'd used a chisel stood out as a light patch against the dark paint. Cautiously, ready to jump aside if they were behind the door, I nudged it ajar with one foot. I felt for the light switch – and experienced a sense of *déjà vu*. It was like revisiting the offices once more – with one exception. In the midst of my trashed living room was a short, muscular bloke, blinking in surprise at the sudden light.

I decked him.

16

He was the owner of the local plant centre, delivering my sister's birthday present.

It had been overlooked in their order book, and rather than let me be disappointed for a further day, he'd made a special out-of-hours trip. He was quite reasonable about the situation once I'd picked him up, stuck a wet tea towel over the blossoming bruise and re-righted a chair so he could sit down. His cutie-pie voice sat at odds with his burly yob appearance of bulging biceps, gold earring and oil-slick hair.

'The door just swung open when I *touched* it. I was *so* surprised. And I thought I'd just tiptoe in and leave it inside because . . . well . . . one just never *knows* who might want to steal such a *scrumptious* arrangement.'

I stared at the round wooden tub the size of a truck tyre bristling with a collection of weirdly spiky-leaved, needle-sharp vegetation that looked like it had escaped from a

1950s B-movie of *The Cabbage that Ate the World* variety. 'Is this my sister's choice? Or all your own hallucination?'

'It is exactly as specified, I promise. Tierra Caliente succulents. *Very* fashionable this year. All the top interior designers are using them.'

That explained it. She'd have seen them in *Vogue* or *Tatler*. My sister thinks those magazines are obligatory instruction manuals rather than leisure browsing.

'Aren't they just wonderful?' my visitor cooed. 'They're so *butch*.'

'You like them?'

'I *adore* them.'

'Then you keep them. Compensation for my thumping you.'

'Oh, no. I couldn't hear of it. Your troubles are greater than mine.' He waved the blood-stained towel around the chaos. 'I couldn't deprive you of the one delightful thing in this terrible mess.'

'You could. Honestly.'

Unfortunately, he couldn't. 'I shall leave you in peace to call the police. Unless you'd like me to stay? For emotional support? This kind of thing can be so stressful.'

I told him I thought I could bear up OK, thanks. And asked him if he had a business card. 'You've been so great about this, I'd really like to recommend you to all my friends.' (Besides, it wasn't unknown for someone trying to break in to pose as a florist delivery. I'd done it myself.)

He hadn't. However, he promptly whipped out the delivery docket and pointed out the centre's address and phone number. 'And we can arrange delivery over a wide area. Perhaps you might want to thank your sister with a *delicious* little treat for her own birthday?'

'Do you stock triffids?'

'Triff . . . Oh, *naughty*.'

'Talking of naughty, I don't suppose you noticed anyone hanging around? Or running like hell when you arrived?'

'Oh, no. It was all quiet. Well, no, I tell a lie. A vehicle *was* pulling away from the kerb as I arrived.'

'Make? Registration number?'

'I simply didn't take any notice, I'm afraid. A truck, I think. *Disgustingly* muddy.'

'No sweat. Probably just a day-tripper.' I hadn't been home for nearly three days. The break-in could have happened any time between Thursday morning and Wayne's arrival tonight. I thanked him for being such a sport about the belting.

'Scatter seeds not weeds as you walk through the greenhouse of life, is my motto. Be careful not to touch those *gorgeous* succulents, won't you? The spines can burrow through just about anything. It feels like a thousand *red-hot* needles under your flesh. Well, I'll fly then.'

I waved him and his estate wagon off from the steps and turned my attention to the break-in.

It was virtually a repeat of the scene at Vetch's as far as upholstery, food containers and paperwork were concerned. In addition, the old pantry cupboard I used as a wardrobe had been ransacked and my clothes were heaped in a jumbled pile on the main room floor. They'd made a soft landing for the disembowelled television and radio sets. Stepping into the narrow, windowless room I used as a guest bedroom, I found the only piece of furniture it contained, a fold-up bed, had had the same treatment. Lugging the florist's tub in there, I shut the door on it.

There wasn't much to wreck in the bathroom, but they'd given it their best shot anyway. The medicine cupboard where I kept all those little things that keep a girl sweet had been ripped from the wall, and there were lighter spots around the floor by the toilet bowel where liquid had dried. I didn't want to think what it might have been. At least they hadn't deposited anything worse in the basin and bath.

Returning to the main room, I ducked down into the alcove where the old range had stood, felt in the roof area, located the loose stone and drew it out carefully. There must, I think, have been some kind of stack pipe running through the bricks here at one time. When it had been removed it had left a small space up here that was just the right size to keep a bundle of building society passbooks.

(OK – I know I never spend any if I can help it, but Annie had been right: I did have a cache of savings. I just had an almost pathological terror of spending it.)

They didn't seem to have found them. But after the fake photos fiasco I eased them out and checked anyway before carefully putting them back and turning my attention to the drifts of cornflakes, washing powder, coffee granules and rice I was wading in.

I started to clean up, intending to see what I could salvage, but in the end dragged in the rubbish bin from the back yard and threw every consumable thing inside. There was no way I ever wanted to touch any of it again.

I wanted a bath. But I couldn't bear to use the towels and I'd got nothing to scour out the bath with anyway. About the only thing that was still intact was the phone. Annie wasn't answering, either at home or on her mobile. In the end I dialled the office without much hope. And was surprised when Vetch answered.

'It's eleven thirty at night.'

'Thank you, sweet thing, but I've been able to tell what the big hand and the little hand mean since I was four.'

'My place has been trashed.'

'I know that too. I'm here supervising the activities of an extortionately overpriced twenty-four-hour security service. Is your new hobby stating the obvious?'

'Not there. Here.'

I filled him in on the situation at the flat and was disgusted to hear a quaver in my voice. Up until then I really thought I'd been handling it.

The little diamond came up trumps for once. After he'd persuaded the security firm to bring round a new front door and fit it (an activity that was enormously popular with the rest of the street at one o'clock in the morning), he offered me a bed at his place for the night, and when I declined (I wasn't *that* traumatised), drove home and returned with soap, bleach, food, clean towels and a sleeping bag.

'Don't forget we have a date with your latest client tomorrow.'

'You'll have to make my excuses, Vetch. I'd not be very good company.'

'You often aren't. Nonetheless, I'd advise you to make the effort. Barbra has a tendency to take offence rather quickly. And you really can't afford to lose this job. Consider your debts.'

'What debts?'

'Now you mention it, that door I've just paid for. I'll take a cheque.'

I wrote him one and told him he'd have to give me a lift to Wakens Keep.

'I'll pick you up at twelve thirty. Good night, sweet thing. Or good morning, rather.'

There was no way I could turn up at Barbra's in this outfit. My clothes had been on me since Thursday and were showing signs of being able to walk into the washing machine by themselves. But the only alternative was the stuff that had been pawed over by my visitors.

In the end I extracted a silky oyster-shaded dress splashed with red poppies from the heap and spent twenty minutes scrubbing it after I'd finished the same operation on myself. I even washed the strappy red sandals I was going to have to wear with it. Finally I rinsed out the panties I'd been wearing. The sun was just coming up when I hung the lot out in the back yard and crept into my sleeping bag.

I woke again four hours later. Annie still wasn't answering. I tried her several times whilst I sorted out what I couldn't face doing last night and splashed bleach in all directions. In passing I bailed a couple of mugs of water over the sulking succulents and wondered what on earth I was supposed to feed them on. Pit-bull burgers, by the looks of them.

By the time Vetch arrived, I'd dumped the rest of my underwear in the garbage and hauled every other blessed thing around to the service launderette (*everyone* works seven days a week in high season).

'What did the police say?' Vetch enquired, his eyes out on stalks as I scrambled into the passenger seat. I'd chosen this dress because it dried fast and crease-free, forgetting quite how short the skirt was.

'I didn't report it. Nothing's missing; I've no insurance anyway; and I don't feel inclined to give the local station a good laugh.'

'Are we being paranoid, sweet thing?'

'It's not paranoia if they really do despise you, Vetch.'

'If you say so.'

The sun was unbearable through the glass and I could feel the damp patches where I was touching the car upholstery. With the flat fields and almost no trees out here, there were no welcome patches of shade to break the relentlessly solid heat. I lowered my window to cool things down a bit and could almost smell the tarmac melting. Vetch opened his side, creating a through draught, and remarked it would storm soon.

I peered up at yet another cloudless sky. 'You reckon?'

'I have an instinct for troublesome atmospheres. Speaking of which – you haven't offended anyone recently, have you, Grace? More than you usually do, I mean?'

'Not that they mentioned. Why?'

'I couldn't help wondering about our visiting vandals. As you so rightly observe – theft doesn't appear to have been the motive. And they do seem to have been remarkably persistent in their efforts to enter the office.'

'What makes you think it was the same lot that hit my place?'

'Oh, come now. You don't really think it was coincidence, do you?'

'No. I guess not. But that's not to say they're after me. Maybe they'll come calling on you – or Annie – today.'

'Possibly. However, you were their victim of first choice. Have you given out your address to anyone recently? Or been tailed home?'

'Not that I noticed.'

'Phone number?'

'Occasionally, but . . .' But nothing. We both knew it was possible to back-track from a phone number to a subscriber's address – if you knew the right people.

'Sloppy, sweet thing. Sloppy.'

'The rest of us can't reach your level of perfection all the time, master. And get your hand off my knee and back on the gear stick before I break a few fingers.'

I felt more cheerful. When I analysed the mood, I realised it was because I suspected Vetch might be right and I had been targeted for some reason. Somehow it made me feel better, thinking whoever had been grubbing through my things was out for revenge rather than sexual kicks. I wondered if it was too late to retrieve my knickers from the rubbish bin.

17

It was a while since I'd been out to Wakens Keep, and I'd forgotten how busy it could get in the tourist season. It was an oddly arranged village – with the front wall of the keep entrance on one side of the square and meandering lines of lopsided oak-beamed cottages on the other three. I suppose the central section must have been a village green once, but it had long ago been filled in and was now a flat expanse of reddish stones and asphalt.

It was already full, but with a bit of creative parking

Vetch managed to squeeze us in by the war memorial. Without the rush of air through the car windows, the heat out here was ten times worse. Pulling sections of polyester off my damp skin, I took a quick glance around the square.

Most of the tiny strips of front gardens were planted up with rose bushes and assorted shrubs with tubs sitting on the doorsteps (I counted three identical to my birthday succulents – my sister wasn't the only botanical fashion victim around here). Only one owner seemed to have broken the trend. Their strip was a gnome sanctuary. Two dozen of the pointy-eared little charmers were gardening, fishing and posing around a miniature windmill and toy-town wishing well. It was plastic naff, big time.

It looked like Barbra had invited a houseful for lunch. Confidently following the stream of people who were heading for the door that was being opened every few seconds to admit those clutching bottles of sparkly plonk, I summoned up my best party smile and headed into canapé canyon.

'This way, sweet thing.' Vetch grabbed my elbow and used it to change my course towards the gnome sanctuary, where Barbra had just opened the door.

'Hi, sweetheart.' The smacker she landed on Vetch was the full tonsil-tasting variety. It gave me the chance to congratulate myself on my choice of outfit. Short and tarty was *in*. Hers was cerise pink and floaty.

I caught a glimpse of movement on the stairs out of the corner of my eye and looked up as the scuffed trainers and jeans descended far enough for his head and shoulders to duck under a large beam across the first landing. There was enough resemblance to his dad for me to guess this was Lee the Loser, although he'd inherited Barbra's pre-op broad nose and wider mouth. He opened it at that minute, to say he'd never met a model in the flesh before.

'Corny,' I said.

'Who's talking to you, darling? I meant the dwarf. It was

you posed for statues in my mum's garden, weren't it? You forgot yer pointy hat, mate. Brought yer little rod though, I see.' He slouched down a few more stairs and leant his crossed arms on the banister rail.

'You remember Lee?' his mum said, letting Vetch up for air.

'Yes, indeed. Still searching for that elusive spark of originality, I see.'

'We met then?' Lee enquired. He seemed to be having a bit of trouble staying upright and sank to a tread so he could lean his face against the struts and peer at us through the bars. There was a sweet aroma of burning cannabis mingling with the scent of Barbra's perfume in my nostrils.

'Vetch was one of my best customers at Lucinda's Lingerie. You were probably too busy nicking the stock to notice. Come through to the garden.' Barbra pulled Vetch's arm around her waist and headed for the back. Assuming I was invited too, I followed.

She was right about it not looking like a millionaire's place. The main room had been knocked through from several smaller ones and came complete with brick inglenook fireplace, low beams and open-plan staircase. The back room was a fitted kitchen/dining area with a door leading on to the long, narrow back garden that most of these cottages tended to have. Given the areas it was in, it undoubtedly hadn't come cheap. But then again, it wasn't the indoor-pool-and-three-car-garage job I somehow associated with the mega-rich. Maybe it was time I stopped thinking in clichés.

There was a young man in dark trousers and a chef's three-quarter-length white coat at the work surface, transferring delicious-smelling nibbly bits from an oven tray to a large silver platter.

'This is Andreas. From the caterer's,' Barbra announced. 'Do you want a drink before lunch? How about champagne? I've got champagne.'

Actually, I didn't. The sight of the bottle brought back Thursday night's fiasco with sudden painful clarity. 'Have you got a beer?'

'Don't be daft. We'll have champagne, Andreas.'

Like the summons to lunch, it wasn't an invitation. It was an order.

'Out here,' our hostess said, opening the back door. 'Fetch us the *hors d'oeuvres* out, Andreas.'

She stalked out, and we foot-soldiers fell into line behind her. A third of the way down the garden was a pagoda-style blue-and-white-striped tent with a dining table and chairs set up inside. Net curtaining had been drawn around the open sides, but it was transparent enough to let us see there was no plastic picnic cutlery here. It was all silver, crystal and linen.

The buzz of laughter, music and shrill voices from next door indicated that their party had also spilled into the open. The two houses were divided by a tall hedge but the vegetation nearest the house had died back to reveal glimpses as the guests tripped out of the french doors.

'Stand here,' Barbra commanded.

We stood on a square patio stone that looked like . . . well, every other square stone on that patio, actually.

Andreas emerged from the kitchen with a tray of glasses. He'd taken off the white coat and was now sporting a black waistcoat and bow tie to match the trousers.

'Is that champagne properly chilled?'

'Yes. Fridge. Yes, madam.' He folded stiffly from the waist and offered it.

'Only you don't want to spoil the good stuff by serving it warm,' Barbra informed us. I wondered which of us she thought was hard of hearing. 'You ever had the really good stuff before?'

'Thursday. It was supposed to cost ninety pounds a bottle. I can't tell the difference myself.'

'Yeah, I know what you mean. Taste one, you've tasted

them all. I can't stand these wine snobs. Pretentious ponces most of them. How's yours, Vetchy?'

'Delightful, thank you, Barbra. But I think I'd better stick to the Perrier over lunch. I'm driving. Fortunately Lee is obviously determined to see that your expense does not go to waste.'

Lee sauntered out swigging champagne from the bottle. 'Where's the food? I'm starving.'

'Canapés, Andreas.'

Andreas duly returned to base and returned with the silver platter, and we went through the bow-serve-bow-serve performance again. I began to suspect Andreas didn't speak much English. He'd grown a wispy little moustache to make himself look older. He was probably another moonlighting foreign language student.

Lee took a handful of the round toasted whatevers and dropped to the patio where he could zip them up like frisbees and play catch with his mouth. For someone who was supposed to be stoned, his co-ordination was suspiciously good.

'How's my investigation going?' Barbra asked me.

'OK.' I cast a wary eye in Lee's direction, unsure how much he knew. He seemed absorbed in his game of field-the-food.

'That's it? OK? I want a bit more than that for me money. What have you done so far?'

I considered. 'I've been threatened by a lunatic with a shotgun. Held captive for hours thinking I could get my head blown off any second. Been shot with an arrow by a tribe of miniature savages. Bonked a total stranger in the interests of research . . . and oh yes, my flat's been trashed, which may or may not be relevant to your job.'

I had began to suspect midway through this moan that Barbra wasn't really listening to me. Her attention was somewhere beyond that hedge.

'. . . So after I got snatched by the aliens from Zog and

they'd finished the truly disgusting reproduction experiments, I joined the morris dancing team and knew real horror . . . Hello?'

Barbra refocused. 'What? Yeah. Fine. Just stay in touch. Let's eat now. Lee, shift your arse.'

Her offspring responded to the kick by unpeeling himself from the patio and flopping down in one of the dining room chairs. I ended up next to him. Sitting down hoicked that damn dress up again.

Lee gave me an appreciative leer before yelling: 'Hey, Andreas, you wanker, what's keeping you?'

Given Barbra's opinions on scrounging foreigners, it seemed strange that she should take offence. But she did. 'Don't bloody well call him that. At least he's not just a waste of skin. He's got talent.'

'For what? Shoving pâté up quails' jacksies? Or has he got other uses? You renting him by the hour for that too?'

'Don't be so bloody coarse.'

'I thought that was why we were here. Add a bit of coarseness to the fun. Same as the garden ornaments.'

'Don't be so daft,' Barbra said. 'Shut up if you want to eat. Otherwise – get lost. Nobody asked you to stop here anyway.'

We had lobster, crab, salmon and prawns. Not portions, you understand; full-sized beasts that looked like they'd romped around Dounreay as baby spawn. In the end we had more sea-life out there than the local aquarium. Dessert was fresh strawberries and crêpes Suzette – cooked at table by Andreas, who'd wheeled out a gas-fired trolley so he could do the performance with brandy and matches to an appreciative audience.

By this time I was aware that quite a few of next door's guests were more interested in our party than their own. I also had a pretty good idea that that was the whole idea.

It was a theory I tried out when Barbra and I paid a visit to the little girls' room upstairs. 'What's the occasion next door?'

'Wedding anniversary. Ruby.'

'Looks like the whole village is in there.'

'Except me, yer mean? Yeah, I noticed that too.'

She helped herself to a cigarette from a box on the landing table and lit up, leaning against the loo door. Blowing a stream of smoke down her nostrils, before saying: 'What do you think of the front? It was seeing Vetchy again gave me the idea. You should have *seen* their faces. I was watching from the window up here.'

'Have things always been like that?'

'No. They were OK when I was the live-in help. It was when I started to get . . .' She ran one pink-tipped nail from hair to waist. 'Designer clobber and make-up sort of tipped off that me and Barney weren't sticking to our own bedrooms any more. It wasn't the sex that bothered them, you understand. It was the idea of losing an available bloke. Eligible widowers are rarer than Hell's Angels around here. And then Barney's brother dripped a bit more poison into the wounds when he got caught with a severe case of credit shortage.'

It was the first I'd heard of Barney having any living relatives. Somehow I'd got the impression that his first wife's death had left him alone in the world. Hence all his goods and chattels to Barbra when he dropped off.

'They weren't close,' Barbra said curtly. 'At least they hadn't been for years. Then Barney came into all that money and suddenly brother Karl and his family are popping up all over the place like an eczema outbreak. They'd talked him into putting money into some daft business scheme. Said it needed a cash injection. More like the whole flaming blood bank. Even got the contracts drawn up. And a will in their favour – just in case he died before they'd conned the lot out of him. That was when I decided we'd have to get married. So I popped the question.'

'You asked him?'

'Sure. Don't tell me you're one of those old-fashioned girls think blokes should make all the running?'

'No.' (Yes, actually. I don't care how far equal opportunities have come, that was one of two things I don't think I could ever do. Admitting it was the other.) 'This wasn't a popular move with the in-laws, then?'

'Like hell. Even started to put it about the village that I was looking for the fastest way to see Barney out of this world. In a way, they did me a favour. Soon as Barney got to hear, he told them not to bother calling round again.'

'And did they?'

'Came to the funeral. Kicked up a fuss when they found out I'd got the lot. Made a few threats. It was pussy-cat stuff. That will's watertight, I saw to that.'

'Talking of threats . . . any activity in that direction from Lee?'

'Not as far as I can tell. No rat poison in the milk; no leaky car brakes.' She lit another cigarette from the fag end of the previous one and offered the box.

'No thanks. I don't.'

'I didn't. Gave it up years ago. Started again after Barney . . . you know. I don't half miss him. I hate this bloody dump without him.'

'Then move.'

'Why should I? I'm not letting them push me out and win. I'll stop here as long as I want to.'

'But you don't want to.'

'What's it got to do with you?' Opening the door behind her, she flicked the half-smoked cigarette into the toilet bowl. 'You really not got any further with me photos? No names at all?'

Asked straight out like that, I had to admit to Harry Rouse being a local farmer. 'I can't say for certain, but I think it's unlikely he's ever been involved in anything criminal. The local grapevine has nothing on it.'

'What's he like?'

'Divorced. Short of cash. His dad's on the fast track to senile. Needs professional care. They could really use some help now, I'd say.'

'No dice. I told you, no hand-outs until I'm gone. You haven't told him about me?'

'No. That was the agreement.'

'Too right it was. What about the two women?'

There was no way I was going into the Daniel/Rainwing saga. 'I'm following some leads on the Indian squaw. Nothing on the first woman yet.'

''S funny. I had a sort of feeling I knew her from somewhere. Couldn't place her though. 'Spect she works in one of the shops or something.'

That was the first good news I'd had on Numero Uno. At least it sounded like she might be fairly local.

'Look, I'm bursting here. Can I go first?'

'No. I'll not be a sec.'

She whisked inside. Definitely not the hostess with the mostest. I jigged around the landing until she finally re-emerged, and bolted inside gratefully. My skin was flushed with a touch of sun and a sheen of perspiration. After splashing cold water over my face and neck, I dabbed dry and re-opened the bathroom door.

The entire space was blocked by Lee. He was so close his nose must have been pressed against the wood.

'Are you desperate? Or do you just get your kicks out of listening to people tinkling?'

'I know who you are.'

'Of course you do. We just had lunch together. It's good to know there's nothing wrong with your short-term memory.'

'She'll leave them naff-all, you know. You're wasting your time.'

'No, actually, I'm wasting your mum's time. At an excellent daily rate.' He was leaning with his left forearm above his head on the door frame and his crossed feet touching the bottom of the frame on the opposite side. Despite missing out on his dad's nose, he really wasn't a bad-looking bloke. If he could just stop giving the impression he had more chips than McDonald's on his shoulders, he would have been halfway fanciable.

'She's only doing it to wind me up.'

'You really do think you're the centre of the universe, don't you, Lee?'

'No. I just know me mum. She's narked 'cos of something that happened – or didn't happen, rather – a few weeks back. She can be a sulky bitch.'

'From what I heard, she had every reason to be upset. This will isn't so much sulking – more self-preservation.'

'What d'yer mean?'

I'd apparently overestimated the depth of the mother/son confidences. Barbra hadn't had the nerve and/or the assurance to accuse her only offspring of trying to push her under moving traffic.

'Talk to Mummy. And get out of my way. Now.'

He eyeballed me for a moment just to establish he wasn't the sort to be intimidated into backing off. Then he backed off. 'It won't do you no good. I know exactly how to fix her little game if I wanted to.'

'And do you want to?'

'That's for me to know, ain't it? Wait and see.'

'With bated breath, Lee.'

18

In the kitchen, they were on the coffee and *petits fours*. Barbra was pouring whilst Andreas was up to his armpits in soapy water. Looking at the debris of gourmet dining spread around the serving area, I had a nostalgic yen.

'I could murder a cheeseburger.'

'Me too,' Barbra said unexpectedly. 'Or egg and chips. That mate of yours in the rock-and-roll café does the best egg and chips I ever tasted. It was a belting party you missed there. Coffee.'

It sloshed in the saucer as it was thrust in my hands. Picking up another cup and the plate of *petits fours*, Barbra marched into the garden. She didn't exactly call 'heel' but the implication was there. I made up my mind to bill her for every hour of this farce.

Vetch was sprawled in one of the garden chairs with his little legs stretched out in front and his hands over his stomach. The resemblance to the plumper gnomes out front really was amazing.

Barbra seized his face in both hands and planted a pink-lipstick smacker on the bald top. 'Knew it was a good idea to invite you. I wish I'd done it months ago. You'll come again, won't you?'

'Who could resist such an inducement? However, I do think it's time we were making a move. I have rather a lot of work on at the office.'

'Not Sundays? You're turning into a right little workaholic, Vetchy.'

I started to explain: 'It's since the—'

A fast raise of Vetch's eyebrows warned me he hadn't mentioned the break-in. He must have kept her downstairs when she came round with my replacement snaps yesterday. I suppose it doesn't inspire confidence in the clients to discover their murkiest secrets are open to browsing by anyone with a crowbar and a head for heights.

'Since the recession,' I finished. 'Competition. The job is full of amateurs. I blame those PI correspondence courses.'

'Oh? OK. I'll give you a call, then, lover. Fix up another date.'

Vetch agreed that would be best. They explored each other's tonsils again while I stood around feeling surplus to requirements. Then Vetch headed for a last call in the bathroom and I wandered out to wait at the car. There was no sign of Lee, but Barbra came through to the front with me.

Perhaps it was the food and wine, or perhaps it was simply that the sun had had several more hours to beat down since we'd arrived, but the temperature in the square seemed to have climbed at least ten degrees. Heat was palpably radiating from the bricks and asphalt and there didn't seem to be a breath of wind anywhere. Sweat started trickling between my shoulder blades and rolling into the cracks around my nostrils.

'God, it's bloody unbearable out here,' Barbra groaned. 'I wish the storm would break and get it over with.'

'Speaking of storms and breaking things – when did Lee turn up?'

'Same day I came to see you. He was sitting on the doorstep when I came back from our breakfast. Told you he would, didn't I? He's like a recurring cold sore.'

'And you told him about the new will? And the photos?'

'Course. Wouldn't be no fun otherwise, would it?'

'So he's right. You are trying to wind him up.'

Barbra shrugged and used her fingers to massage the nape of her neck. 'Why shouldn't I? He's done it to me for long enough.'

'You don't think it might encourage him to try something before you sign on the dotted line?'

'Not now he knows you and Vetch are watching him. You're my insurance.'

It was what everyone tended to think. Unfortunately, it's a theory that doesn't allow for the fact that a hell of a lot of people assume they're much smarter than they really are and there's no chance they'll ever get caught.

'Has Lee seen the photos?'

'No. Why?'

'I just wondered. You're holding the negatives here . . . he could have taken a look. Checked out the competition.'

'He's had a search around. I've seen him doing it. But he ain't found them yet.'

There was a gleeful note in her voice. It was beginning to seem more and more as if Lee was right. This was one of those strange family games that outsiders have to play without getting a look at the rules. Which was fine, unless it involved my personal possessions. The office address was listed in the phone book. And for all I knew, Vetch had mentioned my home address to his latest girlfriend. Had Lee already come calling, looking for those snaps?

She darted back inside as Vetch and I climbed into the oven-hot car and then reappeared just as we were pulling out to thrust a carrier-bag through the window into my lap.

'Here. They're new; never worn, I promise. You can't wear your old stuff, can you? Not after someone's turned them over. Makes yer sick.'

I investigated. There were half a dozen bra and pantie sets; all seductive designs in silk, satin and lace. Vetch cast a sideways look and informed me they'd probably cost her not less than two hundred pounds for each set. It was the classiest lingerie I'd ever owned.

I asked Vetch if he'd given her my home address.

'I wouldn't do that, sweet thing. You should know me better than that. I assume you're entertaining the theory that the lovely Lee trashed his way through Seatoun on Friday night? Why would he do that, exactly?'

'Teenage tantrums? He strikes me as twenty-four going on fourteen. Maybe he thought I'd already found the names and addresses of those legatees. Perhaps he intended to carry the showing-off to the enemy. You know – yo dudes, don't think you're going to enjoy my inheritance. I – Lee Delaney – will be in your face every time you take out a chequebook.'

'*Yo dudes?* Good heavens, who have you been mixing with?'

'Pseudo Red Indians – or Native Americans if you prefer.

And a half-American film producer. That reminds me, can we stop off in St Biddy's, I've left the bike at his place.'

'Your every wish is my delight, sweet thing.'

'Great. Can I borrow your mobile phone then? I want to check on Annie. Have you heard from her since last night?'

'The only way I'm going to hear from Annie at present, I fear, is via a message tied to a brick.'

'Something's up with Zeb. I didn't get the details.' I punched in the number for Annie's flat and listened to the answerphone inviting me to leave a message. It was the same with the mobile service again. On an impulse I dialled the local CID office. Even if Zeb was undercover some-where, the local grapevine might know what was supposed to be wrong with him. Given the state of my relations with most of the police around here, I decided to pretend to be one of his other sisters (I had a choice between Tennessee or Tallahassee, if you'll recall).

As it turned out, however, I didn't get the chance to decide which unlikely alias I preferred, because I recognised the voice that picked up at the other end. And he knew me.

'How come a chief inspector is working Sunday after-noon?'

'Even the great and the good have to take their turn on the duty rota,' Jerry Jackson informed me. 'What can I do for you, Miss Smith?'

'I heard Zeb was in trouble. And I can't get hold of Annie. Any idea what's wrong with him?'

'DC Smith isn't working in this office at present.'

'I know that. Annie said,' I added quickly, in case I got Zeb into trouble for blowing his cover. 'But I thought you might have heard something.'

'I think it would be best if you waited until you are able to contact his sister.'

Little tingles of alarm connected the beads of sweat rolling down my spine. Something was wrong. I was quite fond of Annie's youngest brother, in a big-sister sort of way. 'Do you know where Annie is now?'

'If I see her, I'll tell her you're trying to reach her,' Jackson said. Did he think I might not notice how he'd ducked the question? Or maybe he realised there was nothing I could do about it. The latter, probably – as demonstrated by the fact he then hung up on me.

Even the draught zipping through the open car windows wasn't making much impression on the stifling heat now. My head was starting to pound. I prayed for the storm to break and was answered by a roar as a flash of forked lightning ripped down and appeared to strike the heart of the village just as we approached the turn down to St Biddy's.

'Next left, opposite the shop,' I instructed Vetch over the roll of thunder that followed a few seconds later.

He steered the car down the rutted track. We bumped up on the narrow verge by Brick Cottage just as the first welcome spots of rain splashed down. The bike was where I'd dumped it, held upright by the stone wall and the row of bushes. Vetch helped me haul it back on to the lane. Then we hit a snag.

'What do you mean, ride it back? I thought you could put it in the car?'

'Be reasonable, sweet thing. It won't fit inside and I don't have the roof rack fitted.'

'Luke tied it to his boot.'

'Then I assume he wasn't driving this model.'

He was right, of course. The smooth, rounded lines of Vetch's car provided no obvious holds on which we could lash the damn thing.

'The exercise will be good for you,' Vetch said.

'Pneumonia won't. And the crispy-fried look is right out this season.' The thunder and lightning were now letting go with a vengeance. And the raindrops would shortly merge into a full-blown downpour. There was no way I was cycling three miles in that lot.

I considered the cottage. If Luke was in, then perhaps I could persuade him to offer shelter to a woman in distress until the downpour was over. After which, with any luck, I'd be able to cadge a lift for me and the metal monster. Or at least the loan of some clothes more appropriate for cycling than four-inch stilettos and what was beginning to feel like the shortest dress in the hemisphere.

There was no answer to my ring. I knocked and tried the door. It opened.

'Anyone in?' My voice echoed back at me. There was no scuffle or creak of floorboards inside the house as someone responded to my intrusion. 'Luke?'

The rain was coming down hard now, the parched lawns and overblown flowerbeds absorbing it gratefully and the meandering stones of the path bouncing it back to break into rainbow-coloured droplets. I was debating whether to make a dash for the car when Vetch solved the question by racing up and joining me under the mini-porch.

'Do you think your friend would mind if I used the bathroom?'

'I don't suppose so.'

'Thank heavens for that. I really must cut back on the fizzy water. It seems to have the oddest effect on my bladder. Where is it?'

'Your bladder?'

'The lavatory, sweet thing.'

'I've no idea.'

'I thought this was a friend's house.'

'We've not done home visits yet.'

We both gave a gasp of shock as the garden was lit up with a flash of vicious light and the cottage shook to an ear-drum rattle of thunder. As one, we took a hop sideways and landed in the relative safety of the hall. And discovered the small pile of junk mail and newspapers that had been pushed back when I swung the door. Vetch checked the dates on the papers.

'Saturday and Sunday. Looks like he's away for the weekend.'

'And didn't lock up?'

'Some people are delightfully casual about such things. Now, where's that lavatory?'

Halfway down the short hallway, we both smelt it – not the lav, but a distinctive putrid aroma.

'Is that . . . ?'

Vetch was scenting the air delicately. 'I'm afraid it is. It seems to be strongest over here.'

'Here' was the door at the end of the hall. Neither of us wanted to open it, but one of us had to. In the end, Vetch did the honours.

It was the sitting room. An ugly open fireplace and high plastered ceilings making it feel unwelcome, but saved by the mismatched furniture that had the air of being carefully chosen and cared for over the years.

At present a lot of it was liberally daubed with blood. The detached part of my mind noted that it had smeared thinly where it touched rather than soaked in pools. The stains had already dried brown over the red velvet upholstery of an old chaise-longue, the rugs and floorboards, and the length of the two streaks down one wall – the imprint of the separate digits showing where he'd attempted to drag himself upright.

A copper umbrella stand that had been caught by the opening door rolled forlornly away, and broken glass fragments scrunched under its progress.

I tried to assess the situation coolly, but it's very difficult when a bloke you last saw alive, well, and chatting you up is lying at your feet with the tip of a spear protruding obscenely through his breastbone and several feet of shaft sticking out of his back.

The exceptionally warm weather and the fact that all the

windows and doors had been closed had speeded up the decomposition process. His face and neck were a sickly shade of greenish red, and there was a festering blister on one cheek. When a beetle crawled out of his partially open mouth, I knew I had to get out of there – fast – before I started whimpering.

In the end I huddled on the porch with Vetch's mobile and had my second chat of the day with the local CID office.

19

'Last person to see the victim is usually the murderer. It's common knowledge.'

'Then I'm not surprised you've heard of it. You can't get much commoner than you, Rosco.'

If he'd been on duty in time to catch my dawn-slot skinny-dipping adventure a few days ago, then Terry Rosco should have been off duty at nine o'clock on a Sunday evening. But of all the gin joints in all the world, Rosco kept strutting into mine.

'And I think you'll find that's the last person to see the victim *alive*, Terry. Otherwise the maximum-security wings would be full of undertakers.'

'You saying you had nothing to do with it, Smithie?'

'Should you be questioning me about the murder?'

'Who said it was murder?'

'Well, if it wasn't, it was the strangest way of committing suicide I've ever seen.'

'Stabbed, they reckon . . . ?'

There was an interrogatory note in his tone and a hopeful gleam in his eyes that he was doing his best to hide.

'Haven't they let you go and play with the big boys, Terry?'

He straightened the immaculately pressed jacket. Peacocks had tail feathers; Terry Rosco had creases you could cut cheese on and a shiny cap peak that touched the bridge of his nose. 'Someone's got to keep an eye on the suspects. See you don't do a runner.'

'Tsk, tsk,' Vetch reproved. 'I thought we were simply witnesses assisting the police with their enquiries. Now I find I'm a suspect. Should we complain about this confusion to the Chief Inspector, do you think, Grace?'

The flush on Terry's face darkened. He knew he'd blundered (he should do – he got enough practice), but he didn't want to apologise to me. On the other hand, Vetch was a different matter. Vetch always gave the impression he KNEW PEOPLE.

'Sorry, sir,' Terry muttered through gritted teeth. 'Slip of the tongue. I'm sure Mr Jackson's grateful for your patience.'

We hadn't really been given much choice. Impatience would have left us in exactly the same position – viz., stuck in one of the spare rooms in the Bell that Keith Benting had put at the police's disposal.

Benting was having the place refitted, and services such as running water, electricity, and flushing loos were only available on an erratic basis. Hence we had the deserted Bell to ourselves whilst Kelly's dad chalked up some Brownie points with the local law-and-order brigade.

I stood. Terry moved into his aggressive-barrier mode. 'Where you going?'

'To get some air. Any objections?'

'Mr Jackson said—'

'That we should keep ourselves available. Well, I can be just as available on the doorstep as in here. Now shift it.'

He sidled a few inches sideways, forcing me to squeeze past. No doubt he thought I'd enjoy the experience. Despite all my efforts to dissuade him, Terry Rosco still lived under the delusion that he was God's gift to those born with a genetic ability to breast-feed.

Overhead, the first stars were emerging together with a pale sliver of waxing moon. The storm had passed an hour ago, leaving behind it cooler air and dripping gutters and leaves. The lights in the Royal Oak opposite were already blazing through the leaded windows and reflecting in puddles on the oily black road surface. Down to the left, the stronger white headlights of the patrol car blocking the access to Cowslip Lane illuminated the few sightseers still waiting patiently for the next stage of the entertainment. Most had wandered into the pub, where they could keep an eye on things in considerably more comfort.

I watched the angle of the beam change as the car rolled forward just far enough to let out the van that appeared a few moments later.

Luke Steadman's departure from St Biddy's was a sad contrast to the last time – all the power and energy of that sports car replaced by the sedate crawl of the plain white mortuary van as it set off to deliver what was left of Luke to the pathologist.

Drawing a deep breath of the air that was laden with the smells of wet earth and damp vegetation, I took a few steps down the road and felt the wetness seep over the soles of the stilettos. Goosebumps zipped up and down my arms. The stifling heat of the day had been trapped inside the Bell, but outside the night was beginning to feel chilly. I couldn't even beg the loan of a car blanket from Vetch. They'd made us leave his vehicle parked up by the cottage whilst the forensic team swept it.

At least talking directly to the head of CID had bypassed the initial stage of a uniformed officer arriving to look over the scene and agree that a body with several feet of metal and wood stuck through its upper torso did indeed qualify as a suspicious death.

Jerry Jackson had turned up himself with the troops to

find me and Vetch in the hall watching the shrubs bending under the onslaught of the storm. We'd shut the door to the sitting room and left the front door open, but the smell still seemed to be permeating everywhere.

They'd taken initial statements from us at the cottage and then we'd been driven up here, the patrol car's windscreen wipers struggling to cope with the downpour, as it crawled close enough to the Bell for us to dash inside.

I wanted action. It was, therefore, a relief to see other figures emerging from Cowslip Lane. I thought I could make out Jerry Jackson and a female detective sergeant he'd had in tow. With any luck we could stop being 'available' and head back to Seatoun soon.

The spectators at the edge of the lane sensed the action was moving away from the cottage as well. They started a drift in my direction. One seemed familiar. It wasn't until he got within a few yards that I realised why. My stomach did its second loop-the-loop of the day as my subconscious reminded it of our last encounter with Harry Rouse Senior. Surely with all these uniforms around he ought to be re-enacting the St Valentine's Day Massacre any minute.

'Hello, Atch,' I said loudly.

He looked up, blinking underneath his tweed cap. And then smiled tentatively. 'It's you, isn't it?'

'It was last time I looked.'

'You come up the farm the other day.' He shuffled forward a few more steps. 'I scared you.'

'You can say that again, Atch.'

'I'm sorry. I . . . I . . . forget, you see. How things are. Times and places. They all get muddled inside my head. I'm that sorry. Blast this thing.' His fingers fumbled uselessly at his jacket buttons. It was unevenly fastened, one side of the coat low and the collar twisted. He looked ashamed as he assured me he could do it.

He wasn't scary any more. Just a frightened old man. 'It's getting chilly out here, I expect your hands have got cold.

Let me.' I bent over and rapidly unfastened and realigned the buttons.

'Thanks.' He took my hand trustingly and stood waiting. The next move was plainly up to me. Even if I'd wanted to walk him home, there was no way I could have made that farm track in these shoes. Finding him another minder seemed my best option.

'Why did you come into the village, Atch?'

'For a pint.'

'Good plan.' I started towards the Royal Oak, but Atch didn't budge. He was looking at a uniformed PC who was talking to one of the spectators a few hundred yards away. I found myself tensing, hardening my grip on him to take control if there was another panic attack.

But Atch simply swung our linked hands like a lively toddler and said: 'They're not looking for me, are they?'

'No, they're not.'

'Are they looking for the others?'

'I shouldn't think so.'

'Dad!'

The other half of the Harry Rouse duo was approaching in an awkward half-trot, half-walk, his Wellington boots slapping and squelching as he hurried past the knot of approaching CID officers and arrived in a shower of water that splashed over my bare legs.

'Watch it.'

'Sorry. Oh, it's you!'

'Hi. Tied up anyone interesting recently?'

'No. Look, I explained that. Said we were sorry. What more do you want?'

'She's having a joke with you, son,' Atch interrupted. 'Can't you tell a joke when you hear one?'

Harry didn't look convinced by his dad's assessment of the situation. But since I didn't contradict him, he turned the pent-up nerves on Atch instead. 'I've been looking all over for you. I told you I'd fetch you down the pub when I'd finished up at the farm.'

'I don't need to be fetched. Been coming here for over fifty years.' His fingers twisted in mine and his lips acquired a mulish pout.

The CID officers had been following him up the lane and were now in earshot. The woman was wheeling Grannie Vetch's pride and joy.

'Does this mean I can go?' I asked, ignoring her and speaking directly to Jerry Jackson.

'Just a few more questions, if you don't mind, Miss Smith. In the meantime, I'll send someone down to drive Mr Vetch's car up here.'

He was staring at the Rouses. Introductions were plainly expected.

'This is Harry Rouse. And his dad. Also Harry, but known as Atch. They own a farm up the road. Detective Chief Inspector Jackson.'

Jerry nodded. 'Pleased to meet you both.'

For the first time Harry seemed to notice that things were not as usual in downtown St Biddy's. 'What's going on?'

'We're investigating, sir. A suspicious death. At Brick Cottage. Did you know the occupant?'

'Eric Groom? He's dead. Died last winter.'

'We were told the name was Luke Steadman.'

'Twenties,' I prompted. 'Blond streaked hair, gorgeous eyes. American accent.'

'Oh, him.' Harry's tone was dismissive. 'Flash prat. Always burning the tyres off Eric's old car. I know who you mean, but I can't say I knew him. Just saw him around sometimes. What's happened to him?'

'As I said, sir, we're investigating. If you live locally, I'm sure one of my colleagues will be calling on you.'

It came out before I could stop it. 'Best make it a plain-clothes one.'

'Why's that?' Jerry asked.

Atch was oblivious to the danger; his son's eyes, however, had become large with alarm. I saw the unspoken plea in them. A couple of days had dulled my initial anger. I dropped Harry a reassuring wink. 'Getting to their farm involves at least three changes of direction. I doubt uniform could cope with the navigation.'

It wasn't very original, but it was the best I could come up with at short notice. I got a tight-lipped smile from Jackson and the bike from the female officer.

She wasn't getting me that easily. I indicated the outfit. 'I'm not dressed for it. You couldn't drop it off in Seatoun, could you?'

'No. We couldn't.' She wheeled it forward a further few inches.

'I'll take it.' Harry reached for the handlebars. 'I'll stick it in the truck. Be coming into town in the next couple of days. What's the address?'

I opened my mouth. And then shut it again. Normally I'd have given the agency's, but I was supposed to be a student as far as Harry was concerned. However, after yesterday's adventures in vandalism, there was no way I was spreading my home address any thinner. 'Can you leave it up at the farm? I'll collect it tomorrow.'

'My pleasure.' He took the cycle with one hand and retrieved his dad with the other. 'Good night, then.'

'Night.'

I watched him wheeling the thing into the Royal Oak, as if I really cared that someone might steal it. Jackson touched my arm. His fingers were cold on my flesh and I gave an involuntary jump.

'You seem nervous, Miss Smith,' Frosty-face remarked.

'This isn't nerves. This is hypothermia.'

'Won't be much longer, Grace,' Jackson said, steering me back towards the Bell's front door. 'Do you mind if I call you Grace?'

'You always do, Jerry.'

Mind you, I didn't normally call him Jerry. But I couldn't resist putting it across to Frosty-face that I was on intimate terms with her boss. I'll bet she had to call him 'sir'; there was no way I could imagine anyone ever calling Jerry 'guv'nor' or 'boss'.

He installed me in a corner of what had been the lounge bar before they started taking up the carpets and running wires under the floorboards. Ms Frosty-face perched on a spare stool within earshot. Slipping off his wet coat, Jerry removed his suit jacket and held it out to me. 'Here. Try this. I've only got a few more questions.'

Whilst I snuggled in polyester warmed by his body, he read rapidly through a set of handwritten notes.

'According to your statement, you called at Mr Steadman's to collect your bike . . . ?'

'Yes.' Despite the fact I liked Jerry Jackson and I'd always sensed he was one of the few senior police officers in the area who liked me, I felt all my old resentments at the representatives of my former career hardening inside me. Part of me wanted to help Jerry out, but the devils were already whispering, '*Stuff it . . . Let them sort it out themselves . . . They won't believe a word you say anyway . . .*'

'Despite the fact you aren't able to ride it in that outfit?'

I looked down. 'That outfit' seemed to be shrinking by the minute. 'It was a failure of communication between me and Vetch. I thought he was going to carry it on the car; he thought I was going to ride it back. That's why we went into the cottage. Luke fitted the bike on his car before – I thought he might do it again.'

'How well did you know him?'

'Hardly at all. I met him here the other day and he gave me a lift into Seatoun.'

'But he offered to keep your cycle for you?' Frosty-face said.

I had to admit he hadn't exactly offered. I'd just dumped it in the garden and hoped he'd understand.

'Was he the understanding sort?' she asked.

'How would I know? I've told you, I scarcely knew him.'

'You didn't have a more intimate relationship with him?'

'No.'

'And yet you were worried he was being unfaithful to you.'

'You what?'

'We found his mobile in the bedroom. There's a message on it,' Jerry Jackson said, reclaiming the initiative. 'It sounds like your voice, Grace.'

I remembered. The call Annie had made me make after my little romantic fiasco with Rainwing/'Daniel'. I'd made some flippant remark about Luke staying true to me.

'It was a joke, right? Luke asked me out. I was accepting. A little light-hearted banter, OK?'

I found myself talking to Frosty-face despite the fact Jerry had picked up the questioning. She asked me to define my relationship with Luke.

'How many more times do I have to say it? Our "relationship", as you put it, was confined to fifteen minutes of conversation between here and Seatoun.'

'But you were prepared to date him. Why was that?'

'Well, let's see. He was tall, good-looking, in terrific physical shape.' I ticked them off on my fingers. 'He had a great car. He seemed to find me attractive. Nope, it's a mystery, isn't it? Why on earth would I want to go out with a man like that?'

'I can imagine you might,' she agreed calmly. 'And if he wasn't keen – or was messing you around, perhaps – well, these things can escalate, can't they?'

'What things?'

'An argument. Not even that. Differences in the way you saw things, perhaps. Blokes can be like that, can't they? They can say, or do – or not do – something that turns your whole world upside down, and not even know they've done it. It was just a big laugh to them. No big deal. Can't understand what you're making such a fuss about.'

I couldn't believe it. Now she wanted to play the all-sisters-together card? She had to be kidding. I looked at Jerry. 'What the hell is she talking about?'

'We were wondering about the two other calls, Grace.'

They played them back for me. *'Where are you, lover? We had a definite date, remember, and I'm getting pretty pissed off standing here freezing my little arse off. You'd better not stand me up or I'll kill you.'*

And then again: *'Last chance. Either you get yourself to Seatoun P-D-Q or I'm coming looking. And believe me, if I have to, you won't like what happens next.'*

My skin tingled. I tried to keep it cool. But even I, who was nominally in charge of the mouth that was supposed to have made that call, had a momentary doubt. People committed murders whilst sleep-walking, didn't they? Did they also make phone calls?

'I'll give you there's a slight resemblance in the voice. But it's definitely not me. When were they made, before or after the fir . . . the one that I made?'

'We don't know until we check with the retrieval service. Some play back the last call first. Others do it in reverse order,' Frosty said. 'And I'd have said the resemblance was rather more than slight.'

'Well, you would. But then I'll bet you'd have done Mother Theresa for vagrancy.'

I wasn't seriously bothered. If they'd really suspected me of involvement in that death, they'd have cautioned me before asking their questions. Nonetheless, I could feel all my nape hairs standing up. And so, I guess, could Jerry.

'Can you give us a minute, please, Emily?' he said. 'Go over Mr Vetch's statement with him, will you? See if anything else has come to mind.'

Emily allowed herself to be dismissed with grace. Or in

her case, I guess, without Grace, since I was left alone with Jerry.

'You really should attempt to do something about that attitude, Grace,' he said quietly. 'Tell me about Luke Steadman. The early gleanings of the team seem sparse. He wasn't a local, I gather?'

I told him all I knew. The uncle who'd left the cottage to him; the American dad who'd owned a meat-processing business; the upbringing in the States that had so nearly led to a walk on the wild side and been turned around after he'd been packed off to the wide-open spaces; the film studies; the production company; the plans to move across the Atlantic permanently.

'So no immediate family that you know of?'

'Both his parents are dead, but I suppose he might have other relatives here. He said his mum was English – I think. You're wanting identification of the body?'

'Amongst other things. Well, thanks for your help, Grace. We'll be in touch.'

'I suppose you want your jacket back?'

'Please. Otherwise I shan't be able to remove it and see the team's faces collectively hit the floor when they realise they're in for early starts and late finishes for a while.'

'Perhaps you'll get lucky and solve it before you hit the overtime budget.'

'I doubt it. In order to solve it in one bound, I'd have to be a lonely maverick whose disregard of the rule book exasperates my superiors. And who works all hours rather than return home to a lonely flat . . .'

'Festooned with the half-empty whisky bottles and ageing takeaway food cartons that form your staple diet . . .' I suggested.

'To listen to the recordings of my obscure musical icons . . .'

'While your ex-wife – who divorced you because she

couldn't take the pressure of the job and is now married to a decent, but dull, nine-to-five type – is secretly still in love with you?'

'The minimum requirements for a truly brilliant detective these days.'

'And you don't measure up to these standards?'

Shrugging his way back into his jacket, Jerry sadly admitted he didn't even come close. 'My career assessments have been rather good over the past few years – even if I do say so myself. My wife shows no signs of wishing to leave and the house is as tidy as is compatible with the needs of our inquisitive first-born; I don't like whisky and I cook a pretty mean shepherd's pie.'

'Musical preferences?'

'Radio Two.'

'You're a hopeless case, Jerry.'

'I know.'

He smiled at me and I found myself grinning back. I knew he'd done it to relax me and wind me down from the everybody-hates-poor-little-me soapbox – and it had worked. I really did like Jerry. He wasn't my type in a million years, but I envied Cathy Jackson at that minute for being his.

'What's the news on baby number two?' I asked as he showed me to the front door. 'It must be due soon.'

'Eight weeks. Everything's going very well, thanks. Here's your car. Emily?'

Vetch and the sergeant emerged from a side room in response to Jerry's interrogatory whistle, Vetch making a big play of saying goodbye with a handshake that he held a fraction too long, judging by the expression that touched Frosty Emily's face.

Whilst Rosco backed the car into the car park, I asked Jerry what was happening with Zeb. 'Oh, come on', I said. 'Do you think I didn't recognise the brush-off when I phoned you earlier about him? I've been trying to get hold of Annie since yesterday and it's no go. Is Zeb in serious trouble?'

'As I told you when we spoke on the telephone, DC Smith is not currently working out of Seatoun.'

'But you're his boss. Don't tell me you don't know what's happened to him. Please, Jerry. Annie's my best friend. If something is going down with Zeb—'

'Then I'm sure the family will tell you should they wish you to know. Good night, Grace. We'll be in touch.'

20

After paying an extortionate ransom to the laundry for the return of my freshly washed and pressed clothes, I spent the best part of Monday trying to restore some sort of order to my office. Even with the minimal filing system I employ, the paperwork had accumulated to amazing proportions over the past few years.

In the end I became so damn depressed I decided a bit of colour therapy was called for. Perhaps if I slapped some paint around the room it might seem more cheerful. On the other hand, if the business was about to go bust, as Annie had predicted, I certainly didn't intend to spend any money on it. The logical course of action was to find someone with a collection of those half-used tins of paint that are left after the decorating.

Jan's desk was empty, but the internal door to the basement was wide open.

'Anyone home?'

'What do you want?' Jan was halfway up the stairs, her arms clasped round a box of copy paper. The orange and lime of the past week had gone. Once more Dracula's bride rose up to meet me; a vision in black boots, black shorts, black tights, black leather waistcoat, white blouse and a raven-black barnet.

'You dyed again, then?'

'No. I'm just really tired.'

'I meant the hair.'

'I know you did. That was a joke, see? I can do that sarky stuff as well as you.' She emerged into the light, using her back to walk the door closed again. 'I went to a posh hairdresser. It took them hours to get it back the way it was. Cost a flaming packet. It'll take me weeks to pay Ifor back.'

'Ifor-squared loaned you money?' I revised my opinion of the Grim Reaper. He was beginning to sound like my sort of person.

'Yes. But only because I've been giving him a hand with his decorating downstairs. He won't give you any.'

'Why not?'

'I told him you never pay people back.'

'Cheers, Jan. Is he in?'

'No. He's gone up the nursing home to see his sister. That's why he's set up in this dump. So he can be near her.' With a grunt of expelled air, she dropped the box of paper on a handy chair. 'He said he might come back this evening.'

Somewhat belatedly it occurred to me to ask whether our burglars had done any damage in the basement.

'No. Alarms went off when they came down here, Vetch said.'

'I was thinking they could have used the outside entrance.'

'Wish they had,' Jan said, punching up icons on her computer screen. 'Me and Ifor can't get that door open most of the time. The lock keeps jamming. Did you like my card?'

'What card?'

'Me birthday card. I left it at Pepi's after the party. Didn' you get it?'

'You went to my party?'

'Everyone went. Even that big-headed policeman you can't stand. He tried to grope my bum.'

Terry Rosco had been to my birthday party? What the hell did Annie think she was playing at?

If I ever found her, it was something else I'd have to ask. In the meantime, her absence was really beginning to niggle at me. I was assuming she was somehow involved in Zeb's mystery problem, due to the evasive answers I kept getting from the local CID office. But what if that wasn't it? She could be in trouble somewhere and no one would know. On my last case I'd ended up chained in a wine cellar (I attract that sort of client), contemplating just how long it might take before anyone in my life would notice I was missing. I'd concluded it would probably take several weeks of decomposing before they sent out the search parties. I decided to start making enquiries via Annie's numerous relatives if I hadn't heard anything within the next day.

My mind wouldn't settle. Since I couldn't paint the restlessness out, I jogged it. On my way back I spotted a notice in the window of the mini-market advertising a portable TV for sale at £25. It meant a trek home to get my savings passbook, but it looked to be a bargain, and my old one hadn't survived my visiting vandals. I stocked up with some groceries at the same time and staggered home with plastic carrier-bags dangling from each forearm and the set clasped to my chest.

I took the side streets because it was easier to negotiate the relatively empty pavements with this lot rather than weave amongst the lager lizards on the promenade. Back here, one in four B&B properties seemed to be empty – their boarded windows mutely testifying to the previous tenants' blind faith in their ability to 'make a go of it' despite all the previous evidence to the contrary. The necessity to stop and redistribute my load every few minutes meant that I happened to be outside one such crumbling dream when the basement window's plywood shutter slid aside and a familiar figure wriggled out and dropped to the ground.

'Hi, Lee. Doing a spot of window-shopping?'

He brushed dust off his clothes and hair whilst he strolled back up the outside steps. The paint on the double-fronted building looked relatively new and the door furniture and roof tiles were intact. Even the 'Lease For Sale' board hadn't been half dragged off the wall by bored kids yet. It all suggested a property that had only recently been closed up. There were probably still a fair amount of goodies inside worth stripping out, although to be fair, Lee's hands were empty as he joined me at pavement level. Perhaps he'd just needed a place to crash for the night after one row too many with Barbra.

'Hi. Earned me mum's thirty pieces of silver yet?'

'Nope. But I'm still giving it my best shot.' The slippery case of the telly was heading ever floorwards. I tried nudging it back with a knee.

'Give it 'ere.' Lee dragged it out of my arms and swung round to walk beside me. 'Want to know why me mum really wants you to find them punters?'

'Is there a real reason?'

'Natch. She can be a right nutter at times, you know.'

'Takes one to know one, Lee.'

It occurred to me it might not be a good idea to wind him up when he was carrying my newly acquired TV. But he merely said: 'Yeah, OK, so we both got a mouth on us. Better than being one of them sad bunches that sits staring at the telly all night never opening their gobs. You want to hear this?'

We had to step apart to let a couple of skate-boarders belt past.

'Go on then,' I invited when we re-joined.

'She tell you about Carly— What the hell . . .' He just managed to leap aside again as the boarders hurtled back, cleaving between us like a bow wave splitting the ocean swell.

The old girl coming towards us wasn't as fast on her pins. By the time we'd righted her and restored her walking stick, Lee and the boarders had both run out of screamed suggestions as to what they were all going to do if they ever got within gobbing distance again.

'You were saying . . . ?' I prompted when Lee and I had resumed our original course down the street.

He opened his mouth . . . and this time was interrupted by a wail from behind. 'My purse. Oh, my purse. It's gone.'

The old girl was swaying on the walking stick, frantically delving in the capacious handbag hanging from her fore-arm. I couldn't help it. My eyes racked Lee for a tell-tale bulge anywhere in his pockets. He saw me looking and his mouth twisted. Thrusting the telly into my arms, he strode back with a stiff-legged gait, cast around the site of the original collision – and retrieved the purse from where it had fallen in the gulley by the kerbstone.

Ignoring its owner's thanks, he came back towards me with the same impatient stride. I tried to apologise.

'Forget it,' he snapped. 'You're just like the rest. Who needs yer?'

I dragged my guilt home along with my groceries and my new TV.

I was aware I'd wasted a lot of the day when I should have been working on behalf of my client. But finding a dead body yesterday had knocked my professional concentration off balance. I was fine doing mundane, routine tasks, but as soon as I started any serious thinking, I kept getting flashbacks.

I could see Luke, his face distorted with terror and pain, his body curled into a half-circle as he died, and the metal tip of that awful spear erupting through his chest. It wasn't one of those flat-bladed types of the kind usually brandished by the masses in medieval crowd scenes. This one had had a long, thin spike like ... *Well, go on, say it*, my subconscious urged ... like the sort carried by Native American Indians?

There were deep slashes on Luke's hands too. It was funny, I hadn't consciously noticed them at the time, but now they floated into my mind and stuck there: curved and bloody and lying palms together near his face as if he was praying. One of the little fingers was almost severed; the bone gleaming whitely through the raw flesh.

He'd tried to drag the spear out – or perhaps push it back. I doubt it would have done any good if he'd succeeded – probably just have caused him to bleed to death faster.

I was aware that the chills were setting in again. Pulling a baggy cardigan on over the sloppy T-shirt and trainer bottoms I'd reverted to after yesterday's flash-the-flesh fiasco, I made myself a coffee, turned on my new bargain, and sat wide-legged on the floor in front of it, dealing out Barbra's photos face down like a set of tarot cards.

I played a game with myself – turning the snaps face up as each new item was featured on the early-evening news. Luke's death hadn't made the national slot. The biggest story was still the diphtheria scare. Two more victims had been hospitalised. Serious-faced scientists explained technical details with multicoloured wriggly graphics, and Ministry of Health officials told everyone there was no need to panic, whilst I turned up shots of Rainwing/whoever.

Despite the way the jerk had set me up, I couldn't help feeling a certain tingle at the memory of that night. He might be a chronic liar – but he'd been a terrific lover.

The national news-readers signed off and the programme switched to the local news. At least Luke got a mention there. There were long-distance shots of the cottage with the police tapes fluttering across the lane, and an earnest-faced blonde doing general background-type interviews with a couple of locals from St Biddy's – neither of whom seemed to know much about Luke. Both spoke about the late uncle, however, with more fluency.

For some reason I was surprised to find Uncle Eric had been an optician before his retirement. I think I'd subconsciously had him tagged as another son-of-the-soil.

An enterprising researcher had managed to dig out an old black-and-white picture of him posing outside his shop for some charity event. It looked like it had been taken in the mid sixties. There was no discernible resemblance to Luke, but I recognised the car his well-polished shoe was resting on immediately.

The report switched to the diphtheria scare and returned to an interview with Faye Sinclair, who seemed to have been elected our rent-a-quote MP on the subject. They'd caught her in the garden this time; there were trees and bushes waving around in the breeze as she held her hair back with one hand and chatted to a mike being waved under her nose.

I turned up Mrs X's portraits and willed her to give me something . . . anything . . . to help me find her.

The shots Barbra had taken were all partials. In the first couple, Mrs X had dropped her head to meet the sunglasses that were being raised towards her nose. The upcoming arm and spectacles had shielded sections of her features in the later shots, and in the final one, as she'd passed in front of Barbra's lens, the glasses were in place and there wasn't much beyond an ear and the angle of a chin to recognise her by.

I picked up one of the earlier snaps and tried to imagine

what she would look like without the arm cutting across her cheek and eye.

A sense of disorientation swept over me again. The face that was in front of me was also floating six feet away. Blinking to try to refocus, I attempted to bring both images together. It wouldn't work. There were two Mrs Xs – one in my photo . . . and one on the screen.

21

'. . . *as a child of mixed race myself, I know how pernicious racism can be. It's so easy to blame those who don't seem to understand the rules* . . .'

I sat forward, oblivious to the interviewer blabbing on about another attack on an immigration hostel in Dover, whilst I studied every millimetre of Ms Faye Sinclair's features. Why the hell hadn't I seen it before? Because I'd only ever seen her in formal interviews, that's why (and not taken much notice of them). The public Ms Sinclair, with her carefully groomed suits, discreet jewellery, immaculate make-up and hair that seemed to have been engraved from ebony, was very different from the casual, relaxed woman in the photo I was holding.

As a final confirmation, the cameraman pulled back slightly to reveal the distinctive abstract pattern of 'that' T-shirt.

Surely Barbra must have known who she was snapping? Or possibly not. I wouldn't know our MP if I fell over them. By her own admission, Barbra found politics (and therefore politicians) boring. And seen out of their normal context, it's not always possible to place well-known faces. In fact, Barbra *had* thought she'd known Mrs X. She'd taken her for an assistant who'd served her in a shop.

I felt a small flicker of joy. At last something was going right. I'd have to check her out, but if Mrs X really was

Faye Sinclair, and I was ninety per cent certain she *was*, then the rest would be a cinch. All I had to do was look her over in the flesh and get her to confirm it was her in the picture. Perhaps I could pretend to be a political groupie and ask for her autograph?

My forward planning ran full steam into a brick wall. I couldn't get anywhere. I'd forgotten the damn bike yet again.

A root through the local telephone directory revealed that the Rouses were ex-directory. I'd just have to issue more apologies tomorrow for not collecting today as arranged. In the meantime, I dialled the local library and found I'd hit lucky – it was late-night opening.

Reading wasn't a popular pastime on warm summer evenings. The woman on the information desk was so pleased to have something to do, she not only located the relevant biographical details on Faye Sinclair but volunteered to look through back copies of the library's magazines since she was sure she remembered an article on the Sinclair family a few weeks ago.

I scanned the *Who's Who* typed entries eagerly. Mrs Sinclair, I discovered, had been born Faye Chang forty-four years ago. Daughter of David and Susan Faye Chang (née Becker). The girl had done good. Educated St Paul's Girls' School and Kent University. Called to the Bar when she was twenty-five. Married Hamish Alistair Sinclair. Three daughters, one son. Became an MP at thirty-two; various assorted political committees, under-secretary of this and that; and a clutch of ministerial jobs that I hadn't known existed. Disappointingly, her address was given as the House of Commons. I wondered if that would do for Barbra. Probably not, since she was planning to live through at least another ten general elections.

'Here you are, then . . .' The assistant bustled back. A glossy mag was pushed under my nose, the pages open at the relevant section. 'She's lovely, isn't she? And such a nice person. I wish she was our MP.'

'Isn't she?'

'Oh no. If you live in Seatoun, that is. Our Member of Parliament is Jack Fisher. Horrid little man, and no help at all when they were going to close the Breast Cancer Unit. Whereas Mrs Sinclair was so supportive.'

'You wouldn't know where she lives? Apart from the House of Commons?'

'It's all in the article.' She flipped pages eagerly and I'm sure would have read the thing out loud to me if she hadn't been summoned back to the information desk.

I scan-read, eyes alert for addresses and telephone numbers. Basically it was just an extension of the condensed facts in the *Who's Who*. Hubby Hamish, I found out, was an 'international jet-setting lawyer' (who made big bucks, judging by the 'luxurious London town house'). They also owned another house in Ashlyn Steeple, which was a village about twenty miles south-west of here, and were currently renovating a holiday home in France.

I read back up the columns again, filling in the gaps I'd skipped over on the first pass. Faye looked to have gone down the usual student route – which is to say she'd rejected her parents' 'wealthy lifestyle' to spend a few years slumming it in some hippy commune – before cutting her hair and her losses and embracing mortgages and power showers once more. Both Sinclairs were active in charity work: he favoured cancer research; she had helped to set up and run a day centre for disabled teenagers.

I read on. The Sinclairs adored each other, adored their daughters (Amy and Victoria, aged twelve, and Phoebe, ten), and regretted the family couldn't spend more time together. As a final teaser, there were a few coy references to an autumn reshuffle and a move to a HIGH-PROFILE APPOINTMENT (Faye herself couldn't possibly comment).

I'd half convinced myself it wouldn't be necessary to do a physical check on Faye, I was becoming so certain she was Mrs X. Doubts set in again as I looked over the illustrations.

Hamish was one of those chiselled-jawed, broad-shouldered hunks. The thick – just going grey – hair and light tan must have gone down a bomb with the female jurors. This guy could have got Attila the Hun off with a caution for public nuisance.

The twins had inherited their dad's colouring of blonde hair and brown eyes. Little Phoebe was a real throwback to her oriental ancestors with her thick blue-black hair and big black eyes. Despite the supposedly informal nature of the interview, all the girls were dressed in Laura Ashley-type frocks, their neatly crossed feet twinkling in patent shoes and white socks.

It was the same with the parents: near-identical double-breasted blazers topping grey slacks for him, a pleated check skirt for her. It was all so stiff and unlike the relaxed, happy woman in Barbra's snaps. What if I'd got it wrong and she was just some look-alike? There was only one person who could say for sure: I was going to have to show Faye the photos.

In response to my query as to whether she thought Mrs Sinclair would be sitting in the House of Commons tomorrow, the librarian informed me Parliament was currently in recess. 'That's on holiday,' she explained with a patronising smile. I sensed she was going to be asking me if I wanted some books with plenty of pictures in them very shortly. 'If you wish to contact her, I suggest you try her local address. The number's in the phone book.'

She was right. It was. But disappointingly what I got was an answerphone inviting me to leave a message and a member of Mrs Sinclair's office would contact me. As a bonus, however, it gave the times and dates of her clinics.

The next one was tomorrow afternoon in Ashlyn Steeple's church hall. Pay-dirt!

I gave a small skip as I left the phone box and set off back to the office. Things were going right for once, two down and one to go! The light was just beginning to fade; the tide halfway out and the beach almost empty. On an impulse, I took off my shoes and walked over the wet sands, squidging soft worm casts between my toes, until I reached the first waves. Down here, with the sea breeze pulling at my clothes and just the bobbing gulls and an oil tanker gliding over the horizon for company, I felt almost light-headed with happiness. Perhaps solitude really suited me.

I'd intended to drop into Pepi's and scrounge supper. It wasn't until I reached the locked door that I recalled Shane closed every Monday except for Bank Holidays. In the end I settled for double cheeseburger and fries in the amusement arcade and strolled back via the office in case Ifor-squared had returned.

His business was called Romani's Dragon Kwik Print Service according to the green and gold sign that was now affixed by the front door. It was a large, glossy sort of come-on – full of swirly characters and gilt overlay. It completely dwarfed our own modest brass name-plate, so it should fulfil Vetch's plan to provide camouflage for those too shy/guilty to be seen going into a private investigator's office.

There were no lights on but I tried the door on the off-chance. Recalling Jan's remark that it regularly jammed, I applied a hard shove as I turned the handle. It worked, and the door swung inwards on Ifor's freshly painted kingdom (the colour scheme wasn't quite as bad as I'd anticipated, although it did seem heavily dependent on Celtic symbols).

'Anyone home?'

It seemed rather strange that he'd have left all this

expensive equipment in an unlocked office. Unless, of course, he hadn't, and our friendly neighbourhood vandals were back.

I trod quietly up the internal stairs to our offices. The heavy wooden door I'd seen Jan bolt shut earlier swung open on the dark and deserted reception hall. I eased inside, intending to take them by surprise – and something hooked one ankle, threw me off balance, and slammed me face first into the wall with my right arm twisted up into the small of my back.

I rolled one eye as far backwards as I could. 'You missed me, then? Could we can the hug?'

With a soft exhalation, Annie let me go. 'Sorry. You shouldn't creep.'

'Creeping is the way I sustain my lifestyle.'

'How did you get in? I secured the basement entrance. You haven't picked Ifor's lock?'

'No need. It's still not locking.'

'Damn. I need to go out that way.'

'Why? What's wrong with our own front door?'

'I don't want to be seen coming out of here. The print shop is safer.'

'Safer for what?'

'Not here. You'll have to block Ifor's door after me and go out the front. I'll meet you by the ladies' loo next to the lifeboat statue in fifteen minutes. If I ignore you, then we don't know each other. Just keep walking – OK?'

'Whatever you say, Mata Hari.'

I heaved the copier and a couple of cabinets across the back of Ifor's door once she'd slipped away up the basement steps and took my time resetting our own alarm and letting myself out.

Annie was between the squat white loo block and the promenade rails. Without speaking, she took my arm and herded me back across the main road.

'Where are we going?'

'Your flat. We can talk there.'

'It's in a bit of a mess.'

'It always is.'

'More so than that.' I brought Annie up to date on my break-in. And Luke's death.

She refused to say anything else until we reached my flat. Settling her on the slashed mattress, I made coffee and looked her over. Her hair needed a wash, there were dark circles under her eyes and her clothes looked like they'd been slept in. In fact, her outfit was odd altogether. Battered jackets and jeans were more my style than hers.

'You look like shit.'

She didn't argue. Instead she took a few sips of scalding coffee and made a face. Her mouth twisted. For a second I thought she'd burnt her tongue. Then she burst into tears.

Annie wasn't a blubberer. In all the time I'd known her, I'd never seen her even close to tears. Now she was sitting on my bed bawling her eyes out – and I was just no good at all this empathising stuff. I felt bad – for me.

Awkwardly I squeezed in beside her and put an arm round her shoulder. 'Hey, come on. It can't be that bad.'

Apparently it could. Zeb had diphtheria.

'He's been undercover,' she gulped when she finally got her voice under control.

'I know. Craig Stillwell,' I added, recalling the identity tag that I'd glimpsed on his belt.

'Meet Ann Stillwell. Sister of the aforementioned waste of space.'

'Pleased to meet you. Craig's not much of an asset to the community, then?'

She gave me a watery smile and told me the rest. Zeb had been undercover on a joint operation between the police, Customs and Excise and the Immigration Service. He'd been working for a container company in Gravesend with a cover that included a habit that required more money than he could earn. Just the sort of low-life, in fact, who'd be susceptible to a bit of strictly illegal moonlighting.

'They know this company is the British end of a racket that's bringing in illegal immigrants. Not the usual vanload dumped at a motorway station and left to fend for themselves job. This lot offer the full monty – passports, birth certificates, social security numbers, job history and references. You too can be an occupant of this wonderful country – without ever having to go through all that boring business of proving you deserve asylum or citizenship. Providing you have serious cash.'

'Then all those morons baying for blood on the news were right? The diphtheria was brought in by immigrants?'

'Looks like it. But they can't trace the carrier. Or carriers. And they're not exactly going to come forward, are they? The chances are, they don't even know they've got it. You can carry without showing symptoms, apparently.'

'But Zeb's been immunised against it, hasn't he? Everyone gets the shots when they're a kid. He'll be fine.' I hoped I sounded more confident than I felt.

'There's no record in his medical notes. It's horrible, Grace. He was bleeding from the throat . . . he couldn't breathe . . . they had to give him a tracheotomy. And I couldn't even hold his hand, they'd got him in an isolation room. I had to look at him through a window. And I just kept thinking, what am I going to say to Mum and Dad if he dies . . . I mean, how'd you tell something like that . . . and I knew they'd blame me for not saying so they could be there . . .' She gave another enormous gulp and visibly swallowed the threatened tears. 'Then this afternoon, he started breathing easily again, and they said he was going to be OK. I dashed back to grab a few things.'

I gave her another hug. 'Where is he?'

'Paddington. They wanted him well away from this area

to minimise the chance of anyone recognising him accidentally. At first they didn't want anyone going to the hospital at all. Just Craig the lonely loser with no next-of-kin. But I managed to persuade them that Craig's equally socially inept sis had to put in an appearance.'

'How?'

'I threatened to blow their whole operation by making a fuss outside the hospital,' Annie admitted. 'I think I might have aimed a Glasgow kiss at the Customs Controller's nose at one point. Jerry Jackson had to get between us. He's lucky he's got fast reactions.'

'Jackson's involved as well?'

'He's local police liaison. Some of the raids will be in this area. I know I'm being paranoid, but I keep getting these visions of someone following me and finding out who Zeb really is. I circled ten times before I came into the office tonight. I mean, I don't care about the Customs operation . . . well, I do . . . but it's if they got to Zeb in the hospital . . . Hell, I'm babbling, aren't I? I shouldn't have told you any of this, I don't know what's the matter with me.'

I did. I asked her when she'd last eaten.

She admitted she didn't know. 'There were snack machines at the hospital but I wasn't hungry.'

So there was a good chance she'd had nothing since I last saw her on the beach Saturday evening. No wonder she was floating in never-never land here. I prescribed a bath and a Grace Smith Double-Decker Sarnie Special.

'Ok.' There was a pause whilst she drank the rest of her coffee and drew her legs up to sit cross-legged on the bed. I sensed there was something else she wanted to say. And for some reason she didn't want to look me in the eye when she said it.

'Grace, you didn't know any of that before tonight, did you?'

'About Zeb?'

'The immigration scam.'

'No. How would I?'

'No reason.'

I was sitting on a kitchen chair opposite her. Raising a trainer, I nudged the edge of the mattress. 'Give, Anchoret.'

'It's . . . they asked me about you.'

'*They* being?'

'The Customs and Excise team. And I know they asked Jackson too.'

'What did they want to know?'

'Everything. You've not got yourself mixed up in anything fishy, have you? You could tell me, you know.'

'Annie, I haven't a clue why Customs and Excise should find me that interesting. Cross my heart and hope to go to a hell without chocolate if I'm lying.'

She held my eyes for several long moments. Then her shoulders relaxed. 'OK. Can I stay here tonight? I don't fancy an empty flat.'

'You'll have to sleep on my other slashed mattress or the floor.'

'Let's take a look at the mattress.'

I showed her into the guest cupboard.

'What the hell's that?'

I'd forgotten all about my birthday horror. If ever a bunch of plants were capable of radiating resentment, this lot were doing a great job.

'It's my sister's birthday present. I don't think they're really at their best.'

'I'm not surprised. Have you ever heard of plants that are indigenous to coal mines?'

'No. Why?'

'Because it must be pitch in here when the door is shut. Didn't anyone tell you plants need light? Put the poor things in a room with a window.'

'But I live in those. And I'm not rooming with a refugee from *The Little Shop of Horrors*. I'll stick it outside.'

'Someone might steal it.'

'My luck isn't running that well at the moment.'

We heaved the tub into the basement area out front and then I made us sandwiches whilst Annie had a bath.

'What is it?' she said suspiciously, twisting the plate at eye level.

'A fried bacon and sliced Snickers bar double-decker toastie. I dreamt it up myself.'

'During a particularly lurid nightmare, I assume?'

But she ate the lot, and after testing the mattress, elected for folded blankets on the floor.

I curled into my sleeping bag and listened to her breathing in the dark for a while, before saying, 'Annie?'

'What?'

'Are you OK? With the diphtheria thing?'

'They screened me. I'm clear.'

'Good.' I brooded for a few more minutes before asking, 'When did the Customs lot ask Jackson about me?'

'A few days ago, I think. I only picked it up on the rumour mill. Why?'

'He never mentioned it when I saw him at St Biddy's yesterday. He's in charge of the Luke thing.'

I heard a huge yawn crack in the darkness as Annie remarked that it was unlikely Jerry Jackson would want to have a chat, then, when he was up to his neck in a murder inquiry.

'We did chat, but not about that.'

'What, then?'

I reran my interview with Jerry in the Bell *vis-à-vis* the antisocial qualities needed by a hot-shot police officer. 'We sort of came to the conclusion I was ideally qualified to make Chief Constable.' That reminded me of another unlikely scenario. 'Annie?'

'Mmmm?'

'What the hell was the idea of inviting Terry Rosco to my birthday party?'

There was no answer; just quiet, rhythmic breathing.

After a while, it became quite hypnotic.

22

Annie was heading back to Paddington. Via public transport, as befitted the down-on-their-luck Stillwells. She declined to lend me her car, so in order to retrieve the bike I ended up on the bus route that provided evening transport for the thrill-seekers of St Biddy's.

As promised, it deposited me on the main road about a mile beyond the turning to the village. The storm had left the ground damp and rejuvenated the insect life. Clouds of midges rose up from underfoot and danced tauntingly in front of my nose. Halfway to the signpost down to St Biddy's, I came across a small unmade track meandering off at a right-angle that should lead it somewhere near the village.

I hadn't really intended to go into St Biddy's, but the urge to see how they were getting on with the investigation into Luke's death got the better of me. After all, we'd practically dated – that had to count for something. (Another entry under the largest section in your love-life diary, 'The Ones That Got Away'? my personal demon suggested.)

Once I'd cleared the tall hedgerows that blinkered the first hundred yards of the track, I could see across country to the rooftops of the village, with the disproportionately large church spire thrusting between them at the left-hand edge. A little closer and I made out the individual bleached red bricks of the nearest building. Blue and white fluttered from the lane side of the house, snapping out in the breeze and then lying flat against bricks again. My first assumption, that they were banners or deflated balloons signalling it was party-time inside, was revised as I got closer. It was plastic tape. The ripped remains of police tape, in fact. I was on the other end of Cowslip Lane, approaching Brick Cottage.

I'd never seen it from this angle before. There was a smaller garden at the back, separated from the open farm fields by a hedge that had grown dense and high over the years.

The cottage was surprisingly ugly: a plain red-brick structure with no softening climbing plants to add a bit of rural charm. Whoever had built it seemed to have been trying to squeeze it on to the smallest area of land possible. Its height somehow appeared out of proportion to its base area, an oddity which no doubt accounted for the high plaster ceilings inside. The garage had been tacked on to the section abutting on to the lane like a pimple that had erupted on party night. At present it had Carter's eyes fixed on it with an expression of lust only slightly less intense than that he bestowed on Kelly Benting's butt.

He was perched on a fence post on the right side of the track, drawing a scrappy bush branch through his fingers and rubbing the leaves to nothingness.

'Hi, Carter. How's it going?'

He gave me an odd look before dropping his head so that most of his face was concealed by the peak of his baseball cap.

'Question too difficult for you?'

'I don't truck with liars.'

'That must make your conversational opportunities few and far between. What am I supposed to have lied about?'

He raised his head and pulled at his bottom lip. 'One of the coppers told Kelly you were a private investigator. Are you investigating those people in the photos?'

'In a manner of speaking.'

'Why? What's Harry Rouse done?'

'Nothing that I know of. Private investigations don't always have to be bad news, you know. We do good as well,' I said sanctimoniously (and largely untruthfully).

'Like when they trace the long-lost heirs to a fortune or something?' he asked, getting closer than he knew to the truth.

I touched a finger to my lips.

'Wow! Neat!'

'Not a word, mind.'

'Total lock-down, I swear!'

We exchanged a high-five. Communications re-established, I asked Carter if the police were still in the village.

'No. They pulled out last night. They've been all over the place, poking around in the bushes and ditches. They took stuff out of the cottage. I made a statement. And they took my fingerprints. For elimination, they said.' He sounded proud of the fact. 'We could have been the last people to see Luke, I reckon.'

'Who's we?'

'Me and Kelly. The first time. We came up here Friday afternoon. I wanted to ask Luke about something in one of those books he lent me. He gave me this.' He tweaked the cap peak. 'For my birthday.'

'And Kelly came with you?' Obviously she was a girl who didn't do things half-heartedly. Having decided to stake a claim on Carter, she'd gone for it like a limpet on speed.

'She can't get enough of me,' Carter said. 'I reckon she was waiting until I was sixteen. So she could, you know, open up . . . let me know she was keen. I can respect that. It's cool.'

'Totally cool. Where is she now?'

'Lying down, her mum said. Woman's problems. He was killed Friday night,' he said, abruptly switching the conversation back to Luke.

'The police told you that?'

'No. But they were asking people where they were then. You don't have to be Inspector Morse to work it out, do you?'

It tied in with the weekend papers Vetch and I had found in the hall. I was surprised no one had discovered the body earlier. Carter wasn't. 'No reason for anyone to come here, was there? Not to go inside. And he didn't like people just dropping by. Said it broke his concentration when he was working.'

'Except for you.'

'I kept an eye on the car for him. He knew he could trust me.'

He didn't seem to be taking the death as hard as I'd have expected. But I suppose it didn't seem real yet. Seeing the body as I had makes death very real. But if you haven't that tangible proof in your eyes and your nose and your dreams, it's easy to think of the dead as simply being in another place for a short while.

'What did you mean by seeing him the first time? Did you and Kelly come back later?'

'No, not Kelly. It was me. Me that saw him, I mean, not came back. He came in the shop just before we closed. I was minding it. Gran said she had to see to some ironing but I knew she was really doing my birthday cake.'

'Nice. I never got to eat mine.'

Carter offered me a slice of his. 'There's loads left. Gran only eats a little. And Kelly didn't want any.'

'Kelly came to your birthday party?'

'It wasn't a party really. I mean, no one else from school lives around here . . . and what with my birthday always being in the summer holidays . . .'

I got the message. Carter had no friends to speak of.

'But Kelly came. She brought me a card. And I showed her all my space stuff.'

Lucky old Kelly.

'Then we hitched up later and went into Seatoun. She's really hot for me, you know.'

'You said.'

The surface of the lane was muddier here. The storm's

downpour had softened the ruts into a consistency that caused a sucking, glooping sound every time I lifted my trainer. It was doing the same with Carter's. Idly I followed the patterns of our respective shoes. Mine were in a straight line, but Carter's trampled up to the doorway. The last imprint disappeared half under the door. I looked at him and saw him knowing that I knew.

'You've got a key.'

'No.' He ducked under the baseball cap again.

'You're a lousy liar, Carter. Remind me to give you lessons.'

He looked up again. 'I didn't steal it. Luke gave it to me.'

'So what's the problem?'

'I never told the police. I mean, they never asked, but I thought it might be like . . . concealing evidence or something.'

'Shouldn't think so. Unless you killed him?'

'Course I didn't! We were mates. We talked.'

'About what?'

'Films. And the States. And . . . you know . . . stuff. He had this, like, really wild time when he was a kid. Hung out with some mean guys.'

'He said.'

Carter was visibly disappointed that he wasn't the only one Luke had confided in. Something had to be done to re-establish his position as Luke's number-one buddy. 'Want to see inside?'

Before I could decline, Carter had taken the key from his pocket and was heaving the up-and-over open.

The shelves were lined with all those half-used decorating tins that tend to accumulate, plus assorted garden preparations, car polishes and shampoos. A neat line of gardening implements were hanging from a row of hooks and two black motorcycle helmets with smoked visors sat on pegs above an old motorbike.

The car was sitting in the centre of the concrete floor. Beyond it was a door to the rest of the cottage.

'You can't get in,' Carter said, following my eyes. 'Luke always kept it locked.'

'Didn't he give you a key for that?'

'No. Just the garage.'

'What about the bike? Was that his uncle's too?'

'Do me a favour. He was ancient. That's Luke's.'

I hadn't ridden one for years, but perhaps his next-of-kin might be persuaded to let it go for a bargain price. It wasn't a very noble thought when its late owner was probably still being reassembled into a tidy package by the pathologist, but a girl's got to eat, and somehow I had the feeling that a PI who cruised up in leathers and metal was going to be perceived as cooler than a puffed-out female on Emmeline Pankhurst's bike.

Talking of which . . . 'I've got to split, Carter. Do you know if the Rouses are in?'

'If they aren't, they'll be back soon. They're planting out this week.' He smoothed a final caress over the car's headlight. 'You won't tell anybody, will you – about me having the key?'

'Not my business, Carter.' But something else was. 'Did Luke ever talk about his girlfriends?'

'No. The police asked me that.'

And probably for much the same reason as I had. Somebody had made those other two calls to Luke's mobile service complaining about his failure to turn up for a date. And she was a somebody with a voice very like mine. Coincidence or deliberate?

I asked Carter again if he was absolutely certain Luke had never mentioned any female friends. 'Couple of blokes together. They usually compare the talent. See who's ahead in the pulling stakes.'

I hoped the implied compliment – that he and Luke were on equal footing when it came to pulling power – might make him chattier. But instead, he ducked his head beneath the cap peak again and mumbled a denial. I was almost certain he *did* know something. I was equally sure he wasn't about to open up to me. I left him mooning over the car and made my way back the way I'd come until I rejoined the main road.

Life around Tyttenhall Farm was buzzing compared with my last visit. There were three kids – mid teens – wandering around one of the ploughed fields, apparently fussing over rows of limp green plants that seemed to have been spewed out by a large yellow farm machine of some description.

The farmyard itself was as lifeless as before. Nobody seemed to be paying me any attention. I edged towards the barn, still half convinced Atch was going to jump me any minute despite the fact I'd taken care to wear a plain white T-shirt, grey jogger bottoms and a pink cardi today. (I figured the cardi was a clincher. How many military policemen were going to be into sugar-mouse pink?)

The barn showed signs of activity. Empty plywood boxes were scattered over the floor and full sacks of some kind of chemical were piled in one corner. The concrete was smeared with clumps of mud and boot marks, indicating the regular tramp of feet in and out since the storm's downpour. As I'd hoped, Grannie Vetch's bicycle had been stored in here too.

I scooted it out, one foot on the pedal, and heard the sounds of an approaching vehicle. I stood and waited while the truck bounced and bucked its noisy way up the rutted track. There were more of those plywood crates stacked in the back.

Harry climbed out of the driver's seat whilst his dad decamped from the passenger side. My 'Hello, Atch' received no more than a suspicious sideways glance before he shuffled to the back of the vehicle. I wondered if rumours of my real job had reached the Rouses as well – hence the cold shoulder. But when I looked at Harry there was no hostility. He shook his head fractionally. 'Bad night,' he mouthed.

'I took the bike. Sorry I couldn't make it yesterday.'

'Not a problem. Dad, leave that!'

Atch had pulled one of the crates half off the pile. It crashed to the floor and split open, spilling what looked like more of those sickly green seedlings into a heap. Atch backed away with a look of alarm.

'It's OK, Dad,' Harry sighed. He sounded tired.

'Can I help?' I asked, indicating the mess of soil and greenery.

'It's OK. I'll get the kids over.' Inserting two fingers in his mouth, he summoned a couple of the field workers and set them to unloading crates and sweeping up the spillage.

'What are they?' I asked curiously.

'Cauliflowers. We buy them in as seedlings from the wholesaler's warehouse. It's a bloody useless way to live, but it's the only one I know and I'm too old to start at something else now.'

'What's useless about cauliflowers?' I couldn't stand the stuff myself, but somebody must be eating the tasteless squidge and chewy stalks.

'Nothing,' Harry said. 'If anyone was going to eat them. We harvested the early crop six weeks ago. At least there was some point to them. The market wholesalers took it off soon as it came out of the ground. There's satisfaction in that. Seeing food being harvested and gathered in. Knowing it's going to feed folks . . . be part of the cycle, same as it's always been since folk's started growing things. But this . . .' He kicked a dying seedling that had been overlooked in the clean-up. 'Know what's going to happen to this? It'll be tended, protected, harvested and thrown into a great big pile with another four hundred and ninety-nine of its friends. Then a man will come along, count all the piles of five hundred, and write me a cheque for them. After that, this little fellow, and all the others, will be carted off – and burnt to a cinder. Such is the joy of the Common Agricultural Policy.' He gave me a mock bow.

It was plainly a sore point with him. But not one I felt like kissing better. 'I'll be off then.'

I swung a leg over the bike. Harry asked if I was heading back to Seatoun.

'Steeple Ashlyn.'

'That's a good twenty miles. I can take you part of the way if you want. I've another load to collect anyway.'

Atch was squashed between the pair of us in the front but he seemed determined to ignore me today, keeping his eyes fixed ahead through the windowscreen and his hands clasped over his knees. Each time we went around a corner, his knuckles tensed, opening up the festering grazes along them.

'Did you have an accident, Atch?' I touched the reddened skin. The old boy flinched as if my fingers were red-hot.

'He hit them against the door,' Harry said. 'I locked him in his bedroom last night.' Anticipating my response, he snapped: 'I had no choice. He wanders off. I had to get some sleep.'

'Sure.' I paused to let him negotiate a narrow turn between stone garden walls spilling over with the exuberance of summer's growth. The flowers shed their petals like confetti over the bonnet. 'No luck getting any nursing help at the farm?'

'I told you. It costs.'

'There's respite care . . .'

'He's my dad. Nobody's putting him in a home.' His tone was final. And then it changed and he said awkwardly: 'I've not said thanks. For not saying anything to the coppers the other night about Dad and the gun. I'm grateful.'

'It's OK.' I asked if he'd heard anything more about Luke's death.

'Policeman came up the farm. Asked if I'd seen anything. Told him I didn't even know the bloke. Which, now I think about it, might not have been true— Bloody idiot, are you blind!' This final remark was directed at a tractor that had pulled out of a concealed gate and nearly rammed us. The truck's bearings squealed in protest as we rocked, rolled and righted ourselves.

Atch whimpered in fright and grabbed my hand. I whimpered right back.

'Sorry,' Harry panted. 'Everyone OK?'

'Terrific. We must do that again sometime. You were saying – about knowing Luke?'

'Not him. But years ago Eric Groom used to have a sister come stay sometimes. She had kids, couple of boys and a girl. This Luke must have been one of *their* kids, the way I see it. Make him Eric's great-nephew.'

'Gillian,' Atch said, unexpectedly returning to Planet Reality. 'Gillian, the girl's name were. Fast piece. Come up the house showing everything she had. Not the sort you want on a farm. That kind don't settle. Soon got tired and moved on to the next lad. You needed a steady local girl, Harry.'

'I had one. She divorced me, remember,' Harry muttered into the windscreen. 'Well, it's too late now . . . a long way too late.'

I thought that was the end of the conversation. But Atch said: 'That was Gillian's boy in the red car, was it? Don't surprise me. She always had plenty to say for herself too.'

'You talked to him, Atch?'

'Harry did.'

This would seem to be at odds with his son's recent statement. Harry said shortly: 'We had words – once.'

'About what?'

Atch had really achieved splash-down on Planet Normal. He said in that soft, rational voice he'd used when speaking to me the night of Luke's death, 'Trespassing. He had that car of his up my place. Drove it around the yards. Over the fields too.'

'What did he do that for?'

'Show off, these youngsters, don't they? Wheelies. Hand-brake turns. Neighbour had them running drag races over his fields a few years back.'

'Is that what Luke was doing?' It was hard to picture.

'Said he wasn't there at all. Said we must be seeing things.'

'Did you? See him, I mean?'

'Saw him pulling out of the lane one evening. We'd been up the cycle place, hadn't we, Harry?'

Harry gave a noncommittal grunt.

'Do you ride a bike too, then, Atch?'

'Not had one of them for years. I mean the cycle place with the big metal bins. We puts the rubbish in them. Tins and the like. We drive it all into town for the bins.'

It just goes to show: I would never have put Harry Rouse down as a born-again recycler.

Atch chattered on happily. 'That red car of Eric Groom's came out of the lane as we come back along the main road. Saw it plain as I'm seeing you. And where else is there to go up there but our farm? I looked round next morning; there was tyre tracks all over the place. Fancy ones. Not like truck tyres.'

Harry pulled over abruptly, dragging on the handbrake with more force than was necessary. 'I'll drop you out here. Wholesaler's down the other way.'

It wasn't as close as I'd hoped, but at least the land in this area had the flat dullness of unbroken marshes. It made for boring scenery but easy cycling. I figured to an experienced cyclist like me it should be a breeze. A couple of miles into the trip, I knew distance had lent a rosy hue to my biking memories. Now the rock-hard saddle was doing the same to the more personal areas of my anatomy again. By the time I rolled into Steeple Ashlyn I was sore, out of breath, and sticky with sweat. And not all of it was down to pumping the pedals. The temperature was creeping up again and so was the humidity. It looked like we were in for a period of cyclical storms.

There were already a few people hanging around outside the church hall. I took them to be the queue for the clinic until I got close enough to hear the discontented mutters and see the scrawled notice pinned to the closed doors: 'MRS SINCLAIR'S CLINIC HAS BEEN CANCELLED DUE TO ILLNESS. SHE SENDS HER APOLOGIES.' I swore.

'You can say that again,' one of the crowd said. 'I have to see her. The lot next door is driving me mad. Yelling, screaming, music, day and night. And the filth they come out with when you tell them to shut up. She's got to tell the council to throw them out. It's only fair. I voted for her and I know for a fact they didn't.'

I figured I might as well make use of her by asking if she knew where Faye Sinclair lived.

'What? Go there, you mean?'

'I thought I could put a note through her door.'

It was plainly a novel idea. But she was game. And more importantly, she knew the address.

Number 14 Chestnut Avenue proved to be a thirties semi. Not really what you'd expect for the combined incomes of an international lawyer and a Member of Parliament.

My new friend answered to Cheryl. Slapping a bottom that was already packing more fat than Sainsbury's chiller cabinet on to the garden wall, she dragged out an old envelope and proceeded to list her grievances and what she expected Faye Sinclair to do about them. I pretended to do the same with a scrap of paper I dug out of my bag. Together we marched up the crazy paving pathway, posted our notes through the letter box and stepped back. There was no sign of movement behind the net-curtained bow windows, but I was sure I'd caught the faint notes of music inside as I'd bent to open the flap. Cheryl didn't seem to have noticed, but that was probably down to the ear-plugs I'd glimpsed under the fuzz of badly permed hair.

'What now, d'yer reckon?'

'Go home and wait for her to get in touch,' I said firmly.

Cheryl wasn't keen. She seemed to have come with the notion that Faye could get the council hit squad to evict her neighbours by closing time tonight. Eventually, however, I managed to get rid of her. As soon as she turned the far corner, I scooted back. There was absolutely no way I was cycling back here again. I didn't care if Faye Sinclair was on her deathbed. I intended to get a good look at her today.

Ringing and knocking on the front door produced no response. But there was now no doubt that the music was coming from the back of the house somewhere. Two ornamental stone urns and some dodgy trelliswork provided just enough support for me to climb on to the flat garage roof, run along it and drop down into the back garden.

It was as ordinary as the front had suggested it would be: lawn, shrub beds and stepping stones with a small patio in front of the french windows.

Still working on my story, I shielded my eyes against the sun and pressed my nose against the glass. It took a second for my pupils to adjust to the darker shapes inside. It took ten times longer for my brain to do the same. Whatever I'd been expecting to see, it sure as hell wasn't this!

23

Faye Sinclair – supermum, super career woman, super-cool – was dancing around her lounge stark naked apart from a towelling bath robe.

I tried the patio door and discovered it was unlocked. Faye was waltzing barefooted to Whitney Houston's assurances that she would always love her. She seemed oblivious to everything but the music. The reason was standing on the coffee table. Faye Sinclair, Member of Parliament, minister for something-or-other, was smashed out of her tiny skull on vodka.

Humming the tune under her breath, she extended her arms and moved towards me, swaying unsteadily to the rhythm. I was half afraid I'd have to fend off a drunken embrace, but a tricky change of balance threw her just as she passed the sofa and she flailed sideways into the cushions.

'Damn.' She hiccuped, sniffed, looked around as if she'd lost something, and burst into tears.

I'm not the sort of girl who regularly carries a packet of tissues in her bag in case the public loo roll has run out. I pulled a lacy mat from under a plant pot and handed it to her.

'Thanks.' Her eyes were red with crying and with the remains of make-up smudged liberally above and below. There was more multicoloured stuff smeared at random places over her face. She looked like a melting Picasso portrait.

'Who are you? Well, never mind. Have a drink.' She scanned the room vaguely again. 'I seem to have misplaced my glass.'

I was impressed. Fancy being able to pronounce 'misplaced' correctly in that state. The woman had class.

The trouble was, I wasn't sure she was Barbra's Mrs X.

Her partial Chinese ancestry was more obvious in the flesh than it had been on the screen, and at present her face was swollen and blotched by misery and all those haphazardly applied cosmetics. I was going to have to clean her up and calm her down before I could compare her to Barbra's snaps. I turned the music off and asked Faye if there was anyone else here.

'No.' She hiccuped and tied the bath robe more securely. 'I'm all alone. I'm always alone. Even when I'm with the people who ought to be closest to me, I'm still alone. Do you understand that?'

Completely. However, an in-depth discussion on the realities of loneliness wasn't in my current game-plan.

Perceived wisdom says the quickest way to sober up a drunk is a cold shower and hot black coffee. Perceived wisdom has never suffered from a stonking alcoholic overload.

Since Faye seemed unalarmed by finding a total stranger wandering in her house, I went in search of the bathroom and turned the power shower to a pleasantly warm temperature. By the time I got back to Faye, she was half passed out on the arm of the sofa.

'I've run your shower.'

'I don't want a shower. I want another drink.'

'Fine. I'll pour us a couple while you shower.' She was too drunk to think of a coherent argument why I shouldn't lead her upstairs and bundle her into the cubicle. I unscrewed the shower gel bottle, put it her hand, stuck a lump of sticking plaster over the bolt on the bathroom door so she couldn't lock herself in there, and left her to it.

Coffee was no good in her state. It would just increase the dehydration. I found two large glasses, added quarter of an inch of white wine, and topped them to the brim with soda water. Rooting around further in the kitchen produced cream crackers and cheese. I carried the lot back into the lounge and mooched around with one ear open for the sound of the water stopping. I decided to give her ten minutes then go up and compare whatever had rinsed out with Barbra's photos.

The lounge was pink and pale green with display cabinets in some kind of pale wood. Dotted around the place were assorted co-ordinating lamps, ornaments, wall mirrors and silk flower arrangements. It was pleasant enough but gave the impression whoever had furnished it had walked into a display room in a furniture retail park and told them to deliver the whole caboodle. The kitchen had had the same oddly impersonal air about it: there was just enough food and utensils in the cupboards to suggest a self-catering break rather than a family home.

The only truly personal items were a collection of framed portraits scattered over walls and furniture. Faye and hubby Hamish were sparsely represented, but the three daughters were there from babyhood to present day. There were a couple of a boy of about eight who I assumed must have been the 1(s) mentioned in the *Who's Who* entry. I wondered why he'd been left out of the at-home piece in the magazine. Perhaps he wouldn't wear the Laura Ashley outfit.

I explored across the hall and discovered a small dining room with the same 'furnished let' feel to it. Faye's glass was sitting on the polished wood of the table, amongst half a dozen water-marked rings where she'd put it down after each swallow. Scattered around it were a dozen dark green and white bullet-shaped capsules.

Cursing softly, I hunted for the container to give me some clue what they were. No luck. The water was still running. I took the stairs two at a time, expecting to find Faye unconscious in the shower tray. She was, however, perched on the bathroom stool bundled in a couple of bath towels and using the corner of one to rub at her hair.

I thrust a capsule under her nose. 'How many did you take?'

'I have no idea. Who cares anyway?'

Grabbing the tops of her arms I made her look at me. 'What were they? What's in them?'

She frowned with concentration. 'Sea kelp.'

'What?'

'Kelp. It's good for you. Makes you feel ever so much better. Says so on the packet. Didn't make me feel better. I feel bloody awful.' Her face twisted and her lip trembled as the tears welled up. At this rate she was going to get all swollen up again before I could get the snaps out.

Kneeling so that my face was on a level with hers, I said slowly and clearly: 'Are you sure they weren't something else? Sleeping tablets? Or tranks?'

'Tranks?' Water dripped from her fringe and trickled down her nose as she tried to make sense of the question. Finally she got there. 'You think I was trying to commit suicide!'

I admitted the idea had crossed my mind. The concept seemed to sober her up slightly. At any rate the slightly away-with-the-fairies expression was replaced by a spark of anger in those jet-black eyes. 'My mother died when I was ten. Do you seriously imagine I'd deliberately put my own daughters through that kind of pain?'

There it was again. That enviable ability to form coherent sounds when tanked to the gills with booze.

'Sorry, but you're not exactly . . . I mean . . .' Oh, to hell with it, why did I need to bother with tact. 'You're smashed. Drunks don't behave rationally.'

'Am I?' Faye Sinclair considered this idea. 'Good. I haven't been drunk since I was nineteen. Perfect little Faye Chang mustn't get drunk. Mustn't do anything to prove them right. Little Chink tease. Bet she's desperate for it. They know tricks, these oriental babes. Know how to get a man going. I'm the wrong way round, you know.'

I was still holding on to her. Mainly because she seemed in danger of sliding to the carpet if I didn't. Impatiently she pushed me off and stood up. Using a corner of the towel, she polished a porthole in the steamed-up mirror and examined her own reflection.

'Usually in mixed marriages it's the man who's English, woman's Chinese. It's all right that way round. Well, almost all right. Not other way, though. My father had two first-class honours degrees. He ran one of the most successful import/export companies in the country. But it didn't matter. My mother's family never spoke to her again after the marriage. Never wanted anything to do with me. I had to be so bloody perfect. The perfect daughter to prove them all wrong. My father's living legacy to my mother's memory. Well, I don't want to be perfect, OK? I want to be bloody normal! I want to feel something!'

Before I could stop her, we both felt the effects of a tooth mug shattering the mirror. Having made her gesture, she seemed at a loss to know what to do next and stood staring at the fragmented reflection behind the spider's web of shattered glass. That's the trouble with these one-day anarchists. They stick their heads above the rut of normality and they can't follow through.

'Watch your feet.' I slung the discarded bath robe down à la Walter Raleigh, and marched her out of there into the bedroom opposite.

The double bed was unmade. Newspapers and colour supplements were scattered over the duvet and floor and the remains of a half-eaten breakfast were still sitting on the bed-tray. The TV was muted but on.

Dumping Faye in a chair, I opened the wardrobe. It had that 'just here for the holidays' feel I'd noticed in the kitchen. No clutter, just neat rows of clothes.

I selected black trousers and a white T-shirt. It was the colouring of Mrs X's outfit in the photograph and would give me a better comparison. Taking some underwear from the drawer, I bundled the lot on her lap. 'I'll tidy the bathroom while you dress.'

It wasn't that I liked housework (you'd probably noticed), but there was something voyeuristic about watching other women dress. By the time I'd turned off the water, opened the windows and located a vacuum cleaner to pick up the glass slivers, Faye had got herself clothed and was sitting on the floor tracing the lines of text in a single-paragraph article in the open newspaper pages.

I peeped over her shoulder. It was this morning's

Telegraph. The headline read: *Film producer dies in bizarre slaying*.

And I finally saw what I should have seen days ago. If Faye had been heading past Barbra the morning she'd taken those snaps, she must have been walking down Cowslip Lane. And there was only one place she could have been going. 'Luke?'

'Luke.' She whispered it like an echo. 'Oh, Luke!' With a cry of despair, she wrapped her arms around herself and rocked back and forth.

I did the only thing I could do in the circumstances. I slapped her.

The stinging mark of my fingers was still visible on her cheek when I returned with the drinks and crackers. 'Spritzer,' I said firmly. 'Drink. Eat.'

She was too disorientated to argue. Once she'd nibbled her way through most of one biscuit and downed half the glass, I asked her how she'd met Luke.

'He's a friend of my son's.'

'The boy in the pictures downstairs?'

'Peter, yes.' She picked up a morsel of cheese that had fallen to the carpet and popped it in her mouth. 'He's a lot older than that now, of course. My little mistake. First affair. Only affair. Confirmed all the old prejudices, didn't I? My father threw me out. Literally. His chauffeur turned up at my college rooms with all my things. Put them out on the pavement. I had to sell most of them to keep us both. And move into that awful commune.'

We were sitting cross-legged opposite each other. I'd slipped Barbra's half-dozen shots of Mrs X into my back pocket when I'd collected our snack. I wasn't sure of the etiquette for bedroom picnics, but taking them straight out and staring at my hostess seemed like bad manners. A bit of social chit-chat was surely called for first?

'I thought you liked the commune. I read this mag piece; said you found it an enriching experience.'

'I read that too. I *said* it. What else could I say? That they were mostly a bunch of self-indulgent no-hopers who were hiding from real life? God, you should have heard them . . . sitting there night after night droning on about how they were going to save the world and not doing one single damn thing to try to change things. But I had to stay. How else could I have finished my degree? Everyone wanted me to have an abortion. Or have him adopted. But I wouldn't. He was mine. No one was going to take him away from me. I even had to leave Peter with them for a few years after I joined chambers. There was no possibility of affording a child-minder on what they were paying me for the hours I worked. And God, how I worked. I had to: female; unmarried mother; ethnic minority. Believe me, I had to be ten times better just to stand still, let alone get ahead.'

'You seem to be ahead of the field now.'

'Don't I just. Successful husband, adorable children, lovely home, high-flying career. No . . . I tell a lie . . .' She wagged a finger and rocked forward slightly. 'Two careers. Barrister and Member of Parliament. Didn't like the law. Stupid profession. Mr Bumble was too kind. It's not an ass . . . it's a whole herd of asses. Politics is better . . .'

The alcohol was really starting to kick in now. Even that impeccable diction was beginning to slur. Any minute now she was going to lie down for a few hours – and wake up with a thundering headache, queasy stomach and the words 'never again' on her lips.

Sure enough, she started to bend sideways from the waist as I watched. Her head touched the carpet, whilst her legs were still crossed in the lotus position. Amazing suppleness; I just hoped Luke had appreciated it. There was no resistance when I straightened her out into the recovery position and tucked the duvet over her.

She'd more or less confirmed she was Mrs X, and any criminal skeletons in her cupboard would have been unearthed by the press long ago, surely. There was really no need for me to stay any longer. But those capsules bothered me. I ended up rooting around in the waste-paper containers before going outside and tipping out the rubbish bin on to the patio. I finally found the wet and disintegrating blister pack tangled in the remains of a smashed jar of olives. As she'd said – sea kelp.

Reloading the muck into the wheelie and straightening up, I became aware of the sweat trickling down my back. The heat wave was building up again with a rapidity that promised it would break in another electrical storm. I was hot, sticky and facing a very long bike ride home. There was only one thing to do in the circumstances. Invite myself to stay.

After I'd helped myself to the shower and the towels, I checked on Faye. She must have come round after I'd originally left her since she was now cuddling one of the photos from the bedside cabinet. It looked like Daddy Chang – hugging the blonde twins with a baby moppet on his lap that must be the youngest kid.

I stuck her back in the recovery position and sauntered downstairs. Opening the french windows wide, I put my feet up and settled down to a few hours of hard relaxation.

The sofa was delightfully squishy and the room was very warm. I suddenly became aware how tired I felt. Vandals and cycling can be a powerful combination when it comes to draining a girl's energy banks. Maybe a little snooze was called for.

I felt myself going down into a floating half-awake state. Part of my mind was mulling over Barbra's commission. I'd found two of her lucky legatees – and faster than I'd have expected. Now there was just the elusive Rainwing to pin down and I'd have the complete set. And that lovely fat finder's fee.

All I needed was to figure out how I was going to track down my transvestite Hiawatha. Images of that narrow face loomed over me. I could feel the silky skin of his hairless chest under my hands and taste that mouth probing mine.

Fired up with remembered pleasures, my body flexed in anticipation while my mind told it it was a dream and to get real. I opened my eyes and proved to my mind it was a damn liar.

Rainwing was standing two feet away, staring down at me.

24

'What the hell are you doing here?'

We spoke simultaneously, but I like to think my self-righteous snarl had the edge. Neither of us apparently felt like answering. The silence was becoming awkward when Faye decided to join us.

I guessed she was still barefooted because I hadn't heard her coming downstairs. Instead her arrival was announced by the crash of a door sliding from the grasp of someone whose booze-blitzed co-ordination couldn't handle relative distances yet. From my present position (flat out on the sofa) I couldn't see her at all; but I sympathised with that groan of pain as the bright light from the french windows hit her eyes.

Rainwing said: 'Hello, Mother.'

Mother?

'Peter, darling. How lovely. You should have let me know you were coming down. Oh, God, I feel so ill . . . Draw those curtains, please.' Her progress had brought her far enough across the carpet for her to see over the back of the sofa. 'Oh? I'm sorry, I didn't know you had company.'

Her fingers were tidying her hair whilst her shoulders were pulling back, her backbone was straightening and that professional politician's sincerely-bothered-about-you smile was materialising like the Cheshire cat's. Our previous encounter seemed to have been erased from her memory by the hangover.

I sat up and gave her my own best cheesy grin. 'Hi! I'm Grace.'

'A friend of mine,' Rainwing/Daniel/Peter/whoever-the-hell-he-was-today said. His hand on my shoulder squeezed a plea for silence.

'We met earlier.' I smiled, shaking Faye's hand and contriving to dislodge her conniving son's paw at the same time. 'You may not remember. You were a bit . . . under the weather.'

'You've not caught anything, have you, Mother? From the immigrant hostels?'

'No, of course I haven't, darling. I'm just a bit stressed.'

Stressed as a newt, I was tempted to say, but didn't.

Faye said ruefully, 'I'm so sorry. I don't usually behave so badly.'

'Forget it,' I said. Before remembering that she already had.

She was still trying to switch into perfect hostess mode, but a problem with gravity was sabotaging her efforts. As she swayed forward, I stood up and steered her on to the flattened cushions. 'Take a seat. I'll fix something. Tea, coffee, bicarb?'

'Tea would be lovely,' Faye said, curling into the hollow I'd just vacated. 'And an aspirin, if you wouldn't mind.'

'I'll help,' whatever-his-name said.

'Thanks.'

We both waited until we were out of earshot in the kitchen before resuming hostilities.

'How bloody dare you come here?' he snapped.

'Why shouldn't I? Your mum's an MP. We hoi-polloi are allowed to crave a boon once a year. It's in the deal.'

'She doesn't represent Seatoun.'

'How'd you know I come from Seatoun? No! Don't tell me – you found something when you searched my bag to nick those photos. No, that can't be it. I don't keep anything with my home address in there. Did the great spirit in the sky send a messenger to you, Rainwing? Or is it Daniel today?'

'It's Peter Chang, as you very well know.' He reached round me for a tin of teabags and flicked them two-fingered into the pot – dealing them out like a card sharp. 'And Luke told me you lived in Seatoun.'

'You know Luke?' Daft question. Of course he did. His mum had just told me her lover was a mate of his.

'He's a friend. Practically my only male friend, if I'm being truthful.'

'They say you should try everything once except incest and clog-dancing.'

'Do the words pot, black and kettle ring any bells?'

'Here!' I thrust the filled kettle at him and contrived to slosh a lot of the contents down his sweater. It was a pale grey silky V-neck today, with matching trousers in a soft jersey fabric. Very understated and not at all Rainwing's style.

'There's no need to behave like a bitch.'

'You should know – Rainwing, dear.' I hadn't intended for my tone to be quite so arch.

His expression changed. He looked . . . hurt? 'I really thought you understood about that. But you're just as bad as the rest of them – pretending to empathise, and making jokes about men like me behind our backs. I think I'd rather you just made the snide remarks to my face. At least that's honest.'

'Don't you get all holier-than-thou on me, you bastard,' I hissed. 'What about that pack of lies you fed me – or are you Daniel as well in your spare time?'

'No. I'm not. That was a one-off performance. I'm sorry, but you have to understand – when Luke saw those pictures you'd taken of me—'

I didn't correct him; Barbra's existence was none of his business anyway.

'We thought you were a journalist. Out to do a spoiler story on my mother. They've tried before, you see. She's a good target – glamorous, well-off, a touch of the exotic. Be much more fun to bring someone like that down rather than one of those boring grey suits. And ever since the rumours started about her getting a cabinet post in the autumn . . . well, let's just say Rainwing would have been an absolute gift for the muck-rakers.'

The kettle was boiling. I passed it across. 'You could,' I pointed out, 'have given up the frocks.'

'I can't. I have tried, believe me. But I just have to. It's like a junkie needing a fix, I suppose. Luke understood that. But when he saw those photos of me . . .'

I recalled the couple of snaps Carter had passed to Luke after my dive off the churchyard wall. There hadn't been a flicker of recognition when he'd looked at them.

'He tried to chat you up himself. But he said you blew him out. So he warned me. I had to get close to you somehow. Find out what your agenda was.'

'How did you manage to set me up with Daniel?'

Peter was setting out a tray with cups and milk jug. He flicked a glance in my direction. And my heart did a little hop-skip-jump as other parts of my anatomy recalled that considering look.

'You were talking to that weird kid that hangs around Luke. Luke had a word with him and found out you'd been asking about the local bus. It didn't exactly take Einstein to realise you'd figured out I'd used it. Luke went down to the bus station and bribed the driver to point you in the direction of Auntie Vi's house. He promised to get him a part in the films. It's amazing how many people fall for that I-can-get-you-in-the-movies routine.'

'Violetta the bird lady is your aunt?'

'Honorary aunt. She used to be my child-minder when I

was a kid – well, one of many at the commune. I always stay with her when I'm being Rainwing. She'd do anything for me, Vi.'

'Including slipping me a book of poetry with Daniel's address in it.'

'That was her idea. She likes a bit of intrigue, does Auntie Vi. Thought you were more likely to believe it if you had to work for it.'

And I thought I'd been so bloody clever tracking down that flat! I just hoped all her budgies got the mange.

'You really were incredibly easy, you know,' Peter said silkily. I got the impression he wasn't only referring to the misdirections.

'So who's Daniel Sholto? Another mate who was in on the joke?'

'No. He's exactly as I played him – apart from the cross-dressing, of course – a stressed-out banker who can't climb off the treadmill. I occasionally work for a housekeeping service when I'm resting.'

'Really? I've never found housework particularly restful.'

'Technical term, love. Sounds better than out of work. I'm an actor.'

That would certainly explain the Shakespeare. Who else but an actor could quote great chunks of the stuff off the top of their head? It probably accounted for the way he found it so easy to slip into a convincing Rainwing as well.

Peter sniffed the milk delicately before adding it to the jug. 'We on the housekeeping circuit are a matey lot. One of my clients has a fantastic wardrobe of designer gear – just the sort of thing an out-of-work actress needs to gatecrash the hottest parties – so when she's out of town my friend borrows them. And in return, when the invest-ment banker she scrubs for – if you'll pardon the expression – is off on his travels—'

'She lets you borrow his keys?'

'Absolutely.'

'And his credit cards?' I asked, recalling the champagne supper.

'I doubt he'll even notice. Those sort of people don't check card statements. And if he does complain, the restaurant will write it off as a mistake.'

'You hope.'

'Well, no. You'd better do that. It was you who opened the door to the delivery man. Still, never mind – I daresay all you blonde westerners look the same to the Chinese.'

'Bastard.'

'Oh, don't get all bitchy on me, Grace. You must see I had to find out if you were planning to screw my mother.'

I was tempted to tell him his best mate, Luke, had already done that. But the memory of Luke's body, twisted and skewered on that spear, intervened. We were both speaking about him as if he were still alive. I wondered if Peter had heard about the murder. Not everyone browses the *Telegraph* (I certainly didn't).

I rested my forehead against the window, needing to feel the coolness of the glass on my skin. The kitchen was in the front of the house, overlooking the road. When I'd arrived, the shadows from the trees lining the pavement had formed truncated pools of blue over the flagstones. Now they stretched like streams of spilt ink over the road, their tips nearly touching the opposite kerbstones.

'What's the time?'

He cradled the tray on one arm in order to consult a large plastic watch on his left wrist. 'Nearly seven. Why?'

I couldn't believe it. Normally I find it difficult to sleep during the day. I'd assumed I'd dozed for no more than a couple of hours. Instead of which, I must have been out for nearly six.

'It doesn't matter. Where's the aspirin?'

'Paracetamol. That drawer, I think.'

There were only two left. When I turned back, Peter was

blocking my way. 'Grace . . . look . . . I know you're mad at me, but please don't tell my mother about Rainwing.'

'She doesn't know?'

'Obviously not, or I wouldn't need to ask. If she knew, I think she'd try to persuade me to get treatment or something. I have a right to my own life . . . don't you think?'

Yep. If there was one thing I could empathise with, it was the curse of the parents who KNOW WHAT'S BEST FOR YOU, DEAR.

'Stay out of my reservation in future,' I said. 'And I'll stay out of yours. Kapeesh?'

'Kapeesh.'

During our absence, Faye had pulled herself together sufficiently to plump the cushions, hide the vodka bottle and apply a slick of lipstick. Ankles crossed, back straight and eyes bright, she exuded poise as she poured with a steady hand. Only the grateful way in which she gulped down the paracetamol indicated that all was not well chez Faye.

'So how did you two meet?' she asked me, playing the Mummy-entertains-the-girlfriend role to perfection.

'At a mutual friend's. Daniel Sholto. Maybe you know him?'

'I don't think so. He's not that actor you were in the fringe thing with last year, is he, Peter?'

'No. You've never met him.' Peter threw me a dirty look and I gave him one of my best adorable eyelash flutters.

'Are you in the entertainment business, Grace?'

'In a manner of speaking. I'm writing a novel.' I smiled innocently at my new beloved. 'Peter keeps going on at me to show him the first chapters. But I'm just not ready for that yet.'

'That sounds very challenging. Does it have a theme?'

'Betrayal.'

'Grace still has a lot of research to do, don't you, my love?'

'Mmmm. And Peter has been *so* helpful.'

We exchanged loving looks that could have stripped the varnish off any furniture that had been unfortunate enough to stray into range. But since we were sitting in the half-dark in deference to Faye's current allergy to bright lights, she wouldn't have seen.

'Oh? Well, good. You couldn't be helpful to me too, could you, darling? It's just that there's scarcely a teaspoon of petrol left in the car and I daren't risk driving it in this condition . . .'

'No problem. I'll fill her up first thing in the morning.'

'Can't you do it now? I may have an early start.'

'Er . . . well, OK. Shall I put the bike in the garage?'

'What bicycle?'

I'd left it propped outside when I climbed over into the back garden and promptly forgotten all about it again.

'It's mine. I'd best be going anyway.'

'Don't be silly. There's no need to rush away. Peter won't be ten minutes. And we can compare notes on him while he's gone. The keys are in the kitchen, darling. I'll get you some cash.'

I assumed that she wanted reassurance I wasn't going to give my loving other half a blow-by-blow account of his mum's extramarital confessions and had my comforting speech plus sympathetic smile in place when she returned from shooing Peter out of the front door.

I didn't get a chance to use either. The heart-broken lover and/or perfect political hostess had gone. Swallowed up by a hot-eyed spitting she-cat.

'I think,' she hissed, her body vibrating with so much rage I could practically feel the heat oozing from the pores, 'that creatures like you should be buried alive.'

25

'I'll tell Peter an engagement's out of the question, then?'

'Is that supposed to be a joke?'

'A small attempt. But then I'm not really on top form,' I said truthfully. 'What exactly am I supposed to have done?'

She removed a clutch of crumpled snaps from her trouser pocket. They were Barbra's shots of her emerging from St Biddy's store. My hand went instinctively to my own back pocket. Which was as good as admitting they'd fallen out of there in the first place.

'I found these in the sofa. I shan't even bother to ask if they belong to you,' Faye said coldly. 'I assume you struck up a friendship with my son for much the same reasons as you took these.'

'Actually – he latched on to me.'

'After you'd put yourself somewhere he couldn't fail to fall over you, I'm sure.'

(Well, that was true enough, I guess, since I was picking the lock to Daniel Sholto's flat at the time.)

Faye ripped the snaps in half. 'I'm certain you have other copies, but never mind – this makes me feel fractionally better.'

Balling them up, she slung the missile into the empty grate. 'And you may as well know right now that I don't intend to pay you one single penny. So if you were hoping for an easy bonus, you can put the idea out of your mind.'

'I wasn't.'

'Then to quote Lord Nelson, "Publish and be damned" and you can pass that on to whoever you work for.'

'Wellington.'

'What?'

'It wasn't Nelson. It was the Duke of Wellington. Right war – wrong service. And I'm not a journalist.'

'Then what are you?'

I was beginning to lose track myself, I'd told so many cover stories in the past week. In such circumstances there is only one thing to do. Resort to the truth. 'I'm a private investigator.'

At least that wiped the self-righteous expression off her face. It took whatever colour she had with it. She sat down quickly. Her voice had lost the crisp don't-mess-with-me edge when she asked who'd sent me. 'Was it my husband?'

'I've never met your husband. Nobody sent me. At least, nobody sent me after you; you just got caught up in another case . . .' It was the best explanation I could come up with that didn't violate the promise I'd given Barbra on complete confidentiality.

Needless to say, it didn't satisfy Faye, who wanted to know who, why and when.

'We don't give out that information.'

She picked me up immediately: 'We?'

'My company.'

'So other people have seen those photographs?'

'One or two. But it's OK, honestly. Nobody's going to start ringing the hotlines to the tabloids. What would they say? I've got a picture of Faye Sinclair coming out of a grocery shop? I mean, big deal . . .'

'Of course it's a big deal, you stupid . . . Oh God, I'm sorry.' Silent tears welled and that lost expression flooded her face. 'I'm sorry,' she whispered again. 'But you just don't see—' She caught her breath sharply at the sound of a car engine and the automated rumble of the garage door lifting. 'Peter doesn't know about me and Luke. Don't tell him, *please*.'

I didn't intend to tell Peter the time of day if I could help it (although there was one intriguing question I'd have liked an answer to – once we were on spitting terms). All I really wanted to do now was put space between me and Barbra's weird legatees. That wasn't going to be as easy as it sounded.

Peter wanted me to stay for supper. Oddly enough, for once in my life I wasn't that hungry. Perhaps it was another consequence of turning thirty; pretty soon I wouldn't be able to so much as look at a cheeseburger without fretting about cellulite. On the other hand, the alternative was a gruelling cycle ride home, and the oppressive humidity was showing no sign of abating now evening was setting in. On the contrary, it was showing every sign of delivering another humdinger of a thunder and lightning show.

Faye was surprisingly receptive to the suggestion – perhaps she had hopes of planting me six feet down with a stake through my heart before sunrise. She'd already got the garlic to hand.

'There isn't much in, I'm afraid,' she said, adding tomato paste and a packet of herbs to the garlic bulb on the work top. 'We don't really live here.'

'It's Mother's constituency address,' Peter explained, seeing my puzzled expression. 'She's got a four-storey in Islington she calls home. And *une petite maison* in Brittany for those get-away moments.'

'It's *une petite* cow shed at present,' his mother said, shaking oil into a pan. 'I was over there last week trying to get some sense out of the local builders.' Her head was bent over the bulb she was peeling, but I saw the slide of her eyes under the fringe and the silent plea in them. Now I knew where she should have been when she was shacked up with Luke.

I gave her a noncommittal half-smile and asked if there was anything I could do.

'Perhaps you could lay the table in the dining room? There's cutlery and things in the unit.'

I hadn't got the first spoon in place before Peter followed me in. 'Salt and pepper.' He extended the two glass mills. Moving closer, he dropped his voice. 'Listen, can we talk—'

He broke off as his mum appeared with the place mats. 'I forgot to give you these.'

'Thanks.'

I doled out three place settings. An activity that took as many seconds. When I looked up, both of them were watching me. I was tempted to take a bow.

Neither seemed inclined to move. It dawned on me that neither wanted me to be alone with the other. To test my theory, I started edging towards the kitchen. They followed like a couple of iron filings drawn by a magnet.

We played the same daft game whilst we made pasta with tomato sauce and a rather sparse side salad. As soon as I showed any signs of breaking away from the trio, I was quickly swept back into the fold again. We ate with the windows wide open and the unspoken dialogue as tangible as the electrical storm building outside.

Faye cracked first. 'Did you see that piece on the news, Peter? About the death at St Bidulph's-atte-Cade? Wasn't that a friend of yours? Luke something?'

'Steadman,' Peter replied with equal lack of interest. 'Luke Steadman. I introduced you at the pub in King's Cross.'

'Peter was doing an experimental piece there. They have this one-room theatre over the bar. Do you know it at all?' Faye asked me with a tight smile, being the perfect little hostess again as she drew me into the conversation.

'I don't get to London much. And quite honestly, I've always found the performances I have experienced up there haven't been worth the train fare. Not much content and a disappointing climax.' I smiled blandly at my new beloved.

'Really?' Faye said. 'I am surprised. I'm sure you've simply been unlucky.' She chewed a forkful of salad without enthusiasm before angling the conversation back to the subject she really wanted to discuss. 'I was so sorry to hear about your friend, Peter. Do you know how it happened?'

'I know as much as you do. That piece in the paper more or less implies it was murder.'

'I do hope not. Such an awful way to die.'

'Is there a good way?'

'No, I suppose not . . . It's just . . . well, never mind, let's talk about something more cheerful, shall we? Grace?'

I couldn't believe it. They expected *me* to provide a diversion? OK. 'Is the rest of the family coming down?'

Just what she wanted to drive the pictures of her lover out of her head: a reminder of the relationships she'd been putting at risk.

'No,' she said after a moment's pause. 'My husband is travelling abroad at present. And my daughters are in Scotland with his parents. Your grandparents have bought a boat, Peter. A dinghy. Did I tell you?'

'They're not my grandparents.'

'They've always thought of you as a grandchild. As much as the girls. You know that.'

'Pity everyone didn't feel the same, isn't it, Mother?'

'There was nothing I could do about that, Peter. I tried. You know I tried.'

'OK. Not your fault. Water and bridges long gone now, eh?' He twirled a forkful of pasta against a spoon. The moment turned into one of those silences where you notice the clock ticking and the sounds of traffic way off. At least Faye seemed to realise it this time. She apologised, adding she was sure I hadn't expected to be caught up in a family disagreement.

'No, I go home if I want to do that.'

'Do you come from a big family?'

'Not really. Two parents, one brother, one sister, one brother-in-law, two nieces, assorted distant aunts and cousins.'

'Are you close?'

'Not in the slightest.'

Having killed off that topic of conversation, I figured I'd done my bit. It was someone else's turn to find a subject that would make us all feel uncomfortable. Since no one volunteered, we ended up leaving it to the approaching storm – which obliged with yet more stifling heat and no breeze.

'This is unbearable,' Faye said, fanning herself with a magazine. 'You can't intend to cycle home in this, surely? Why don't you stay the night?'

'Yes, do,' Peter urged. 'You'll get soaked out there.'

To confirm his prediction, the unhealthy yellow illumination of lightning flashed over the garden, bringing uncomfortable memories of that evening at Luke's cottage. We'd moved back into the lounge and left the french windows open in an effort to get some air. Now a sudden gust caught one and rattled it. There was no reason to associate the storm with rotting bodies, but suddenly I didn't want to be alone in my flat – even if I had been able to get back to it.

They put me in the front bedroom. With its double and single bed, girlish white-and-gold furniture and more photos of Grandaddy Chang cooing over his granddaughters, I guessed this was the twins' and little Phoebe's bedroom on their visits to Mummy's constituency. Which probably meant they were trotted down every four years to be paraded for the election pictures.

I'd scarcely climbed into the knee-length nightshirt Faye had loaned me and lugged the duvet off the double bed before she tapped lightly on the door and slipped in.

'We need to talk.'

Well, she might, but I didn't. My head was aching and I was feeling more washed-out than I could remember in a long time. However, short of lifting her bodily back on to the landing, I sensed I was going to have to provide an audience until she'd got her confession off her chest. Wedging the pillows against the headboard, I leant back and hugged my knees.

She sat on the edge of the mattress and said: 'I love my husband. And my children.'

'Fine.'

'But . . .'

Why did I know there was going to be a 'but'.

'But . . . have you ever felt driven by something totally outside your control? I can't describe it . . .'

Try lust, I thought cynically.

'With Luke, I was someone else.'

'Smart move. Checking in as Faye Sinclair might have been a bit of a giveaway.'

'We never checked in anywhere. It wasn't like that. We walked, we talked. It was wonderful – like finding the other half of yourself. Can you understand that?'

'You mean there was no sex involved?'

'Well, yes, there was. Of course there was. Wonderful sex. It was spontaneous. Crazy. Fun. I didn't know it could be like that. I was thirty when I married Hamish, and until then I'd only ever slept with one other man.'

'Peter's dad. At college.'

Her colour faded slightly again, emphasising the ivory shade of her skin. It was strange how the different sides of her parentage dominated depending on her moods. 'How did you know that?'

'You told me. When you were stressed as a newt this morning.'

'I did? What else did I say?'

'Not a lot. Just that your dad had thrown you out when you brought disgrace on the family name. I thought that sort of thing had gone out with Victorian melodramas.'

'It didn't.' Her gaze fixed on one of the bedside photos. Her eyes became wide and thoughtful. I got the impression she was talking more to her father's image than me. 'I have never been so *scared* in my entire life. I was the original spoilt princess. I hadn't even cooked a meal. We had servants to do that sort of thing. Before I started university, I'd never lifted a finger for myself. And then suddenly I was standing on a pavement with a couple of suitcases and a baby growing inside me. If Win hadn't found me crying my eyes out on the station platform, I honestly don't know what I'd have done.'

'Who's Win? Someone from the commune?'

'Win taught the younger children. Amongst other things. We all did jobs around the place. I helped look after the pigs and worked in the kitchens some evenings. It fitted in with my degree.'

'Sort of like a kibbutz?'

'In a way.'

'You said you couldn't stand them. The humans, I mean. You didn't volunteer any opinion on the pigs.'

'Did I?'

'Self-indulgent were the words you used.'

'Yes. They were in a way. Please don't misunderstand. I'll always be grateful to them. But they were so inward-looking – always complaining about injustices in the world, but never doing anything to help. It's changed now, of course.'

'In what way?'

'A healthy dose of greed rather took a hold when they realised all those self-sufficiency and lifestyle skills were marketable. Nowadays the commune is more of a limited company, from what I hear. I haven't been near the place for years.'

'How long did you live there?'

'Just over two years. Although Peter was there until he was nearly ten. At least at the commune I knew there were plenty of people around who cared about him. It was no different really from leaving him with my parents, say, and visiting at weekends. Lots of single mums do precisely that.' Her voice acquired a slightly defensive edge, as if child-abandonment might have been something she'd been accused of in the past. 'And as far as Peter was concerned, that *was* his home. It was truly kinder to leave him there.'

'But you liberated him in the end?'

'Hamish and Win talked it over and decided he really needed the discipline of proper schooling.'

'Didn't you get a say?'

'Of course I did. But with the best will in the world, it's hard to empathise with what a ten-year-old boy wants or needs, when you've never been a ten-year-old boy. Hamish was better qualified. And he really did want to be a proper father to Peter.' She gave herself a visible shake and said briskly: 'Anyway, I don't know how we come to be talking about that time. Did you know Luke? I thought perhaps you did. Is that why you were in St Bidulph's taking those pictures?'

'Yes, I did. Although not well. And no, it wasn't.' I didn't see any necessity to tell her I hadn't taken the photos.

'Do you know how he died? The papers don't say much and I can't ask without drawing attention to myself.'

'He was stabbed.'

'Oh, God. Do the police know who did it?'

'As far as I know, they haven't a clue. Do you think they're likely to come looking in your direction?'

'Why should they? I told you, we were very careful. Luke insisted. He was very sweet like that. He didn't want to cause any trouble for me. From the beginning, I think we both realised that it couldn't ever lead anywhere. I mean, we dreamt, but at the back of our minds was the knowledge that it would only ever be this one summer. In fact, we'd already said our goodbyes. Those few days at St Bidulph's were our last. He wanted us to spend some time as if we were a couple, instead of just snatching a few hours when we could. It was magical. We locked all the doors and there was just the two of us in the world. We never went out of the house.'

'Except for visiting the shop.'

'Yes. That was so *stupid*. I came on. And if there's one thing you can't find in a bachelor's house, it's a packet of tampons. I was only out for a couple of minutes at most.

There was no one around except for the woman in the shop. I don't see how you could have photographed me without my seeing you.'

'There's a seat in the wall in Cowslip Lane. It's hidden by shrubbery,' I said, ducking the question of the photographer again.

'It must have been a surprise. Stumbling across an MP down there.'

'Not really. To tell you the truth, it took me a week to recognise you.'

'But it can't have done. I mean, I'm all over the papers and television at present with this diphtheria business going on.'

'I'm not really into politics.'

She stared blankly. Her face was expressionless. Then she managed to surprise me again. She laughed.

'Oh, heavens,' she said when she'd got her voice under control. 'I wish some of my colleagues could have heard that. Or perhaps, in the circumstances, I don't. We all think we're so vital to the country. When the truth is, there's more chance of the voters recognising a soap star than the Chancellor of the Exchequer.'

There certainly was in my case. I found myself desperately trying to pull up a picture of him/her. I could just about recall the faces of the major party leaders and a few other politicians who seemed to get a lot of air time – although I hadn't a clue what jobs they held.

'I really only remember the ones who do something a bit different. You know, marry their mistresses, or get picked up kerb-crawling, or, em—' It occurred to me I wasn't being very tactful here.

'Quite so,' Faye agreed dryly. 'And I'm sure you'll understand why I'd rather not be remembered in those circumstances.'

'Sure. But listen, you were supposed to be in France doing a bit of DIY – *oui*?'

'Yes.'

'So you came back early. Or left late. And stopped off in St Biddy's for some shopping. No big deal.'

'Unfortunately it's not that simple. I chose to be in Brittany deliberately because we don't have a telephone line installed yet. I'm only contactable on my mobile.'

'Which could be anywhere.'

'Precisely. I spoke to my husband that morning. In fact, I became quite lyrical describing the garden in Brittany. And I had a call from a reporter who wanted to know if I could do a slot on the local lunchtime news. I had to explain I was currently sitting in a cow shed in France so it wasn't really feasible. If she were to get her hands on photographs that proved I was really in St Bidulph's on that morning . . . Well, let's just say she's been looking for the next step up for some time now. And believe me, she doesn't care whose face she steps on to get it.'

'Well, she won't get them from me, if that's your point.'

'Then you'll give me the negatives?'

So that's where this was leading. Dead end, I'm afraid, lady. 'I don't have them.'

'Please. I'll pay whatever you think is reasonable.'

'What happened to publish and be damned?'

'Common sense. Being brave is all very well if it only affects yourself. But if this became public property, my daughters would have to deal with it too. And my husband. I do love him, you know.'

'You said. But listen, they really are rotten shots of you. Your face is partially obscured in all of them. Why not just claim it's someone with a vague resemblance? You were in France.'

'It won't work, unfortunately. Did you notice the T-shirt I was wearing?'

'Very colourful.'

'And totally unique. I'm involved with a respite centre for mentally impaired teenagers. Some of them painted it especially for my birthday. It's my lucky shirt. There's not another one like it in the entire world.'

'Not so lucky then.'

'Let me have the negatives? Please, Grace.' She leant forward and rested her hand on mine. 'Please.'

'I'll see if I can get hold of them,' I promised weakly. I had no great hopes of prising them from Barbra, but my energy seemed to be draining through the soles of my feet and I just wanted to get rid of her so I could close my eyes.

She gave my fingers another squeeze and slipped out, wishing me a good night's sleep.

Some hopes. I'd left the curtains undrawn and the tops of the bay windows open to let in whatever air there was. Switching off the lights, I lay on the fitted sheet watching the raindrops sliding down the glass, back-lit by the streetlamps and flashes of sheet lightning. Silently I chanted the formula we'd learnt as kids – counting the heffalumps between lightning and thunder clap – to estimate the position of the storm centre.

I'd hardly got enough heffalumps for a small-sized herd when the door opened again. I was lying facing the window and didn't bother to turn over as the mattress dipped under another weight.

He curled against me spoon-fashion. 'Hi.'

'Hi, yourself.'

'I'm glad you decided to stay. I've missed you.'

He nuzzled my ear. (There was no doubt about it. This guy could make the Olympic nuzzling team. Hell – he could captain it.) 'There's something I wanted to ask you.'

'There's something I wanted to ask you too,' I murmured.

'Really? Ladies first.'

'Is that why you left the frock off?' Now his body heat was penetrating the cotton nightshirt and my own sweat, all my senses were telling me he'd left pretty much everything else off too.

'Don't be bitchy, it doesn't suit you. What did you want to ask me?'

I levered myself free and wiggled round to face him. 'When you stole my snaps in London, you got a complete set. So how come you've never wondered what your mum was doing in St Biddy's?'

'I know what she was doing. Sleeping with Luke.'

His face was next to mine on the pillows. In the light from the windows, I couldn't see much beyond the darkness of his pupils against the whites. 'You're not supposed to know about that.'

His breath tickled my nose as he said that of course he knew. 'Luke told me months ago. He thought it was the right thing to do.'

'But you didn't tell your mum?'

'How could I? It was embarrassing, finding out your mother was sleeping with someone young enough to be her son. Would you want to discuss your mother's sex life with her?'

'Probably not.' I wasn't even sure my mother had one any more. Not since my dad had been confined to that wheelchair.

He eased the length of his body closer to mine. 'Luke promised me it was all finished anyway. One last fling and farewell, my lovely. He was moving to the States and she was going back to my stepfather. On a full-time basis, I mean.' There was a small silence when he seemed to be holding his breath. Then he released it in a gentle sigh and said in a different tone of voice, 'Who do you think killed him?'

'How would I know? He was your mate – who'd want to?'

'No one. He was all right, Luke. Everyone liked Luke.'

'Somebody didn't.'

'I don't suppose it was personal. These things are usually burglaries gone wrong, aren't they?'

'Are they?'

'I had an idea . . . That story you spun me about being a trainee investigator – was that on the level?'

'More or less. Although I'm not training any more. I'm fully fledged.'

'Even better.'

'For what?'

'I thought you could help me get into his place. Take a look around. See if there's anything to connect him with my mother.'

'And nick it.'

'Well, basically . . . yes.'

'Forget it. If there was anything, the police will have found it by now.'

'But they might not have realised it was important. A quick search wouldn't hurt, would it? You've no idea what it would do to her if all this came out. Please, Grace.'

He drew me in tighter and started easing up the hem of my nightshirt. The storm was working itself to an ear-bashing finale outside. I heard myself saying I'd think about it.

'I knew I could count on you. There's something special between us. I can feel it. Can't you?'

'You think so?' I nuzzled into the hollow of his neck. 'There is one special thing I'd like you to do for me.'

'Name it.'

I eased away from him and started sliding the soles of my feet up over the front of his feet, his shins, knees, thighs, and into the groin. I was quite proud of my own flexibility. I got my knees right up into my chest. Putting every ounce of energy behind them, I kicked him straight in the stomach.

The cotton undersheet was smooth and tightly woven. He skidded off it and hit the floor with a very satisfactory thud.

Flicking on the bedside lamp, I bent over his groaning

form and hissed: 'Nobody cons their way into my bed twice, sunshine. Now get lost.'

At least he had the sense not to argue. With some relief, I flopped back on the pillows and gave myself up to an aching head, rising temperature, and the shivers. I couldn't remember when I'd last felt this rotten. Eventually I went downstairs, found the phone, and dialled.

The answering machine at my parents' house picked up the call and invited me to leave a message.

'Mum? It's me. Can you ring me back at this number—' I rattled off the figures on the receiver. 'I really need to know – have I been immunised against diphtheria?'

26

It wasn't diphtheria. I had food poisoning. The doctor couldn't identify anything in the past twenty-four hours that might account for it. In the end, he decided I probably had a strange metabolism that had taken an abnormally long period to absorb the bugs, took a variety of bodily samples that made me glad lab-technician hadn't been my career of choice, and left me to suffer in peace.

I spent the next three days curled up in bed with just the cramps, diarrhoea and boiled water for company. The high spot of the seventy-two hours was the undignified whack of a syringe full of anti-emetic in a very personal place.

By Friday night I was able to sit up in bed and groggily scoop up the clear soup and toast Faye had prepared for me. Saturday morning had me sinking into a bath with a grateful sigh.

My clothes were neatly stacked on a chair. When I picked them up I discovered they'd been washed and pressed. I was relieved I'd had to wear one of Barbra's wildly overpriced lingerie sets. The idea of a Member of

Parliament washing out my off-grey knickers with their dodgy elastic didn't bear thinking about.

Padding downstairs with my knotted bundle of whiffy sheet and duvet cover clasped to my chest, I located the washing machine in the kitchen and Faye in a small study tucked into the back of the house.

'Well, hello. And welcome back to the world of the living. How do you feel?'

I did a quick mental check and discovered I actually felt quite hungry. And embarrassed. 'I'm really sorry about crashing on you like that.'

'It couldn't be helped. Hang on until I've finished this letter and I'll cook you some brunch.'

I was lounging by the door whilst she was sitting at a well-worn desk sorting through files and tapping information into a laptop computer. There was a bookcase next to the desk which seemed to contain mainly legal text and folders labelled with the names of assorted voluntary agencies and government departments.

Today she looked like the woman who made all those public appearances: silver-grey coat dress, matching court shoes, the sheen of pearlised tights, the discreet touch of silver jewellery around her throat and on her ears. Even the hair was sitting in an ebony cap that no split end would ever dare to disrupt.

She closed down the laptop screen and ejected a disk. 'I hope you don't mind eating early. I've rescheduled my surgery for this afternoon.'

'Don't fix anything specially for me. I can always grab something on the way home.' Another niggling thought emerged in my partially comatose brain. 'You didn't stay down here because of me, did you?'

'Well, I could hardly leave you on your own. Imagine if we'd opened up the house again next month and found you decomposing in the front bedroom.'

A spasm of pain twisted the immaculate make-up as the

import of what she'd just said brought to mind another body – both alive and dead. She recovered with another of the brave-little-trouper smiles and said, 'I have to eat anyway. You're more than welcome to join me.' I hesitated. 'Please stay, Grace. There's something I need to discuss with you.'

My conscience doesn't allow me to refuse meals more than once. Perched on a kitchen stool, I watched my sheets spinning and Faye whipping up some kind of savoury potato pancakes with warm salad. From a girl who couldn't peel a spud, she'd come on amazingly.

There was a portable TV on the corner of the work surface. She used the remote control to surf the channels until she found a local-interest programme. The diphtheria scare was still the number-one story, although no new cases seemed to have been detected. Nonetheless, the camera panned down queues at the local clinics and doctors' surgeries that had stocks of the vaccine.

'You'd think they'd have had the sense to have those children immunised as babies,' Faye said, muting the television before shaking a pan of crisping pancakes and flipping them with a wrist-action that would have got her a job at Pepi's, no questions asked. 'Thank the Lord mine have had all their shots.'

'How are they? Your daughters, I mean,' I added hastily in case she thought I had the slightest interest in her first-born.

'Having a wonderful time. I spoke to them on the phone last night. I'm joining them in Scotland next week. With my husband. As a matter of fact . . . that's what I wanted to talk to you about.'

She flipped the food on to plates. Three of them. And set one to keep warm in the oven.

'There doesn't seem to be any progress in Luke's case. At least, as far as we can gather from the press reports. Of course I know they only release a fraction of the information, but I can't ask, you see. It's not even in my constituency. And if I were to make enquiries, no matter how discreet—'

'It could trigger off the very sort of questions you're trying to avoid?'

'Yes. That's it.'

'Then why not just keep your head down?'

'Because I can't. Because I have to *know*. If someone you'd loved had died in a particularly brutal way, wouldn't you want to know why? I need to make some sense of this, Grace.'

'Sure. But I don't see what I can do.'

'You're a private investigator. You must have contacts. In the police or somewhere? You could ask around.'

'I could. And I'd be told to get lost.'

Faye considered this whilst she poured two glasses of fizzy water and added ice and lemon. 'Then perhaps you could find out yourself who killed him?'

'The police investigate murders. Any private investigator with an ounce of sense stays well clear.'

'Why?'

'Because a murder indicates that there is someone around who is prepared to kill. Sticking your nose in their business is a good way to hack them off. Believe me – I know. My last venture in that direction left me tied up in a car boot and heading for oblivion over the North Bay cliffs.'

This glimpse of life in the raw seemed to have shocked my hostess into silence. I forked up pancakes greedily as my body demanded replacement calories for all those it had missed out on since Tuesday.

Faye ate with more daintiness. 'Couldn't you just . . . find a few clues,' she said eventually. 'Point the police in the right direction?'

I tried to picture the scene. *'Excuse me, Officer, did you happen to notice that particularly distinctive cigarette ash in the footprints by the south window?*' Oh, yeah – the CID officers at Seatoun would love that!

'It really would be better to leave it to the police, Faye. They'll find him – or her – in the end.'

She sipped her water without smudging the immaculate lip gloss, and asked me if I had any idea how many murders *weren't* solved in this country. 'I sat on a select committee into the use of police resources. And the less the police find, the more they're going to dig around in Luke's life.'

So it wasn't just a need to know who'd taken Luke away. There was a good dose of self-preservation in her desperation. 'I thought you said no one knew about you and him.'

'They don't. As far as I know. We were so careful. We met at different places. Made sure we weren't followed. If we were travelling together, it was always on his motorbike.'

A mental picture of the garage at Brick Cottage flashed into my mind. 'Because you could wear a helmet.'

'Who would have guessed it was me behind that visor?' Her eyes sparkled and the woman momentarily peeped out from behind the professional mask. 'It was fun. We did all kinds of silly, impulsive things. Hamish never does anything on the spur of the moment; it's the lawyer's training, I suppose. Every decision weighed, evaluated, judged. I'd become the same.' She frowned into the distance. 'It's strange how you can change and not even know it until you see yourself reflected in someone else's eyes. When I realised Luke was attracted to me, I took a long, hard look at myself . . . and I just couldn't understand why. What could he see in a middle-aged woman who'd become so obsessed with presenting the right image, professionally and socially, that all the spontaneity had gone out of her life? I love my Hamish; he's been a rock, I couldn't have managed without him. But Luke brought joy back into my world and I'll always love him for that. *Always.*'

'But you'd decided to break up?'

'It was the sensible thing to do. I had my children, and Luke had his whole life ahead of him. I wasn't so naïve as to imagine he'd still feel the same way in ten years' time.'

Make that five, my cynical little demon whispered.

'He'd probably have wanted children of his own eventually. Letting him go now was the loving choice. He'd have found someone else . . . someone of his own age.'

And unless Faye was a saint, a piece of her would have been hoping he'd compare every twenty-year-old he ever slept with with her – and feel he'd got the rotten end of the deal.

'I can't afford the scandal, Grace. I really can't.' She took my empty plate. I looked round hopefully for signs of pudding. 'Apart from the effect it would have on my private life . . . there's my career. I've worked hard to get where I am. I don't intend to lose it.'

'Would it be such a big deal?' I asked. 'I mean, politicians with something on the side are practically the norm these days. It doesn't seem to make much of a dent in their image.'

She served me a small dish of fresh peach slices but took none for herself.

'Those were men. Let me give you a tip here, Grace – in case you ever decide to go for a public career yourself. Forget all-female steering committees, high-profile foreign jaunts and cabinet appointments. When a middle-aged female MP is caught out having a bonk with her toyboy and her family line up to appear in cosy shots for the Sunday papers and tell the world the marriage is as solid as ever – whilst the party leaders rally behind her to say what a marvellous job she's doing for the country and her private life is her own business – then you'll know that women have achieved *real* equality in politics.'

'That's a bit cynical, isn't it?'

'No. That's totally realistic. If my affair with Luke becomes public property, then my marriage and my career are over. At least in their present form. I'm not saying I wouldn't be able to salvage something. But it wouldn't be what I have now. And I want to hold on to what I have. Coffee?'

Without waiting for my answer, she took a foil package of ground from the cupboard. It was new too. She must have done a major shop when she realised she was going to be stuck here playing nurse for a while. My conscience pricked. I told it to mind its own business.

Slicing the top off, Faye took a deep breath of the released aromas before spooning coffee into the cafetière. 'He loved ground coffee.'

A couple of tears spilt over the top of her bottom eyelashes. Grabbing a sheet of kitchen towel, she dabbed daintily, careful not to smudge the make-up. 'It's hard, you know,' she said. 'I was being good; strong. Until I opened that damn newspaper. It was all right, you see – when I could imagine him out there somewhere. Living his own life. Without me . . . but going on . . . being whatever it was he wanted to be. But now . . . I have to go up to Scotland next week and play happy families, and pretend everything's just as it was always was. When it's not, and it never will be again. And I can't even talk to anyone about it.'

'Except me.'

'Yes, well you knew anyway, so there's not much point in being secretive now. And I'm grateful for that, having someone to confide in. Even if you won't help me any further.'

What could I do? The conscience was sticking needles in like a demented acupuncturist. I heard myself saying I'd ask around and see what I could pick up on the murder.

'But no promises, mind? The police really don't welcome amateurs sticking their noses in.'

'I understand. Anything you can do will be very much appreciated. And I'll pay your normal fees, obviously.'

Obviously.

We both heard the sound of the front door lock turning. 'Don't say anything to Peter.'

'Not a word.'

'And you won't forget those negatives?'

'No problem.'

(Well, one big problem, actually. I couldn't think of any good reason why Barbra should want to hand them over to me. And if I started to ask after them, she was fly enough to take a closer look to see what the attraction was. Who knows . . . maybe if she looked long and hard enough, even she would recognise Mrs X.)

Faye was ostensibly retrieving his warming lunch from the oven when Peter sauntered in and we did the hi-how-are-you-feeling-much-better-thanks routine.

She kept her head turned away as she juggled setting the pancakes on the salad and dabbing with more kitchen towel. I knew she was crying. Peter knew she was crying, although he was pretending not to notice. I knew why he was pretending not to notice. The whole thing was beginning to give me another headache.

Blowing her nose noisily into the towel, Faye said in a barely trembling voice, 'Can you give Grace a lift home this afternoon, Peter? I don't think she should cycle that far. She's bound to be a bit woozy still.'

The silence of his non-answer was enough to make her look round in surprise. Incautiously she lifted her head so he could see the lighter patches where her tears had washed away halfmoons of foundation below the lashes. At least he could have done had he been looking at her. But he was staring beyond her, towards the windows.

'Peter? Is something wrong?'

We both instinctively tried to find something odd about the perfectly ordinary street scene framed between the blue-chequered blind and the smudged grey windowsill. There was nothing I could see.

'I was wondering,' Peter said, 'why Grace was famous.'

'Am I?'

'Apparently. Or perhaps you're simply notorious.'

He indicated the muted television. I looked. And then looked again. My face was filling the screen. It was a slightly younger me, with longer hair and less peroxide, but definitely yours truly. I thought I recognised it as the picture from my police personnel file.

Peter flicked the remote control and the announcer's voice boomed over the whirr of the spin cycle on the washer.

'. . . The police are particularly anxious to speak to Grace and anyone with information on her current whereabouts should ring their local police station or Seatoun CID office on . . .'

27

'So what's the plan here? Do we hijack the cross-Channel ferry and tell him to head for Rio? Or will you spill your guts and cop a plea?'

'I think that's an American arrangement, Peter. We don't do that in downtown Seatoun.'

'Just trying to lighten the mood. You look like you're facing the Lord of Death's icy breath. That's Oscar Wilde, by the way. *The Ballad of Reading Gaol*. I was up for that part once.'

'Stage or film?'

'Deodorant advert. Didn't get it. The director was an ignorant S.O.B. who thought Oscar should talk Thames Estuary. Know wha' I mean, darlin'?'

He flicked the wipers and windscreen wash on. They swished in a desultory fashion over the glass before clearing it to give us a view of the squat, soulless building that housed Seatoun's police. I'd ended up having to accept a lift back because as soon as I'd retrieved the bike from Faye's garage, my legs had told me she was right. There was no way I could have cycled.

My first instinct when I'd heard that the police were looking for me had been to make darn sure they didn't find me. Then common sense had kicked in. I hadn't done anything wrong – well, not recently. It had to be some kind of mistake. I had to call the Law.

But I intended to make contact on my own terms. I'd have marched into the front office of the station accompanied by a lot of self-righteous indignation and my lawyer – but I didn't have either – so I had to resort to Plan B, viz., use any edge you can get.

'Ask for DCI Jerry Jackson,' I instructed Peter. 'Say you need to speak to him personally. About Luke's death. And block the sender number on your mobile.'

'Already ahead of you.' He dialled with one thumb whilst I watched the sun sparkling on the ocean. From up here (illegally parked on double yellow lines), we had a good view of the deeper grey swell bucking and rising beyond the small harbour wall. The storm cycle had passed whilst I'd been making out with the botulism bugs, and the British summertime had reverted back to another run of sunshine-filled, breeze-fresh days. It was almost spooky.

'I'm through,' Peter whispered. He held the phone against my ear for me to confirm that it was Jerry's voice calling: 'Hello? Is anyone there? Who is this?'

Nodding at Peter, I slipped out of the car, ran across the road and fronted up the constable on the reception desk.

'Grace Smith. Jerry Jackson's expecting me. Hurry it up, will you, I haven't got all day.'

Luckily he was green and easily intimidated. He also didn't react to my name. So much for being notorious.

Rather than send someone to collect me, Jerry came down personally. I was touched. Jerry was annoyed.

'Are you all right? And where the devil have you been?'

'Fine. In bed. Next question?'

'Do you have any idea of the trouble you've caused me?'

'No. How come I'm featuring on the most-wanted list?'

'Grace, you are not wanted by anyone. Particularly me. I'm quite busy enough without this.'

'I was on the telly. I saw it. Anyone who's seen me to contact you lot.'

'Did you listen to the entire broadcast?'

I admitted to missing the beginning.

'Pity. You'd have found out we were worried about you. "Missing in worrying circumstances" was the phrasing we used.'

'Who's worried?'

'Your namesake, the other Miss Smith.'

'Annie?'

'Quite so.' Jerry's voice took on a sharper edge as he told me he'd appreciate some straight answers. 'I've wasted a lot of valuable time on you in the past twenty-four hours, Grace. Not to mention having to pull in several favours at the local television station to get them to broadcast that appeal. I think the least you could do is come up with a credible explanation. Where were you?'

I was sprawled in his visitor's chair, doing my best to give it the cool, unconcerned, funky-chick attitude. Looking down at my hands, I found I'd twisted all his paperclips into a necklace. I guess I wasn't getting the unconcerned segment quite right.

Linking it over his pen-holder, I muttered that I'd already told him. 'I was ill. Food poisoning.'

'In hospital?'

'No. Friend's house.'

'What friend?'

'No one you know.' I stood up. 'Well, if that's all, I'll be off. Thanks for your concern and all that. But I'm a big girl now, Jerry. I can look after myself.'

He held out his hand to shake goodbye, and like a mug I took it. Once he'd got me pinned, he said, 'If there is anything wrong, Grace, the best thing would be to tell me now. I may be able to help.'

'Appreciate the well-meant lie, Jerry, but we both know that's not true. If I was mixed up in anything dodgy – which I'm not, incidentally – the best thing I could do would be to get myself an ethically challenged solicitor and lie like hell.'

I twisted free and made for the corridor. Jerry stopped me before I reached his door.

'Just a moment. There is something we need to ask you. Where were you last Friday?'

It didn't take a genius to make the connection. 'Luke's death? You can't think I had anything to do with that? I told you, I barely knew the bloke. And those other two telephone calls weren't from me. Believe me.'

'I'm trying to,' he said quietly. 'But you don't make it easy, Grace.'

'Did you ever find out where they came from?' I asked.

'A telephone box in Seatoun. On Friday night. Do you mind telling me where you were, Grace?'

I did a mental back-flip. 'I was in London Friday.'

'Can anyone confirm that?'

Well, Peter could confirm the morning, couldn't he? *MP's son in bizarre slaying mystery* – not quite the anonymity my new client was hoping for. And then there were the other tenants of the block who'd seen me breaking into Daniel Sholto's apartment. Or what about his bitch of a secretary, who was convinced I had the hots for her boss?

'Nope,' I said. 'Unless you count the several hundred commuters I ended up sharing sleeping space with at Victoria on Friday night. But we never really introduced ourselves. So if that's all . . .'

This time I did manage to reach the office door before he could intercept me. And found myself sharing the corridor with Frosty-face Emily.

She was ushering a middle-aged woman towards me. The

narrowness of the space meant I had to step back into Jerry's doorway again. Giving him the opportunity to whisper very quietly into my ear, 'Last chance, Grace. I want to help. Tell me what's going on.'

Leaning slightly backwards, I put my lips near his own ear and murmured: 'You first. Why are Customs and Excise asking after me?'

'Who said they were?'

So he wasn't going to play. 'No deal, Jerry. This confidence stuff works both ways. Nice playing verbal footsie with you again. And by the way, I'm glad we're getting cosier. You didn't ask me if you could call me Grace once.'

Frosty-face had reached reception and was showing her visitor out by the time we got there. Frosty said loudly: 'Lively-looking corpse, isn't she, sir?'

It was obviously directed at me. I hadn't a clue what she was talking about. Jerry enlightened me. 'That was Luke Steadman's mother Emily has just shown out.'

I felt illogically annoyed with Luke for lying to me like that. Heaven knows why I should have expected total truth from a sixty-minute acquaintance. I heard myself apologising to Jerry and assuring him Luke really had told me his parents were dead.

He held open the outer door and told me not to let it bother me. 'I gather the family had problems in their relationships.'

So did mine. But I didn't go around claiming my mum was dead. It occurred to me that his mother might provide a good lead on any enemies Luke might have – in addition to his nearest and dearest, that is.

She'd already disappeared. Peter seemed to have achieved the same trick. Faye's silver Volvo had gone. And with it, Vetch's bike. It was beginning to feel like that damn cycle had a life of its own.

I headed back into the town, with one eye open for the

car and the other scanning for Mrs Steadman's grey jacket and brown hair. The place seemed oddly busy even for a good day in the high season. The parking places along the prom were already taken, with other cars circling in the hopes of picking off a newly vacated space. I was nearly at the end of the prom walk when the hard blare of a car horn, followed by several more variations on the same theme from the motors forced to brake and swerve behind him, caught my attention.

Peter leant across and flicked the passenger door open. 'Hi. Sorry about having to split like that, but the yellow perils were on my case.'

I slipped in because unloading the bike wasn't an option here. Peter drove away purposefully.

'Where are we heading?' I asked.

'St Biddy's. I thought we could start our investigation there.'

'Sorry? *We?*'

'Why not? I could be the Watson to your Holmes. The Lewis to your Morse—'

'The Nit to my Wit.'

'Great; I've never had first billing before.'

My instincts told me to dump him now. But my muscles had other ideas. Even that short walk from the police station had left me more drained than I would have believed. The enervating effects of the bug and enforced fasting had wiped out my inclination to discourage a free chauffeuring service.

'Circle around the town again. I've some thinking to do.'

'Yes, ma'am.'

He threaded into the traffic nudging along the teeth-itching one-way systems. I helped myself to his phone and dialled the office.

'Where the hell have you been?' Annie's angry voice crackled from the mobile. 'And why didn't you let anyone know where you were going? I got back yesterday and found no one had heard from you since Tuesday morning. And it hadn't even occurred to this dipstick Vetch employs to man the phones that there was anything wrong with that situation. I even called your parents.'

'I rang them. Come to think of it, I left a message on the answerphone asking them to ring me back.'

'It's not working. There's just a load of garbled rubbish on it. I've had people chasing in all directions here looking for you.'

'I know. I've just seen Jackson. Thanks for caring.' I said it with sincerity and meant every syllable. I gave Annie the edited version of my trot with the trots (without specifically mentioning Faye) and asked after Zeb.

'He's on the mend, thanks,' Annie said, her tone slightly mollified. 'You'd better phone your parents, incidentally. I tried to keep it casual but think I might have spooked them. Are you coming into the office?'

'Later perhaps. Things to do. STOP!'

I cut off Annie's whimper of pain as her eardrum exploded and congratulated Peter on his reflexes.

'Do you have a death wish?' he gasped breathlessly. 'I only ask because that bus braked at least three centimetres from our rear bumper. I could take the scene again a fraction slower if you like. It will give us a better shot at being shunted into that rock shop.'

'A gumshoe's sidekick needs a thick hide and fast reflexes.'

'A rhino on speed would be your preferred choice, then?' Peter called as I abandoned him again and darted after a familiar grey suit. She was carrying a small tartan suitcase that she hadn't had at the police station.

'Mrs Steadman!'

She looked around her as if she wasn't quite sure I was yelling at her. Which, as it turned out, I wasn't. Luke's mum had remarried years ago. She wasn't Mrs Steadman, she was Mrs Bowman.

I offered sympathy and a vague relationship with her son. 'Are you driving back right away?'

'I don't drive. I'm getting the train. Change in London.'

'Have you got time for a quick coffee?'

'I could murder a cup of tea.'

'Terrific.' I steered her through the expanding crowds, leaving it to Peter to sort out how he was going to follow me.

Pepi's was rocking with chatter, laughter and Chubby urging us all to twist again. It wasn't the ideal setting for a spot of sensitive interrogation of a grieving mum. I'd have backed out, but she jostled forward, using her case to bag across a couple of window seats that were just being vacated.

I got the teas and two cheesecakes piled with mounds of desiccated coconut strands. 'Sorry about the noise,' I yelled.

'I like it. We used to dance to this one when I was in my teens. Seems like a lifetime ago. I look in the mirror and don't recognise the old bat staring back at me.'

She certainly didn't look anything like the teenage tease Atch had described. She'd aged badly, with deep lines from nose to mouth and poorly dyed grey hairs amongst the brown.

'How did you say you knew Luke?'

'Friend of a friend. Peter knows him better. They're both into films, acting, that sort of thing.'

'He was forever going on about being a film producer. Daft idea, my Roy thought. He wanted Luke to get a proper job.' She starting sawing the cheesecake in half, buttering the split sections with frowning concentration.

'Roy's your second husband?'

'Yes. Although I never really counted me first marriage. It was over before the confetti melted. I met him when he was stationed at the American base. Fancied him rotten in his uniform. But truth to tell, I married him to spite my mum. She was always trying to split us up. Said he was just a loser who'd never amount to anything. It's funny, I can hear myself sometimes saying exactly the same things to my Miranda my mum used to say to me.'

This didn't seem to be tying in with Luke's version of his childhood. My tentative suggestion that his dad had owned a meat company brought a snort of laughter. 'He never did. Drove a truck that delivered for them, that's all. Still does, as far as I know. I tried to stay in touch for a while. For Luke's sake. But he never showed that much interest. I suppose it's what with him and his wife having kids of their own.'

'Luke never lived with him, then?'

'Born and bred in Suffolk, same as the rest of my lot. He went out there for a couple of holidays. Stayed in their place in Chicago, but he didn't like it. The local kids bullied him; him having a funny accent as far as they were concerned.'

'I thought he'd experienced the wide-open spaces? Cowboy country . . . yeehah and all that?'

'That was the second time. We saved up. Bought him an air ticket so he could go camping with his dad. Had one of those camper vans, what they call them – Winnie . . .?'

'Winnebago.'

'That right. Hired one for a week.'

'One week?' So much for experiencing the wide-open spaces.

The jukebox displayed a previously unsuspected talent for irony by breaking into 'Red River Rock'. She started swaying in time to the music, humming the melody under her breath. And then caught my eye.

'I suppose you think I'm not behaving like a mum whose son has just died?'

I gave a noncommittal shrug.

'Truth is, I lost Luke a long time ago. I married Roy when Luke was five, and God knows, he tried to be a good dad. But Luke didn't want to know. Right from when he was little, he always acted as if he was better than us. Smarter, like. And he had a tongue on him. Used to say clever things and then sit there with this smirk on his smug little face. To tell the truth, it was a relief when he left home.'

'When was that?'

'Disappeared one morning when he was sixteen. Took all the money I'd put by for bills, and Roy's car. We never did get it back.'

'Do you know where he went?'

'London, I expect. He was always talking about going there.'

'You didn't try to find out?'

'No.' She took a mouthful of tea, using her thumb to clean off the smear of lipstick she left on the rim. 'I know that sounds hard, but we'd the other four by then and things between me and Roy were getting so bad that I don't think we'd have stuck together much longer. Once Luke had gone, it was like an infection had been removed from the house. All that scratching and tearing at each other stopped. We became a real family, the six of us. That makes me sound like a bad person, but sometimes you have to sacrifice one kid for the sake of the others.'

'Did you ever hear from Luke after he did a bunk?'

'Not until Uncle Eric died. That's the first we knew he'd been seeing him. He left the lot to Luke, you know. Me and my brothers were his only close relatives. No reason why he should leave it to us, of course. Like I said to Roy: we hadn't taken no notice of the old boy for years and he could leave his cash to anyone he chose . . .'

'And he chose Luke.'

'Yes. Wicked, isn't it, to hate your own son. But I did . . . Roy'd not worked for over two years and a bit of extra cash would have been a godsend. Roy's gone now – God bless him. That policewoman thought that if Luke hasn't made a will, me and his dad will probably inherit. His real dad, I mean.'

I started toying with wild ideas about checking the movements of a Chicago truck driver, and then realised the police would already have gone down that route. Just like they would have discreetly made enquiries about this woman opposite me.

'Have you been out to St Biddy's, Gillian?'

'The police took me to see if I could see anything unusual in the cottage. But like I said to that policewoman, how would I know – it's years since I've been out there. How did you know my name was Gillian?'

How did I? I searched my memories and came up with the Rouses.

'Harry Rouse! You're kidding. I used to fancy him like mad. How is he?'

'Not very fanciable,' I said truthfully. 'His dad said you tried to lead him astray.'

'Cheek!' She gave a sudden giggle and I glimpsed the girl she must once have been. 'I really thought I was the business: miniskirts up to my bum, enough hairspray to float the *Titanic* and false lashes like loo-brushes. I used to sneak out at night and Harry'd drive us to the discos in that old truck. Magic times. This number was one of our faves.'

Shane was doing serious damage to his knee joints behind the counter, grinding himself into the floor to the sounds of 'Twist and Shout'.

It was ironic, really, I thought. Gillian had turned into the drabby homebody Atch would no doubt have considered suitable daughter-in-law material. I had a brief fantasy of getting her and Harry together. Rosy pictures of the pair of them playing with the kids in front of ye-olde-farm-house-roaring-fire danced behind my eyes before reality placed a call and asked if I'd care for the last seat on the shuttle to Real Life? I refocused on Gillian. Nostalgia had opened her stopcocks in a way that her eldest's death hadn't. I started to panic. We were into that empathy moment that I dreaded.

It was lucky we had a window seat. It enabled me to spot Peter wandering like a lost soul and signal frantically.

'Sorry, boss, had to park miles away.' He slid in beside me and directed a two-thousand-watt smile at Gillian. 'Mrs Bowman, it's wonderful to meet you at last. Even if it is in these awful circumstances. Luke talked about you so often. I know how he deeply regretted the problems between you.' Reaching across the table, he captured both her hands. 'He felt terrible about the way the situation between him and his stepfather had caused you so much trouble.'

'Did he?' Gillian said. She was staring into Peter's eyes, almost mesmerised by them. 'You could have fooled me.'

'You were his stability, Gillian. He knew he'd screwed up, but he intended to make it up to you. It's tragic that he won't be able to now. But I want you to know we're here for you.' He bent her fingers into the palms of his own hands and gently stroked the bases with his thumbs. 'Whatever help you need, Gillian, Grace and I are going to be right there for you.'

Wow, was he good at the empathising. Gillian was lapping it up. I began to feel like a gooseberry.

'Now, is there anything, anything at all, that we can do, Gillian?'

'Well, em . . . this is going to sound real bad . . . but . . . you don't know if he left a will, do you? I wouldn't ask, honest,' she gabbled, her grip on Peter's fingers now turning her knuckles white, 'only with Roy gone and all the toing and froing to the hospital before that . . . We're so strapped for cash at home . . .'

'We understand, Gillian.' He released her left hand and softly stroked one cheek in a gentle gesture of comfort. 'I know he intended to make one. He wanted you to have everything if anything happened. Make up for all the times I screwed up with her, he said.'

'Really?' A flicker of hope lit up her tired face. 'Did he go to a solicitor? They'd have a copy, wouldn't they?'

'Not necessarily, Gillian. But we could look for it for you.'

'I couldn't ask you to do that.'

'It's our job. Right, boss?'

'In a manner of speaking. I'm a private investigator,' I enlightened her.

'I can't pay.'

'We wouldn't ask you to, would we, boss?'

For preference – yes.

'Heh, Gillian, this one is for Luke. We'll have to start at the cottage. You realise that?'

She nodded, scrabbling in the zippered pocket of the battered case to draw out a key. 'I took it when we went up there. The policewoman said it was really up to his executors, but I thought, I'm his next of kin, who's anyone else to say I can't go in my own son's place? I was going to go back and have a look round myself, but Miranda's not doing so well. She's a good kid, but she's only seventeen. The boys are playing her up. Missing their dad. I've got to get back—'

Peter's long, slim fingers closed over hers; he contrived to caress them as he drew out the key. It was a seductive gesture. But then let's face it, he was a seductive sort of guy . . . and I should know. Perversely, I asked Gillian if she was quite sure she wanted to hand over the key to complete strangers.

Peter threw me an exasperated look, before turning the charm offensive up to nuke mode. 'Luke was the best friend I ever had, Gillian. I want to do this for him. But if you feel you can't trust me, then I understand. Perhaps it would be best if you got a solicitor to sort things out. But promise me you'll get a proper quotation out of them. Remember, they're there to make money for themselves – not you. Will you promise me that, Gillian?'

'Yes . . . I promise.'

'And if they ask for a deposit up front, I want you to contact me. I've got a bit in the bank and you're more than welcome.'

'Deposit? You think they might want one?'

Peter raised helpless shoulders. 'If you had a will, it would be harder for them to string it out, of course, still . . .'

You could see caution and greed chasing each other around her face. Guess who won?

'Give her a card, boss. Let her see we're on the level.'

That was easy for him to say; he didn't have to pay for them. I'd only had a couple of dozen printed and I generally like to flash one and return it to my pocket. Now I had to give one up. I also heard myself weakly telling Gillian we'd do an inventory at the cottage whilst we searched.

We took her to the station and waited with her. The parting scene on the platform between her and Peter was like something out of *Brief Encounter*.

'Nice performance,' I said as he spun the cottage key one-handed and caught it. 'Very *simpatico*.'

'It's a gift. I can be all things to all women. And men, if I put me frock on.'

I'd nearly forgotten Rainwing until he said that. It was strange. He was so definitely masculine out of costume.

The road to St Biddy's was reasonably clear, but the incoming traffic was unexpectedly heavy. I said as much to Peter.

'The forecast is another mini heat wave over Bank Holiday.'

I'd forgotten it was the last break of the year. And an unseasonably settled one. No wonder the place was packed.

'How come you're so anxious to help out here, Peter?'

'Various reasons.'

'Name three.'

'One: Luke was my closest friend – and he really did want to make things right with his mother. Two: it gives me the chance to make good with you. Three: Luke had a rather unfortunate habit.'

'Cocaine? Heroin?'

'Poetry.'

I thought it was street slang for a new designer drug. Peter enlightened me.

'He wrote it. Used it to express his feelings.'

'Or who he was feeling?'

'Exactly. For all I know, there are whole epics in that cottage to my mother. And Luke's descriptive powers could be quite . . . crude, to put it kindly.'

'I thought he was supposed to love her? At least, she thinks he did.'

'What's that got to do with it? It's like a happily married man watching porno movies, isn't it? The one has nothing to do with the other as far as he's concerned. I'm going to feel a lot better when I've gone through his place and burnt any odes. Or anything else that might connect him with my mother.'

St Biddy's hadn't escaped the holiday rush to the coast. Cars were squeezed in along the main street but Cowslip Lane was clear apart from us.

Someone had left a bunch of flowers on the cottage step. They were already fading and desiccated, but such was superstition that no one would remove them until they'd rotted to nothingness.

Not so the junk mail. Half a dozen envelopes squeezed back with the opening door, but a larger stack had been picked up and stashed on the hallway table. The ones I could make out were all addressed to Eric Groom. It was oddly eerie seeing garish banners telling a bloke who'd been dead for three-quarters of the year that he'd definitely won a cash prize.

The strange atmosphere must have had the same effect

on Peter: he took the stairs two at a time, muttering about needing a slash. That left me to make the short trip from normal life to murder scene all by myself.

They'd left the curtains partially drawn in the back room. The furniture loomed from the shadows in vaguely sinister humps. It was amazing how your imagination can twist ordinary things into objects from your worst nightmares.

It wasn't cold in there, but an involuntary shudder went through me from skull to toes. A floorboard creaked behind me and I turned back to ask Peter if he could feel anything odd.

Something detached itself from the shadows behind the door and took form: arms, legs, body. And a grinning head half hidden by a baseball cap and designer sunglasses.

28

'Hi,' Carter said.

'What the hell are you doing here?'

'Just hanging out.'

'Behind the door? What are you . . . a coat-hook?'

'Heard you come in. Could have been burglars. I was going to make a surprise attack. Sort them out.'

'Why don't I believe that, Carter?'

'Dunno.' He took off the cap and glasses to reveal a forehead peeling with the effects of too much sun. 'What *you* doing here?'

'That's none of your business, kid,' Peter drawled.

He'd slipped silently back downstairs and was blocking Carter's route to the front hall. Not that Carter showed much inclination to leave.

'Who's he? Another investigator?'

'No,' I said.

'Yes,' Peter said. 'How did you get in?'

'Door was unlocked. I reckoned the police forgot last time they were here.'

'Have you been nosing around this place?'

'No.' Carter's fingers scoured more skin from his forehead, leaving a fresh pink oval between fringe and eyebrows.

'Don't feed me any bullshit, kid.'

'Get lost.'

I interrupted the machismo-rattling contest. 'I've a better idea, Carter. *You* get lost. But hand over the key first.'

'What key?'

'The police don't make those sorts of mistakes. Give.'

Peter hooked his thumbs into his belt. 'Want me to frisk him, boss?'

'No thanks. I can do my own frisking. Only in this case I think he'd probably enjoy it. Anyway, it won't be necessary. Will it, Carter?'

He held my eyes for another second and then shrugged, delved into his jeans pocket and produced a bronze-coloured key.

'Which door is it?'

'One through to the garage. Found it months back stuck up under one of the shelves. I reckon old Mr Groom put it there, case he locked himself out.'

'And you forgot to mention it to Luke?'

'Suppose. I never *took* anything,' he exploded indignantly. 'I just hung out. It's better than home. Anyhow, I thought you said it wasn't any of your business?'

I held up the key Gillian had given us. 'It's become my business.' The last thing I needed was Carter breathing down my neck whilst we searched the place. 'Just push off now and we won't mention the fact those look suspiciously like Luke's shades.'

'They're Armani,' Peter said. 'And that's his hat, too.'

'He gave me that. You know he did. For my birthday.' Carter appealed to me.

'Go, Carter. But hand over the garage key too before you do.'

With a heavy sigh Carter dug out another key and slapped it in my hand. 'I left some stuff around.'

'We'll post it on to you.'

'No . . . don't do that.' Alarm flooded amongst the freckles. 'I could help out. You going to find out who topped Luke?'

I'd have told him the truth – well, partial truth anyway – that we were tidying up a few loose ends for Luke's mum, but Peter got in first again.

'Need-to-know basis, kid.'

'Well, *I* know something. The police asked me loads. They asked me about the Sioux lance. One he used to keep in here. Is that what they used to kill him? I asked the copper but she wouldn't say.'

I didn't intend to either. 'The lance belonged to Luke?'

'Yeah. Kept it in a brass umbrella stand.'

I suppose that made sense. Few would-be murderers go hunting with a six-foot toothpick – unless their intended victim is a buffalo.

'What else did the police say, Carter?'

'Not much. They took some stuff from the house. Did all that crawling around picking bits up and taking photos, like on the telly, and they were asking people about when they last saw Luke. And then they just cleared off. One of them came back the other day, brought this woman with her. They went inside for a bit and then she – the woman, I mean – stood around in the garden and cried. She never went in the garage though. Was that Luke's mum?'

'Probably.'

'Now beat it.' Peter started to propel Carter towards the front door via a grip on his shoulder. It opened before they reached it. Kelly Benting's eyes widened in alarm. 'Oh!'

'It's OK, Kelly,' Carter said, twisting himself free. 'He

works with her. Private investigations, remember? I told Kelly about you. No secrets now we're together.'

'Very new man,' I said, looking Kelly over.

To my eye she'd lost a few pounds, but it might have been just the illusion created by the wide-legged drawstring pants and baggy top. Her face was definitely paler and the dark curls had lost their bounce to hang limply to her shoulders. Only her eyes had any sparkle. And I had a feeling that wasn't due to *joie de vivre*.

'You 'vestigating Luke, then?' she asked.

'Amongst other things,' I intervened before Peter could give her the benefit of his hard-nosed act. 'You got anything to contribute?'

'Me? No, why should I?'

She advanced a few more steps. There was no telltale smell on her breath, but I was certain she was either drunk or stoned.

'Hi, Carter. You miss me?' She snuggled her arms round his neck and hoovered out his mouth with her own.

'Yeah . . . right . . . We'd best push off now, Kelly.'

'I thought we were going to screw.'

'Kelleeee . . .'

You could see conflicting emotions chasing over Carter's face. Embarrassment was just about winning over pride at pulling Kelly.

'Pack it in, Kelly.' Carter was finding himself with more wish-fulfilment than he could handle. Desperately, he tried to unlock her arms from his neck whilst shuffling her backwards towards the door.

I advised him to watch her until the effects of whatever she'd popped wore off. 'That, or tell her parents so they can do it.'

'God, no!' Sheer terror ignited the flat features. 'Her dad would kill me. He'd think I got them for her. He thinks she's perfect. Well, she is, course. Kelly, come on.'

He tried to lever her over the step, but she twisted and

giggled in his grasp. The loose T-shirt sleeves slid towards her shoulders, revealing a circlet of yellowing bruises, like tattoos, around her upper arms.

Carter caught my eye. 'I didn' know girls were so soft,' he mumbled. 'I never meant to hurt her. I wouldn't ever do that. Let's go, Kelly. Pleeeese.'

'OK, Car'er. Did yer tell them about the woman?'

'What woman?' Peter asked.

'No one. She's off her head. Come *on*, Kelly.'

'Stay, Kelly.' I grabbed a wrist. 'Has this woman got something to do with Luke?'

'Yes,' she giggled.

'No,' Carter snapped.

'Is this something you've already told the police? Or something you'd like me to mention you failed to tell them?'

'Yes. No. It was hours before he died. It's got nothing to do with him getting killed.'

'Let us be the judge of that, kid,' Peter said.

If he said 'Spill your guts', I promised myself I'd scream.

'Spill your guts.'

I passed the scream off as a spasm of cramp.

'You were about to say, Carter? And I should do it before your girlfriend passes out on the step and we're forced to go get help from her father.'

'It was that afternoon. When we came up here and Luke gave me . . .' He flicked the cap peak. 'I told you about that. When we got here, the front door was open. It really was this time,' he added hastily. 'So we came inside. And Luke was arguing with some woman in the back room.'

'Arguing about what?'

'I couldn't really hear. Just that she wanted something and Luke wouldn't give it to her,' Carter said quickly. 'Soon as we realised it was all getting a bit heavy, we were going to leave. Only she started coming out, so we dodged inside the coat cupboard in the hall and waited until she'd gone. We didn't want it to look like we were eavesdropping or anything. And then we came out and knocked on the front door. Like we'd just arrived, see? Anyhow, it was hours before he died, so it doesn't count.'

'I daresay you're right. Don't forget what I said about keeping an eye on Kelly, will you?'

Carter received the 'get lost' message. With one of Kelly's arms around his neck and his own encircling her waist, he steered her down the path and displayed the better part of valour by turning right up the lane away from the village.

'So,' Peter said, closing the door behind love's young dream, 'who'd you reckon for the mystery broad?'

'How would I know?'

'Don't bullshit me, Grace. You figure my mother for the part, don't you?'

'Peter, is it my imagination, or are you turning into Dirty Harry?'

Sheepishly he grinned. 'I was trying for Mickey Spillane, actually. Sorry. It's a habit. I like to get inside the skin of a character. Walk it like they talk it.'

'Like you did with Daniel Sholto? Lies to order; scummy action optional?'

'I thought we'd called it evens on that? I conned you into bed – by your standards – and you kicked me out. Quits?' He held his hands up in a gesture of surrender.

'Not even sixty/forty, mate. And for your information, investigators don't generally strut around with a loaded piece, inviting punks to make their day. The idea is to be Mister Average and blend in with the crowd. Now, let's hit those mean streets and get on down.'

'Before we get started, come upstairs a minute. There's something I want to show you.'

'That's a hot contender for worst chat-up line of the millennium.'

'I'm not trying to come on to you, you silly bitch. Come look.'

He led me up to the back bedroom. It was plainly and unfussily furnished, with cream linen, polished floors and scattered rugs. Uncle Eric's taste, I had to assume. I would have liked it – if it hadn't been for the addition of a dozen roses disintegrating over the pillow cases, a bottle of supermarket wine and two glasses on the bedside table, and an overpowering musky scent emanating from a couple of candles.

'Your friend Carter's idea of sophisticated seduction,' Peter remarked. 'There's more.' He ducked under the bed and came up with a paperback entitled *How to Have Her Begging for More*.

'I guess it hasn't got quite the frisson of expensive champagne and cheap Shakespeare. But what the hell – the kid's young, he'll learn.'

Spitting on his fingers, Peter pinched out the candles. 'Keep harping on like that, Grace, and I'll begin to think you really care. Did you say something about hitting those mean streets?'

Or, in this case, we hit those mean rooms. Turning out drawers, crawling under furniture, looking into cupboards, opening boxes, unloading shelves, and generally nosing into all those little places that might conceal a will or sheets of purple poetry.

The strange architectural style had been continued internally. The lower rooms had tall walls and high plaster ceilings that created an optical illusion of narrowness, whilst on the upper floor I could easily put my hand flat against the ceiling, so that the rooms had a rambling feeling.

Luke had moved into one of the spare bedrooms rather than take over Great-Uncle Eric's. The clothes in the wardrobe were mostly designer labels, and the dressing table held an assortment of pricey men's toiletries. He'd also got a laptop computer and printer; a couple of remote-controlled video cameras; and a watch that – if genuine – hadn't left much change from a thousand pounds.

In the bathroom cabinet I discovered a large tube of instant tanning cream and a spray can of hair highlights. It was beginning to look like everything about Luke was fake – including Luke himself.

Most of the papers we came across were connected to Uncle Eric's life. The old boy had been a hoarder. He'd got letters, cards and bank statements harking back fifty-odd years. It was sad in one way and fascinating in another, tracking the life and times of Eric Groom from middle age to death. His statements showed two regular payments coming in each month. I did a bit of mental arithmetic and decided the smaller one was his state pension.

An equal amount flowed in the other direction. Uncle Eric had lived each month as if it might be his last, by the looks of it, and hadn't bothered with any future rainy days. The last statement sheet hadn't been filed; I found it crumpled in the base of the envelope. It was dated this June and showed a steadily increasing balance that was explained by the fact that the larger payment was still being credited in but nothing was being paid out.

A deduction that was rather confirmed by continuing demands from the utility companies over the past eight months that had culminated in threats of legal action and disconnection. It looked like no one had bothered to tell them Uncle Eric was now in a place where not even the bailiffs could reach him.

The only letters I found addressed to Luke were from a classic car restoration company who'd billed over three thousand pounds for work on the MG, and realtors in the States providing details of office space to let.

'He really was living this fantasy of moving to the USA, then?' I asked, dry-washing my hands of grime and cobwebs. 'Has the bloke ever spent more than four weeks out there in his entire life?'

'Sure. He did film studies in New York.'

'You mean that wasn't another one of his fantasies?' On his previous form I'd translated the 'film studies' into a weekend at the flicks in Manhattan.

'No. In fact, that's how we met.'

We'd come full circle back to the hall and were perched side by side on the bottom stair. Peter drew his legs up and rested his heels on the edge of the tread, embracing his knees. 'I went over to tout my arse around Broadway – figuratively speaking. Ran into Luke. We shared a place for a few months.'

'Did you get any takers?'

'No.' He stood up. 'I couldn't get an agent without a green card. Couldn't even begin to get on the bottom rungs of the green card lucky dip without an agent on my case – catch twenty-two. Fancy supper? I'll cook.'

I checked my watch and was startled to find I'd been rooting for nearly five hours. 'Is there anything *to* cook?'

'There's some cheese and eggs in the fridge. Past their sell-by dates, but they look OK to me.'

I popped into the loo while Peter went off to get domestic. On the way back, I guiltily remembered I was supposed to have called my parents to reassure them I was still in the land of the living. I was evidently going to have to do it from somewhere else: the phone was dead. I tried cadging another call on Peter's mobile.

'It's in the car. Do you want to fetch it?'

'Later.'

Straddling a chair in the kitchen, I watched whilst Peter whisked eggs and grated cheese. He had his mum's brisk competency with a recipe, but his movements were more graceful and fluid. Almost feminine, I found myself thinking. Until I recalled that for periods of his life this bloke *was* a woman. I erased Rainwing and concentrated instead on her *alter ego*'s masculinity. He'd pushed up the sleeves of his jersey to cook. The muscles I remembered only too well were rippling along his arms. Stretching to retrieve the salt and pepper from a higher cupboard gave a glimpse of flat midriff. I was beginning to feel like a voyeur.

When he strolled outside and casually picked a few herbs to chop into the omelette mixture, I was really gone. All that and a real chef too. If only he wasn't a chronic liar who wore women's frocks, the guy would be pretty damn perfect.

He slid the omelettes on to warmed plates and suggested we eat in the lounge.

'Why?'

'Because we've both been avoiding it.'

That was true enough. Our joint search of the room had been done in total silence and a gritted determination not to mention the discoloured patches on floor and furnishings.

Thankfully, whoever had tidied the place up had rearranged some of the furniture over the stains. There were indents in the wooden flooring to show where the heavier pieces had once stood and the slightly darker geometric outlines of rugs that had been burnt into the wood by the bleaching effects of many years of sun. The chaise-longue had gone altogether, and the rest of the chairs and sofa had been repositioned to face away from 'that' spot and look out of the back windows.

We ate watching the midges dancing patterns over the blowsy back garden, and flocks of birds rising from the newly planted fields and swirling against the pink-tinged sunset like chocolate chips beaten into marble cake.

When I got bored with that view, I watched from under my eyelashes as Peter forked up softened cheese and perfectly cooked egg. And was embarrassed when he looked up and caught me doing it.

'Something bothering you?'

'I was thinking you don't look particularly Chinese.'

'Quarter Chinese – by birth. By upbringing, not at all. I

think Chinese was about the only nationality not represented at the commune.'

'Did you like it? Being brought up by strangers?'

'They weren't strangers. They were family, as far as I was
concerned. Extended; weird; funny; screwed-up, maybe.
But definitely family. More so than my real one.'

'I gathered you had problems with your grandfather?'

'No. In order to have problems, you have to have a
relationship. Grandaddy Chang simply refused to acknowl-
edge I existed. He behaved as if I was invisible. I was a
bastard by birth; he was one by inclination.'

'And that bugged you?'

'Wouldn't it you? When I was really young I didn't
realise I had a grandfather, so it was no big problem. Later,
after Mother and Hamish hooked up and my sisters came
along, he started turning up at family gatherings. Which,
when you think about it, showed a breathtaking arrogance,
considering he'd literally thrown my mother on to the
street. She should have told him to get lost.'

'Why didn't she?'

'I never asked. But I guess because he *was* her father. You
can dump other halves, but it's not easy to split with your
parents. It's not like you can divorce each other. So Old
Man Chang turned up for Christmas, birthdays and
Chinese New Year, and everyone pretended he'd never
been away. He always brought presents for the girls.
Mother would buy me something so I shouldn't feel left
out. She used to pretend it was from my grandfather at first,
but that rather fell down when he ignored my attempts to
thank him. After a while, we both got caught up in this
stupid game of seeing which of us could ignore the other's
existence best. I guess he won in the end. When he died six
years ago, he made a point of listing the rest of the family in
his will – even Hamish – but not one word about me.
Game, set and match to Grandaddy Chang.'

Levering himself from the large leather club chair, he

walked across to the light switches. The wall sconces glowed softly but the central fixture remained dark. I craned my head back to peer under the shade. 'There's no bulb.'

Switching it off again, he reseated himself. This time he chose the sofa, next to me. His hand draped along the back behind me. It smelt of whatever herb he'd chopped into the eggs. Pretty soon now I was going to have to decide where I was going to sleep tonight. And with whom.

'Do you ever see your real dad?'

'Never. My mother wanted a clean break.'

'You're not really twenty-nine, are you?' I said, recalling that brief hesitation in Sholto's flat.

'I'm twenty-four. Daniel is twenty-nine.'

'Staying in character, eh?'

'Yep.' He leant a little closer. This was turning into a rerun of that evening in Daniel Sholto's flat. All it needed was the poetry.

His lips were practically touching my cheek. I could feel his breath teasing over my flushed skin. This was crunch time. Self-respect or sex?

'Grace?'

'Mmm . . . ?'

'Can you hear anything under these cushions?'

I bounced a little more weight forward. The crackle of paper sounded clearly.

It was stuffed way down the back. Deep enough for us to miss it on our hasty earlier search. Peter wriggled the padded envelope free. The address label had been ripped off, leaving a jagged patch of the inner filling to crumble away.

'It feels pretty substantial. Like books.'

'Perhaps Luke wrote a volume of poetry to your mum. Or – with any luck – a diary listing all the people who might want to kill him.'

It was neither. Two videos fell out. They had crude hand-printed labels: *Whiplash Wendy* and *Naughty Night Nurses*.

'Well, well. Naughty old Uncle Eric,' I said lightly. 'Or Luke?' We were kneeling face to face, leaning on the sofa's cushions. *Déjà vu* swept over me again. And I wasn't even high on champagne this time.

Peter shook his head. 'Not really Luke's style.'

I picked up a video. 'Ever acted in one of these things?'

'Never been asked.'

I snuggled a little closer. 'Fancy auditioning?'

Peter didn't respond in kind. In some way he seemed to have pulled away from me. The intimacy that had been growing before our discovery had gone. Don't tell me he was embarrassed? Or did he have a hang-up about women and adult videos?

'I should be getting back. Mother will need the car.'

'Fine,' I said coolly. 'Do you want to meet back here tomorrow?'

'I think we've pretty well exhausted the possibilities of wills and odes, don't you?'

'There's the inventory to finish off. And Luke's murder: don't you think your mum might ask how we're getting on with that?'

He returned the videos to their envelope. 'Not me, she won't. I'm not supposed to know about her toyboy, remember.'

'True.' Junking the dirty plates and cutlery on a side table, I scrambled up. 'Can you drop me back in Seatoun? I don't fancy the bike in the dark.'

'Yes. Sure. Let's go.'

He already had gone. Far away. It was like sitting next to a stranger on the short ride home. I couldn't figure out what had gone wrong. As soon as the glow of Seatoun's garish neon lights appeared on the horizon, I told him to let me out here. He unloaded the bike without another word.

'To hell with him,' I said to no one in particular.

I free-wheeled through West Bay and down to the wide promenade that bent around the coast towards Seatoun. It was dark along this section, with just the flash of fluorescence on the black sea to illuminate the 'No Cycling' signs, and the perpetual hush and swish of waves over the shingle to provide a counterpoint to the squeak of the left pedal.

I took the ramp up off the prom and cut inland, heading for my flat. For the first time, I found myself privately admitting that I didn't really want to go home. After Faye's house and Uncle Eric's cottage, a partially trashed flat held limited appeal. Did turning thirty activate the gene that made cruising B&Q comparing paint charts on a Saturday afternoon suddenly seem an attractive deal? It was a worrying thought.

The first thing I saw when I drew into the kerb was the tub of highly desirable Tierra Caliente succulents. Despite being so highly desirable, nobody had nicked the damn things.

The second thing I saw was the police car.

29

It was Jerry Jackson's own car. Which rather suggested I wasn't about to be invited to the station to answer a few more questions on Luke's death. Chief inspectors don't provide a personal chauffeuring service unless you're a high-profile serial killer or a relative of the Chief Constable.

I dismounted and glided along the pavement with one foot on the off-side pedal. 'Hi. You waiting for me or just doing a spot of kerb-crawling?'

I regretted that last crack as soon as it came out. Jerry wasn't the sort of bloke you swapped sexual innuendos with. It wasn't that he was strait-laced, just – grown-up, I guess.

'Can we talk, Grace?'

'Sure. Come in.'

'I think it might be best if I didn't. Why don't we drive out somewhere for a drink?'

From anyone else I'd have assumed it was the beginning of a clumsy pick-up. But that wasn't Jerry's style.

'OK. Let me dump the bike. Won't be two secs.'

'There's no hurry. I'll hang on while you change.'

That one hadn't occurred to me. Now I suddenly felt like something the cat had not only dragged in, but buried, dug up, and rejected in favour of week-old Whiskas. 'Make it five minutes, then.'

Somehow I couldn't see Jerry chilling out in the coolest bar scene around town. In the end I settled for my second-best pair of jeans with the flared bottoms and flowery inserts, and a man's blue shirt I'd got from the dump bin at Oxfam. They proved to be a good choice for the country pub we ended up in.

The bar was busy enough to be sociable, but not full enough to be uncomfortable. Which meant we'd be able to talk freely without being overheard. We both had orange juices. Jerry ordered a chicken sandwich. In response to an enquiring eyebrow, I shook my head: 'No thanks, I've eaten. So, what's this about, Jerry? Why the tour of the countryside?'

'I thought it would be prudent for us not to be seen together. Let's move over there.'

He indicated a table by the brick fireplace that had just become vacant. I obediently trotted after him and hitched up a tapestry-covered stool.

He took a sip of the freshly squeezed (i.e., reconstituted) juice, before saying abruptly: 'You remember asking me why Customs and Excise were interested in you? Do you honestly not know?'

'Why else would I ask?'

'It might have been a bluff. A pretence of innocence.'

'I am innocent. Well, of whatever it is Customs are accusing me of anyway. What is that, by the way?'

Jerry seemed to be weighing up his options.

'Come on, Jerry. You've broken the rules this far. Be a devil and go the whole way.'

He nodded – to an internal voice rather than me. 'You know about the illegal immigrant operation? Please don't pretend otherwise, Grace,' he added before I could. 'It's just wasting time. I'm aware that Zeb will have spoken to his sister and his sister will have spoken to you.'

'OK, I know about it. So?'

'A certain number of phone taps were applied for. Including on those in the offices of – well, let's just say someone with serious connections to this unpleasant business.'

'And?'

'Your name came up. There was also a description which made it fairly certain you were the right Grace Smith. A tall, skinny blonde with a mouth on her, I think was the exact wording.'

'Yep, that would pin it down to me, wouldn't it? Where did this call originate?'

'Public telephone. Public house.'

'Local?'

'St Bidulph's-atte-Cade.'

'Did you trace the caller?'

'No. The reception was very poor. It's not even clear if it's a man or a woman. However, they did extract one partial phrase: "she connected with the last shipment".'

'News to me.'

'Is it?' He wiped the grease from his fingers with a red paper napkin. 'There was something else. A suggestion that you could be bought off . . . Were you?'

'There was nothing to buy off.'

I could see where this was going. My departure from the police had been precipitated when I inadvertently provided an alibi for a local villain who subsequently turned out to have been involved in an operation where another officer had been seriously injured. I know I should have owned up, but by the time anyone found out just how badly that other officer had been hurt, it was too late. I'd frozen and stuck to my original story. I don't know whether I was deliberately set up or not, but to add to the suggestion of corruption, several thousand pounds had mysteriously appeared in my bank account shortly afterwards (and yes – I did keep it). The point is, that operation had been a joint one with Customs and Excise too. It would seem that it wasn't just the police who believed in giving a bitch a bad name, et cetera.

'If you have got yourself involved in something ... unethical, let me help, Grace. Tell me now and I'll do what I can.'

'Look, I appreciate the offer, Jerry, and the fact that you've stuck your career on the line here, but I honestly haven't a clue what you're talking about.'

We held eye contact for a few more seconds. Then he shrugged and said: 'If you say so. Shall we go?'

It was a twenty-mile drive back. The sea hushed softly to our right. A few hundred years ago this area had been under the waves, but over the centuries the coastline had silted up, and now we were cruising through waterlogged marsh flats with the moon glinting off pewter pools amongst the reed-pierced islands.

Jerry reached over and snapped the radio on. 'Do you mind?'

'It's your car.' I was aware that had come out rather more off-hand than I'd intended. There was a pair of tiny leather football boots dangling from the switch. To make amends I asked: 'You play?'

'My son does.' He flicked the boots. 'His first try-out for the Seatoun Minnows Under-Fives Playgroup tomorrow. Otherwise known as the Milk-Teeth Marauders.'

'Great.' That was the extent of my social chit-chat. We rode the rest of the way in silence, listening to jazz on Radio Two.

Once we reached Seatoun, Jerry drove past my door, his eyes scanning the pavements. To make sure he wasn't spotted consorting with the notorious Ms Big of the Meat Trade, presumably. I told him to drop me off in one of the back streets. I thought that was the end of it, but as I was about to walk away, he called through the window: 'Grace. Have you got something to write on?'

I located an advertising flyer for a pizza place in my shoulder bag. Jerry passed me a pen and reeled off his mobile number. 'Call me. If you want to talk.'

'I've already said it all, Jerry. But listen, thanks again. Wish the kid luck from me. Hope he scores a hat-trick.'

'That seems unlikely. He's in goal.'

I went to bed feeling good that night. OK, the down side was that Jerry Jackson thought I was a closet smuggler – but at least he'd cared enough to break the rules for me. And anyone who knew Jerry knew just how much that meant. I resolved to return his pen, which was currently in the bottom of my bag.

Huddled in my makeshift bed on the floor, I mulled over the puzzle of who would phone from the Royal Oak about little ol' me.

Come to think of it, they could have used the phones in the Bell. It wouldn't be difficult to slip inside when the refurbishing team were elsewhere and help yourself to the public boxes. If it was one of the Bentings, they wouldn't even have needed to sneak in. Kelly's mum had a foreign-sounding name and an un-English way of speaking. Were they into introducing her fellow countrymen to the delights of the British countryside?

And then there was Luke: a bloke whose phone had been cut off and who didn't pay his bills but had enough cash to splash on expensive electronic equipment and his beloved sports car. And who'd died suddenly and messily recently. He hadn't inherited much spending cash from Uncle Eric if those bank statements were to be believed; the cottage hadn't been sold yet; and he didn't seem to have a job – just grand plans for a career in the movies – so where had he been getting his financing from? Perhaps he'd had a falling-out with the rest of the organisation. Or simply become too greedy.

I felt myself drifting into that dreamy state just before sleep. The police would hardly have missed the connection if it was there. And yet the whole investigation into Luke's murder had always seemed strangely laid-back. Had they been holding off on an arrest in order not to jeopardise the rest of the operation? If they had, what were Faye Sinclair's chances of keeping out of it? Slim to none, probably.

I woke at eight, still with that up-beat feeling that comes when you discover someone really likes you, and an irresistible craving for fried food, ketchup and frothy coffee.

The big news on the television was a series of raids that had taken place early that morning. An operation involving several hundred police, Customs and immigration officers. *'A number of arrests have been made in south coast towns, the Midlands and Home Counties,'* the breathy newsreader informed us. *'And quantities of drugs and firearms have been recovered. A large collection of persons believed to be illegal immigrants have also been held in the swoop. It is alleged that the origin of the recent diphtheria outbreak . . .'* With any luck they'd got the mysterious caller from St Biddy's and cleared my good(ish) name with Jerry.

I sloshed a bottle of water over the succulents on my way to the high street. The kiosk shops were just opening: buckets, spades, sandcastle flags, shrimp nets and jelly sandals were being piled into dump bins marked 'Special

Offers'. It was last-chance weekend before the town sank into the sub-arctic bleakness of low-season desolation.

Pepi's already had a dozen customers. Including Annie, who was halfway through an enormous All-British Fry-Up. I signalled to Shane to bring another plate of the same, and enquired: 'Late night or early start?'

'Bit of both. I drove Zeb over to my parents in the wee small hours of this morning. They discharged him once that container firm he was working in was raided.'

'How is he?'

'Recovering. Won't be returning to CID for a few more weeks yet, though. Mum was in her element pampering her baby when I left,' Annie said, forking up a generous portion of mushroom and black pudding.

'You still not back on the diet, then?'

'I have abandoned diets and men. I am now celibate, fat and happy. What have you been up to?'

Hitching up the chair opposite her, I brought her up to date on the Life and Times of Grace Smith – Not-So-Super Sleuth. In consideration of the big risk Jerry had taken on my account, I left out last night's tête-à-tête.

'It's time you got your life together,' Annie said, licking off a cappuccino moustache with the tip of her tongue.

'Thanks.'

We ate in silence for a while, whilst the jukebox crooned a selection of slower numbers that Shane considered suitable Sunday-morning music. Eventually I raised my voice over Elvis's protests that we gave him fever, and asked what she had planned for the rest of the day.

'I've got to go into the office. I'm working on a couple of Vetch's cases.'

'How come? What's happened to my favourite gnome?'

'In bed for most of the week. Together with the Delaney woman.'

'I didn't think the little letch had the stamina.'

'Food poisoning, you idiot. They've both had it. Dodgy seafood last Sunday.'

I laughed. With the horrors of my own bout of poisoning already fading, I could see the irony in the situation. For years I'd existed on junk food and warmed-up leftovers and I'd never had a single stomach bug. As soon as I hit the high life, I was pole-axed by botulism, or whatever the darn thing called itself.

'It's nature's way of telling you you were born to be common,' Annie remarked as we left to the strains of 'Blue Moon'. 'Talking of being born, I seem to be speaking to your mother more than I do to mine. You didn't call her, did you?'

'I tried. The phone was out. I'll come into the office with you. Do it now. It's closer.'

'And cheaper.'

She checked the answering machine whilst I nabbed Jan's extension to ring my mum. Our conversation was short – if not sweet. Once she'd established I was OK, she couldn't wait to get off the line. I could hear my dad's voice calling to ask who it was as she hung up on me.

'There's a message for you on the tape,' Annie said. She headed across the hall and let herself into Vetch's office. I listened to Barbra Delaney asking where the hell I'd been.

'. . . I've not heard a bloody word all week. I told you to keep in touch. When I spend money on something, lady, I expect to get what I've paid for. You get your arse out here and tell me what's happening, pronto.'

'Firstly,' I said as soon we were connected, 'you haven't paid me – yet. Secondly, if you want something that comes when whistled, try Battersea Dogs' Home. And thirdly, I haven't phoned you because you gave me food poisoning and half killed me.' Even though it was a good two days before I'd succumbed, it was too much of a coincidence for it to be anything else but Barbra's infamous aquarium à la Andreas that had pole-axed me.

'Oh? Sorry. It's shit, isn't it?' Barbra said. 'I didn't mean to mouth off at you like that. I was feeling rotten. I've been stuck out here all week on me tod. No one's been near except the doctor and a couple of calls from Vetchy.'

'No Lee?'

'No, but . . . Look, can you come out? There's something odd been going on.'

'Tell me.'

'I'd rather do it face to face.'

'Are you going?' Annie enquired when I relayed the gist of the conversation to her.

'I suppose I'll have to. She is paying the bills.'

'How lucky someone is.' Annie flicked through a sheaf of papers in front of her. She'd seated herself at Vetch's huge leather-topped desk and was making herself very much at home in his files. 'You don't seem to be. In fact, as far as I can see, I seem to be about the only person in this business who pays up on time.'

'Really?' I wished I'd known that earlier. I'd have held out for even longer. I looked Annie over. She was in casual sweats rather than her normal business suits; with her hair scrunched back and her face shiny behind the glasses. Nonetheless, she radiated efficiency as she pored over Vetch's accounts.

'Any chance of you putting the tycoon act on hold and giving me a lift to Wakens Keep?'

'Go tidy your pit upstairs for a couple of hours whilst I finish up here, and then you have a deal.'

'Cheers.'

We'd shut the main door because we weren't officially open on Sundays. I opened it to take a few breaths of sunshine-touched ozone before plunging into my least favourite occupation – housework.

The day-trippers were struggling down to the beach, lugging picnics and whiny kids. A couple of cyclists free-wheeled past, thigh muscles rippling and sweat crystals glistening on their hairy legs. (They were probably nice girls when you got to know them.) The window of a passing car was lowered as it came opposite our offices and a greasy sack with a motorway services logo was pitched out, spilling half-eaten burgers, polystyrene containers and paper beakers as it spun. It missed the rubbish bin – probably because the nearest one was fixed to a lamppost two streets away.

Perhaps it was the combination of those cyclists and the sack seen together, but fragments of memories started to crowd into my mind. They broke into pieces and then re-formed in my head, making new patterns. It was like watching a kaleidoscope spinning, taking the same segments of colours but making a completely new picture with them. I didn't like the finished result very much. But I had to check to see if I was right.

I sprinted the few streets to the flat, dragged Grannie Vetch's monster up to the road and kicked the pedals into position.

They'd finished the planting out around St Biddy's. Rows of cauliflower seedlings sprinkled the coffee-cake-mix-coloured earth like pale green hundreds-and-thousands. It didn't seem possible that they'd soon fatten up into plump little farm-subsidy magnets, but what did I know?

Harry answered the door to me. He was in his shirt sleeves; a stained tea towel flung over one shoulder.

'Can we talk?'

'About what?'

'Vegetables.'

He led me into the kitchen. There were old china bowls on the table containing peeled and quartered potatoes and cauliflower florets. A pile of scraped carrots was sitting on the chopping board.

'I was getting the dinner ready to go in. Do you want a cup of tea?'

'No thanks.'

'Best sit down, then. What's this about?'

'You remember that day I first came here and ended up in the barn? How did you get home?'

He started to cut the carrots into neat circles, slicing the blade towards the ball of his calloused thumb each time. 'I've a truck. Gave you a lift in it, remember?'

'But you didn't use it that day. You can hear a motor coming up that road of yours. Especially yours; it makes a bigger racket than mine.'

'So I got a lift to the end of the lane. What's it matter?'

I nudged the bowl of cauliflower. 'It matters because of this. You told me yourself you harvested your first crop six weeks back and it was taken straight to the wholesaler's. And you've only just put the next one in. So what the hell was a Timpkin's Farm Fresh delivery truck doing up here that day?'

'I don't know what you're talking about.'

'Come off it, Harry. It's a one-track, one-house road. Where else could it have come from? It was you who ran me off the road that day, wasn't it? When I – quote – "came into contact with the last shipment".'

He kept his back to me, taking a saucepan to the sink to run cold water into it. 'I waited to see if you were hurt. I'd not driven anything with that big a turning circle before.'

'First cargo, was it, Harry?'

He still wasn't looking at me. Fussing over the cooker, he muttered no.

'What went wrong this time?'

'The proper driver took sick. Laid him down upstairs for a few hours, but he just kept worse. I thought he was going to croak on me. I had to get them all out of here fast.'

I recalled the distinctive smell of diarrhoea that first day. I'd unfairly blamed it on Atch. 'So you stuck them in the van and dumped it somewhere.'

'I left them at a motorway service station and phoned . . .

someone . . . to tell them where to find the load. Hitched back. Had to walk the last couple of miles.'

'How long have you been doing this?'

'Eighteen months. I get a load every few weeks; except during planting out and harvesting times. Too many others coming and going then. I watch them, feed them, give them somewhere to sleep, until their papers are fixed up. Then someone comes, picks them up and takes them off. Don't know where. Never wanted to.'

'Why?'

He finally looked at me again. 'I needed the money. To get care for Dad. Dozens of arrests, they said on the radio. I've been listening all morning. Thought somebody would turn up eventually. Carter told me how you'd been trying to find out if I'd been in prison. I guessed you were undercover.'

I should have seen it as soon as Jerry told me about that phone call. It had all been there: that delivery truck when there was no delivery to be collected; the cupboard full of more food than the Rouses could possibly get through and all those tins carefully placed in the recycle bins well away from St Biddy's so the rubbish collectors wouldn't start to wonder about the amount of food consumed up here. And, of course, that bag of mints he'd brought home the day he'd freed me from the barn. It had had a motorway service station logo on it. And nobody gets to those gulags of loos, petrol and fast food on foot.

Harry gave me a slow, sad smile. 'What happens now? Am I going to get arrested?'

'Not by me. I'm strictly freelance. But if you were so sure they were on to you, I'm surprised you're still here.'

'Where would I go? This is my home. I don't want anything more than this. Never did.'

'You telephoned someone about me. From one of the pubs in the village. Who was it?'

'I don't know.' He turned from arranging two pork chops in a much-blackened pan. 'I've a contact number I had to ring if anything went wrong up here. I never knew who they were. Driver told me that's how they operate. What you don't know, you can't tell.' He was smearing lard and salt over the meat. There were no concessions to healthy eating in this household. 'They said not to worry about you. Said you could be bought off if necessary. I thought maybe they'd done it.'

I saw the flicker of hope behind the words. Perhaps he was half hoping I'd come up here in the expectation of being handed a plain brown envelope. But he didn't have one. And I wouldn't have taken it (I think). 'How did you get involved in all this, Harry?'

Quarters of potato were neatly arranged around the perimeter before he set the pan inside the oven and lit the gas. 'A woman came a few years back. After I started advertising for someone to help out. First off she asked about the job. Then later, she came back . . .'

'And suggested you might like to board illegal immigrants instead?'

'Said it was a chance to make easy cash. They'd a dozen or so other houses, all making good money. No one asks questions in this country. All too busy minding their own business. Nobody ever comes here except the casual when we're planting or harvesting. Apart from young Carter, you're the first visitor in five years.'

'What about Atch? Weren't you scared he'd say something?'

'Who'd believe him? He lives in the past. Who's to say who the strangers are he sees?'

That was true enough. He'd asked me whether the police were looking for 'the others' the night of Luke's death, and I'd put it down to his half-crazy ramblings.

'Was Luke involved in all this smuggling business?'

'No. Least, not that I know of. Why?' He seemed genuinely surprised by the question.

'Just seemed like a bit of a coincidence. Two unconnected crimes in one very small village.'

'Don't see why. Big towns don't have a monopoly on nastiness. How long do you think it will be before they come for me?'

'I have no idea.' He was plainly still entertaining the idea I was some kind of undercover super-plant.

Raising a spike-like instrument, he stabbed two holes either side of a tin of treacle pudding and put it in another saucepan before switching the kettle on. 'Sure you don't want a cup of tea?'

'Go on, then.'

He fetched three mugs. I tried not to mind the thick coating of tannin inside. 'Sugar?'

'No thanks.'

Two spoonfuls were heaped into one, three into the last. Milk from an open bottle went into two, but the well-sugared one received a large tot of whisky. 'Dad,' Harry said in answer to a question I hadn't asked. Going to a small cupboard, he took out a medicine bottle. Whilst I watched, he pulled the capsules inside apart and tipped the white powder into the whisky mixture. All twenty of them went in. A cold sensation started to crawl down my spine bones.

'I've done his favourite dinner. If they come for me before I can give it him, can you make sure he takes this lot. Just pour some tea on and stir it up. Give it him with his meal.'

'You've got to be kidding!'

'No.' Calmly he threw the empty capsule bottle into the bin. 'I told you. He'll not last in a home. This way's best. Don't worry. I'll say you didn't know what I'd put in the mug. Just wait until he falls asleep and come away.'

He was serious! He actually expected me to kill off his dad for him.

'I'm not doing it, Harry. Just forget it. They'll sort something out for Atch. You may not even go to prison.'

'All right. I can't make you.'

I was relieved when he gave in so easily. He made my tea and disappeared into the hall. A minute later he reappeared with the shotgun broken over his arm.

'What are you doing?'

Harry took two cartridges from his pocket and loaded the gun, snapping it shut with a decisive click.

'It's the only way now. I'd hoped he could just fall asleep.' He started to leave. I shot up, taking care to keep myself behind him. Grabbing his arm, I gabbled: 'Hang on. You're not really going to . . . you can't . . . he's your *dad*, for heaven's sake.'

'You think I don't know that?' He wouldn't look at me again. I was hanging on to a handful of shirt back. 'If he were a dog – old, sick, miserable away from home – would you put him in kennels?'

'He's not a bloody dog, is he? You can't murder your own father.'

'He won't feel anything. I'll put it in the head. Be quick.'

'You'll get life.'

'I've two barrels.'

'I can't let you do this, Harry.'

'You can't stop me.'

I intended to have a good try. Unfortunately he was a lot stronger than I'd anticipated. All those years of manual work on the farm had built up unexpectedly tough muscles. He might have won – but the sound of the cars brought us both to a frozen stop. We both knew. There was more than one engine and they were travelling far too fast for the single track. And all this for a bloke who never had visitors.

'Is there any evidence the illegals were ever here?' I said quickly.

'No. I cleaned up pretty well after them. There's just the food . . .'

'So you bulk-buy. Very economical. You've a chance. Say you don't know anything about it.'

A brief hope flared in his eyes. 'You think they'll believe me?'

'No. But they have to *prove* otherwise. Get rid of the gun,' I said. 'If you open the door holding a weapon . . .'

It was a very slim chance. They'd probably dig up something to charge him with. But he didn't know that. His head jerked in agreement. I released my hands. The shotgun disappeared amongst the collection of old wellies, coats and assorted household junk in the under-stair cupboard.

I recognised the leader of the Customs posse immediately. He'd covered the biceps with a suit jacket, removed the single earring and washed the grease slick out of his hair, but he was still instantly recognisable as the deliverer of the sulking succulents. His name was Wayne.

He was backed up by three more Customs officers, four uniformed police and – discreetly keeping his head down in the back car – Jerry Jackson.

Whilst Harry was going into his I-can't-think-what-you're-talking-about routine on the doorstep, I wandered over to lean down by the car window.

'You'll miss the kick-off, Jerry.'

'It's not until twelve – I should just make it.'

'What a coincidence, running into you here.'

'Give me your bag, Grace.'

It wasn't quite the approach I'd anticipated. But ever ready to oblige, I handed it over. Jerry tipped the contents into his lap and located what he was looking for – his pen. Silently he unscrewed it and held one section out to me. Nestling behind the foreshortened ink holder was a metal tube.

'Tracker?'

'And microphone. Electronics are amazing these days, aren't they? I'm told they've got one a quarter that size.'

'So much for putting your career on the line to help poor little Grace out.' I tried to keep it light, but I heard the shake in my voice and was horrified to feel a lump forming in my throat. All that matey taking-a-risk-and-giving-away-official-secrets-because-I-like-you-Grace palaver had been a great big act to spook me into tipping off whoever had phoned from St Biddy-atte-Cade. And I had been dumb enough to believe he really liked me.

'I hope,' I hissed at Jerry, 'that you got enough to confirm I knew diddly-squat about Harry being involved until an hour ago.'

'We did. And don't look so upset. He's a grown man. He made his own choices. And . . . Keep very still, Grace, and don't make any sudden movements.'

I was bent towards his open window. Now I cautiously glanced past my right shoulder and oh-so-slowly started to straighten up. Not that Atch was taking any notice of me. His attention was fixed on the uniformed officers. They in turn were mesmerised by the barrels of the shotgun.

'Take it easy, sir,' Wayne said soothingly. 'There's not going to be any trouble. Just lower the gun and let's talk.'

'Do as he says, Dad. Break the gun.'

Atch stared at his son, his eyes going from head to foot and back to Harry's face. 'Who are you? Get off my farm.'

'It's me, Dad. Harry.'

'Harry? Harry who? I want Madge. What have you done with her?' The barrels swung and a collective intake of breath and stomach muscles was taken by one and all. They came to rest pointing directly at me. 'Madge?' He took a tentative step forward. 'Madge, come here. It's all right, my lover. I'll take care of you.'

It seemed simplest to do as he asked. He wasn't going to shoot me if he thought I was Madge, was he? But as I went to move, Jerry reached out and clamped my wrist. 'Stay where you are, Grace.'

'You leave her be. Let go of my girl.'

The barrels dropped to car window height. His intention was presumably to fire into Jerry's head. The chances were he'd have taken out a good portion of my hip and waist at the same time. Neither of us found out. Harry stepped between us.

30

He died instantly.

He must have known they could never have charged Atch with anything in his mental condition, so either he was trying to save me – or he'd realised pleading ignorance wasn't going to work and he couldn't face prison. I like to think it was the former.

The shock of the blast and the blood sent Atch into a frozen state that made it easy for them to disarm him. The last I saw of him was his bewildered face staring through the back window of the police car that took him away.

I ended up back at Seatoun police station making yet another witness statement and congratulating my delivery boy on his performance. 'Very convincing. If a bit non-PC.'

Wayne was a medium-sized cheese in Customs and Excise who had hopes of becoming a king-sized Cheddar if this operation came off successfully. Easing his shoulders in a way that made his jacket seams gape slightly, he said, 'I was checking you out. Your place had already been trashed when I got there. Two seconds later the guy arrives with your plants. What could I do but claim to be G. Smith? I swear to God he talked just like that.'

'Do you think your newly redundant smugglers wrecked my flat?'

'Do you?'

I had to admit that I didn't know. 'Will you tell me if any of them puts their hand up to it?'

'In the fullness of time, no doubt.' (Which roughly translated as I'd read it in the Sunday papers after the trial.)

I pedalled back to the office to find Annie still stuck into the files.

'Hi,' she said, rising from a sea of paperwork spread over Vetch's office carpets. 'Is it that time already?'

'It is well past that time. I have been bugged by Jackson; helped to bust the last link in a smuggling ring; and just avoided having my profile radically altered by a shotgun – and you didn't even notice I'd gone!'

'Of course I noticed you'd gone. I just hadn't realised you were quite that far gone, frankly.' She scooped an armful of files and dropped them into the cabinets. 'Do you know, this place could have potential if it was properly organised.'

'Vetch thinks it is. Can it be that our esteemed leader is not quite the hot-shot business bunny he thinks he is?'

'He's missing out on a lot of work. Personal protection; electronic fraud . . . I must have a word with him. Talking of words, your client phoned again.'

'Which one?'

'You have more than one? That's not on the files.'

Too late I recalled that my arrangement with Faye was strictly on a personal basis. I fell back on Gillian Bowman. 'She asked me to see if I could dig up a will. Preferably one that leaves all Luke's worldly goods to her.'

'And have you?'

'Not so far. I doubt there is one. But I'll give it one last shot.'

'Fixed fee or hourly rates.'

'Aah.'

'I'll take that as a neither, shall I?'

'It's my business.' I was beginning to feel on the defensive. My best mate was turning into a power-crazed tycoon before my eyes. Within the year she'd probably be opening her own airline and flogging her own-brand cola drinks.

'It is at present,' Annie agreed, completing her clearance of the carpet. 'But if this place is to get ahead, it's something Vetch needs to address.'

'What do you care? You're planning to decamp to London anyway. I wonder,' I murmured, 'if you shouldn't go back on a diet? I really prefer you when you're fretting over the way your butt bulges in those sweat pants.'

It worked. 'Does it?' Annie twisted to see her own rear.

'A tad. Is that lift out to Wakens Keep still on?'

I half expected to be dumped in favour of a brisk three hours in the gym after that crack, but luckily she went for the comfort-eating option instead. We munched happily on a pile of chocolate bars stored in her glove compartment on the way out to Barbra's place.

'I thought you were never gonna get here,' Barbra said. It wasn't a protest; she sounded scared.

'Come through.' She led the way to the back of the house. One foot was held stiffly in front of her, the newly painted toenails separated by wodges of cotton wool. The pagoda where we'd all been served seafood salmonella à la mode had gone, but there was a set of white garden furniture on the terrace. 'Park your bottoms,' Barbra invited. 'Have a drink.'

There was a glass jug half full of iced tea on the table. Barbra had collected two more glasses on her way through the kitchen. She filled them two thirds full, ice cubes cascading noisily as she poured. We both took a mouthful and coughed in surprise. It wasn't just water she'd used to dilute the tea.

'Cheers!' Barbra sent half her own glass down on the first swallow and wiped her lips dry with the back of her hand. 'So, how's me job going? You found out who them people are yet?'

'One of them's dead, I'm afraid.'

'Which one?'

'Harry Rouse, the farmer I told you about. His dad shot him.'

She dismissed Harry's life with a casual, 'Yeah, Lee often has that effect on me.'

'Talking of Lee – any sign?'

'I ain't sure. You know I said there's been funny business going on out here?' She leant conspiratorially over the table. I was beginning to suspect this wasn't her first jug of iced tea, and from Annie's expression she'd come to the same conclusion. Still, it wasn't our job to stop the clients getting sloshed. 'Thing is, I've been getting calls . . .'

'Saying what?' Annie asked.

'Nothing. That's part of the problem. Nobody there when I pick it up. First off, I thought the neighbours were playing silly buggers, but I did that' – her finger jabbed a pattern on the white metal scrollwork of the table – 'on one of them.'

'Dialled one-four-seven-one?' Annie suggested.

'Yeah. It was some pub in Dover. I don't know anybody in Dover.'

I helped myself to another slug of tea and asked how long this had been going on.

'Not sure. Started when I was ill, I reckon. I had the answerphone on. There's half a dozen calls on there where they didn't leave a message. Don't know when they came in. I was too bloody ill to care.'

'I remember,' I said, lest she should forget I was a fellow sufferer. 'Have you heard from Lee since last Sunday?'

'Not unless he's the one making the funny phone calls. And I don't think he is. Not his style. Once he's spent ten pence on the call, he'd want to get his money's worth by giving me a mouthful.'

'Don't you think you should make a few enquiries? After all, three out of four of those who attended the luncheon from hell last Sunday . . .'

The alarm that filled Barbra's eyes didn't quite tie up with the couldn't-care-less parenting skills she'd been displaying previously. 'He could be lying sick somewhere? Trying to phone for help?'

'From a pub in Dover?' Annie asked.

Barbra relaxed slightly. 'No. I guess not. He'll be OK. He probably poisoned the bugs.'

She swirled her ice cubes and stared moodily into the whirlpool. It gave me the chance to study her. The illness had taken it out of her, deepening the lines around her nose and mouth and adding a yellowish tinge to her complexion. It was accentuated by her T-shirt and jeans which matched the tan shade of her nail polish.

Turning her attention back to it, she removed the cotton wool, inserted it between the toes on the other foot and resumed painting. 'So the bloke's history. What about them two women? You got the business on them yet for me?'

'Not completely,' I temporised. After all, I didn't have Peter's home address. Not that I wanted it. Just thinking about that brush-off yesterday made me go hot and cold. Or that was what I told myself. The old subconscious kicked into life and suggested perhaps that wasn't the only memory of Peter that was making me feel uncomfortably hot. In a way it was a comfort to find out that turning thirty hadn't stopped the mind recognising a potential bastard whilst the old hormones screamed, 'Yes . . . yes . . . yes – I'll have some of that!'

I became aware that Annie was giving me a funny look, and hastily asked Barbra if she still intended to go through with the will business.

'Why shouldn't I? Anyhow, I paid me deposit, didn't I? I'm entitled to me money's worth. Does *she* know about it?'

I felt Annie stiffen slightly at that 'she' and quickly said, 'The job. Not the legatees. You asked me not to flash the snaps around, remember?'

Barbra rested her foot on the spare chair. 'Listen, if you

two aren't busy, d'you fancy making an evening of it? Bottle of wine; video: girls' night in? You can sleep over.'

I'd intended to ask Annie to drop me in St Biddy's so I could ask a few more questions about the non-event that was Luke Steadman's death. Annie pleaded paperwork.

'I'll pay yer. Going rate.'

My first thought was loneliness. My second was that something else was going on here. Annie beat me to the question. 'It's not just phone calls, is it?'

'Yes. No. Oh, I dunno. Maybe it's just living on me own. I got out of the habit. Started imagining things. Daft cow.' She tried to re-cap the polish and succeeded in tipping a sticky pool of the stuff over the table instead.

Annie fetched some paper towels. 'What are you imagining?'

'I think someone's been in the house.'

'When?'

'I ain't sure. I been in bed for days 'cept for crawling into the loo – well, you know how it makes you feel?' she appealed to me. 'Only . . . well . . . couple of times I woke up and I could have sworn there was someone in the room with me. But when I turned over there was no one there. Another time, I thought I heard the telly going down here.'

'Did you come down and check?' Annie asked.

'No. Could have been Jack the Ripper holding a rave for all I cared. There's something else. When I finally got myself downstairs, I had the feeling someone else had just been there.'

Annie suggested one of the neighbours was being neighbourly. 'If they knew you were ill?'

'Not this lot. Anyhow, how'd they get in?'

'Spare keys?'

'No. I had the locks changed after Barney died. Case his grabbing brother had got his hands on a key,' she explained for my benefit. 'There's only two sets of keys for my new locks and they're all on the ring upstairs. So you gonna stay?'

'Wouldn't you be better off going to a hotel for a while, Barbra?' Annie enquired.

'No. This is my house. Nobody's driving me out. If you don't want the job, just spit it out. I'll phone one of them agencies in the paper. Twenty-four-hour security. I don't care. I'm used to shifting for myself. Just thought you might want the business, that's all. Didn't look like Vetch's place was going too well when I called in. Still, if you're flush enough to turn down my cash . . .' Her pout reminded me of Lee. It became obvious he hadn't got all his in-your-face sulk genes from his dad.

And she was scared. I knew how that felt. I'd had a few reminders in the past few days. Besides, it would be a good opportunity to search the place and retrieve those negatives.

'You can leave me here if you like,' I offered Annie.

'No. It's OK. I'll fetch my spare toothbrush.'

She wasn't kidding. This was truly a woman who was organised enough to carry a spare toiletries kit in her glove compartment.

It wasn't a bad way to spend a Bank Holiday Sunday afternoon. The garden was heavy with overblown scented flowering shrubs (no, I haven't a clue what they were – read a gardening manual if you want a list of herbaceous bushes). Insects droned with the sort of fat, self-satisfied sound that said they hadn't a clue that come the frost it was off to insect heaven. When the light faded, we moved indoors, ate supper, drank the wine and watched the late news.

There was a brief item on Harry's death but no mention of the farm being linked to the immigrant smuggling, so I guess that bit hadn't yet leaked from whatever sources the press had at the police and Customs offices. However, there was a roundup of that story to date; plus an interview with

Faye Sinclair in which she supported law and order whilst hoping that legitimate asylum-seekers would be left in peace.

'I'm glad they caught them,' Barbra remarked from her cross-legged position on the hearth rug. 'I'd chuck them all out. They come over and it's straight round the DSS for a council house and a handout. Bloody cheek. How much have they paid in?'

'Isn't Delaney an Irish name?' Annie asked.

'That doesn't count. The Irish aren't proper foreigners. And before you say it,' she said with a belligerent glare in Annie's direction, 'Barney never claimed a penny off the state. He worked for everything he had.'

'Or married it,' I couldn't resist adding.

'What of it? It's better than standing in the post office with half a dozen kids and a wad of tenners you never paid a bleeding cent towards. They ought to spend it on the homeless and old in this country before they start dishing it out to a load of sponging foreigners. And there's no arguing with that!'

Neither of us had any intention of arguing with her. There very plainly wouldn't have been much point.

'See, I don't mind foreigners like her.' Barbra nodded towards Faye's image on the screen. There was no recognition at all. Faye was in her chic professional feathers tonight; a very different bird from Luke Steadman's relaxed lover in the St Biddy's snaps. 'She's all right. Knows how to do a decent day's work. Anyway, she's only half foreign. Her mum was Chinese.'

'Her dad,' I corrected.

'Well, it makes no odds, does it. She's half and half. I'm off to the loo.' She picked her way past us with bare feet.

'I'm impressed,' Annie said. 'I didn't think you'd recognise an MP if you fell over one in the House of Commons.'

'Normally I wouldn't. But I read one of those at-home-with-the-rich-and-think-they're-famous features the other day. She's married to some superstar lawyer; looked quite dishy in the pictures.'

'He does in the flesh, too. Bit of a cold fish, though. Well, no, not cold exactly … but precise. Everything to a timetable.'

It was pretty much what Faye had said about her husband; but I was intrigued as to how Annie had acquired her inside knowledge.

She checked Barbra was still out of earshot before wriggling closer and dropping her voice slightly. 'You remember my Parsdirp the other week? The one I had to meet at Heathrow between flights …' She flicked her forehead at the TV screen, although Faye had by this time been replaced by the local weather forecast. 'It was Hamish-the-not-so-humble. He felt things weren't quite right in the marriage.'

'Hamish Sinclair employed you to watch his wife?' I asked in a small voice.

'No. Changed his mind.'

'Did he say why?'

'All been a mistake. No case to answer, to use his own terminology.'

'The romantic fool.'

'Quite. I think he just preferred not to know. No doubt he was hoping any affair would soon fade out.'

Or perhaps he knew it would. The room got colder as pictures of Luke's blood-splattered body jumbled around my brain. I had a sensation of swimming in a very dark, deep pool, with no idea at all what was lurking under the surface.

'You chilly?' Barbra asked, returning to the room. 'There's a double duvet on yer bed, but I can get blankets if you want.'

I assured her the duvet was fine. I didn't want to get too cosy anyway, since I had to get up once the house was silent in order to search for those negatives.

Shuffling around in bare feet and Barbra's Italian silk pyjamas some hours later, I wondered whether I was simply wasting my time. Had Faye and Luke been as careful as they'd imagined? And how do you tactfully enquire about hubby's location at the time the lover was being turned into a giant kebab?

There was no sign of the negatives I wanted, although irritatingly, Barbra and Barney had been enthusiastic snappers during their travelling days, which meant I had to check all the strips in those albums just in case she'd hidden them with another set of prints. She hadn't. Apart from Barbra and Barney's Happy Hols, most of the other pictures were of the kid Carly growing taller and thinner with each year of her illness, but enduring it all with a solemn gappy-toothed smile. It made me feel dirty snooping amongst them, but I pushed on.

I'd been looking for over an hour when I fetched up in the kitchen and flicked the light on. And stared directly at a gross, fleshy, disembodied face, floating outside the window.

There was only one thing to do in those circumstances. And I went for it. I screamed the damn house down!

31

'Well, it's no ghost.' Annie played the torch beam over the lawn. The crushed grass showed mustard yellow in the artificial light. 'Might be an opportunist burglar. Or a plain old prowler hoping for a glimpse of something salacious.'

'That's supposed to make me feel OK, is it?' Barbra snapped. She was huddled in the kitchen doorway, watching as Annie and I quartered the area for clues. (The dropped book of matches from a nightclub; the shoe imprint with the distinctive V-shaped abnormality; the cigarette butt smeared with that exclusive shade of lipstick

– you know, all those things that keep turning up in fiction and never happen in real life.)

'No,' Annie said calmly. 'I was confirming that it isn't your imagination. You have had a visitor. Tonight, at least.'

'I had one them other times as well. I'm dead certain now.'

'Then how did he get in? Is it possible you hadn't locked up before you were taken ill?'

'No. I always check me locks. I've seen what walk-in thieves can do. And I take the keys up with me.'

We'd already discovered that when we tried to go after our midnight ghoul. By the time we'd managed to get outside, our visitor had long gone.

'You sure you didn't recognise him, Sherlock?' Annie asked.

'I only caught a glimpse. He had his face squashed flat against the pane – trying to see inside, I guess. It's hard to recognise your nearest and dearest from that angle. Soon as I screamed, he was off.'

'Any impressions?'

'I do a belting Martha Reeves – without the Vandellas.'

Lights were going on in the neighbouring houses. Barbra instructed us to come inside. 'I'm not providing a show for that lot.' We obediently regrouped in the living room for an argument of the 'what next?' variety.

Annie was for calling the police to report the incident. Barbra couldn't see any point since there was nothing to tell.

'I hate coppers,' she admitted. 'Every time Lee pulled something where I worked you could tell they thought I was in on it. No police unless we got something definite to tell them. Now, how about tomorrow – you two OK to hang on?'

Annie wasn't. She had things to do in Seatoun. And I

didn't fancy a whole day in a twosome with Barbra. The more I saw of her, the less I liked her, somehow. On the other hand, it was another opportunity to search for the negatives – and more time at a very generous hourly rate.

(With a chutzpah that left me breathless, Annie had made Barbra pay for one night's services there and then. 'Best to pay as you go along. Saves a nasty shock at the end,' she'd said as we folded our respective cheques into our respective pockets.)

In the end we agreed to do another night's stint. Barbra would spend the day in Seatoun whilst Annie and I hit those hot pavements in pursuit of truth and justice, and we'd all rendezvous back here in the evening.

'I thought I'd pop in and see Vetchy,' Barbra said at breakfast. 'I feel bad about poisoning the little love. Anyhow, I've had a brilliant idea. What you think about me buying into your company? Sort of a sleeping partner?'

Judging by Annie's face, she thought exactly the same way I did about it. No way, José!

'It's none of my business, of course. I probably shan't be there,' Annie said as we followed Barbra's convertible along the dual carriageway. 'And heaven knows, the agency could use a decent cash injection. However, I somehow doubt if Barbra is capable of keeping confidences for more than twenty minutes at a time. And we certainly don't need anyone to slag the clients off. You've already got that angle well covered.'

'Vetch might enjoy the "sleeping" element.'

'No doubt.' She negotiated a roundabout that was encircled by yet more trippers off to enjoy the final day of the Bank Holiday before saying: 'You don't think Vetch would really consider taking her into partnership, do you?'

'She's a rich blonde widow who he fancies the pants off. What would be your best guess?'

'Oh, hell,' Annie sighed. 'Flat or office?'

I chose office. The road outside was full of parked day-trippers' cars – and one red sports two-seater that I recognised instantly. There was no sign of the driver as we swept past. Annie managed to beat a camper van to a space on the promenade.

I told her I'd see her back at the office. 'I want to stretch my legs first.'

'I'm heading back to Barbra's at six. If I don't get a call on my mobile by then, you're on your own.'

'Fair enough.'

I dawdled along, scanning the crowds, telling myself it didn't have to be him. But who else would have access to the car keys?

I found him halfway along the prom, leaning on the blue-painted rails and watching the trippers hammering in windbreaks and disentangling deckchairs to stake their claim on a patch of beach. I'd been looking out for the grey jumper and trousers, which was why I was nearly on top of him before I realised.

'Hi.'

He turned to rest one arm along the top railing, whilst his weight shifted to the right leg, thrusting his hip slightly out.

'Hello,' Rainwing said.

It was the plain buckskin dress and short boots from the end-of-course snap Esther Purbrick had shown me. The black wig was unadorned, although there was a hint of smudgy shadow and mascara around the liquid eyes and a gleam of gloss on the lips.

Shivers went up and down my spine. I *knew* that this was a man, yet all my senses were telling me I was speaking to a woman. Everything about him, his voice, his posture, his gestures, even the way he was looking at me, was pure female.

'If you want to walk away right now,' he said, 'I'll understand.'

'Why should I? I'm not the one who makes a habit of walking away. That's your style, remember?'

'Yes. I don't blame you for being upset. Will you give me the chance to explain? Please, Grace.'

'Go ahead.'

'Let's walk along a bit, shall we?' He linked his arm through mine. And I reacted like he'd got a thousand volts flowing through his elbow joint. He moved away, putting space between us. 'Sorry. I half hoped you'd be all right about . . .' He gestured at his appearance, bringing his hand from his left shoulder to his right hip in an elegant sweeping gesture.

'I am. I'm fine.' I wasn't, and it bothered me that I had reacted like that.

'It's OK, I do understand,' Rainwing said.

I found I was actually thinking of him as Rainwing again, rather than Peter. It was confusing. (It probably is for you too, so I'm going to call him Rainwing until he reverts back again.)

'Could we go somewhere to talk? Somewhere not too crowded?'

That ruled out Pepi's. Its noisy, greasy, rocking-in-the-kitchen atmosphere appealed to Bank Holiday crowds out to cram as much enjoyment as possible into these last hours of freedom.

I suggested the BHS restaurant in the shopping centre. We had to walk through the lingerie department to get to it, and I got another attack of the goosebumps when Rainwing stopped to browse through a display of lacy bras and knickers.

We slid into a window table with our coffees and I asked: 'So what did you want to talk about?'

'A couple of things. I've had an idea about the woman those kids heard in Luke's place the day he died. But before that – I wanted to explain about the way I froze you out.'

'Forget it.' I turned my cool, unconcerned gaze on the harbour beyond the windows. The grey stone walling encircled a few working boats and a couple of weekend sailors. Beyond it, half a dozen empty container vessels were swaying on their moorings and waiting for a summons to move down the coast and pick up a load.

The silence made me look back at Rainwing eventually. He was watching me, his face expressionless.

'Well?' I said ungraciously.

'It's this. The dressing-up. I need to do it. I want to do it. And I don't intend to stop.'

'Did I ask you to?'

'No. But it's already making you uncomfortable, isn't it?'

'No,' I snapped.

'Yes,' I admitted.

'Then you see why I froze up on you? I felt that we were moving towards something rather more than sex. Something a lot closer . . . warmer . . . than that. Didn't you?'

'I guess. Well, OK – yes.'

'I couldn't handle that, Grace. Starting to care and then watching you turn away when I look like this. Or worse still, gritting your teeth and pretending everything is OK when I can feel your skin cringing under my fingers. So I bottled out.'

It was my call. 'Where did you get to?'

'I drove up to my bedsit in Battersea to get Rainwing's things. And then I dropped my mother's car back.'

'How is she?'

'On her way to Yon Hielands to join the rest of the family by now. She said she'd ring you at your office later. Purely to see how your health is, you understand?'

'You mean you still haven't let on you know about her and Luke?'

'And there's no way I shall be doing so. I'm having enough trouble with my own sex life. I don't want to hear about my mother's. You seem to be avoiding the central issue here, Grace. Are we going anywhere? Or shall I sashay off into the sunset now, with a last smouldering look over my shoulder?'

What could I do but tell him it was fine? The situation had certain advantages – I got a date, and possibly a best mate if Annie decamped to London, all wrapped in one neat package.

'I'm not saying we should go choose furniture in Ikea,' I said. 'Let's keep it casual, see how it goes . . . OK?'

'Suits me. Where do we go from here? *Vis-à-vis* Luke?'

I had to admit I wasn't entirely sure. 'I think we can agree the poetry's a non-starter. There are no odious odes to your mum hidden in the cottage.'

'Apparently not. But there's still the small matter of who killed him. And the will. I really should like to find that for his mother. It did bother him, you know – the problems with his family. Not that most of it was Luke's fault. His stepfather was a real pain. Thick and proud of it. Luke said he never forgave him for being ten times brighter than his own kids.'

'What about *your* stepdad?' I asked, recalling Hamish Sinclair's near-attempt to employ a PI of his own. 'What's he like?'

'Hamish? Organised. Good sportsman. Very ambitious. Why do you ask?'

'Just wondered if you had the same problems as Luke.'

'I didn't. We've never had that much to do with each other, me and Hamish. I was off to boarding school when he married Mother and I left home as soon as I was eighteen. We don't have what you'd call a family relation-ship. More like an amiable acquaintanceship.'

'Didn't you resent that?'

'I never thought about it. You accept things as a child, don't you? I doubt if things would have been any different with my natural father. He was something of a repressed stick too.'

'Didn't you say you hadn't met him?'

'As I remember, I said I never saw him now. I met him once, actually. My last year at school. He was looking for somewhere to send his oldest legitimate sprog after prep school. The prefects give the prospective parents a tour. I drew him. I had absolutely no idea who he was until he told me.'

I drained the last cold dregs of my coffee and asked how he'd felt.

'I didn't feel anything. I mean, there was no great father–son bonding session. We had a polite chat, he wished me luck, slipped me a fifty-pound note; and that was the last I ever saw of him. Except on the TV.'

'He's an actor?'

'No. Wouldn't that have been a weird coincidence? He's a barrister. He's done some of the big libel cases. Could you just glance to your left? There seems to be somebody trying to attract your attention.'

I'd sat with my back to the restaurant entrance. Slewing around casually, I saw a horribly familiar face staring intensely at our table. It was all the encouragement Terry Rosco needed. As soon as we linked eyes, he flexed the old pecs and strutted over in macho-man mode.

'Hiya, Smithie. Long time no see.'

'It's never long enough, Terry.'

'D'ya miss me?'

'Unfortunately. But I think my aim's improving.'

'So who's your friend? Morning, darling.'

'Hello,' Rainwing murmured. The voice was sexily husky, the glint beneath the eyelashes a definite come-on.

Terry went up a few more notches in his own estimation. 'The name's Rosco. Terry Rosco.'

'Licensed to bore,' I murmured.

'Call me Raine,' Rainwing invited, tossing her hair in a flirtatious gesture.

'That's nice. Classy.'

'Thank you. Terence is a lovely name too.' Rainwing pushed her chair back and crossed her legs.

'So maybe we could get together sometime? A few drinks? A club? And then who knows, eh, Raine?'

'Oh, I think we do know, don't we, Terence?' The lashes and sexy purr were brought into play again.

The self-satisfied smirk on his square jaw was wonderful. I bit the inside of my mouth to stop myself from laughing.

Rainwing drew one finger lightly up Terry's arm. 'Grace has my number. Promise me you'll call, Terence. I'll be waiting.'

'You won't be disappointed, darlin', I promise.'

'And I do so hope *you* won't be, Terence.'

'Dad!'

Terry came down from his self-made pedestal with a bump as his oldest mutant appeared in the doorway with a tray.

'Mum says you're to come pay. And one of the twins has done a poo again. He don't 'alf stink.'

Rainwing rose from her seat with a graceful fluidity. 'I think we should be going too, Grace.' She ruffled Terry's arm hairs again. 'Don't forget, Terence.'

As we left, Linda Rosco was struggling to manoeuvre a double buggy, full of the two screaming latest additions to the Rosco tribe, down the self-service counter. Her second oldest was throwing a tantrum because his shake had tipped over and was flooding the tray with luridly pink milk, and the eldest had climbed on the metal rails and was being shouted at by the counter assistant.

'Poor cow,' Rainwing said. 'That's one aspect of being a woman I'm never going to regret missing out on.'

'Kids?'

'Being stuck with some big-headed God's gift. I've always wished I had the courage to whip my wig off when they start coming on to me like that. Ah well, some day, perhaps. Let me tell you about Luke's mysterious visitor . . .'

He put his arm through mine. And this time I didn't flinch.

32

'He's a poseur, of course,' Rainwing asserted. He smoothed down the buckskin skirt that was riding up in the car's low-slung seats. It was annoying to discover he had better legs than me.

We'd had something of a row over Luke's car. Rainwing had insisted that Luke would have had no problems with his closest friend driving it. Which I could just about swallow even if it did technically belong to Luke's estate now. However, it then turned out that Rainwing didn't have any insurance.

'I have no car,' he'd shrugged.

I just couldn't help myself. 'What? No silver Audi?'

'No. That is Daniel Sholto's preferred mode of transport. I'm not saying it wouldn't be mine too. But I can't afford it. Or any other model, if it comes to that.'

'How come? I mean, your background isn't exactly DSS, is it?'

'The family money isn't mine. My parents' money is their own and my grandfather's is – or will be – my sisters'. If you were hoping to party with the rich and famous, Grace, I'm afraid you're out of luck. I'm not rich and I'm certainly not famous. What you see is what you get.'

'Well, not quite,' I'd grinned.

In the end, I drove. I'd somewhat over-optimistically

taken out a comprehensive policy on my own car which should cover me in this little beauty for third-party risks.

'And a fake,' Rainwing continued as we sped in the direction of St Biddy's.

'What's fake about him?'

'That title, for a start. "Professor" Purbrick bought his degrees from a mail-order college. Got some impressive certificates with big waxy seals and lots of long words. Esther is the real McCoy, but Wyn is a fraud.'

'Win?' Something his mum had said rang bells. 'Someone called Win introduced your mum to that commune you lived in. I'd assumed it was a she. As in Winifred.'

'Nope, it was our Selwyn.'

'But your mum said he taught you when you were a kid.'

'He did. Very enthusiastically, if not very well. By the time I was ten, he assured my mother there was nothing else he could teach me. Personally I'd thought we'd reached that crossroads a couple of years earlier.'

The wind was whipping his hair all over the place like Medusa's snakes. 'Don't worry,' he shouted over the engine's roar. 'It doesn't blow off. I've road-tested it in here before.'

'Didn't Selwyn recognise you? When you turned up in a skirt?'

'I was a small, skinny ten-year-old boy the last time he saw me. Why should he associate that child with a twenty-plus woman?'

'What about Esther? Didn't she suspect during the girlie chats?'

'She didn't suspect I wasn't a girlie, no. When I'm Rainwing, I *am* a woman. Luckily one positive effect of my Chinese genes is I have very little body hair.'

'I noticed.'

'So you did.' He flexed herself into a more comfortable position in the seat before adding that there was never any danger of Esther recognising him as Peter Chang. 'She arrived at the commune after my time.'

'What about the others? Weren't you taking a big risk going back?'

'I'd have passed it off as role-playing for a potential acting part if anyone had recognised me. But I was pretty certain I could do it. Most of the originals – like Auntie Vi – had drifted away as the place became more commercially minded. That was when Selwyn discovered Indian crafts. When I was a kid, he was just a primary teacher who'd dropped out of the rat-race. They didn't start the Native American studies until Esther joined them. It *was* a shock when I realised where the classes were based, but to tell the truth, after I got away with it the first time, it rather added to the thrill.'

'So what makes you so sure that the woman having a row with Luke was Esther Purbrick?'

'It just seems to make sense. Luke didn't know that many people round St Biddy's. It wasn't as if he was planning to settle there. He was just keeping the place warm until his uncle's estate was sorted out. Even I didn't visit him there. Can you imagine if I'd decided to drop in when Mother was there?'

'Vividly. Particularly if you were in a dress at the time. Why aren't you in the exploded parrot today?'

'Exploded . . . Oh, yes, I see. That was one of my earlier efforts. Later, when I was feeling more secure in the role, I felt able to go for something subtler. Like teenage girls putting the full slap on at sixteen and toning it down at twenty-six. That particular visit, however, I was feeling elated . . . sort of see me and weep, world – this is me. That make sense?'

'I guess so. But getting back to Esther . . . I hadn't realised Luke knew the Purbricks. I don't recall you mentioning it.'

'Why should I? They gave Luke some technical advice –

on his film script, keeping the Native American sections authentic. And Selwyn made an investment in the project. Esther wasn't too pleased about that. I know she'd been giving Luke some hassle about it.'

'You think she's up to killing someone?'

'I don't really have a lot of experience of killers myself. I'd have thought that was more your field of expertise. Besides, according to that fat kid, she left hours before Luke died.'

'True. But perhaps she saw something. Anyway, let's face it, we're a little short of other leads. Let's hope the police aren't – and that all clues lead to Harry Rouse.'

'Who?'

'Local farmer. Now very dead.'

'Why would he want to kill Luke?'

I told him about Luke's habit of cruising the tracks and yard around the Rouse farm, and the possibility he'd seen something of the smuggling operation.

'Wow. Poor old Luke. You think this Rouse character was up to . . .' He mimed a spear throw.

'Not him personally, perhaps. But he had some very unpleasant associates. If he'd let slip to them – even quite innocently – that Luke was where he shouldn't be . . .'

'Heavy,' Rainwing murmured as we glided up to the entrance to the Purbricks'. An amateurishly painted board was tied to the side gate announcing: 'Premises Closed Until Further Notice'. 'What now?' he asked.

'Now? It's written into every PI assistant's contract – thou shalt open the gate when the boss is driving.'

'Yes, ma'am.' He grinned, and for a second Peter looked out of Rainwing's eyes at me.

The house was quiet, with none of the manic music or screaming kids that had been whooping it up during my last visit. Our voices echoed in the half-painted hall. Today, without any activity to add a bit of life to the place, its decay was fighting back with a vengeance. I could smell damp and see where the rust and rot had been hastily glossed over.

'Anyone here?'

'We're closed. Oh, Rainwing . . .' We turned to find Esther standing in the door to the room she'd been using as an office last time I dropped in. You didn't have to be a detective to guess all was not well here.

'Esther, darling, whatever's the matter?' Rainwing walked swiftly over and put an arm around the other woman's shoulder. Esther promptly burst into tears.

'I'm sorry. I don't mean to . . . Oh, hell, I've just had *enough*.'

'Tea, gin, brandy,' Rainwing called to me, steering Esther firmly back into the room and settling her in the desk chair.

He knelt on the floor massaging Esther's hands as if they might be cold, whilst I rummaged. The best I could manage was a few inches of whisky and some more bottles of mineral water.

'Scotch and a splash?' I suggested.

Esther raised red-rimmed eyes and told me to hold the splash.

I stuck to water whilst they sipped from paper cups. (Driving with slightly dodgy insurance cover I might just about get away with, but let the likes of Terry Rosco get one whiff of malted barley and I would truly have made his day.)

'Now, tell me,' Rainwing said gently. 'What's the matter? Why's the centre closed?'

'The Health and Safety made us shut. Somebody reported us for not having the right certificates. Which I know we *didn't*,' she hiccuped. 'But I had to open to catch the school holidays. I thought we could get permits as we went along. Now they're saying we'll probably be prosecuted. God, I *hate* Luke Steadman.'

Rainwing knelt up slightly so he could draw Esther into his shoulder. He made soothing 'there-there'-type sounds.

'What's Luke got to do with it?' I asked bluntly.

Esther raised her head. 'Did you know him?'

Her tone was suspicious, but before I could reply Rainwing intervened to admit that we both had. 'In a professional sense. I act and Grace is in the nature of a technical adviser.'

Esther gave a sharp bark of laughter. 'Technical adviser – oh, yes! He was very fond of those.' She'd finished the whisky. An extension of the cup invited me to refill it. 'Technical advice is the reason we had to move to this dump. His idea of advice comes with several noughts on the end.'

'You invested money with his company?' I asked (even though Rainwing had already told me the answer).

'I didn't. I wouldn't be that bloody *stupid*.' She drew in a deep breath and seemed to take visible control of herself. 'You know how much work we'd done at Owerberry?' she appealed to Rainwing.

'The commune,' Rainwing elaborated. 'It was beautiful. Not the dump most people imagine when you say "commune".'

'It was an extended Jacobean manor,' Esther explained. 'We'd converted part of it for guest accommodation . . .'

'Single rooms, own facilities . . . very private,' Rainwing murmured for my benefit.

'Yes,' Esther agreed, unaware of his hidden agenda. 'And we'd installed proper teaching areas. There were half a dozen disciplines there: Native American crafts, glass-making, organic gardening, metal-working – it was very successful. We'd intended it merely as a means to make a reasonable living, but it turned out to be far more popular than anyone could have imagined. We were making a good profit.'

'And . . .' I prompted.

'And then the owners offered us the chance to buy the freehold. We'd have run the place as a limited company,

315

with each of us holding a share. It was a good deal. Or it would have been – if Selwyn hadn't given our money away.'

'To Luke?'

'Who else? I never really liked him, but Selwyn was flattered when he asked him to be a consultant on his film script. I couldn't see any harm in it . . . until I checked our account for the freehold money. And discovered Selwyn wasn't just advising our precious Mr Steadman; he was now an investor in his film company.'

'How much?'

'Fifteen thousand pounds. I know that doesn't sound like much these days . . .'

It sounded like very much to me.

'. . . but it represented over half of our savings. There was no way we could afford a stake in the freehold with that gone. And Luke refused to give it back. He said we'd get twenty times that amount once the film went on release – but what bloody good was that!' She glared angrily between us as if we were personally responsible. 'The others asked us to leave. They moved some jewellery-makers in to take our share. And we ended up . . .' She made a floppy wrist-sweep of the room. 'Short lease. Council didn't want it empty. Took most of the rest of the savings account. I knew it wouldn't work, but Selwyn was determined. Our own place . . . let's not be beholden to some commune mafia . . . make our own living . . . finance our own research . . . until the film's a success . . . after which, of course, it's first class all the way. God, how could a grown man be so . . . so . . .'

'Stupid?' asked a voice behind us.

'I was going to say gullible,' Esther informed her husband. 'How did you get on at the council offices?'

'They were closed. Public holiday.'

'And you've only just noticed that, have you, Selwyn?'

A pout protruded Selwyn's chiselled lips as self-pity

316

clouded his blue eyes. 'I hardly think sarcasm is going to help. I'll sort matters out tomorrow. It's just a temporary hitch, that's all. Must you be so negative?'

Esther stood up, crushed her paper cup, and flung it straight at her husband's head. 'It is not a temporary hitch. Practically all our money is gone. We are saddled with this . . . slum, which is never going to work, and I am sick and tired of trying to keep everything afloat. So I am going to pack my cases and leave. Is that positive enough for you, Selwyn?'

'Leave? But how . . . where will you go?'

'I'll stay with friends until I get something sorted out. I'm sorry, Rainwing, the centre is closed. Permanently.'

'Oh, don't worry about me, Esther. I'll be fine. I'm so sorry things have ended like this.'

'Don't be ridiculous,' Selwyn protested. 'Of course it hasn't ended. We can soon get things set up again. Once I get our money back from Luke . . .'

'You know he's dead?' I asked.

'Naturally. We do read the papers. His film company will have to be wound up. I'm an investor in that company. I have papers to prove it. It will take a while, Esther, but we'll get the money back.'

'There isn't any money, you idiot. He spent it. And do you know what? He didn't even know what he'd spent it *on*.' Sweeping her hand through an arc in that dismissive gesture again, she said in a fair imitation of Luke's mid-Atlantic drawl: '*Well, I don't know, honey. It just melts away, doesn't it, like snow when the sun comes out.* Fifteen thousand pounds, and he hadn't a clue where it had gone! Can you believe that?'

Recalling the restoration of the car, plus the designer gear and expensive array of electronic gadgets at the cottage, I reckoned I could come up with a pretty good guess. 'Did he tell you this last Friday?'

'Friday before last,' Rainwing murmured. 'Time flies when you're having fun.'

'We haven't seen Luke for some time,' Selwyn informed us.

'You may not have, but I think Esther has. Someone saw you at Brick Cottage that afternoon,' I lied ever-so-slightly.

Esther gave an indifferent raise of her shoulders. 'So I was there.'

Selwyn beat me to the punchline: 'Why?'

'I went to beg him for our money back. Failing that, I had an extremely sharp Iroquois hunting knife with me. Oh, don't look at me like that, Wyn, I wasn't intending to use it on him. Although heaven knows, I was very tempted after he'd stood there with that superior smirk, telling me I didn't understand the media business and the kind of sacrifices it demanded.'

'What were you planning to do with the knife?' I enquired.

'As much damage as I possibly could to that precious car of his. Unfortunately the garage door was jammed. I got it open a couple of inches and then it wouldn't budge. In the end I left.' She looked defiantly around the three of us. 'I'm glad he's dead. I'm sorry if he was a friend of yours, but as far as I'm concerned, he was a parasite. I'm glad somebody swatted him.'

'Skewered, actually.'

'Even better. Now, if you'll excuse me, I have some packing to do. Here.' She flicked a ring of keys at her husband. He caught them one-handed and stepped into her path.

'Esther, please. Don't go. I need you. You know I do.'

'No you don't, Selwyn. You just need a mother. So you can go on being a little boy and let someone else take all the nasty responsibilities. Well, I'm afraid my maternal instincts are all used up. Now get out of my way.' She dodged to the left. He blocked her again. They swayed right. Then left again. The dance ended

318

with Esther bringing her knee up sharply.

With a gasp of pain, Selwyn collapsed.

Rainwing uncoiled himself from the floor. 'I think perhaps it's time we were leaving, don't you, Grace?'

He clamped my arm and led me back to the hall. The hollow reverberation of floorboards above our heads made us both look up. Esther was striding along the first-floor landing, a bundle of clothes in her arms.

'Esther,' I shouted up. 'How was Luke when you left him?'

Pausing to glance down, she said coolly: 'Alive.'

'I know that. But was he happy? Sad? Frightened?'

'Smug.'

'Because he'd ripped you off for fifteen grand?'

'Yes.' A little of the tension faded from her face. 'No. Not entirely. He seemed to think his film deal was "coming together", whatever faith you can put in that.'

'In what way?'

'He'd found a way of raising the rest of the finance he needed. All we had to do was wait a couple of years and Selwyn and I would be percenters in a future Oscar winner.'

'Did he say where this cash was coming from?'

'No. But if you'd like my guess, he was going to put his little pickaxe over his shoulder, trip-trap off to the end of the rainbow, and dig up a pot of gold. Goodbye, Rainwing.'

33

'Does something about this place strike you as odd?'

'Tell me, master. Or should that be mistress?'

'Neither whilst you're in that frock.'

We were perched side by side on the front step of Brick Cottage, staring out over the garden where the flora had rioted under the effects of the recent downpours and heat waves. The vaguely uncomfortable feelings we'd been left with after witnessing the Purbricks' bust-up had been exorcised by flinging ourselves into the inventory. For the past few hours we'd rechecked and relisted every damn thing in that building down to the last bent teaspoon and cracked flowerpot until there was just the garage left to do. As we'd gone along, we'd opened all the windows, releasing the last ghostly traces of Luke and Uncle Eric.

'So what's odd?' Rainwing asked.

'We didn't find any correspondence from local estate agents. Luke was supposed to be keeping the place warm until he found a buyer. So how come there's no agents' particulars?'

'He could have fixed up a private sale.'

'With who? There are no letters from anyone apart from the American realtors, the car restoration lot and threats from the electric and gas to cut the cottage off if he didn't pay the bills. In fact, Luke seemed to specialise in taking what he hadn't paid for.'

'He wasn't like that.'

'No?'

'No,' Rainwing said in Peter's voice. 'I know how it looks, but Luke truly believed in his work. He put everything into it. And he really did intend to pay everyone back. He wasn't a con man; it's just that passion about something can sometimes make you forget that not everyone feels the same.'

'Did he borrow from your mum?'

'No. I asked him.'

'And you believed the answer?'

'Yes.' He slewed slightly on the step so that he was looking directly at me. It was eerie. I could actually see Rainwing receding and Peter emerging. 'I knew Luke. A lot of the time he was my only friend. I'd have known if he was lying about taking cash from my mother. He wouldn't. OK?'

'OK.'

'So what now? About Luke, I mean. Is it too much to hope that you have a cunning plan?'

I admitted to being clear out of plans on that one: 'Cunning or otherwise.'

'You've no theories at all about who could have done it?'

'I haven't a clue. I told your mum, I don't do murders. The general idea is to look at means, motive and opportunity.' I ticked them off on my fingers: means – he provided that himself. Motive – could be anything. Money, I guess. Or rather Luke's somewhat casual attitude to other people's.'

'Esther could have come back,' he offered. 'After those kids left. If they had another row and things got ugly, she knows how to use Indian weapons. I've seen her shoot a hunting bow.'

I duly chalked up Esther as a possible. 'And then, of course, there's good old sex. Always a hot contender in the motive stakes. Any idea where your stepfather was that Friday?'

'Hamish! You are joking? I mean he didn't even *know* . . .'

Maybe not, but he sure as hell suspected, if he'd got as far as putting out feelers for an investigator. However, I'd promised Annie to keep shtum on that one, so I kept it vague. 'Partners pick up signs. Even if they don't know what they mean, they know something is wrong. Believe me, we've had enough of them through the agency.'

'*Suspicion always haunts the guilty mind,*' Peter said in his apt-quotations voice. 'I don't know where he was. I could perhaps find out from Mother. But if it was Hamish . . . I mean, there would be no way of keeping her out of it!'

'It would be difficult,' I agreed, standing up and stretching out muscles cramped by hours of paperwork.

'And as for the third of that trio – opportunity – the guy lived in a relatively isolated cottage: you don't even have to come through the village to get to it. He had no regular habits, so no one was going to miss him for days; and time of death can only ever be approximate in a post-mortem, so there are a couple of hours either way to play with. To sum up, then – a large part of the county could have driven over and stabbed him, if they'd felt so inclined, and then provided themselves with an alibi from a dozen assorted witnesses in a fifty-mile radius. What I wouldn't give for those old clichés: the button torn from the murderer's jacket and the initials scrawled in the victim's dying blood. I think I'll walk along the village and stretch my legs. Coming?'

'No. I'll see you in a minute.' He almost ran inside the cottage, his movements awkward inside the dress now he was no longer Rainwing but Peter.

I sauntered up to the main street and into the local store. Carter was slumped moodily behind the counter, watching a couple of trippers rummaging in the ice-cream freezer. The action caused the sunburned flesh to bulge around the back of their bra straps and from the uneven bottom edges of their shorts.

Grannie was tidying greetings cards in the revolving stand. I saw her mouth tighten in disapproval at all this flashing flesh and then look to check that Carter wasn't being corrupted. His chin went up and he met her gaze defiantly. Surprisingly, it was her that coloured and dropped her eyes away first.

I'd come in to pick up a local paper and, hopefully, a bit of local knowledge. But since I was here, I mooched along the shelves adding milk, a box of jam tarts and bag of mixed toffees to the pile. By the time I'd finished, the girls had left and Carter and his gran had swapped places behind the till.

'It's last week's,' she said, holding up the paper. 'The new one comes out tomorrow.'

'It doesn't matter. I just want to look up local estate agents. I was wondering, Brick Cottage, you don't know who's handling the sale, do you?'

'We've no idea. The young man never said.' She ran the bar-code reader over the cellophane packaging and tsked-tsked in exasperation as it refused to read. 'Carter, this isn't working again.'

Carter was now lounging by the door, his arms folded over those girlish breasts and his attention fixed on the scene outside. Barely glancing our way, he said: 'Flatten out the back and try again.'

It took her a dozen more goes, with the till beeping like a demented electronic orchestra. She had the same trouble with the rest of my collection. The agitation increased the tremor in her fingers. 'Wretched thing, I wish we'd kept the old one. Carter, can't you be a little angel and come and do it?'

But Carter wasn't going to be moved from his attempt to prop up the door jamb with one shoulder. 'Just do as I told you, Gran. It's easy.' He did at least look directly at me this time. 'You were up the Rouses' place, weren't you? When they had the shooting? They're saying Harry was shot by his dad.'

'Are they?'

'Went crazy, they reckon.'

'Do they?'

'Had to call in loads of armed police to catch him. That right?'

I advised him to ask the all-knowing 'they', since they were obviously so well informed.

Carter looked like he was about to argue, but Gran had finally beaten the till into submission and announced the total was two pounds thirty pence.

I handed over three pound coins and checked the printed

receipt the till had spewed out in the hope it had rung up something twice in the midst of all that angst. No such luck. It did, however, thank me for my custom, tell me the date and time and inform me my assistant today had been Kar the Klingon.

Carter seemed reluctant to part with me. Either that or he was too tired to lever himself off the back of the door. 'You going to buy Luke's place, then?'

'No. Just curious. I'm sorting things out for his mum. Thought she might be interested in the asking price.' I also hated inconsistencies.

'Oh?' Carter twisted to put his back against the door and give me his full attention. 'You living there now?'

'Nope. Just passing through.' I was about to add a warning that I'd be back and forth, in case he'd got any more keys, but I realised his mind wasn't on me any more.

St Biddy's was the sort of village that attracted a better class of day-tripper. It was a place for browsing, leisurely drinks and cream teas. The souped-up roar of the Escort, plus the thundering rhythm of the sound system, tended to stand out. It was dangerously overpacked again, but I thought I caught a glimpse of Kelly Benting squashed in the centre of the back seat.

Carter was dead certain he did. 'Kelly! Wait!'

The accelerator pedal was slammed to the floor. Wheels spun. The ice-cream sign went flying in a metallic crash. The Escort raced away, forcing an approaching car to sound its horn and bump to a standstill at the entrance to Cowslip Lane.

'Kelleee . . .' Carter's voice rose in desperation. 'Wait. Come back. *Kelleeee . . .*' He ran several ungainly steps up the street and then realised it was hopeless. Kicking the air in a futile gesture, he slouched back.

His grandmother called to him from the doorway to pick up the sign.

Carter stopped, fists balled into his fleshy waist. 'Pick it up yourself, you stupid cow,' he said loudly and clearly.

'Carter! Where's my Master Smiley gone?'

Carter didn't even bother to answer. Hands in pockets, he slouched off. I glanced at Grannie and made an interesting discovery. She was scared of Carter.

Her eyes slid away and refused to meet mine. Without a word, she righted the sign and dragged it back into position. I'd have probed a bit further if the driver across the street hadn't whistled to attract my attention.

'Oi. Supersnoop. You know those bozos in the Escort?'

'Afraid not, Lee.' I walked over to where he was picking out the shards of a shattered wing mirror. 'They're just passing bozos as far as I know.'

'Prats!' He banged the mirror with a balled fist and the remaining pieces fell out into the bag he was holding under it.

I expected him to lob it over the nearest wall. Instead he wrapped it carefully and walked over to the rubbish bin outside the store. It was a strangely conventional thing to do. In fact, when I looked him over, everything about Lee Delaney seemed oddly normal, if that isn't a contradiction in terms.

He was dressed in a pair of light trousers and overshirt that looked to be clean and recently pressed. His hair was pulled back in a neat ponytail and the twisted sneer had been surgically removed from his upper lip. Even his eyes had lost that slightly spaced-out expression.

He looked . . . I groped for a comparison, and realised he looked like what he was – a young man in his mid-twenties, rather than the superannuated teenager I'd been introduced to at Barbra's unforgettable lobster and listeria luncheon.

'You still working for me mum?'

'Yep.'

'Wasting your time. I told yer.'

'And I told you – it's not my time I'm wasting; it's your mum's money.'

Reaching into the car, he removed a bouquet of flowers from the front seat and locked up. 'This where she found 'em? The ones in her will?' Without waiting for me to reply, he nodded and said: 'Makes sense. The daft biddy just can't let it go. Want to see what this is really about?'

He started to walk deeper into the village, not bothering to see if I was following. Cradling my goodies, I caught up with him.

'You feeling OK, Lee?'

'Top of the world, thanks. 'Ow about yourself?'

'I'm fine now. But I just spent most of the week in bed with food poisoning. In fact, everyone at your mum's that Sunday had it. Except you, apparently.'

He hefted the bouquet on one shoulder and twisted round to walk backwards so he could look at me. 'So you reckon what? I've been sprinkling lightly chopped toadstools over the salad?'

'Just a thought.'

'Scrub it. It was probably the prawns. I reckoned at the time that wanker had defrosted and frozen them twice. That's why I didn't eat none.'

'Couldn't you have warned the rest of us?'

'After the way my mum had talked me up to you? Would you have believed me?'

'Probably not,' I agreed.

'There you go, then.' Spinning back, he bounced away, whistling 'Bohemian Rhapsody'.

Given the flowers, I half expected a girlfriend. But Lee managed to surprise me yet again by heading for the church and making his way to a grave nestling under the shade of the trees near the boundary. Its edge was delineated by a row of white-washed stones and the shrivelled flowers in the sunken holder still retained some colour. Evidently it was a double plot. There were two inscriptions.

'There you go. The reason for me mum's latest tantrum.'
I read silently:

Sacred to the memory
of
Matilda Ann Tanner
Beloved wife, mother and gran
1898–1968
and
Her great-granddaughter
Carly Ann Delaney
Fell asleep 1st August
aged 9 years
Sleep safely my precious in
Nan's arms

'This is where your sister is buried?'

'Nicely spotted, supersnoop.' Lee started dragging the faded flowers from the holder and replacing them with his own. 'That's me mum's gran. Her old man should have been in there with her, but he went and got himself lost at sea, so Mum got them to put Carly in instead. Thought it would be less lonely for her. Daft idea, really, but I suppose I can see where she was coming from.'

So could I. It was odd I'd never wondered before why Barbra had chosen St Biddy's for her morning photography excursion.

Lee stabbed a chrysanthemum into a waiting hole. 'See the date she died? Well, that's special. Sort of sacred. We always had to come up here then. Make a big show of putting flowers out, telling Carly how we'd been doing all year.'

I guessed what was coming. 'You missed this year?'

'I was *busy* this year. I got a life, all right?'

'Who's arguing? So you think that's why your mum is trying to leave her money to a load of complete strangers?'

'Course it is. Carly was always more important than me. She still is. Even when she's been dead for seventeen frigging years.' He started rolling the dead blooms into the cellophane wrapper from his own bouquet, kneading them in with vicious little stabbing movements. 'It was always Carly. There was never nothing left over for me. When I was kid I used to get really excited about something I'd done at school – like winning a race, or getting a good mark in me book – and I'd go running home to tell me mum and she'd not even hear me. It was always: I'm busy, Carly needs this, Carly wants that.' Smashing the crackling parcel flat, he knelt up on it. 'Don't get me wrong. I loved Carly. She was my big sister, weren't she? But sometimes I used to dream how it would be if it was just Mum and me. And then she died and it was. Only me mum still didn't have any time. She started doing all these poxy jobs instead.'

'She says she needed the money after your dad walked out. Single-parenting doesn't come cheap.'

'What did she expect? She never had time for him either. He weren't even allowed to pick Carly up in case he bruised her. She bruised easily. Big purple and yellow marks on her arms and legs like flowers. I remember that.'

Snatching up the parcel, he stalked over to the rubbish bin, then filled a plastic bottle from the standpipe. 'This is why she's writing that daft will,' he said, dribbling water into the flower holder. ''Cos I phoned her and said I couldn't make the first of August.'

'Not entirely it's not, Lee.' I wondered just how far I ought to trust him. 'Have you been prowling around your mum's place this past week? Or making funny phone calls to her?'

'Is that what she's saying?'

'It's not just her. I'm saying someone is.'

'Well, it ain't me. I told yer, I've got a life. If my mum ain't, that's her problem.' He looked down at the stone-edged oblong. 'Well, so long, kid. See you again one day, eh?'

He strode off, leaving me to catch up again. Approaching the Royal Oak, he asked if I fancied a drink.

'Better not.' I raised the shopping I was still cradling. 'I'm expected back.'

'See yer then. Oh, and give me mum a message – tell her she can leave her frigging cash to anyone she likes. I don't need it. And I don't need her no more. Cheers.'

He headed for the pub. I headed for Cowslip Lane. As soon as I stepped into Brick Cottage, the old subconscious picked up the signals and was issuing a danger warning.

34

For a split second I thought I'd walked in on one of those private moments where three is a crowd, or the answer to a personal ad in the *Swingers' Gazette*.

Peter was kneeling on all fours over something on the sofa. Since the back was to the door, all I saw at first was his head and shoulders. He was panting with exertion, his weight forward on his outstretched arms.

A fist lashed from below and whacked him on the chin. He jerked his head away and lost his grip. Carter erupted up, his hand slapping sideways hits, which mostly failed to land. Peter was trying to block on his forearms. I'd seen more violence in the qualifiers for the Senior Citizens' Indoor Bowls Tournament.

Stepping between them, I jabbed an elbow in their respective chests. They both collapsed, Peter on a footstool and Carter on the sofa.

'Are you both crazy?'

Peter concentrated on drawing his bath robe tight rather than look at me. 'I was running a bath. I heard him down here. Thought it was you. He was looking for things to steal again.'

'I was not,' Carter said. 'I just wanted my stuff back. I thought the place would be empty. I didn't know he was here.' Tears were filling his eyes. 'He's mad. He wants locking up. I'm going to call the police. He tried to kill me.'

'If you feel you must, Carter. Mind you, we'd have to explain you were trespassing. And not for the first time. I'll just get your bits and pieces.'

We'd stashed the seduction kit in a carrier in the hall. I retrieved it. 'We had to throw the roses out, but you can check the rest is still here.'

I laid them across the coffee table. A pair of candles. The bottle of sparkling wine. And one paperback, title: *How to Have Her Begging for More*.

'The police will want to see them.'

'They will?' Carter said doubtfully.

'They're proof that's why you came in. To get your property. You'd best warn your gran. They may want her there if you're making a statement about an assault.'

You could read the hesitation all over Carter's pudgy face. His burgeoning confidence didn't quite stretch to sitting in a room with his grandmother and a police officer leafing through that paperback.

'You can keep the stuff,' he mumbled. 'I don't want it now that perv's touched it anyway.'

He thrust past me and fled. The crash of the front door reverberating was the only sound, apart from a clock I hadn't noticed before and Peter's short, shallow breaths.

He and I finally looked directly at each other. What had happened was painfully obvious. He'd taken off Rainwing's clothes and wig but hadn't got around to removing her make-up. The lipsticked mouth, smokily shadowed eyes and blushed cheeks that had looked so sexy on Rainwing gave Peter the appearance of a camp drag artist. And Carter had walked in on that.

'You didn't need to be so rough with him,' I finally said. 'You could have caused him some serious damage.'

'I meant to. I'm sorry. But what he said . . . the way he looked at me . . . and I really did think he was stealing . . .'

'He's just a kid. You overreacted.'

He hunched defensively into the robe. 'Don't lecture me. You're not my mother.'

'Just as well. She'd have got an even bigger shock.'

'I'm going to finish my bath. Shall I make up a bed?'

'You'd better make it a single.'

'Bit too real for you, is it?' He made one of those elegant circling gestures over his face of the kind used by mime artists.

'It's not that. I've a job on tonight. Bodyguarding.'

'Sure you do.'

'Peter, I don't play those sort of games. If I say I'm working . . . I'm working.'

'If you say so.'

This was more mood than I wanted to handle. 'Maybe it would be best if I went now. I'll catch up with you tomorrow.'

'If you like. Leave the car keys.'

'We've had this conversation. You aren't insured.'

'I'm not being stuck here without transport. If that kid starts spreading it around that there's a pervert camped out here, I want an escape route in case the rent-a-bigot brigade start burning crosses on the lawn.'

'He wouldn't. At least,' I amended, 'I don't think he would, but if you're worried, come back and use my flat. You'd have it to yourself.'

'No thanks. I'd rather stay here. And since Luke was my friend, I think I've more right to the car than you. I'll take the risk on being picked up.'

'So how do you expect me to get home?'

'Bus? Taxi?'

'Cheers, Peter. You're a real star.'

As far as I was concerned, there was only room for one moody sulker in this relationship – and I'd got that corner covered. I stalked out with a satisfactory front-door slam.

My intention was to check out that bus stop along the main road and hope the Bank Holiday service included a late-afternoon run to Seatoun. It didn't.

I'd have to hike back to the village to find a phone box and ring Annie. Still in a huff, I refused to use the lane past Brick Cottage even if it did mean another half-mile to the main approach turning.

As I reached it, it belatedly occurred to me that I could have taken the motorbike from the garage. On the other hand, that would mean I'd have to go back to Brick Cottage. Whilst I was weighing convenience against swallowed pride, Lee's car bowled up to the white stop lines. 'Wanna lift?'

'I'm going into Seatoun.'

'Hop in.'

I hopped. In doing so, I rammed my knee into the glove compartment – which snapped open, releasing a cascade of junk on to the floor. Had I found myself knee-deep in controlled substances and porno magazines I shouldn't have been at all surprised. But once again it was the lifestyle of Mr Ordinary. I started stuffing back the sweet wrappers, tissues, sunglasses, and half a dozen of those free toys they give away at burger restaurants.

'Don't break 'em,' Lee said sharply when I attempted to force a brontosaurus into the last remaining corner.

'You collect them?'

'Not for myself, OK? It's for the kid.' Delving in his shirt pocket, he fished out a slim leather holder. There was a photo in one side of a girl with long dark hair clutching a boy of about three years. 'That's my Jenny. And Rhys. He ain't mine. Her bloke walked out, didn't want to know. We're engaged.'

'Congratulations. She's pretty.' She was actually a dead

ringer for his mum in her first wedding pictures to Sean Delaney.

'Yeah. Not bad. And Rhys is a brilliant kid. He already calls me Dad.'

'Best of luck,' I said. There was something else in the other side of the wallet. An identity pass for the Silver Springs Health Resort and Country Club in East Sussex (RAC and AA ****; two Michelin stars). According to the lump of plastic I was holding, one Lee Delaney was the assistant chef at this posh fat farm.

'You've got a job?'

'Had it nearly four years now. Started off as general dogsbody in the kitchens. Chef trained me up. Me and Jen's thinking of going for our own place after the wedding. That's why I was checking out that B and B place in Seatoun the other day. But it's not a goer. Right price, wrong area.'

'Your mum thinks you're a no-hoper who can't hold down a toilet flush, much less a steady job.'

'I know.'

'So what's the idea?'

He spun the wheel, taking us into the streets of West Bay that I'd last driven down with Luke. The kamikaze pedestrians were even more in evidence now that the tag end of Bank Holiday fever was gripping the place.

'She thinks I'm rubbish. Always has. Every time something bad went down where she worked, she'd reckon it was me. Most times it weren't. Not after I was sixteen or so. I really tried to get my head together, but she never noticed. Just kept rubbishing me to everyone she met. So in the end I thought, right, give the public what they want.'

'So you turn up every few months, play the moody ratbag, and then change back into Mr NiceGuy on the way home. Don't you think that's a bit childish?'

'What's it to you?'

'Nothing. It just seems an incredible waste of time and energy, particularly when your mum is . . .'

'Is what?' he asked, gunning the car round the curve that took us on to the cliff road that ran parallel to the promenade. Down below me I could see the wet sands and seaweed-encrusted groynes of the bay where I'd skinny-dipped to prove thirty wasn't a one-way ticket to respectable oblivion.

'Is lonely,' I said. 'Since your stepfather died, the neighbours have been freezing her out of the cheese-and-wine wing-dings. I bet she'd like a family around.'

'Yeah, sure. She's so keen on me company, she'd rather leave her money to a bunch of people she don't know from sweet FA. And then rub my face in it by telling me all about it. Over and over in case I missed the point that she still thinks I'm worth less than what sticks to the bottom of yer shoe.'

'That's not why she's doing it.' I made a quick decision. Somebody had to stop this daft carousel Lee and his mum had got themselves on. 'Do you know where your mum's solicitors are?'

'London. Strand way. Why?'

'Did you know she was visiting them a few weeks ago?'

'She said when I rang to say I weren't coming to see Carly this year.'

'Did you follow her?'

'Why the hell would I?'

'She thinks you tried to kill her.'

There are times when having no bust to speak of is a definite advantage. When a seatbelt locks like an iron bar across your chest during an emergency stop is one of them.

'You *what*?' Lee snapped.

'I nothing. Your mum thinks. Great brakes, by the way.'

'Are you taking the Michael?'

'Not at all.' I filled him in on the mysterious bloke who'd

334

tried to push Barbra under the London taxi a few weeks ago and led to her decision to make that bizarre will.

'And she thinks it was me? That I tried to top her?'

'Who else would benefit from her death? There is only you.'

'That's a load of bull. It could have been an accident. Or some nutcase. You read about them. They hear voices telling them to kill someone.'

He was trying to talk me down, but there was something in his voice that wasn't right. He sounded unsure. Whatever had gone down that day in London, Lee knew more about it than he was letting on.

'Any ideas?' I prompted.

'No.' He leant across and opened my door. 'You'll have to shove off now. Hike it from here.'

I didn't have to hike it very far. We were only a few minutes' walk from the flat. It was as I remembered it: depressing, too full of bicycle and guarded by a tub of spiky succulents that were clinging to life with the tenacity of a soap star with lousy plot lines.

I rang Annie's mobile. She was still at the office. 'We're just doing a bit of tidying and decorating. Come round now if you want a lift.'

'We' I'd assumed to be her and Vetch. But it turned out the little gnome was still poorly.

'It really hit him hard,' Barbra said, pushing hair behind her ears with paint-engrained nails. 'I feel dead guilty. Do you reckon the lobster was off?'

'Prawns, according to your Lee. I saw him at St Biddy's. Visiting Carly.'

I half expected she might feel the need to explain her tantrum over the will. I should have known better. Barbra Delaney only played to her own rules and didn't care what anyone else thought. Particularly anyone-elses who she was paying to dance to her tune.

'Let's go then, girls. We'll have a barbecue tonight. I

bought some steaks and stuff when we went up for the paint. When me and Vetchy go into partnership, I might get a proper interior design whatsit in to do down here; scarlet and black, I thought. And your business stationery needs jazzing up. What d'yer reckon to this: a plain white card with the silhouette of a pistol and "This Gun For Hire" under it? I've been telling Annie here all me plans to get this place on its feet again. It's going be brilliant. I'll see you back at Wakens Keep.'

I caught Annie's eye as our potential partner breezed out. She gave me a despairing shrug and started resetting the answerphone and alarm systems. 'So how's your day been? Did you get this mysterious client that you don't want to talk about – or put through the books – sorted out?'

'There's nothing mysterious about this one. I've been doing an inventory up at Brick Cottage for Luke's mum. She's strapped for cash and needs every penny she can raise. Pronto.'

'I doubt if she's going to get much from that place.'

'Oh?' She had her back to me, relocking the front door, but I knew her well enough to recognise that slight telltale pink stain on the back of her neck. She'd said something she hadn't intended to. 'Give, Anchoret.'

'It's confidential.'

'I'm a naturally discreet person.'

'No you're not.'

'Don't quibble. Confide in me or I smasha ya face. What have you heard?'

I had to wait until we were in her car and pointed towards Wakens Keep before she told me. 'I had to collect a few things from the police station for Zeb. And Emily and I got chatting.'

'Emily? You mean that frosty-faced detective sergeant?'

'She's a very pleasant person.'

'She doesn't like me.'

'Lots of people don't – what's that got to do with it? Do you want to hear this or not?'

'Shoot.'

'They took some correspondence from your friend Luke's cottage. Only it turns out it isn't his cottage. It belongs to some finance company. Luke's uncle—'

'Great-uncle.'

'Not-so-great in this case. He'd used the property to buy an annuity. Which stopped when he died. Or some months afterwards, actually. It seems they didn't know he'd died and continued to pay. They'd been threatening legal action to evict your friend Luke from the cottage. I guess they've saved themselves the court costs.'

'So what's Emily doing now? Looking for a hit man from the finance people?'

'Don't be daft. We're not talking a back-street loan shark. It's a multinational business. And Emily isn't looking for anyone in connection with Luke Steadman's death.'

'How come? She off the case?'

'No. It's simpler than that, Sherlock.'

There was only one other possible answer. 'The police know who killed Luke!'

'Give the lady a cuddly toy.'

35

'Do you think I'm weird?'

'Is that a serious question?' Annie stopped shaking out the spare towels in the bathroom rack to look up at me.

She had to look up, because I was currently standing on the loo seat, fishing in the cistern tank with my yellow Marigolds. Or Barbra's yellow Marigolds, if you want to be pedantic.

I hate period houses when it comes to an investigation. Modern rabbit hutches with their low-level bathroom suites and flimsy built-in furniture with lousy locks are so much easier to search. The only real advantage to hefty walls and tree-trunk timbers is they muffle noise and hopefully stop you waking your hostess as you turn her home upside down. (Although in Barbra's case, the couple of bottles of Valpolicella she'd knocked back with the steaks was a big help in keeping her out of our faces.)

We'd had another girlie supper party. Barbra had entertained us with her vision of the new agency: 'Vetch and Delaney'. Annie looked about ready to stick her head in the waste disposal unit by the time we could reasonably plead terminal tiredness. After checking all the locks and rigging a couple of rudimentary booby traps in the back garden, we'd settled down for the night.

My plan had been to do a thorough job on locating those negatives for Faye when the other two were asleep. Unfortunately the third step of the staircase creaked like an ogre with indigestion under my weight. Annie had appeared on the landing, dragging her sweat pants on over her pyjamas.

'Did you hear something?'

'No. I've just remembered something I left downstairs. Go back to bed.'

'I can't sleep. Things to sort out – you know?' She'd twirled a finger by the side of her head.

I'd sensed there were two ways to go here. Spend the next few hours thinking up increasingly unlikely excuses for prowling, or recruit her help to search this place.

As you'll have gathered, I'd gone for the second option. Which meant I had to tell her I was going to take those negatives – without being able to tell her the reason why.

'So you're planning to steal from your client? That's unprofessional conduct, even for you.'

'What do you care – you're leaving the agency anyway. And what the hell do you mean – even for me?'

'Your ability to rewrite the rule book in a language

unknown to all law-abiding investigators is legendary, Sherlock.'

'I'm an innovator,' I'd murmured back. 'Are you going to help? It's important, honestly, Annie. I'd do the same for you.'

'I don't burgle my own clients.'

But she agreed to be the burglar's apprentice, bless her. We'd already spent a few hours creeping around downstairs, delving into drawers, freezer compartments, sofa backs and all those other places everyone always think are finder-proof. Now we'd moved to the upper rooms.

'Well?' I repeated. 'Do you think I'm weird?'

'In any particular way?'

'Man-wise. Take Luke Steadman. He was a good-looking bloke. He was easy enough to talk to; fancied me – or at least he did a good job of pretending to; great car; apparently in an interesting career. But something never really clicked. OK, he turned out to be an Olympic-class scrounger in the end—'

'So you had common interests as well,' Annie said, returning the last of the towels to the rack and starting to check the toiletry canisters to see if any had false screw-on bottoms.

I ignored the jibe. I was well into my little bout of self-analysis here. 'But I didn't *know* he was like that at the time, did I? I should have been shaving my legs and checking my roots when he started the chat-up. Instead of which, I didn't even bother to phone him back until you prodded me. When it comes to Peter, however . . .'

I'd told her all about Peter. Without mentioning who his mother was.

'When it comes to Peter, you get the hots every time?'

'Yes . . . no,' I said. 'Well, not when he's in the frock. The point is, I don't see how I can blow out a grade-A bloke with no hang-ups, and then fall for one with better legs than me. And a better bust, if it comes to that. What am I going to do?'

'Ask him if you can borrow it when he's not using it. At least you'll start off with a couple of things in common.'

'This isn't funny. I'm trying to have a serious conversation here.'

'So what do you expect me to say? Who knows why people fall for each other. Look at the odd couples you see around. Nobody can imagine what on earth they see in each other. If I could explain sexual attraction I'd quit this job, write a book on it, and make a fortune. Maybe it's your guardian angel keeping an eye out for you. If you had fallen for Luke, you'd be feeling ten times worse now. Dating a bloke in a frock isn't half as tricky as dating a corpse.'

I guess she had a point. When I thought of Peter I saw golden skin, sloe-eyes and tapering fingers that made my skin tingle. When I called up a picture of Luke, however, the sun-tanned bloke in a sports car had gone. All I could see was that blood-soaked body with fingers cut raw by the barbed spearhead and flesh starting to putrefy in the Turkish bath atmosphere.

Accidental death, the police were calling it. Not officially yet – that would be down to the coroner's inquest – but that was what it said on frosty-faced Emily's paperwork. Hence the strangely laid-back investigation. Annie had spelt it out for me on the drive over to Wakens Keep.

'There was this chaise-longue in the police property store. I thought at first it was stolen gear, but it turned out Emily had had it taken out of Steadman's place. It's evidence for the coroner's court. It seems your Luke was trying to change a light bulb. They found the new one still in its carton behind one of the chairs. Instead of getting some steps, he pulled the chaise under the fitting and tried to balance on the curved section. He went over backwards on to that lance. It normally stood in a brass canister, apparently. Kept it partially upright.'

She'd taken one hand from the steering wheel to show me, palm flattened, the angle of the spear.

'According to the post-mortem, it nicked the corner of his heart. He'd have started bleeding to death pretty fast. I mean, he might have yelled for help or tried to reach the phone—'

'The land line was cut off.' I'd tried to imagine what it must have been like. Had he realised he was dying and known it could be days before anyone found him? Had he tried to get to the outside door? What must it have felt like knowing that whatever plans you'd made for the next forty or fifty years were never going to happen now? This was it – check-out time.

'They think it would have been quick,' Annie had said as if she'd read my thoughts. 'All that blood pumping from a heart chamber. He'd have passed out fast. Even if medical help had got there almost immediately, it's doubtful they would have been able to save him. Emily is going to ring his mum; let her know how things stand. But keep the details to yourself until after the inquest, OK? You know what prima donnas some of these coroners can be if anyone pre-empts their moment of glory.'

'There's nothing here,' she said now, replacing the toiletries in their correct positions in Barbra's bathroom cabinet. 'Just how well is our new partner likely to have hidden these negs?'

'She stashed them so that Lee wouldn't find them during his stay. It's a game with them; making each other's lives as miserable as sin. There's no way she'd make it easy for him.'

'Then I figure we're wasting our time like this. You know the score, Grace. Somewhere like this needs an attic-to-basement job. It's going to take the best part of a day and it can't be done when we're tippy-toeing like there's a bomb with a sound-sensitive detonator in the walls.'

She was right: this was hopeless. I was either going to have to get Barbra away from the house for a clear day and risk breaking in. Or find some way to make her hand those negs over.

The phone bell sent my heart bouncing into my mouth. After becoming attuned to the small-hours silence, the whole house seemed to be acting as an echo chamber for the strident ringing.

'Hell, it sounds like it's right outside the door.'

'It nearly is,' Annie hissed back. 'Is there an extension in Barbra's room?'

'How would I know? Let's get out of here.'

We were too late. Barbra answered the extension question by coming out of her room and padding down the upper landing to pick up the receiver. Annie flicked the light in the bathroom off quickly.

Through the heavy door we caught fragments of Barbra's end of the conversation. It sounded like another crank call; although this time, whoever was on the other end had graduated from heavy breathing, judging by Barbra's suggestions that they 'Get off this line before I call the police, you pathetic creep.'

There was more of the same before it went quiet.

'Has she gone?' I murmured in Annie's ear, since she was crouched closest to the keyhole.

'I'm not sure. Give it a minute.'

We waited, trying to control our own breathing. There was no sound from the landing.

'Clear,' Annie murmured.

We were straightening up and reaching for the door handle when we heard the unmistakable click of the receiver being replaced. She'd been out there all the time, listening to whatever was going on on the other end of the line.

Barbra's footsteps were on the move again. Unfortunately, instead of heading back to her bedroom, she was coming this way. Annie just managed to click the light back on again to prevent the door being thrust into our faces.

There are few plausible explanations as to why two women would be together in a bathroom, in the dark, in the early hours of the morning. Particularly when one of them is wearing a pair of rubber gloves.

I was hoping Annie was about to come up with one of them when Barbra said: 'I want you to leave now.'

My first thought – that she'd taken exception to supposed kinky goings-on amongst her sanitary suite – was soon discarded. She didn't look shocked so much as distracted. And hung-over.

'Pardon?' Annie said.

'You heard. You can push off now.'

'It's two o'clock in the morning, Barbra.'

'So? I'll pay you for the full night if that's what's bothering you.'

Annie stiffened. 'It wasn't the first thing that sprang to mind, no. What about your mystery prowler?'

'Stuff him. I'll get me chequebook while you two get dressed.' She whirled away in a sweep of peach satin and coffee lace négligé.

'Curiouser and curiouser,' Annie said.

We had no choice but to get out of there. Sitting in Annie's car with Barbra's cheque safely tucked in my pocket, I asked her if she wanted to hang around to see what happened next.

'No. To hell with her.' She turned her ignition and lights on and felt for the seatbelt. 'You can lurk if you like. Personally, I've had enough of the Barbra Delaney story.'

'That's no way to speak of the saviour of Vetch's Investigations.'

Annie stomped on the accelerator and did a three-point

turn. We left the square in Wakens Keep at the acceleration rate of a speeding bullet.

She dropped me off at my flat. The slashed mattresses were still ... well ... slashed. The floor hadn't got any softer. I used to be able to sleep on a clothes line. Insomnia seemed to be another side effect of turning thirty. After four hours of intermittent snoozing, twisting, and screwing my eyelids closed, I gave up.

Despite the fact it had the rest of this week to fatten on trippers' cash, Seatoun already had a slight air of low-season famine. There was a sense of something slipping slowly away – like water seeping through a pinprick in a plastic container.

I wandered along the promenade, watching the tide hushing over the drifts of tiny white shells as it retreated from the swath of newly swept and cleaned sands. The early-morning masochists' swimming club was frolicking in the spume again, and the joggers who utilised the near-deserted pavements at this time of day pounded past with grim determination. Occasionally one of the chambermaids or breakfast waitresses at the private hotels would hurry past me. I was the only person out here at this hour who seemed to have nothing much to do and all the time in the world to do it. With one exception.

Sipping from a lager can, Kelly Benting was sitting on the closed cinema's steps, watching the early-morning breeze bowling rubbish down the underpass passage until it flattened against the locked entrance doors to the amusement park.

I raised a casual hand from across the road, but she ignored me. Shrugging, I left her to it and continued to drift up and down the front trying to sort out my future (if any) with Peter.

On the plus side, I fancied him and I enjoyed his company – when he was Peter. On the down side, I wasn't so sure about spending time with Rainwing. They called

344

them 'sh'ims' in the States someone had told me – man one day, woman the next. I wasn't sure I could handle the jokes if the truth came out. On the other hand . . .

I got through more hands than Madame Tussaud's turning things over and over in my mind. Without any conscious effort on my part, my feet took me from the sloping pedestrian section to the start of the climb to the area where Seatoun's finest in blue hung out, and back again. Clock tower, public loos, roped-down deckchair stacks, silent children's playground – all slid over my gaze without my really seeing them. Only objects that were out of place made any impression.

Kelly Benting came into that category. I kept passing and repassing her. She'd crossed over the road to the seaward side and was wandering the same stretch of promenade as me. She looked terrible; worse than the day Peter and I had broken up her rumble in the bedroom with Carter. I don't know what she'd taken but I doubted if the can of strong lager she was now sipping as she shlepped unsteadily from one end of the prom to the other was going to help.

Eventually she slowed from crawl to full stop. I finally caught up with her drooped on the prom rail near the harbour.

'Hi.'

At first I thought she wasn't going to bother to answer. Finally, however, she turned dull eyes on me and said: 'Hi yourself.'

'Made it up with the boyfriend, did you?'

'Yeah. Sort of.'

'Carter will be gutted.'

Her indifferent shrug consigned Carter to history.

'So where is he? The boyfriend? Ricky, wasn't it?' I had to elaborate when she looked puzzled.

'Dunno. We had another row, I think. Don't really 'member.'

She took another swig from the can and continued to stare moodily at the sea birds probing the wet sands.

I could recognise a 'get lost' message with the best of them. 'Well, been lovely chatting. We must do it again sometime. Good luck in the Miss Sullen Contest.'

I moved past her. She called sharply: 'Wait!'

So I waited.

It took another couple of sips of lager before she finally blurted out: 'The police station's up there, isn't it?'

'Certainly is. You can't miss it.'

She pushed herself off the prom balustrade. 'Do you know any of them?'

'Some.'

'I got to go shee them. About Luke. About Luke's death. I have to tell 'em what happened.'

Her tongue was tangling in her sentences and she was plainly thinking better of that decision to let go of the railing.

'They know what happened. It was a stupid domestic accident.'

She frowned, turning over this information in her head. And then she came up with a statement that I couldn't really argue with. 'The police are pretty thick, aren't they?'

'Some of them certainly are. Why d'you think so?'

She put her chin up. 'Isn't that obvious? It wasn't an accident. I killed him.'

36

Kelly wanted to confess to the police. I wanted her to confess to me first. Principally because I'm terminally nosy. But also, having discovered the horror, I figured I had a kind of moral right to hear all the details first-hand rather than have to wait months for the court case. I didn't put it to Kelly in quite that way.

'You realise they probably won't believe you?'

'Why not?'

'Take a look at yourself. You're breakfasting on nine per cent proof and I'd guess you've popped something as an aperitif.'

'That was hours ago.' She shook the can. The contents fizzed out of the opening. With an impatient flick, she sent it into a pool below us left by the retreating tide. 'I'm not stoned.' She pushed her fingers through her long hair, drawing it back from her face. Without the tumbling brown curls, the gaunt cheekbones and eye hollows were even more noticeable. 'I know what I'm saying. I killed Luke. And I'm going to tell the police.'

'Take some advice? If you want to be taken seriously, tidy yourself up and get rid of the lager breath; have some breakfast.'

'You reckon?'

'I certainly do. Come on.' I got hold of her arm whilst she was dithering and marched her to Pepi's.

The early-morning dippers had already bagged three of the tables. The aroma of bacon, eggs and spitting sausages filled the place. Kelly's olive complexion turned to dirty green.

'The loos are out back.' I spun her in the right direction and she fled.

When she came back ten minutes later, she still looked rough, but she'd scrubbed off the final traces of yesterday's make-up and she'd made an effort to comb out her hair.

I pushed out the chair opposite by stretching a leg under the table. 'Tea? Coffee? Cyanide?'

She chose coffee. And double poached egg on toast. Seeing my face, she explained: 'My dad says you should make yourself eat after a bender. Balances the blood sugars.'

I ordered the same and let her sit quietly, hugging her

sore midriff and staring blankly out the window until the food came.

She was wearing a tiny leather bag on a thong across her chest. The contents were tumbled on to the formica surface as she sought for money (I hoped). A comb, crumpled tissues, lipgloss, mascara and mints. 'I had a tenner.' She turned the whole thing inside out and shook it.

I took the two mugs from the tray before Shane could retreat. 'You'd better put them on my tab, Shane.'

'What tab?'

'Start one.'

I half expected Kelly to bolt for the loos again when faced with runny poached eggs, but after a second's hesitation she tucked in to her own plate. I guess being raised amongst the alcohol fumes increases your tolerance levels.

'Tell me about Luke,' I invited.

'I want to tell the police.'

'Think of this as a dress rehearsal. Get it straight in your head. Make it sound true.'

'It is true. You think I'm gonna invent some story about *murdering* someone? What sort of sad sicko do you think I am?'

Her voice had risen with indignation at the idea I actually might doubt she wasn't capable of driving a six-foot spear straight through someone's chest. Luckily the jukebox switched from 'Itsy Bitsy Teeny Weeny Yellow Polka Dot Bikini' to 'Sea of Love' at full volume so the surf-bunnies didn't share in her confession.

'So tell me. Take it from the top.'

She thought for a moment, chewing rhythmically and washing down the mouthful with a gulp of coffee, before saying: 'It was Carter's birthday, that Friday.'

'I remember. I was outside the pub when he told you. He wanted to take you out. You said you'd think about it.'

'I only said that to get rid of him. Otherwise he hangs

around staring at me for hours. Only he came back, didn't he. Not then. On his birthday, I mean. He kept going on and on. In the end I told him to push off. I weren't nasty about it,' she assured me earnestly. 'I mean, I never said he was pathetic or anything. I just said I wouldn't ever go with a bloke who didn't have wheels. And then he said would I if he had a car? Well, I figured he had no chance. Where was he going to get a car? So I said, sure, give me a call soon as you get a motor. And then he said . . .' She leant into the eggy plate, lowering her voice. 'He said he'd driven Luke's car loads of times.'

'Did you believe him?'

'As if! I told him, like, yeah, in his dreams. So he said he'd prove it me if I came up Luke's cottage with him. I thought, right, call his bluff – and I told him let's go.'

'When was this? When you collected his birthday present from Luke?'

'What present?'

'Baseball cap. Luke gave it to Carter just after the pair of you overheard him arguing with Est— with your mystery woman.'

'Oh, that. No. We made that up. He never gave Carter a present. Look, you're getting everything out of order. Do you want me to tell this or not?'

I held my hands up in a gesture of peace and surrender. 'Fire away.'

'He had a key to the garage. Carter did, I mean. Luke gave it to him. So he could wash and polish the car. At least that's what Luke thought he did. But Carter says Mr Groom used to hide spare keys in the garage. He found some for the car months back. He showed me. And he's got one to the house too.'

'Not any more he hasn't. So Carter's been doing a bit of joy-riding, has he?'

Over the hills and far away, no doubt. No wonder Luke hadn't known what Harry Rouse was raving on about when he'd had a go at him about wheelies in the farmyard.

'When Luke was away – he used be out all day sometimes, and come back really late at night – Carter said he'd take a baseball cap and sunglasses from the house and go for a spin. People see what they expect to see, Carter said. And a bloke in a cap and glasses in Luke's car must be Luke. He *said* it was dead easy and he'd take me out in it if I liked. Only he couldn't do it then because the motorbike was still there. That's how he knew Luke would be gone for ages. He always took the bike and the cycle helmets.'

'OK, the car wasn't on. What next?'

'I got him to prove he could really get into the house. He opened the door at the back of the garage. That's when we heard Luke arguing with that woman.'

'You mean you weren't lurking in the coat cupboard?'

'No. We never went inside the house. Not then. Carter wanted to leave soon as he heard them. But I wanted to listen.'

'Eavesdropping is one of my favourite hobbies too.'

'It wasn't that. I thought she was a girlfriend. And if they were having a row and breaking up, Luke might want, you know . . .'

'A bit of consoling.'

'Sort of. Can I have another coffee?'

I waved to Shane, who was demonstrating the hand jive with a couple of sugar shakers, and told Kelly to go on. 'What happened after she left?'

'Carter wanted to bolt again. Anyhow, we'd just started to leave when we heard her outside. She was trying to get in the garage. She even got the door up a couple of inches before Carter managed to grab it and hang on. She went away after a while, so we could get out again.'

'And this wasn't the point where you dashed back and flung an enormous – and rather heavy – lance at Luke?'

'No.' She'd caught the scepticism in my voice. 'And I didn't have to fling it. But it wasn't then. It was much later.

Carter asked me to come up to his for tea. It was a birthday tea. His gran does them. It was gross. Stupid little iced fancy cakes and dinky sandwiches cut into stars and circles and things. I'd just die of embarrassment if my mum did that to me. I mean, it's like she thinks he's nine or something.'

'But you hung in there.'

'Yes. I did. And I bought him a card. *And* I had to look at his stupid space stuff. I mean, like I'm really going to be interested in quasars or black holes. I even put up with him drooling down my dress. He went to the loo once. I'm sure he – you know – did it to himself in there.'

'That when you took the keys?'

'Yes. How did you know?'

'Just a lucky guess, Kelly. After which you dumped Carter and made straight for Luke's?'

She nodded, less sure of herself now she was getting to the nastier details. 'I thought he'd be *pleased*. He was always saying these things – chatting me up, like – when he came to the pub. Only my mum and dad are always around there. I thought he wanted to see me on me own.'

'What about your boyfriend? Or had you already had a row with him by then?'

'Ricky? No. We never really had a row, I just had to dump him because . . . Look, you're getting it muddled again. I went up Luke's because he was a film producer. And he had this great car. And it's not like Ricky and me were engaged or nothing.'

'Fair enough. Go on. You used Carter's keys to let yourself in.'

'Luke was in the sitting room. At first I assumed that woman had come back. He'd got the curtains drawn and there were noises – like someone making out, you know? Only it wasn't that. He was watching a video.' She did her best to look cool. 'It was no big deal. Some of the boys bring that sort of stuff into school.'

'Did Luke know you were there?'

'No. Not then. I didn't want to embarrass him or anything, so I stopped in the junk room. That's where the door from the garage comes out.'

'I know.'

It had been one of the rooms Peter had searched during our futile hunt for evidence of his mum's affair with Luke. It was on the left side of the sitting room, opposite the kitchen, which led off to the right. I'd poked my head in briefly during Peter's exploration, noted the accumulated junk of years that was kept because it 'might come in handy one day', and the big stone butler's sink under the window that suggested it might have been the original kitchen or laundry room of the cottage.

'Anyhow, when Luke had finished and gone into the kitchen with the video, I slipped inside and sort of got comfortable on that red velvet couch thing.'

I could see it now. Had she gone for the sideways hip thrust with the dress hitched to thigh level or lain on her stomach, one foot waving and plenty of cleavage on show? All heaving hormones and moist lipgloss?

Lots of blokes might have thought that an attractive package to find on their sofa. But not Luke, apparently.

'He went mad. I mean, really off his head. I've never seen him like that before. He was scary. Asking me how long I'd been there. And what I'd seen. I tried to tell him it was OK. I said why didn't he bring the film back and we'd watch it together? Sort of get in the mood.' Her eyes grew larger and the pupils seemed to expand as she left Pepi's fuggy breakfast atmosphere and travelled back to that early evening in Luke's cottage. 'He was shaking me and shouting what had I seen.'

Unconsciously her hands slid up her arms to massage the faded bruises that had supposedly been caused by Carter's enthusiastic necking technique.

'I was really scared. He looked like he was going to kill

me. He just wouldn't *listen*. I was screaming at him to let go but it was like he didn't even hear. I managed to get free for a sec, but he lunged towards me again. So I did a Tomoe-nage on him.'

'A what?'

'A stomach throw. You stick your foot in the stomach, drop, and flip them over your head. He was coming at me so I got a good momentum. He really went high.'

I remembered the trophy-filled bar room at the Royal Oak. And all those plaques inscribed to 'K. Benting' that I'd assumed belonged to Keith.

'How long have you been doing judo?'

'I don't no more. But I was junior county champion. Will that make it worse?'

'For what?'

'With the police,' Kelly said impatiently. 'Because I knew what I was doing. Even though I never meant to kill him. I didn't know he was going to land on that lance, did I? It's not like I aimed for it or anything. I just wanted to stick it to him and get out of there.'

Instead of which, she'd skewered him. 'Did you try to help him?'

'I don't think so. It was all so fast. I didn't know what was happening at first. There was like all this blood going everywhere and Luke was making these *sounds* . . .' She shuddered. 'I'd never heard anything like them before. He was gurgling and writhing around on the floor. And then he pulled himself up and he came at me again and his hands were all blood . . . and . . .' She held her own fingers wide, palms towards me to demonstrate the horror that had staggered towards her. 'And he kept saying "mob . . . mob", only I didn't understand.'

'Mobile,' I suggested. 'The police found his mobile phone in the bedroom.'

'Oh?' A self-pitying tear slid down her cheek. 'I couldn't move. I really couldn't. I mean, not if he had been going to kill me, I couldn't have.'

'Did he try to?'

'No. He sort of lurched at the phone on the table. And he was banging his hand up and down on the buttons like . . .' She slapped the table to demonstrate Luke's growing disorientation as he tried to beat life into that disconnected line.

Shane took it as the call of a fellow rocker. With a wink in our direction, he took up the rhythm on his counter and finger-drummed his way through 'Have I the Right?'.

'Luke?' I prompted. 'Unconscious. Dead?'

'I don't know. I couldn't bear to touch him to find out. I thought he might be faking. If he'd have grabbed me with those awful hands, I think I'd have just freaked . . . And then Carter came.'

'Came how?'

'Same way as me. I hadn't locked it behind me or anything. He was brilliant. He told me to stand very still so I didn't spread the blood, and then he went and got these plastics bags from the garage. We put them on our feet and hands.'

'While you moved the chaise-longue under the light fitting?'

'That was Carter's idea too. He said it had to be something heavy that had left marks in the floor. So they'd spot it had been moved and that would make them start thinking along the right lines.'

'Or in this case, the wrong ones.'

'Carter was great. He did something to the old bulb to make it blow. He really knows about all that science stuff. And then he put on a pair of Luke's shoes and jumped around on the chaise so they'd pick up the right dirt and stuff from the seat and arm. Then he . . . he . . .'

Her voice got tighter and she had to gulp a mouthful of cold coffee dregs before she could describe how Carter had carefully trodden in Luke's bloodied footprints before he'd exchanged the shoes with the ones Luke had been wearing.

'He couldn't use those, see, because they already had blood on them and they wouldn't have had when Luke was climbing on the chaise.'

'Yes. I got all that, thanks, Kelly. What happened to the old pair?'

'Carter chucked them. He was so brilliant that day . . .' she said yet again. 'He went back to the shop to get a new light bulb. He said he'd tell the police Luke had come in for it just before they closed. I didn't like that bit much. I had to stay in there with Luke. I really kept thinking he was going to get up. Like in a horror movie.'

'Why on earth didn't you call the police? Or at least an ambulance?'

'I don't know. I was *scared*. I thought I'd go to prison. Carter sort of took charge. And once we'd done it all, it just seemed easy to go with it. We made up that story about going in for the birthday present to explain why my fingerprints were in the house. Carter said we shouldn't mention that woman. Not first off. Keep it simple, he said. The less we tell, the less they can prove is a lie. If the police got too near the truth, we could sort of mention her casually and send them off in the wrong direction again.'

'Why'd you tell me about her then?'

'Don't know. Yes I do. I was fed up with Carter being so pleased with himself. I thought I'd screw up his plan a bit.'

'It was your plan too,' I reminded her.

'I guess.'

I prompted her again, reminding her she was supposed to have been at the amusement park with Carter that evening.

'I was. After we'd fixed things at the cottage, he made me go tell my dad I was going to the park with him. We had a taxi. And we went to all the places that have security cameras in Seatoun – so we'd have plenty of alibis. Carter said they can't really tell exactly when someone died – not like in the TV programmes. Is that true?'

'More or less.'

'Nice one. All that science stuff comes in handy sometimes, doesn't it?'

I asked her if she hadn't been covered with Luke's blood.

'A bit. Most sprayed the other way. It was lucky the bar was getting busy. I sneaked up the back stairs and got in the shower. Me and Carter put the clothes I'd been wearing in a rubbish skip in Seatoun. That weekend was awful. I kept thinking, when are they going to find him? But Carter said there was no way we should go near the cottage. He said the police always suspected the person who discovers the body.'

'He's a right little fund of knowledge, our Carter, isn't he? Lucky I called in, wasn't it? Put you out of Luke's misery.'

'I'm glad you found him,' Kelly said simply. 'I wanted him to be buried properly. It was horrible thinking of him lying there like that. Even if he did turn out to be a nasty shit.'

'So why have you decided to confess all now? Conscience?'

'No. Well, a bit. It's Carter. I was really *grateful*. I was even going to stop the rest of them getting at him at school. But . . . but . . .'

'But Carter wanted a lot more.'

'Yes.' She stared through the windows. 'He's awful. Sweaty and horrible. And he *hurts* me.' Tears threatened as she recalled what must have virtually amounted to rape. 'I try not to mind. I take some stuff before I see him and just sort of block it out until he's finished, but I can't do it no more. I'd rather tell the police and go to prison.'

'Why don't you just tell Carter to go stuff himself in future?'

'He'll shop me.'

'Then you'll be no worse off than if you shop yourself. And who knows? Maybe he won't. Tell him you'll tell everyone what he made you do if he tries it.'

'You think?' Hope filled her eyes. A sunny morning and breakfast were starting to make the world look less bleak.

'It's worth a try,' I suggested.

'I guess.' She bit her lip doubtfully. 'But . . . what am I going to tell my dad? He's going to go spare about my not coming home last night.'

In the end she borrowed telephone change from me and managed to rustle up a school friend who was prepared to swear she'd spent the night. 'Her parents are away. She's got a floor full of people sleeping over. If I get round there before me dad drives over, he'll never know. 'Bye. Ta for breakfast.'

Her mood had already changed. I'd offered her a lifeboat and she'd gone from a third-class ticket-holder to Kate Winslet in seconds.

'Hang on a minute,' I called as she headed for the door. 'Who moved the videos to the sofa?'

Kelly looked blank. 'Sorry?'

'You said Luke took the video into the kitchen. But I found Whiplash Wendy and her friends stuck down the back of the sofa.'

'No. Those are Carter's videos. He wanted me to watch them with him. Pathetic little creep. I don't know what happened to Luke's. I suppose it's still in the kitchen.'

So how come we hadn't found it when we searched the place?

37

It was like a rerun of that first morning that I visited St Biddy's. Only then I didn't have a clue what was at the end of my bicycle ride, and now I did. I wasn't sure the first option hadn't been preferable.

Since my initial visit, Harry Rouse and Luke Steadman

were both dead; Atch had been carted off to a psychiatric ward somewhere; Kelly Benting was nursing a guilty secret and Carter was an accessory to concealing evidence. On balance, I reflected, pedalling into another fine morning, the inhabitants of St Biddy's probably regarded my arrival in much the same spirit that their ancestors viewed the appearance of the plague cart.

I'd popped into the office before heading out to Brick Cottage. Life in Vetch (International) Associates Inc. was returning to normal. Which is to say, Jan was slumped in reception prepared to repel all comers with an Olympic-class performance in the sulk, snarl and supine event; Vetch was huddled behind his overlarge executive-style desk wrestling with a sheaf of notes in Annie's handwriting and wearing that smug expression that managed to suggest he knew something the rest of us didn't; and Annie herself was upstairs slapping paint on her office walls.

'Pink,' I said. 'How do you know the next tenant won't want something a bit more butch?'

'Hibiscus. And I like to leave things tidy.'

'You're still relocating to London, then?'

'Possibly. There was a call for you earlier. I left the number on that pad.'

I didn't recognise it, but attempting to dial it on Annie's phone brought a sharp 'no' from the decorator in question. 'Use your own extension. And by the way, I'd just painted that door you were leaning on.'

Luckily most of the pink – sorry, hibiscus – had missed the sleeveless singlet. I swabbed with turps whilst I punched in the unfamiliar numbers. Faye answered on the second ring.

'Grace, thank heavens. I was just about to switch the phone off. I went for an early walk, but I'm almost back at the house. I can't talk for long. Have you got the negatives?'

'Afraid not. But I'm still working on it.'

She said something under her breath. Even over the erratic connection I could hear she was agitated. 'Has something else happened?'

'Yes. Well, perhaps not happened. But there's something not quite right. I can't put my finger on it, but I keep getting this odd feeling that Hamish *knows* something.'

I was darn sure he did. 'Is he giving you a hard time?'

'No. In fact, he's being particularly charming.'

'And this is a problem?'

'You're not married. You don't understand. I really need those negatives, Grace. They are the only real proof of mine and Luke's . . . friendship.'

Friendship? Nice one, Faye. The great passion was fading already. Isn't it amazing how self-preservation kicks in again as soon as sex is no longer an option? But I owed the woman: how many people would nurse a virtual stranger through food poisoning rather than pack her off to the local hospital sharpish?

I swore to Faye that I wouldn't stop looking until I'd prised the relevant incriminating evidence out of my client. (Although how I was going to do that without alerting Barbra to the fact there was something rather special about her portrait collection was still beyond me.)

Faye rang off abruptly as she reached the pathway to her in-laws' house, I assumed.

Annie had declined to give me a lift to St Biddy's. Instead she'd delivered another lecture on the subject of replacing my car. It was back to Grannie Vetch's pride and joy again.

I'd left it too long between rides. My calf muscles and thighs were aching with the strain; someone seemed to have taken a lathe to the saddle and sharpened it to an even more impossibly narrow angle, and the shock absorbers had decided they'd absorbed enough shocks for one lifetime, thanks a lot – from now on, my bottom could do the job.

By the time I reached the general store I was glad to

dismount and wheel it the last stretch down Cowslip Lane. A car glided past as I was disentangling myself from the pedals. I glimpsed a subdued Kelly in the passenger seat. Her eyes met mine briefly, and imperceptibly she touched her forefinger to her lips. I nodded.

There was no answer at Brick Cottage. I tried doors and banged on windows but couldn't raise any response. Even the garage was shut down tight. It looked like Peter had gone. I experienced a twist of disappointment in my chest. Up until then I hadn't realised quite how much I'd been looking forward to seeing him. I realised my mind had made itself up – without any conscious effort on my part as far as I was aware – to go with the relationship and to hell with what anyone else thought.

I'd done a complete circuit of the cottage and convinced myself there was no legitimate means of entry available. So I used an illegitimate one – a half-brick.

Somebody should have told Uncle Eric about his security arrangements. Once the small square of window pane had been carefully wriggled from the crumbling putty, it was laughably easy to reach inside and disengage the latch.

I'd chosen a window facing the fields at the back, which meant that the room I dropped into was the one Kelly had described as the junk room. The butler's sink provided a handy step from sill to floor on my way through to the sitting room.

No matter how much I wanted to, it was hard not to look at 'that' light fitting. It was still bulb-less. And the shiny indents left in the wooden floor by furniture that had stood in the same place for years until the clean-up squad had rearranged them leapt out at me now I was looking for them. Carter was right – people *did* see what they expected to see. Just add a displaced couch and a couple of bulbs and I'll bet I'd have worked out that 'accidental death' scenario too – and preened myself on how fast I'd done it!

He really was a smart little cookie. By keeping it simple

and making old Frosty-face Emily do just enough detective work, he'd led her by the nose. My earlier prediction to Kelly that Carter would be earning megabucks in ten years' time probably wasn't that far-fetched.

There was a plate and a cup drying on the draining board in the kitchen. I tested the kettle and thought I detected a faint warmness on my skin. Peter hadn't been gone long. The hormones woke up and sniffed the flowers. I told them we weren't picking any today and got back to business.

(Well, strictly speaking it *wasn't* my business. But now I knew about that video – and the fact Luke had hidden it so well it had evaded our original search – I just had to find out what was in it.)

But first I had to find the damn thing. We'd looked in all the likely places. In fact, as far as I knew, we'd rooted around in all the unlikely places, and we'd come up empty-handed. So where was there left to search?

The memory of our tidy exploration of this cottage brought back memories of my own visiting burglars trashing my flat and not finding my building society books.

I examined Uncle Eric's cooker with new interest. It was sitting in an alcove much like the one at my flat that had housed the boarding house's old Edwardian range. Sitting on the top, I squirmed round and peered upwards. The gap above my head was almost identical to that in my flat. Kneeling up, I fished at the brickwork, feeling dust and crumbling mortar and . . . hallelujah!

That missing stack-pipe must have been a common feature of early kitchen fittings. The two bricks came away easily. No shower of gritty dirt fell into my upturned eyes and mouth. They'd been moved recently – too recently for any more debris to collect along the joints. Standing at a half-crouch on Uncle Eric's Aga, I thrust my hand in up to the forearm.

The hole was completely empty.

*

There were two possibilities as far as I could see. Firstly, Peter had found whatever was in there and that was the reason he'd taken off this morning. Or secondly, the only other person with access to this cottage had located that video before we started our search.

Carter wasn't in the shop. His grandmother was serving a small queue at the sub-post office counter. Another group of customers were huddled near the till, their hands full of things they'd have bought if only someone would take their money. One of them saved me the trouble by asking where Carter was.

'He went out.' Grannie concentrated on counting out the benefit money, her fingers sweeping the ends of the notes into a blur.

The tremble in her hands was even more pronounced today. She fumbled the delivery of the cash under the grille. The coins slid off the notes and bounced to the floor. Everyone diving to collect the spinning change left Grannie and me face to face through the bars for a split second.

'So where is Carter?'

'I have no idea. But I don't want you to talk to him. You're a bad influence. Everything was so much simpler before you came.'

She took a tiny lace-edged hanky from her pocket to dab spittle from her lips. Her hand missed the pink choppers by a mile and wiped a pathway through a strawberries-and-cream cheek to reveal the network of broken thread veins underneath.

'That's a bit rich, isn't it? I've hardly had three conversations with your grandson.'

'It doesn't matter. Carter is a different boy. He wasn't like this before.'

I felt like telling her he was – he'd just covered up his exploits rather more carefully. Now he'd ceased to care whether she knew or not. 'He's growing up, kicking out; everyone does it.'

'Carter doesn't. We had rules and he was content to abide by them . . . but now . . .'

'Now . . . ?'

'Nothing. Can you move aside, please. It's not your turn.'

I held my position. 'Sure you don't know where I can find Carter?'

'He'll be hanging around the graveyard again,' the owner of that pile of cash said. 'Funny kid.'

'Cheers.'

I escaped, conscious once more of an odd shift in her relationship with her grandson. The woman was definitely scared – but for him, or of him?

There was no sign of life in the churchyard – unless you counted trilling birdlife and the glimpsed scuts of rabbits scuttling away. I tried to check out the church but found the huge wooden doors locked and all the lower windows covered with mesh grilles.

Hitching myself on a large ornate monument to some long-dead inhabitant of St Biddy's who'd obviously decided that if he couldn't take it with him, he was damn well going to have most of it where he could see it, I considered my next move.

'I could check out the pubs. He could be lurking and lusting after Kelly,' I told the po-faced angel piously looming over *Eugene Thomas Tanner – Gentleman Farmer of This Parish*. One of Carter's distant relatives had been a Tanner, I seemed to recall. And Barbra's grandmother. It must have been hell trying to find a partner who wasn't too close for the Church's comfort in these small villages. I wandered through the overgrown grasses, reading the worn names etched in crumbling stones. Between them the Tanners, Coopers, Carters, Windrows, Rouses, Tillys and Turners had gone forth and multiplied until the land was full. It was fascinating tracing which family had been top dogs in which period. The larger the ego, the larger the gravestone, as far as I could see.

The Coopers had reached the peak of their pretensions about the time of Carter's great-uncle Carter Cooper, who was planted under a large cross set on a stepped plinth. I wondered if Carter's surname was Cooper. It must be odd to see your own name already on a tombstone. Totally freaky, in fact. Was that the 'special connection' Carter had meant that stretched between him and that earlier Carter? Or was there something else?

Squatting down, I peered closely at the plinth. There were four steps, each slightly smaller than the one beneath it. They were all carved from some kind of rough dark stone that had held a century and a half of dirt and moss. Except that on a quarter of the lowest step, the staining seemed slightly discoloured. Rubbing a finger on it, I found that the brownness loosened easily and left an oily deposit on my skin. It was ordinary soil mixed with some kind of grease and slapped on to hide the fact that underneath the original engrained dirt had been scraped away.

Putting both hands flat against the stone above it, I pushed hard. It wouldn't budge. The graveyard was still deserted apart from a few lunching bunnies. Standing, I hugged the cross like it was my closest pal and twisted. This time it came with me, disclosing a cavity in the lowest step. It was plugged with plastic sheeting.

Pulling it free, I discovered several thick plastic bags wrapped around half a dozen packages. The first held magazines full of the kind of girls you didn't take home to Grannie; the second held about forty pounds in notes and a packet of condoms; number three was wound round a pair of trainers. He'd cleaned them up, but squinting along the tread I could still make out a few dark flecks caught up against the sole. The videos were in the fourth packet: three unlabelled proprietary-brand tapes. It was always possible, of course, that none of them was the one that Kelly had seen Luke watching that night. Maybe they were just a few more mucky mail jobs like Whiplash Wendy and her friends. There was only one way to find out.

I quickly checked the last two packages. Number five held the sunglasses, cap and the keys to the car. The sixth was full of photos. There were a few of a younger Carter with a man and woman who'd I'd guess were his parents. There was nothing in them to shock Grannie, so I assumed that Carter just needed to feel close to them somewhere away from the old girl's influence. The other snaps were in a Boots folder like the one Barbra had handed me at the Rock Hotel a few weeks ago. I flicked through the glossy contents. At first I didn't believe what I was seeing.

And then I didn't want to believe it.

38

I used the video player at Brick Cottage to check the tapes. The first was of Carter running through an exercise programme in this room. The camera mercilessly dwelt on the sweating rolls of lardy flesh as he bent, twisted and used a couple of cans of baked beans to pump iron. He was only wearing his underpants, giving the high-tech lens the chance to capture yards of the freckled skin with each grunt and gasp. The programme was way out of his class. By the time he finished he was practically crying.

I expected more of the same on the second tape. Which in a way it was. Vigorous physical activity certainly; but with a different end in mind, if you see what I mean. I couldn't take more than five minutes of this one before I fast-forwarded it. Number three was more of the same.

Wrapping the tapes and photos back in Carter's plastic bag, I improvised a hiding place under the bushes at the far end of the garden before mounting up and pedalling into the village. I tackled Grannie again, this time in an empty shop.

'I have already told you, I don't know where Carter is.' She sat down heavily on the stool by the till, the fingers of one plump hand splayed just below today's floppy bow, which was electric blue. 'I asked him where he was going. He is supposed to help me in the shop in his holidays. He told me to . . . to . . .' She raised bewildered eyes. 'We don't use those words. Those words aren't nice.'

'Have you any idea at all where he went? He could be in trouble.'

The fingers clawed at her blouse. 'What kind of trouble? Carter wouldn't do anything bad. He's my little Mr Manners.'

'Actually, he's not all that little any more. And a kid who cared for you less would probably have told you where to stick Mr Manners long ago. You do know you're making life hell for him at school, treating him like he's a nine-year-old stuck in some nineteen-fifties time warp?'

'I don't know what you mean. Good manners are important.'

'I daresay. But you have to adapt them to the situation. And Mr Manners is about the only person Carter has to hang out with at present, Mrs . . . Cooper?'

'Tilly. My daughter was Mrs Cooper.'

Good guess, then. Carter's surname was Cooper, just like his graveyard safebox.

'OK, Mrs Tilly. Any ideas where Carter might have gone? He's not at the church. I checked.'

'I truly do not know. He visits Brick Cottage. To take care of the motor car.'

Once again her voice had slipped into that old local accent that made it come out 'Oi truly'. It gave me an idea.

'What about the Rouses' farm? Carter told me he used to play up there. Atch taught him how to drive in the farm truck.'

'Did he? I didn't know that or I'd have been Mrs Cross. It doesn't surprise me, though. Atch Rouse was troublesome as a child. Always into where he shouldn't be. And a devil with a catapult. He put out every window in the village. The times his dad took a strap to his backside.'

The idea of Atch as a small boy brought an unexpected lump to my throat. It was probably lucky we couldn't see what fate had in store for us at the end.

'I suppose Carter might have gone up there,' Grannie conceded. 'But I hope he hasn't after all those nasty goings-on. Drugs, someone was saying. You don't think Carter . . . ?'

'No. It wasn't drugs. Anyway, I'm sure Carter's got more sense than to turn into Mr Crackhead. I'm going to pop up there and take a look. Can you do me a favour? If I'm not back in an hour, ring the police station at Seatoun and tell a policeman called Jerry Jackson where to find me.'

It wasn't an instruction designed to turn a worried old lady into Mrs Happy, but after my last prolonged stay on the farm, I wanted to be certain someone came calling this time.

At first glance Tyttenhall Farm was deserted. The tracks of the police vehicles that had churned up the yard that night were still visible, baked into the hardening ground. So was the discoloured stain where Harry Rouse had leaked away his life.

The house was locked up, but shouting and rattling the handles did flush out one inhabitant. The cat sped around the corner and twisted itself frantically between my legs, yowling with all the force of a cat that had got the message that it was time to move on to another mug with tin-opening skills.

'Sorry, puss. I'm not a cat sort of person.'

Arching its back, the ginger tom spat in a way that indicated he wasn't a people sort of puss if it came to that.

But we all had to lower our standards sometimes. He gave me his best shot at an impression of terminal starvation.

'No food.' I spread my hands. 'Nothing concealed up my sleeve. Go latch on to some gullible old lady, ginger.'

With a last disgusted hiss, the cat trotted away towards the barn. I followed it. Despite knowing that the police would have taken away the shotguns, I couldn't help twisting as I walked. My eyes flicked all over the place, and my ears were straining for the sounds of anyone trying to sneak up on me.

Rather than open the doors wide, I slipped inside and let my eyes become accustomed to the gloom. There were a few of those wooden pallets that had held the seedling cauliflowers smashed on the rough floor. Apart from that, the interior appeared as deserted as it had been during my enforced stay a few weeks ago.

'Hello? Anyone here?'

I didn't expect such a violent reaction. A squeal that outdid the cat's effort rose to the vaulted roof, accompanied by a rhythmic crashing.

He was tied to the last stall. Unlike me, he'd been bound by his elbows with his back against the wooden bars and a lump of sticky tape across his mouth. I peeled it off.

With a noisy rasp, Carter tried to get his breath. It wouldn't come. You could almost hear the air stick at the back of his throat while his lungs desperately tried to draw it in. His eyes bulged with panic.

'Take it easy and try to breathe slowly. Come on . . . do it with me. In . . . out . . . in . . . out . . .'

He was struggling, but he had the sense to try to relax. I felt the taut muscles in his arms losing their rigidity as he deliberately let his body go limp. It made it easier for me to get the knots untied and for the alveoli in his lungs to receive a shot of oxygen-laden blood.

'Good. Nice going, Carter. Now just lean back here for a minute and take it easy.'

He tried to speak and couldn't. Turning out my jeans pockets, I unearthed one of the toffees I'd bought in his gran's store, tangled up in the till receipt. Pushing the sweet into his mouth, I studied the receipt whilst he gulped gratefully on the returning spittle. When I judged he was able to speak, I held the receipt up.

'Do you know, Carter, I've been wondering what spooked your gran. It's the receipt, isn't it? Or rather, the lack of one. You never rang the light bulb Luke supposedly bought on that Friday evening through the till. Well you couldn't, of course. Those electronic tills have a memory, don't they? It would have shown the time was long after the shop shut. Mind you, smart operator like you, I'm surprised you couldn't fiddle the electronics or whatever it is you do.'

Carter sucked in and swallowed before saying: 'I could have, but I thought the police might have it checked and spot it had been tampered with. I decided it was better to say I'd pocketed the money if they asked. They expect kids to steal.'

'Your gran doesn't. Do you know, I wouldn't be surprised if she thinks you killed him.'

'What?' Carter's eyes widened. His face was shiny with sweat, much like it had been in that very cruel video. 'No kidding?' He considered this for a second. And a slight smile tilted his thick lips. 'Good. She's been much easier to live with.'

'She's also scared. And old. Since you had the story about nicking the price of the bulb all rehearsed for the police, why not use it on Grannie instead?'

'Might.' Carter's chubby chops masticated the sweet. 'How'd you know?'

'I had a long chat with Kelly.'

Light fired in his eyes. 'She's back? Her dad come round this morning looking for her. She never came home last night.'

'That's because she got smashed trying to work up the nerve to go confess to the police.'

'She never did!'

'No. She's decided on a new tactic. If you split on her she's going to tell the whole village what you made her do. Blackmailing someone into sex is pretty nasty, Carter.'

'I didn't. It wasn't like that.' To my horror, he suddenly burst into noisy sobs. The tears poured down his freckled cheeks whilst his asthmatic lungs pumped in and out with noisy wheezes.

'I really love her,' Carter managed to gulp out. 'I know I look funny and everyone thinks I'm some kind of geek, but I thought if Kelly could see how much nicer I'd be to her than the others, then she'd love me too. And I *was* good to her. I did everything I thought she'd like. Those other blokes just treat her like rubbish.' He turned a face white with misery to me. 'She has to love me. I love her so much it hurts. All the time.'

'I know.' I hugged his fleshy shoulder. 'But it doesn't work like that, unfortunately. People you wouldn't want to share the same planet with spend their entire time in your face, and the ones you really fancy don't know you're alive.'

He sniffed in another noseful of misery. 'I knew it was all over really when she went off yesterday. I hate her.'

'No you don't.'

'But I wish I did,' he burst out. 'If Kelly doesn't want me, I wish I was dead. What am I going to do?'

'Get out of here for a start. How did he get you up here?'

'He phoned me. He wanted a quiet place to meet. He was going to pay for . . . something.'

'I've got the something, Carter. I paid a visit to Great-uncle Cooper this morning.'

He twisted free. 'You had no right! Those are my private things!'

'Actually, Carter, a large number aren't yours at all.' I

was relieved to see that normal colour was returning to his face and his breathing was back to a regular rhythm. 'When did you take those tapes from Luke's cottage?'

'That night,' he muttered sulkily. 'I nipped back when Kelly went home to wash and change. When she said Luke had taken one into the kitchen, I guessed he was using that hole as a hiding place. Loads of the old places around here have that gap. Everyone thinks they're the first to find it. Did you watch Luke's tapes?'

'A little.'

'I'm glad Kelly killed him. I wasn't at first because I really liked him then. If it hadn't been her who'd done it, I'd have called the police straight off that night.'

'If it hadn't been Kelly, you wouldn't have been following her up there in the first place.'

'She took my keys. She pretended to be all friendly coming for my birthday and looking at my space stuff, and then she stole them. I knew she'd go up there. I mean, I could never figure her liking those losers she hangs with, but Luke was a cool guy. I thought he was my friend, but he was just laughing at me like all the rest. I bet he showed that tape to all his friends. I bet they had parties to laugh at me.'

'I doubt it. Why'd you keep it?'

'Dunno. Didn't believe it. I thought if I kept watching it enough it would change, be something else. That sounds really stupid, doesn't it?'

'No. I do that with films with unhappy endings. One day I figure the *Titanic* is going to make it to New York. Did you watch the other tapes, Carter?'

He flushed a guilty pink. The tip of his tongue moistened his lips. 'A bit. It was that bird in your photos, wasn't it?'

Rather than answer that one, I asked him if he recalled the day he'd looked through Barbra's snaps. 'I dived off the church wall under Luke's car, remember?'

'Sure.'

'Can you remember who was in the two pictures you hung on to? The ones you passed to Luke while I was pulling myself together?'

'The women.'

'Both of them?'

'Yeah. One of each. Why?'

'Never mind, I—' We both heard it at the same time. The distant throb of a car engine. 'Move.'

I dragged Carter to his feet and hustled him to the door. The bike was still propped against the front of the farmhouse.

'Get it out of sight. And as soon as it's clear, split.'

'What about you?'

'I'll be fine. And listen, Carter, there's something else I want you to do . . .'

I gave him his instructions. He wasn't keen, but the threat of someone murmuring in a vengeful Keith Benting's ear was enough to send him trotting across to drag Grannie Vetch's pride around the back of the farmhouse before the car bonnet appeared at the top of the rise.

39

I wasn't sure which of them I'd be facing. I sat quite still in the barn stall, my chin on my knees and my arms hugging my shin bones, betting with myself, until I caught the blur of movement at the corner of my eye.

'I win,' I said. 'You move differently.'

'Differently from what?' Peter asked.

'Differently from Rainwing. She glides, you saunter. Walk it like they talk it, eh?'

He squatted on his haunches beside me. The grey trousers and sweater blended into the background, so that I was conscious once more of the gleam of gold skin in the V between throat and breastbone. 'Something like that. Where's the kid?'

'Gone. What the hell did you think you were doing, trussing him up like that?'

'He stole something that belongs to me. And he wanted five hundred pounds to return it. I don't have five hundred pounds. I barely have one hundred at present. I wasn't going to leave him here. Just give him a few hours to think about it.'

'He has asthma. A few minutes could have been enough with the gag on.'

'I didn't know. Truly, Grace. I don't want to hurt anyone.'

'Don't you? You could have fooled me. Well, let's face it, you *have* been fooling me – or helping me to fool myself. This whole bloody seduction scenario was to make sure I didn't spoil your little blackmail scam, wasn't it?'

'You've seen the tapes.'

'I've got the tapes.'

'Carter said—'

'Forget Carter.' I unfolded myself and rose. He followed me so that we ended up looking into each other's eyes. 'It's me you have to deal with now. If you're thinking of tying me up here, forget it, sunshine. Been there; done that; got the T-shirt.'

'I wouldn't hurt you, Grace. Even if I wanted to, I couldn't.' He reached over and tucked a strand of hair behind my left ear. ' "*Give me that man that is not passion's slave.*" '

I knocked his hand away. 'Can the performance. It stinks. I'm not surprised nobody ever casts you.'

That one hurt him. I saw the flicker in his eyes and wanted to hug him better. 'Let's get some fresh air. I need it.'

He allowed me to lead the way back to the yard. The car was parked by the house. Perching on the still warm bonnet, I waited for Peter to join me. 'So tell me more about this scam. When did you and Luke put it together?'

'When we realised there wasn't going to be any pot of gold from Uncle Eric. The stupid old bastard had promised to invest in Luke's production—'

'There really was a film?'

'Of course there was. I told you, Luke had real talent. He could have been another Spielberg or Tarantino. Old Eric was tickled pink at the idea of being involved.'

' "I can get you in the movies"?'

'Exactly. But it wasn't a con – he would have got his money back. We thought he was loaded. He sent cash out to the States regularly when Luke was there. And then when he checked out—'

'You discovered he'd sold the cottage to a finance company – and the payments died with him.'

'There was hardly anything left. We were desperate, Grace.'

'So you came up with the idea of blackmailing your own mother?'

'It wasn't blackmail.'

'What was it, then?'

'A publishing deal.'

'Excuse me?'

Up until then he'd been facing me. Now he came to sit next to me on the sun-warmed bonnet. The hand nearest me lightly brushed mine.

'A publishing deal,' he repeated. 'A book. Serialised extracts in the newspapers. Possibly an electronic package – Internet publishing. My mother is attractive to the media now; she's different, a bit exotic, rather sexy. A cabinet post would have added the final gloss. Give it a few months to get her face on all the right covers, and then . . .'

'Dump on her?'

'It wasn't like that.'

'Isn't it? I've seen the tapes, remember?'

'Where are they?'

'Safe. The photo collection too. That's how I knew you were in on it with Luke, if you're interested. You used the uncompromising ones when you pulled that switch on me in Daniel Sholto's flat.'

They'd all been there. The pagoda-shaped pavilion with its curly red roof; the lake with its protective swan; the cliff with the teapot rock; the anonymous street with the van propped on bricks. Only in the collection Carter had lifted from Luke's hidey-hole, Luke and Faye were included amongst the scenery. They were almost charmingly innocent: in one, his head was bent to hers, the highlighted strands mingling with her ebony; in others they were walking hand-in-hand or with his arm around her shoulder. The one kiss was of the peck-on-the-cheek variety.

'I had to improvise fast,' Peter said. 'The discards from those reels was all I had at the bedsit.'

'Did you take them?'

'Who else?'

'And it didn't make you feel grubby sneaking around after your mum and her lover with a long-range lens?'

'No. If you've seen them, you know there's nothing salacious in the whole collection. My mother's too naturally discreet to behave improperly in public. I doubt she even kisses my bloody stepfather outdoors.' His voice had changed. There was a bitter edge to each word, like hoar frost riming leaves. 'That's why Luke had to get her down here. Give the public something worth salivating over. Who'd have thought the oh-so-cool Faye Sinclair could be such a tart.'

'You watched the tapes!'

'You sound shocked. You really are just an old-fashioned girl under that mean-chick performance, aren't you?'

'Thanks for the "girl". How did Carter's work-out get in on the act?'

'Luke wanted to test out the cameras. See he'd got them

set up correctly for my mother's . . . performance. I didn't know he'd kept it. It probably gave him a buzz – all that boyish flesh.'

There was only one way to interpret that last remark. 'Luke was gay?'

'Ragingly so.'

'Are you?'

'I already told you – no. Although I think Luke always had hopes of converting me.'

'But he had an affair with your mum!'

'One of us had to for this to work. And I don't think she'd have jumped into bed with me. Although I'll grant you, it would have added a few noughts to the publisher's cheque if she had.'

'You really are the pits, Peter.'

'What the hell do you know about it? Have you any idea what my life has been like?'

'Pretty cushy, I'd say. Even that commune wasn't exactly brown rice and loos in the vegetable patch, was it?'

'The commune was great. I loved it. I wanted to stay there. But that didn't suit Mr Hamish Alastair Sinclair. Didn't fit the image to have a stepson hanging out with the hippies. Might look too much like child neglect. So he put pressure on my mother to send me to that goddamn-awful boarding school. And when she wasn't convinced, he recruited good old Selwyn to the cause. There are some people who thrive on being patronised by the great and the good – and believe me, Selwyn is one of them. Between them they managed to convince Mother my best chance lay in the public education system. Children sense things. They know when you're different. That's where I first realised I could act. Believe me, I acted for my life at that school some days.'

'Did you tell anyone?'

'You don't, do you? Because it will make things worse. You just hang in there and pray you'll get through it. And the vacs weren't much better. Do you know what it's like to always feel like the odd one out? The child that doesn't fit into the cosy family set-up?'

Actually – yes. But I wasn't in the mood to start slagging off my own lot, so I let him keep going, pouring out fourteen-odd years of resentment.

'They never said anything – well, apart from my maternal grandfather, who didn't say plenty, if you see what I mean – but I felt it. How much they'd prefer it if it was just my sisters in all those family snaps and official party pictures. I was a living reminder of the skeleton in the closet. I kept popping up like a fault in the lens that leaves a trace on every print.'

'I think you're being a bit hard on your mum, Peter. She seems to care about you.'

'What would you know? Do you know what my father told me? My real father, I mean, not Hamish. He wanted to marry my mother. I'd always thought I was a case of hard-luck-sweetie-and-here's-five-hundred-for-the-abortion.   I was actually *grateful* to my mother for having the courage to go ahead and have me. I could have been the oldest son; the oldest *legitimate* son. Instead of being invisible, I'd have been my grandfather's favourite. But it seems my mother decided she didn't want to ruin both their lives by tying them together in a loveless marriage. She didn't care about ruining my life, though, did she? So why the hell should I care about ruining hers?'

'It's hardly ruined, is it, Peter? You've got the career you wanted. This time next year you could be the next DiCaprio.'

'Or I could be cleaning up after rich bitches. Or working split shifts as a waiter serving Hooray Henrys and bored bimbos who lunch.'

'That what you usually do?'

'Mostly.'

'I thought you had a professional touch with those champagne bottles.'

His hand moved fully over mine. 'That was a magical night for me, Grace.'

'Oh, sure. Just two kindred souls touching across the glorious infinity of space – and lying like hell to each other.'

'I thought we'd sorted that.'

'The only reason we met at all was based on a lie. All that rubbish about worrying that I'd taken pictures of Rainwing that could embarrass your mum. It wasn't the picture of you in your frock that bothered Luke that morning I met him. It was the shot of your mum. The pair of you thought someone else was about to break the news of the big affair and ruin your scam. It's lucky that bus didn't run thirty minutes earlier. You could have bumped into her yourself and trashed the whole plot.'

'Luke was supposed to keep her in the house. We didn't know she'd even been out until—'

'Carter waved the evidence under Luke's nose that morning and launched you both into conniving mode. Was it you who trashed my flat?'

'I'm sorry about that. I'd never done anything like that before. I was panicking. I wanted to find those negatives and get out as fast as possible. I kept expecting you to walk in on me.'

So while I'd been looking for clues about him in Daniel Sholto's flat that Friday, he'd been doing the same in mine. 'How'd you get the address? I don't keep anything with it on in my bag.'

'There's a man off Tottenham Court Road . . . If you give him a telephone number, he's got this computer program that can back-trace to the address. Some of the crowd use him to find the homes of producers, casting directors and the like. Means you can work out which is their local and start hanging out there.'

'Same trick with the office as well?'

He nodded. 'I had to wait for it to close. Even then, I wasn't sure I could get in.'

'You were lucky you didn't kill yourself swinging across the gutter.'

'I know. I nearly *did* die when I saw the alarm systems. All the time I was listening for sirens. That's why I smashed my way around. I couldn't be neat – I hadn't the time. Especially when Luke had flunked it. Or I thought he had.'

'Luke was supposed to be there?'

'Of course he was. I didn't see how I could do it by myself. I rang him up and told him to meet me at ten. I thought it would be dark enough by then. Only he didn't show.'

'So you left him a couple of reminders on his mobile. Using my voice.'

'Did I? It wasn't deliberate. I like to practise other voices when I hear them. Yours was in my head. It has been a lot recently, Grace.'

He squeezed my hand gently. I moved it away. 'Didn't you wonder *why* he hadn't shown up?'

'I thought he'd bottled it. He didn't want to do it in the first place. He was terrified.'

'Of getting caught.'

'That. But more of slipping from that gutter and ruining his precious face. He was a vain bitch. We had words. I was going to go out there and tell him what I thought of him, but I didn't have the price of a mini-cab. I had pictures of him refusing to answer the door and the cab driver calling the police when he found out I was broke. It was the last thing I needed. I couldn't even get home. I'd only bought a single train ticket. Luke was supposed to drive me back after we'd—'

'Stolen my photos?'

'Yes. Sorry.'

We sat in silence for a few minutes, then I asked how he

had got back. 'Slept in a prom shelter that night, hitched back Saturday.'

We'd probably passed each other. Me fuming on the train because he'd taken me for an idiot. And him on the motorway because he hadn't taken me for as much as he'd wanted to.

Abruptly Peter said, 'I thought he was sulking. When he didn't ring me. He could sulk, you know. I was going to let him stew in it over the Bank Holiday and then stage the big reconciliation scene. He liked those. Always raised his hopes that he could get me to cross over to the other lot. And then suddenly there were those news reports of a suspicious death. I knew it was him before they named him – I just knew.'

'So you thought you'd rush down to Mummy and see if the police had been round yet with a set of dodgy videos?'

'Partly. Although to be honest . . .' He paused at my involuntary snort of derision. '. . . to be honest, I needed to bum some cash and the use of her car to get over here and find out what the hell was going on. It's not easy being a crook when you're flat broke and you've got no wheels.'

'It's not easy catching them either,' I said with feeling, recalling the past weeks' adventures with Grannie Vetch's bike.

We exchanged a grin. Without meaning to, I'd let him under my guard. And he knew it.

'Just because I met you under false pretences, that doesn't mean that my feelings towards you were false, Grace.'

I wasn't ready to let him off that meat hook yet. 'You mean, when you shared your soul with me the other day and claimed you'd bolted because you couldn't handle the possibility we'd break up later over the frocks, that was really genuine? Call me a cynic, but I had this nasty little idea you'd dumped me after we'd dug Carter's Whiplash Wendy and friends out of the sofa because you thought they were Luke's home videos – albeit in camouflage packing. And then when you watched them and realised they weren't, you decided you'd better hang in there and keep an eye on me in case I found the star prize before you.'

'Yes. All right, there was an element of duplicity in what I did.'

'Duplicity. Lovely word.'

Peter grabbed my wrist and jerked me off the bonnet so that we were face to face again.

'Listen. I love you. I don't want to. It's probably as big a bummer for me as it is for you. You weren't in my plans at all.'

He was still hanging on to my right wrist. Now he captured the left, raising both hands to his shoulders. Leaning forward, he locked his lips on mine, kissed me hard and kept on kissing until I relaxed and responded.

To be honest, if you're going for outdoor sex, a sun-baked rutted farmyard isn't recommended. What with lumps in your skin, dust in your teeth and ants scuttling for cover, it takes away some of the magic. When Peter reached for the waistband on my jeans, I called time, sat up and started rebuttoning.

'What's the matter?'

'Wrong time, wrong place.'

'And wrong man?'

I shrugged.

'I meant what I said about caring, Grace.'

'But then you're ace at faking it, aren't you, Peter? Esther Purbrick thought Rainwing was her friend. And it was all just to get close to Selwyn and find out the best way to stick the knife in.'

'No it wasn't. I do like Esther. We needed some investment capital, for the cameras and things. They'd have got it back in spades when the film took off. How was I to know they'd need it to buy that freehold?'

'Did you tip off the Environmental Health about their latest place?'

'No need. I should think anyone who'd been near the dump had done that. I've probably done Esther a favour. Once she's free of Selwyn, she'll fly a lot higher. Some people hold you to earth and others carry you to the stars.'

'If you start quoting the lyrics from "The Wind Beneath My Wings", I'm gonna belt you.'

He laughed and pulled me into his lips. This time it was a gentle kiss – more tenderness than passion. 'Come with me, Grace. We can still pull this off. You and me – together. We could travel. New York, California, Florida. Have you ever been to the States?'

'No.'

'You'd love it.'

'Would I? Knowing I'd ruined your mum's life back here?'

'If that's all that's bothering you, I won't go through with the deal.'

'You mean that?'

'Of course.' We were still sitting on the yard floor – a few yards apart so at least one of us could keep temptation at arm's length. Now, however, Peter shuffled closer.

I tried to move back, but was defeated by the car bumper in the back of my shoulders.

'We'll sell the tapes back to them. We needn't be too greedy. Say two hundred thou? Hamish can afford it. Hell, they can both afford it. They don't even need to know it's us.'

'So we *are* back to blackmail?'

'It's not blackmail. It's just what I'm entitled to. What I'd have got legitimately from my grandfather if she'd married my real father. You don't think Hamish is going to practise any of that standing-on-your-own-two-feet philosophy on his own daughters, do you? They'll spend that sort of money easily on my sisters over the next ten years. Believe me, darling, we'd only be taking what's morally mine.' He slid right in against me and took another kiss. 'I love you, Grace. I really do. We'd be good together. And what have you got to stay here for?'

What indeed? My family found me an embarrassment; my flat received sympathy cards from the Salvation Army; my car was knackered; my career looked to be going the same way if Vetch's closed; my best mate was heading for a new life in London; and the only thing sharing my life was a bunch of vicious succulents. Now I'd decided I could handle the cross-dressing thing, Peter and I could have a lot going for us. (Not least a shared wardrobe and joint Valentine's Day cards from Terry Rosco.) I kissed him back.

When we eventually came up for air, Peter said: 'What are we going to do about Carter?'

'What had you in mind? Adoption?'

'I meant in connection with Luke. I wouldn't be surprised if he killed him; he had access to the cottage.'

'But no motive, until he saw that nasty little tape. And the official theory is that Luke was killed by a light bulb.'

I filled him in on the line of police intelligence (without mentioning Carter's contribution to that oxymoron).

'A light bulb. A bloody *light bulb*. All that talent and he dies over a light bulb.'

'That's life for you. Always ready for a laugh at your expense.'

'At least the finance company will be happy. We held them off for months by not telling them the old boy was dead. They finally found out a few weeks back. They check the death registrations in each district periodically. Can you believe that? Well, they can have their property now and good riddance. We'll be long gone. Won't we?'

'I guess we will.'

'What about Carter? Do you think he'll have called the police about me grabbing him?'

'I think Carter could be persuaded to keep his mouth shut.' I rubbed my middle and forefinger against my thumb.

'You'll have to deal with that. Just until we get the cash for the tapes from Hamish.'

'Are you so certain he'll pay? He may tell your mum to take a hike.'

'He'll pay. He enjoys the kudos of being married to a successful politician. And besides, he deals with corporate negotiating. It's not a field where you can afford to look like the biggest chump on the block. Talking of those tapes . . . ?'

'They're in the village.'

Standing, he held out a hand to me. 'Shall we?'

'Can I drive?'

I took the route along the main road rather than going through the village, and turned right to crawl and bump down the rutted track to Brick Cottage. I put us on to the verge outside the closed garage door and led the way to the garden gate. Grannie Vetch's bike was propped a few yards further along the wall, with the Rouses' ginger moggie treating the front basket as his own personal snooze pad.

Carter was standing in the centre of the overgrown patch of cottage lawn with an old tyre lying at his feet. He must have packed something into the bottom, because the three video tapes and the stack of glossy photo prints were clearly visible at the top of the centre ring.

'What the hell?' Peter struggled with the gate catch and then vaulted over it.

Carter didn't even bother to look at him. To me he said: 'Now?'

'Now.'

He lit the twisted spill of paper in his left hand with the disposable lighter in his right, threw the flaming brand into the tyre, and leapt backwards. The result was incredible. A tower of flame shot eight feet into the air with a throaty roar of joy at being activated.

'Bloody hell, Carter! What did you use?'

'Mixed petrol with lighter fuel. Not bad, eh?'

'No!' Peter tried to make a grab for the tyre but the heat drove him back. Dragging his sweater over his head, he beat at the flames. It had the effect of fanning them out like flower petals. One petal explored his trousers. The material caught.

Hopping on one leg, he beat at the other with his bare hands. He managed to extinguish it at the expense of some charred flesh. Carter laughed. With a snarl, Peter took a kick at the fiercely burning tyre. It merely had the effect of shifting the bonfire a fraction and setting the bottom of his trouser leg on fire again. This time he had to collapse to the grass and really hit on the blaze to douse it.

When he started crawling over to the pyre, I had to shout: 'Peter! Leave it. It's too late.'

He turned bewildered eyes on me. 'Why?'

'Because I just don't have your talent for being a bitch, I guess. Goodbye, Peter. Break a leg. In fact, break two.'

Wheeling Grannie Vetch's pride, I headed for the village. Carter followed me. So did the stink of burning rubber. There were already a couple of people pointing to the column of black smoke when we reached the main street.

'It's OK,' I said, trying to smile. 'Just getting rid of some rubbish.'

I turned left. Not because I had anywhere to go, but because I had no other immediate plans for my life.

Carter's asthmatic breathing was still in my right ear. 'It was that politician woman in those photos, wasn't it?'

'Look, Carter, do everyone a favour and forget the whole thing.'

'What about that perv? I'm going to report him to the

police. He tied me up. And he hit me. He ought to be in prison.'

We were nearly at the Royal Oak. A subdued-looking Kelly was sitting on one of the front benches, sipping a bottle of fizzy water. As soon as she spotted us, she got up and went inside.

I looked back at Carter and caught the disappointment on his broad freckled face. Despite everything, the kid still had hopes that some fairy godmother was going to sprinkle magic dust in Kelly's eyes and turn him into Brad Pitt.

Slotting my free arm through his, I drew him along. 'You're right. Peter does deserve to be arrested for what he did to you. But if he is, the police will want to know why he did it, won't they? And once they find out about those hidden tapes, they'll probably start wondering if Luke's death was quite as straightforward as it seemed. I don't think Kelly could stand up to much questioning, do you? She's not as smart as she thinks she is. She'll probably start contradicting herself. I know she never intended to kill Luke, but . . .'

Carter considered this, crease lines denting the raw pink peeling skin of his forehead. 'You mean I should keep quiet for her sake? She don't even *like* me.'

'But you love her, Carter. You'll be making a big sacrifice for the sake of Kelly's happiness.' (And keeping Faye's name out of it – although I didn't mention this essential point to Carter.)

We'd reached the churchyard. By unspoken mutual consent we headed for Carter's namesake and sat on the cross steps. The cat selected a patch of grass and settled down to groom.

'You mean . . .' Carter said slowly, 'it would be like that bloke in *Casablanca*. When he makes her get on that plane with her husband even though he really loves her like mad?'

'You watch films like that?'

'It's my gran's favourite. She thinks it's dead romantic.'

He thought about my idea for a few more seconds and then said: 'OK, I'll do it. For Kelly.'

I gave him a hug. 'Here's looking at you, kid.'

His face twisted and large tears spilled over his sandy lashes. 'It's rotten being in love.'

'I know.'

Watched by the cat, Carter and I had a good blub together.

40

Hello there.

I bet you thought I'd forgotten my promise to retrieve those negatives from Barbra, amongst all the angst and heart-wringing of the last couple of days?

Well, I hadn't, but it took a while before I could get a lift out to Wakens Keep. There was no way I was going to manage a twenty-mile cycle ride there and back, and 'borrowing' Luke's car would have involved returning to Brick Cottage, which I couldn't face. In the end Vetch agreed to drop me off on his way to a meeting in Tunbridge Wells.

'I trust you have the taxi fare home, or an appealing thumb to attract the passing trucker, sweet thing, since I shall not be passing this way again for some hours.'

The parking bays were half empty in Wakens Keep's central square, and the weather had reverted to normal British summer conditions – sulky grey clouds and threatening showers. Even the gnome colony in Barbra's front garden had hauled their little painted butts off to explore elsewhere. There was an air of approaching shorter days and autumnal nights about the place this morning.

I asked Vetch if he didn't want to come in for a minute and say hello. 'You don't have to eat anything.'

'I think not, sweet thing. Barbra has been rather –

distant, shall we say, when I have telephoned recently. I suspect she has found someone else whose charms are even more irresistible than mine. Hard as that may be to believe. Ah well, once more into the breach. My new partner is a hard task-mistress.'

'I thought that was one of your favourite fantasies, Vetch.' I waved him off before heading for Barbra's front door.

Vetch was right. There was another man in her life.

'Gardener, handyman, bodyguard, whatever,' she said, gesturing through the kitchen window at the figure who was snipping off the heads of perfectly formed roses.

I'd had to practically force my way into the house and charge through to the back like a thick-skinned gatecrasher in order to find whatever it was she so obviously didn't want me to find as she tried to shut the door in my face. (A PI who needs to find the dirt on her client really can't afford to be a sensitive soul.)

A live-in lover seemed an unlikely candidate for cupboard skeleton. Barbra Delaney wasn't the sort who'd have been put out if I'd found her romping in the Jacuzzi with an entire paratroop regiment. But something about the situation had definitely spooked her. The casual tone was just a shade too nonchalant.

'I decided I needed a bloke around the place. Comes in handy for all sorts. Want a drink?'

'Is the beer finished?' There were a couple of bottles standing in the sink, both half full.

She took another from the fridge, levered off the top and passed it to me. 'What do you want? If it's about yer fee, I'll give you a cheque now.'

'What about your will? I haven't given you those names and addresses.'

'I've been having a think about that. Maybe I was being a bit daft. My Lee's getting married. He's not going to risk prison by trying to bump me off, is he? Best to leave it. I'll pay you for what you've done, OK?'

'OK.'

Visibly relieved, she went to fetch her chequebook. I took my beer and wandered outside to watch the demon gardener hacking down what looked like a healthy clematis. He had his back to me, but something about the worn and faded denim jeans and jacket nudged a memory.

'Hello again.'

He glanced over his shoulder. 'Sorry, miss, I don't . . .' Then the memories clicked in for him too. He faced me full on with a broad smile spreading from his mouth to his eyes. 'Well, hello there, darling. I didn't recognise you with your clothes on.'

Barbra's return coincided with this last sentence. You could have fast-frozen fish fingers in the look she gave me. Plainly the woman was possessive when it came to the domestic help.

'He caught me skinny-dipping off Seatoun beach the other week.'

'And a glorious sight it was.'

'Where's your mate? Been taken on as the butler?'

'Moved on. He's not one for staying put.'

'And you are?' I looked consideringly between him and his new employer. He was quite relaxed about the whole situation. Barbra, however, was still making like the ice-queen. But then she knew just how dangerous this situation was – and he didn't. Yet.

'The lady was kind enough to offer me a rare little deal here: bed and board.'

'And extras?'

'What the hell's that to do with you?' Barbra snapped. 'We're both free, single and over the age of consent.'

'Well, one out of three, at least.'

She still tried to bluff her way out of it. 'What's that supposed to mean?'

'Oh, come on, Barbra. I saw the wedding snaps, remember? Both sets. Or are they doing Mix-Your-Own-Man kits now? Add eight pints of water to the ashes, stir thoroughly and leave overnight for the perfect mate? You're looking pretty good for a nine-year-old corpse, Sean.'

He wasn't in the slightest jot embarrassed. With an easy grin, he winked and said: 'It's Mike these days, darling. Mike Smith.'

'Fancy that. I'm a Smith myself. We could be related.'

'Well, isn't that wonderful. It's me long-lost sister.' He plonked a kiss on my cheek before I could fend him off.

'Pack that in,' Barbra said. 'I've told you, you're on probation. Any of that and you're out. Come inside,' she ordered me. 'Out here the bloody bushes have ears. And if you stop out here with them clippers much longer, Sea— Mike, it's about the only thing they will have.'

I let myself be led back to the privacy of the kitchen. Barbra rescued the two bottles from the sink and plonked them on the table. 'Sit down.'

We both sat. Sean tilted the beer to his lips and used it as cover to drop me another wink. I kept a straight face and looked him over. The lush Viva Zapata dark brown hairstyle and moustache had gone, replaced by grizzled grey locks cropped close to his head. And the luminous skin was now tanned to the shade of cream toffees and seamed by paler lines like leaf veins. The eyes were the same, though: deep brown and just inviting a girl to jump in and drown in their twinkle.

I must admit that if I hadn't seen him in the same place as Barbra, I wouldn't have made the connection. (Well, I hadn't during our earlier encounter, had I?) But now I had. And it gave me a particularly self-satisfied glow deep inside.

'So what do you want?' Barbra growled.

'The formula for raising the dead, for a start.'

'Now don't you be giving her a hard time over that,'

Sean admonished. 'She'd to identify me from no more than my da's old watch and a ring. How was she to know I'd lost the pair to my old mate Bri at the cards?'

'This would be Bri the best man, would it? The one who looks to be at least six inches taller than the bridegroom in those wedding pictures?'

'He was *burnt*,' Barbra said forcibly. 'How close do you think I looked? Have you ever seen someone who's been charred until you can see their bones falling out? I just read the engraving in the jewellery and said yeah . . . that's my old man, now get me out of here.'

She sounded genuinely shaky. I gave her the benefit of the doubt; even if six inches was rather a lot of benefit to be conceding. 'Doesn't explain why you decided to join us Smiths, Sean.'

'The tax, darling. And the insurance. And the cards. And the losing. There's many reasons why a man should want to leave his old life behind. Not that I'd want you to be thinking I left my family with it. I always kept an eye out for them. My Lee's done all right for himself. You should see the fancy place he works. And he's got himself a little cracker of a girl there.'

'Lee knows you're not crispy barbecue?'

'Well, course he does. We kept in touch. He's my boy, isn't he? What sort of father would I have been to let him go thinking he'd lost his da? And he always saw there was work and a meal for me at his place when I was passing by. A bit of washing-up and regular dinners for the week can set a man up nicely for the road.'

Barbra caught my eye. 'Sounds cosy, don't it?' she said bitterly.

'Now don't be like that, Babs darlin'. I told you, I always kept a watch out for you. And you've done well for yourself too. Look ten years younger now than the day I married you. Would you believe, I didn't recognise her? Followed her down the street and didn't dare say hello in case I was accosting a supermodel.'

'Stop up the syrup valve, Sean. You knew it was me all right. I wouldn't be surprised if Lee tipped you off where to find me. You were just trying to work out the best way to tap me for a loan. You nearly tapped me into bloody oblivion.'

'It was him shoved you under that taxi in London?'

'It was an accident, I swear on my mammy's grave.'

'Your mammy is alive and well and drinking herself stupid in Killarney,' Barbra pointed out.

'God bless her. But you know what I'm saying. I never meant to hurt her,' Sean assured me. 'I'd just screwed up meself to tap her on the shoulder and say me hellos when some eejit pushes me and next thing I know my Babs is sailing into the road.'

'Nice of you to pick me up,' his other half muttered.

'I was scared. Blokes look like me, they take you for a head-case. Or a mugger. Lay in first and ask questions later. So I made meself scarce while they dusted you down. I watched from round the corner,' he informed me. 'Saw she was all right. I'd not have left her if I'd have thought she was hurt. It's a man's job to be looking after his woman when she's hurting.'

He tried to take Barbra's hand. She snatched it away. 'I managed to hurt all by myself for years, Sean Delaney. Without any help from you.'

Something else had occurred to me. 'Is it you who's been hanging around, haunting this place?'

'Not haunting. Just nursing Babs when she was poorly.'

'He got a spare key from Lee, would you believe?' Barbra said. 'The little B only had some cut when he was down.'

'And isn't it just a blessing that he did? With you here all by yourself without a soul to fetch a drink of water? I told her – she needs someone to look out for her.'

This time Barbra didn't evade his hand when it linked with hers on the table.

'It was him phoned up and spooked you that night Annie and I stayed over, wasn't it?'

It was Sean who answered: 'I couldn't be carrying on sneaking about outside any more. I had to know whether we still had a chance, me and Babs. Or if I should be moving on again.' He twisted his tanned and scarred fingers more tightly into her softly manicured ones. 'I've always had feelings for you, Babs. You know that.'

'Feelings for Barney's money, more like,' Barbra said. 'Don't think I don't know why you've blown back, Sean.'

Her protests didn't sound too convincing to me.

Sean didn't think so either. His hand slid up her forearm and continued until it was massaging the side of her neck. The shrug with which she tried to dislodge it was distinctly half-hearted. There was no mistaking the fact that she still fancied the jeans off him. And she was lonely. I was beginning to get the feeling that they'd both like me out of the way so they could put the kitchen table to more inventive uses.

Time to get down to business.

'Talking of Barney . . . doesn't the fact you weren't legally married to the bloke alter things a tad?'

'I *was* legally married. I was a widow. I've a death certificate to prove it. You can't get me on that one. It's not like I knew it was bigamy.'

'Lee did, though. And Sean. But I wasn't thinking of the bigamy so much – I was thinking about the will. All left to you as his lawful wedded wife, wasn't it? But now it would seem you aren't.'

'I'm still entitled. I lived with him for over two years. That entitles me to a share.'

'Checked already, have you? I think you'll find it doesn't entitle you to the whole cake. Didn't you say Barney had made an earlier will leaving the lot to his brother . . . ?'

'His brother is a sponger. That family would have bled him dry and then spat him out. That's the reason I married Barney . . . to keep him away from the bloodsuckers.'

'So you won't mind handing the lot over to Barney's family – seeing as how his welfare is no longer an issue?'

She didn't need to answer. Her face said it all. Few people who've suddenly gone from poor to rich want to make the reverse journey. Otherwise all those lottery winners who've been made miserable by their fortunes would be showering cheques on all and sundry, wouldn't they? The chances were if Barney had left it to her by name she'd easily be able to fend off any challenge by his family anyway. Hopefully she didn't know that yet.

I nudged a little harder whilst she teetered on the precipice. 'And then there's the tax man. There are different inheritance rules for those who aren't *legally* married.'

'It *was* legal,' Barbra snapped. She sounded worried. Her emotional attachment to her cash was serious. It would need major surgery to separate her and her gold credit cards.

'Maybe. But while you may beat off Barney's family in the courts, have you ever heard of anyone beating the Inland Revenue?'

That was the killer punch, she didn't want to take the chance.

'How much, you bitch?'

'Takes one to know one, Barbra. I'll take my fee, for a start.'

She scrabbled the chequebook open. 'As we agreed?'

'Not a penny more. Not a penny less. Here's my invoice.'

She wrote out the figure for my billed hours and expenses – less the fifty per cent discount I'd negotiated if she'd pretend to be interested in putting money into Vetch's business.

(Oh, come on, now – you didn't *really* think Barbra wanted to be a partner in the agency, did you? I knew

Annie wouldn't be able to resist the temptation to save us all from Barbra's meddling. She's now Vetch's new junior partner. I'm hoping the power-crazed-tycoon effect will wear off soon.)

With vicious stabs, Barbra scrawled her signature and flung it over.

I folded my prize. 'I'll take that as the close of this case. Which brings me to a little custom of mine. I always keep a souvenir of each job. It's a sort of superstition. Your snaps are a bit dog-eared by now. Is it OK if I have the negatives?'

'I guess.' Barbra took a leather (and I'm sure ridiculously expensive) shoulder bag from a hook behind the kitchen door, reached inside – and drew out the wallet of family snaps she'd flashed at me that first morning in the Rock Hotel. From a pouch in the back she took out a handful of negative strips and threw them down. 'Here. Sort them out yourself.'

I squinted down the tiny squares until I'd hived off what I needed.

'Did yer ever find out who they were?' Barbra asked.

'Not really. Apart from the one I told you about. Harry Rouse; the bloke who died.'

'Right waste of money then, weren't you.'

'But you still have so much to waste, Barbra.' I stood up and smiled sweetly at her. 'Speaking of which, there is one more thing.'

'I thought there might be.' She reached for the cheques again.

'Can you ring for a cab to take me back to Seatoun? The fare's on you. I'll wait for it out front. Enjoy yourselves.'

I winked at Sean and walked out. Blackmail can be fun, but I didn't want to make a habit of it (as a profession, it was too crowded already).

Epilogue

Atch died. Three weeks after they took him away from the farm. I tried to visit him, but they'd temporarily committed him to a unit on the other side of the county whilst they waited to assess him, and other things got in the way – as they do. By the time I got myself and my bunch of visiting grapes together, he'd collapsed and was already in a coma, connected to plastic tubes and oxygen mask. I kept seeing the kid with the catapult who had terrorised St Biddy's sixty-odd years ago, and made an idiot of myself blubbing in the visitors' car park.

They carried out a post-mortem and the cause of death was listed as Alzheimer's. Although it was never officially released, I heard via the grapevine (otherwise known as Zeb's big mouth) that the hospital pathology department had a ten-minute major alert when they found the old boy was a diphtheria carrier. Whether he'd caught it from one of the illegals Harry hid on the farm or he'd been the original carrier I don't think anyone ever ascertained. But there were no more cases that year and the bug went back into the 'Dormant Diseases' files.

Luke's inquest made the coroner's court just four months after his death, when guilty consciences were still raw.

His mum came down for it. She sat at the front of court, listening as the medical and forensic details were read out. And wept quietly during the coroner's tedious exercise of his own voice whilst he droned on about statistics covering accidents in the home.

As you'll have gathered, I went to the inquest. So did Kelly Benting and Carter. I'd like to give you a nice romantic ending to that relationship and tell you they sat hand in hand, united in mutual recognition of each other's good qualities. But let's not kid ourselves. As far as Kelly was concerned, Carter was still a plump, dull, awkward geek who'd managed to blackmail her into sex. She came to that inquest to make sure he didn't change his mind at the last minute and blurt out the truth about Luke's death. And Carter? Well, I guess he came because for that hour he had some power over Kelly again.

They sat at opposite ends of the rows of spectators' chairs and only looked at each other once, exchanging a half-ashamed, half-triumphant glance when the verdict of 'accidental death' was announced.

Were you expecting me to leap up at the last minute and tell them what really happened? Truth and justice at all costs sort of thing?

What would have been the point? It *was* an accident. Carter and Kelly would probably have had their knuckles smacked for messing around with the evidence and ended up with a criminal record, but in the end who would have profited by the truth coming out?

That's my high moralist argument for keeping my mouth shut.

The other argument goes like this – Luke Steadman was a nasty, lying, low-life slug, and as far as I can see, he got exactly what he was asking for.

But I managed to keep this opinion to myself and sound genuinely sorry as I wished Gillian Bowman the best of luck and apologised for not finding a will at the cottage. 'To be honest, I don't think he got around to making one.'

'It doesn't matter.' She huddled inside a cheap raincoat against the north winds that were now whistling around the Christmas-decked shopping parades. 'There's not that much left. Just bits and bobs of furniture, a few pounds in Uncle Eric's bank and Luke's old motorbike. The finance company took the cottage.'

'There's the car. That must be worth something.'

'What car?'

'The red sports car.'

Gillian shook her head. 'There was no car. I should think Uncle Eric got rid of that old thing years ago.'

I knew he'd taken it. Who else would know it wasn't on the contents inventory? But I guess a tiny part of me had been hoping he'd returned it. I saw him the day I met his mum to return those negatives.

Faye couldn't get back down to the constituency house, so we met up in London. She chose a café in the Parkway, Camden Town. She arrived ten minutes after me, very much the chic, cool MP; all pale grey trouser suit, silk blouse and discreet silver.

'I hope you don't mind this,' she said. 'It's close enough for me to walk from Islington.'

'And small enough for you to check who's eavesdropping?'

It was just one tiny, narrowish room with half a dozen stainless-steel tables ranged down the sides and a serving counter at the far end displaying the myriad combinations that could be packed into your lunchtime sarnie.

But the coffee was good and served in unexpectedly large cups. I slid the negs across the table and idly watched the world go by whilst Faye swiftly checked the minute squares. The glass doors had been folded back to let in the September sunshine, and smells of petrol and diesel mingled with the roar of traffic. It was moving fast for a London street, so I only caught a brief glimpse of the red sports model before a black taxi cut it off from my view.

'Do you have to leave already?' Faye asked.

I realised I'd half risen from my chair, and sank back. 'No. Thought I'd seen someone I knew. My mistake.'

'I'm always doing that. There are so many people around here, aren't there? You don't notice until you've been somewhere gloriously peaceful. And then it's a real lifestyle adjustment when you get back.'

'How was Scotland?'

'As I said . . . peaceful.'

'And uneventful?'

'If you're referring to my relationship with my husband – yes. Perhaps it was just my guilty conscience making me think he was behaving strangely. Things are back to normal. We're very happy.'

She sounded like she really believed that. Or was trying to. It seemed a pity to spoil it. But I did. I told her about Luke and Peter and what they'd intended to do to her.

It had taken me a lot of sleepless nights to decide. But in the end I figured if she wasn't on her guard, Peter might try it again. She didn't take it quite the way I expected.

'I do understand why you're doing this, Grace.'

'You do?'

'Peter told me.'

'He did?'

'Yes. We're very close. And I value that closeness. It's very precious to me. That's why I can understand how much it must have hurt you to lose that.'

'You can?'

'Of course. But believe me, lashing out may be satisfactory now, but you'll bitterly regret it later. And hate yourself for doing it.'

I was beginning to see where this was going. 'Peter told you we'd split up?'

'It happens, Grace. Let it go.'

'Or to put it another way – you think I'm a vindictive bitch trying to get back at Peter for dumping me?'

'No, I understand how much it hurts to give up someone you love. But sometimes you have to. For both your sakes.'

'Believe me, Faye, I can understand how you don't want to admit that your son is capable of doing that to you. And

Luke was just a great actor. If you don't want to believe – fine.'

'Can you prove any of this, Grace? Do you have the tapes you claim they made of me?'

'I burnt them.'

'The photographs Peter supposedly took?'

'They're history too.'

'I see.'

Even a non-equestrian like me knows what not to do with a dead filly. 'It's up to you, Faye. Believe or don't believe. I have life to get on with elsewhere. 'Bye.'

'Goodbye, Grace. And good luck. This is for you.'

She passed me an envelope. It was cash. It would be. She wouldn't want to have to explain a cheque to a private investigator at some later date.

I left her sitting there drinking her coffee with careful sips that didn't smudge her lipgloss. She looked totally serene. I never did decide whether she was a far more talented actor than her son, or she genuinely believed Luke had loved her.

(There was no cabinet post for her in the reshuffle. She got one of those obscure appointments no one has ever heard of and a lot of media speculation on why she was no longer flavour of the month. I'd never believed before in all this conspiracy theory about the mysterious 'they' watching the great and good, but now I'm not so sure. Somebody tipped her husband off.)

I walked through Regent's Park after I left her, to catch the tube to Victoria at Great Portland Street. There was a red sports car waiting at the lights as I left the gates to cross over Marylebone Road. But so what? There must be hundreds of them in London. It's a big place. I didn't bother to look at the driver. I had a date to keep with another bloke in Seatoun.

Annie met me there. She was sitting on a wall waiting when I bowled up on Grannie Vetch's bike.

'Ready?'

I swallowed hard and nodded. I didn't want to do it. But there was no way out. 'Which one?'

'There.' She pointed over the forecourt. 'Five years old. Low mileage. One year's MOT. And they throw in six months' road tax.'

I stepped over the low wall to examine the Micra, with its red and white balloon decorations and large banner announcing that it was the 'Bargain of the Week'.

Annie crowded in behind me. 'And he'll knock three hundred pounds off the price on the board. What do you think?'

I tried to think of something positive to comment on. 'It's . . . it's blue.'

'Good colour for tailing jobs.'

'Yes.' I walked round. It gleamed with car-showroom wax and loving attention. So did the ten-year-old black Porsche just beyond it.

'Leave,' Annie said.

'It's practically the same price.'

'The insurance isn't.'

'I'd be paying it.'

'Grace, for heaven's sake, be practical. I'm trying to put this agency on a viable footing. How can I use you on a surveillance job in that? And why do you want it anyway? It's the kind of motor that's driven by sad middle-aged Peter Stringfellow wannabes and bleached-blonde twenty-two-year-old bimbos trying to pull soccer players. You need a more mature vehicle. If you don't like the Micra, what about that grey Toyota?'

'There's a Morris Minor over there. Only two previous owners. Let's see what kind of deal we can get on that. Maybe he'll throw in a Zimmer frame too.'

Annie folded her arms. 'That's what this is all about, isn't it? You've still got the hump about turning thirty?'

'I hate the idea of getting old, Annie.'

'You're not *old*, for heaven's sake.'

'I don't qualify for the car of choice of a twenty-something bleached bimbo any more, though, do I?'

'Not if you want to stay at Vetch's. We need to get the place on a professional footing if we're going to survive. Cheer up.' She punched my arm lightly. 'Take my word for it, being in between has a lot going for it.'

'It does?'

'Definitely. The Micra?'

'I guess.'

She had to prise my fingers from the three hundred deposit. But in the end I did it. We arranged to collect the car after it had been taxed and insured in my name. As we left, the dealer called me back.

Squatting down, he ran a hand over the front wheel of Grannie Vetch's monster. 'Do you know what this is?'

'At a wild guess . . . a bicycle?'

'It's a Military Sunbeam. In the original WD green paint . . . and, oh my God . . . it's got the original Joseph Lucas rifle clips!' He stroked two irritating metal clips on the frame whose purpose I'd never been able to figure out.

He raised the eyes of a fanatic to my face. 'Tell you what, I'll take another three hundred off the price of the car if you want to trade?'

'Done.'

I left it with him. Together Annie and I strolled back through the back streets towards the front. Halfway there, a police car cruised to a stop just in front of us and the window slid down.

'Oi. Sexy arse.'

'I think it's for you,' Annie murmured.

Stooping, I looked across the WPC in the passenger seat to the driver. 'Hello, Terry. Still taking that bond-with-the-public course?'

'Where's your mate? Not seen her around lately.'

'I take it you don't mean Annie, who is currently

standing behind me and who even someone with your limited powers of observation could hardly fail to notice?'

'The dark-haired bird with the legs. Fancied me something rotten up the BHS restaurant. Been thinking I might give her a go.'

'Oh, Peter.'

'Peta? Thought she was called something to do with the weather. Misty or something.'

'Raine. Short for Rainwing. That's when he's exploring his feminine persona, of course.'

'He? Who he?'

'He Peter. That's Peter with an "er".'

Terry's face paled under the tan. 'You mean that was a queer?'

'If you want to put it that way, Terry. But I'm glad you liked him. He really fancied you. I gave him your number at the station. I'm sure he'll be in touch really soon. See ya.'

I gave the WPC a broad wink. She grinned back. Within thirty minutes it would be all over the police canteen that Terry Rosco fancied a bloke. Life was getting sweeter by the second.

'Do you know,' I informed Annie, 'I think you could be right about being in-between. It might have something going for it.'

'I'm glad to hear it. It's just a question of thinking positive and eliminating anything negative.'

'Done that all week. In fact, you're talking to the Arnie Schwarzenegger of the negative-eliminating business. Both photographic and human.'

Annie was wearing dark lenses. She tipped them so that I could see her eyes when she asked: 'You OK? About this Peter character, I mean.'

'I'm fine. Do I strike you as the sort to let one rotten bloke mess up the rest of my life?'

'Quite right. Just tell yourself there are a lot of good men out there. And one day we're going to find one.'

'For heaven's sake, Annie, go back on the diet before I have to start calling you Pollyanna.'

We'd reached the promenade. I crossed the road to the seaward side. The tide was out, leaving a large stretch of mainly deserted beach glinting where the sinking sun was catching the stranded pools of water and drifts of white shells.

Kicking off my shoes, I rolled my jeans up and dashed across the soft powdery sand and wet ridges beyond the high tide limits. Annie flew after me. In fact, she overtook me easily. Not being on a diet never seemed to have any effect on her superfitness.

We reached the first waves; their lacy, cream crests folding over into the grey troughs.

I looked at Annie. 'Ready?'

'Ready.'

'Let's do it.'

Plunging in up to our shins, we startled every passing gull and dog walker by splashing and kicking our way the entire length of the beach, singing at the tops of our voices:

'*Eliminate the negative . . . accentuate the positive . . .* AND DON'T MESS WITH MRS IN-BETWEEN!'

THE END

Well, not quite the end.

Remember Luke's film script? It turned out it really did exist. It was part of the property removed from the cottage by the police for some reason. It was returned to his mum eventually. I saw a copy of it some time later. It was absolute rubbish.

A year later, a major film company bought the option from Gillian Bowman. They're hyping it as a future smash blockbuster.